# THE POSEIDON TRIALS

## THE COMPLETE COLLECTION

ELIZA RAINE

ROSE WILSON

*You're not broken.*
*You just haven't found what brings you to life yet...*

# SECRET OF THE
# BROKEN KING

# CHAPTER 1

*N*ever underestimate a librarian.

My lungs burned. My feet pounded the wooden flooring, but I could see the massive ornate doors looming closer. I willed my muscles to hold out, pushing through the pain and racing through the museum hall toward the stairwell that led up and out to freedom.

"Stop! Come back here!"

I had thought I was lucky that the archives in the museum didn't have security guards. Little did I know that they didn't need them - because the librarians were built like frigging Olympic athletes. If I wasn't desperately trying to escape with the ten-pound book I'd stolen, I might have taken some time to admire the biceps of the guy chasing me. As it was, I kept my focus forward and dug into one of the many pouches on my leather belt. I pulled out a small plastic sphere and without turning around, threw it over my shoulder, crushing it as I did so.

The smell only just reached me as I propelled myself away from the stink bomb. I heard coughing and spluttering behind me, and as I reached the doors to the stair-well, I risked a glance over my shoulder. There were three of them now, two guys and a girl, and throwing a bad smell at them had not slowed them down.

I took the stairs two at a time, trying to take deep breaths, the book heavy in my grip.

*It's gonna be worth it, Lily. Totally worth it,* I thought.

The wide, spiraling staircase opened out onto a new hallway at the top, and right at the end of the corridor were the large exit doors.

I dipped my hand into a different pouch and pulled out a handful of ball bearings. Once I had put a few feet between myself and the staircase, I dumped them on the carpeted floor behind me. A second later, I heard a yelp, and then a thud. This time, I didn't risk a look back. I pictured my sister's sleeping face and ran as fast as my malnourished ass would carry me.

I reached the doors, twisting my body and throwing my shoulder against them to keep as much momentum as I could. I blinked as I stumbled into the bright light, momentarily disoriented before the vista of the Oxford street on a sunny day settled before me.

"Stop her!" The librarian's voice was loud enough through the open doors that a few people passing by paused and looked at me. I pivoted, trying to find the direction of the road I'd parked my shit-heap car on.

A tall woman in yoga pants and a vest turned to me, frowning. Her eyes moved to the leatherbound book under my arm, and she took a step closer. From my peripheral vision, I caught the motion of a figure bursting out of the museum doors.

I drew on what little strength I had left and sprinted down the road to my right.

*Please be the right road, please be the right road,* I chanted in my head, too out of breath to make the plea aloud.

A vision of my sister wearing her scolding face filled my head. *You should remember these things, Almi! You're always making life difficult for yourself!* The mental image of Lily spoke firmly, and I sucked as much strength from her as I could as I pelted down the leafy street.

All the roads in the university area of Oxford looked the same to me, and I had no idea if I was racing along the one I'd actually parked my car in. Praying I was, I dug into another pouch on my belt and yanked my car keys out. I could hear footsteps pounding behind me.

*Might be time to use the big guns,* said Lily in my head. *Get the elephant projector.*

I bared my teeth through my panting breaths. Reluctantly, I pulled the most expensive weapon I had from my belt. It was a small plastic box, not much bigger than a credit card, and it had taken me days to work out how to use it in my cramped little trailer. Not to mention the effort to steal the thing in the first place.

My attention snagged on something thirty feet in front of me. A small, rusty yellow Ford. *My car.*

There was no way I could unlock it, get in it, and start it, without the hunky librarians catching up to me, I conceded. I would have to use the elephant projector.

Pressing the little button on it, I launched it over my shoulder. I heard the clatter of plastic on asphalt, then a small cry. The footsteps stopped, and I launched myself at my car door. I rammed the key in the lock, cursing the fact that my ancient car didn't have remote locking. It didn't even have a certificate to say it was roadworthy. As the handle clicked open and I threw myself into the driver's seat, I saw two librarians staring, bewildered, at a massive hologram of an elephant, throwing its trunk in the air and rearing up onto its back legs.

It would only distract them for a few seconds. If I could have fitted decent speakers in the little device, I could have made it better. But I didn't have the money for speakers. Hell, I didn't have the money for anything.

I turned the key in the ignition, squeezing my eyes closed and pleading for the rust-bucket to start. I gave an involuntary squeal of relief as the engine roared to life, and the two librarians stopped squinting at the electronic elephant to snap their eyes to mine through the windshield. I gulped, rammed the car into gear, and put my foot on the gas.

"Shit. That was close," I said aloud as I pulled onto the freeway. Adrenaline was buzzing through me, and my lungs still burned. I was used to being hungry, but I wasn't used to being hungry *and* doing a bad impression of an athlete.

*Too close. You really should have remembered where you parked the car,* Lily said. I always saw her in my mind with vivid blue hair and shimmering skin. The way she had looked *before*.

Before she fell unconscious. Before I was sent away and hidden in the human world.

My exile hadn't stopped me trying to wake my sister up though. And after years of research, I finally knew where I might find the answers to curing her sickness.

This book was the key. This book was going to tell me what I needed to save her.

# CHAPTER 2

*I*t was almost dark by the time I pulled into the trailer park I reluctantly called home. In England, they called it a caravan park, but when I'd first been dumped in the mortal world, I had found myself in California, USA, and that's where I'd tried to learn how to fit into a world without magic.

I had been born in Olympus, a world where the Greek gods ruled, and magic and mythology was as real, and as dangerous, as it could be.

Home was the underwater realm of Aquarius, and the first thing I had done when I found myself stranded in America, was try to find a way back there. A way back to my sister, so that I could cure her sleeping sickness.

Back then, in my lowest moments, I'd wondered if I'd invented my home world, just to escape the shitty reality of my life.

That was when Lily had begun talking to me in my head. At first, I had assumed I was going crazy from grief and frustration. But I'd started to wonder if it really was her, talking to me through some mystical sibling bond.

After all, before she fell unconscious, Lily had been one of the most powerful sea nymphs I knew.

*This is it, Lily. This time, I'm sure,* I told her as I switched off the ignition.

I grabbed the book and my backpack, climbed out of the car and let myself into my trailer. I called her Betty Blue, because she had a blue stripe around the top of her peeling fiber-glass hull. There were six bolts on Betty Blue's unassuming door to unlock - all discreetly installed so it didn't look like there was anything inside worth stealing to my less-than-savory neighbors.

Truth was, there was plenty worth stealing - most of it stolen by me in the first place.

I had a decent moral compass, but my need to get home and save my sister was greater than my distaste for breaking the rules. I had only stolen things I really needed, and nothing of sentimental value to anyone, or that couldn't be replaced. And only stuff I could never afford, no matter how many hours I put in at cafes, bars, supermarkets - and anywhere else a girl could get casual work with no bank account. I bought food and paid the rental on Betty Blue with honest cash, but the rest...

It had taken me a few years to find my first Olympus artifact in the human realm, which I had subsequently stolen.

I looked over at the metafora compass hanging on a peg on the wall after I locked the trailer door behind me and flipped on the lights. It allowed me to move between the human realm and Olympus, and it was worth a fortune. Not that I would ever part with it.

It only had three uses, and I was down to just one left.

Moving to the bed at the back of the trailer, I pulled my sketchbook out from under my pillow. It wasn't actually my sketchbook, it was Lily's. But other than the compass, it was the most valuable thing I owned.

Drawing in the little book transferred a memory to it, to be relived as and when one liked, and Lily had used it when I was a child so she could show me her memories of our mother. Through it, I had been able to see exactly what our mom had been like, at least through Lily's eyes.

I had taken the book with me when I'd been exiled from Olympus as a way to be closer to her, but I'd found myself so overwhelmed by my own thoughts that I'd begun drawing my memories into the book too.

My sketches were crap compared to hers, but it seemed to work all the same.

I flipped the pages until I saw a rough pencil sketch of a woman lying in a bed. Blotches that had once been tears smeared the drawing, but it didn't stop it from working. Swallowing, I touched the sketch.

It heated under my fingertips, and I was no longer in the trailer. Instead, I was standing in a small bedroom in a house that wasn't mine.

This was an image I knew wasn't projected by some

grief-stricken part of my psyche. This image was real; my own memory of the last time I had seen my sister.

There, lying on a narrow bed, was Lily. I watched her a moment. No breath came from her lips, and there was no shine on her sallow skin. Her blue hair was dull, and her eyes were closed. I knew that if I could reach out and touch her, she would be as cold as ice. For all intents and purposes, she could be dead.

But she was alive. The Oracle had said as much before I'd been dragged away.

*'The Nereid will sleep, until the gods weep.'*

Tears of frustration burned at the back of my eyes as I stared uselessly at Lily's image. "Fucking Oracle," I spat, and the image faded, the trailer returning around me.

*It's not her fault,* my mental projection of Lily said gently.

"It's someone's fault."

*Maybe.*

One tear leaked down my cheek and I scrubbed it away angrily. Before I could stop myself, I was flipping back the pages of the sketchbook.

*You don't need to see it again,* said Lily.

"There might be something I missed before." There was an edge of desperation to my voice.

*Almi...* Lily's voice faded away as I touched a sketch of a platform floating on the sea, a line of indistinct, badly drawn stick figures standing on it. My fingers felt hot, and then I was eighteen again.

# CHAPTER 3

*E*IGHT YEARS AGO, IN POSEIDON'S REALM OF AQUARIUS

"Tell me again why we're here?" I hissed to my sister under my breath.

"Shhhh." Lily stared ahead, avoiding my look.

I scowled. Lily had spent her whole life telling me to stay under the radar, make sure nobody knew that I was... broken. Powerless. Able to do *nothing* with magic. I couldn't even sense it.

*"It could be the death of you if anyone finds out,"* she had told me. *"We must do whatever it takes to keep it a secret. Nobody must know."*

And yet, there we were on my eighteenth birthday, lined up with two-hundred other sea nymphs on a giant floating dais in the middle the sea, being inspected by the king of the ocean himself. The almighty, and utterly terrifying, Poseidon.

I leaned forward just an inch, looking past the other women in the line, to peer at the god.

He was seven feet tall, at least, with long white hair loose over enormous shoulders. I couldn't see his face, but I could see that he was wearing a robe that looked like the ocean, aqua and turquoise waves crashing over the fabric as he solemnly made his way down the line of women.

"This is bullshit," I whispered to Lily.

"Almi! Be quiet!" She finally broke her stare ahead and glared at me. "This is serious. Poseidon called us here, and we have to answer. Now, behave."

She loaded the command with so much uncharacteristic authority, I shut my mouth.

Lily had been playing the role of my mom for as long as I could remember, but she wasn't very strict. Mostly, she left me alone to mess around with things that covered up the fact that I had no magic, while she honed her own considerable power at the Academy. Lily was everything I wasn't. She was beautiful, with bright blue hair, skin that shone like mother-of-pearl, and a tattoo of a nautilus shell across her chest that was so vividly colored I never tired of looking at it. And she had an almost godly magic over water. She was a true representative of our kind. Of the Nereid.

I, on the other hand, had dark hair with the tiniest hint of blue, pale skin from being inside so much, and my shell tattoo was just a thin black outline. No color at all. No color, and no magic.

I sighed and peered out to get another glimpse of Poseidon.

My breath caught as I turned my head and looked straight into the bluest eyes I had ever seen.

Not just blue... They were every hue of the ocean, and silver swirled amongst the greens and blues, drawing me in, taking me deeper-

"Your name?" The ocean god barked.

Power washed over me as Poseidon approached, but unlike Lily's power, which felt like a light breeze across the ocean, carrying the faint tang of salt, his power was heavy, oppressive even. Whirlpools swirled in my mind, dark crashing waves dragging down everything in their path as they tore through my head.

Oh gods. Oh gods.

*I'd forgotten my own name.*

Poseidon took a step toward me, holding my panicked gaze, and I felt Lily stiffen beside me.

"Lily," I gasped, pulling on the only name I could remember.

"You would lie to your king?" His voice was an echo of thunder over a stormy ocean, and I couldn't breathe properly.

He stopped before me, the fabric of his robe flowing, muscular shoulders widening. Entrancing blue eyes churning with volatile power.

"I-" I choked. But his magic was overwhelming. The skies seemed to darken behind him.

"She is young," Lily said, her calm voice cutting through the storm. I saw her bow her head in my peripheral vision as I tried to suck in air. "My apologies, my king."

Poseidon finally removed his gaze from me, and the air flowed easier into my chest.

"What kind of nymph are you?" he asked my sister.

She hesitated a second before answering. "Nereid."

This time, Poseidon stiffened. He held his hand up, his fingers fluttering as though feeling for her power in the air. "You speak the truth," he murmured. His eyes moved back to mine, but this time my throat didn't close.

When he continued to stare at me, I nodded. His eyes were mesmerizing, and I was struggling to concentrate on anything else.

"You are aware of the prophecy from Apollo's Oracle at Delphi?" His voice was a hoarse whisper.

I looked to Lily, confused, and she shook her head. "No, my king."

He flicked his wrist, and a white flame burst from his hand. When it died away, there was an image left behind. A woman with dark skin, wrapped in layers and layers of cloth, and only her youthful face showing, was chanting nonsensical words. Her eyelids fluttered open to reveal pure white eyes. I instinctively reached for my sister's hand, and I felt her grip mine back.

"He who possesses the heart of a Nereid shall possess the Heart of the Ocean. True love is not a necessity, pure possession will seal the deal." The woman's eyes rolled in her head, and tendrils of red began to bleed and spread across the milky white.

I squeezed Lily's hand harder.

"But be warned. True love will never go unnoticed. Should-"

Poseidon flicked his hand again, and the image vanished before the woman finished the sentence.

Lily drew in a deep breath, and I felt her hand shaking around mine.

"You have never heard this prophecy before?" Poseidon asked.

"No, my king."

"You are what I have been seeking." His tone had turned steely, and Lily gripped my hand so hard it hurt. Fear spread through me as I looked at her frightened face. Lily was never frightened.

"How do you possess someone's heart?" I couldn't help the question from tumbling from my lips, though my voice was barely a whisper. Surely Poseidon, one of the three most powerful gods in the whole of Olympus, wasn't about to cut out our hearts?

The god locked his eyes on mine again. "Marriage," he said, eventually.

I thought that would have lessened my sister's fear - relief that our hearts were staying firmly within our chests was coursing through me. But her hand continued to shake.

"That was the purpose of today?" Lily asked. "To find a Nereid?"

"There are very, very few of you left. In fact, you two might be the last."

Sadness jolted through me at his words. Lily had always been evasive when I asked about our kind, but I didn't think she had known we were the last.

"And now?"

"You will address me as your king." His words were

firm, but the lethal power lacing his voice when he had first approached us was gone.

He lifted his hand again, and all the other women gawking at us on the floating marble platform vanished. "I will return tomorrow. And I will wed one of you. I care not which."

There was a flash of light, and we were back in our home.

"What just happened?" I stared at my sister, my mind reeling as she stumbled backward and collapsed into one of the squishy armchairs in our small living area. Her eyes were wide with fright, and I moved to her, bending to throw my arms around her. She was stiff for a moment, then she wrapped her arms around me, pulling me tight against her.

"Oh, Almi. I'm sorry. We shouldn't have gone."

"Did you know about that prophecy?" I pulled back, looking into her eyes. They were misty with unshed tears as she shook her head.

"I knew that the women of our kind were hunted over the years, but I never knew why. I knew that nobody could know that you were vulnerable, and that we had to be strong to defend ourselves. I didn't know that *possession of our hearts* was the reason." She looked sick as she spoke the word possession. "But… But there is no defense from Poseidon. He is a king and a god."

And not just any god.

Olympus was divided into twelve realms, each ruled

over by an Olympian god, and the three strongest were the brothers who ruled the Underworld, the Sky, and the Sea.

Hades, Zeus, and Poseidon.

"Did he really say marriage?" I breathed.

Lily nodded. "Yes."

I frowned, trying to work that through. "Would that make whoever married him a queen?"

"Yes. A queen in a gilded cage."

"Queens have power and wealth. We would be protected." I was trying to see a bright side, but when I remembered how the god had made me feel, the dark, stormy, drowning waves of power he'd sent through me, I shuddered.

"Almi, we should marry for love, not be forced into it! What of sharing a bed? Would you give that away to someone you didn't love, for a lifetime?"

"No," I said, shaking my head. I had yet to experience any kind of physical love, but I knew I wanted to be the one to choose.

"We would be beholden. Trapped. Creatures of the ocean are not meant to be trapped." She drew in a long breath and stood up out of her chair. She began to pace the small room we'd lived in most of my life.

"I'm not a creature of the ocean," I said, aware of how small my voice was. I tried to make it stronger. "I'll do it."

Tears spilled from Lily's eyes as she turned back to me. "Of course you won't."

"I will. It makes no difference to me. I have no future in Aquarius anyway. Not without any magic. I don't feel the call of the ocean like you, or have the potential to change the world." I forced a smile onto my face. "I'll do it."

"Almi, it's exactly *because* you have no power that I can't let you do that. If he found out, I don't know what he would do."

I swallowed, knowing I couldn't keep the question clawing its way out of my throat in. It was the same question I asked my sister whenever I couldn't understand why I was broken. "Am... Am I really a Nereid?"

Lily gathered me up in her arms again. "We've been through this. Of course you are. You think I put that shell tattoo on your chest, silly?"

"You could have," I mumbled into her shoulder.

"Well, I didn't. I don't know why you don't have your colors or your magic. But they will come one day. And you will not be the trophy wife of an arrogant, entitled god, I swear." She kissed me on the top of the head, her blue hair falling over my brown.

"I love you, Lily."

"I know. I love you too."

"What are we going to do?"

"We can't run. Not from one of the three most powerful beings in the world."

"So...?"

She sighed against my head, all the breath leaving her body. "So, I marry in the morning."

I squeezed her. "I mean it, Lily. I'll do it. You could do so much good with your magic."

"No, Almi. He can never know that you don't have your power. That's our secret, okay? And you never know, maybe I can do more good from the palace. And maybe

Poseidon will not turn out to have a heart of ice." Her voice turned bitter, and I pushed back to look into her face.

"Is that where we'll live? In the palace?"

She nodded. "I assume so."

"I'll come with you, won't I?"

Her soft features hardened. "That will be my only stipulation."

"What if he says no?" Tears filled my eyes at the thought of being separated from Lily.

She brushed my cheek and smiled. "Nothing will keep us apart, I promise."

# CHAPTER 4

The trailer appeared around me, the memory fading before I could feel the pain of reliving what happened next.

*Anything new?* Lily asked.

"No. Poseidon is still an asshole."

*You say that every time. I don't know why you do it to yourself.*

"I can't help it," I muttered. Maybe I was a masochist. Maybe I needed the constant burn of anger to keep me going. After all, he was the one who had exiled me, and was the reason I had to hide in the mortal world.

"Book," I said firmly, shaking my head and dragging my hand over my face.

I pulled the book I'd so nearly been caught stealing from the bench onto my lap.

My heart beat fast, and butterflies fluttered in my stomach as I ran my fingertips over it. *Please. Please be the final piece.*

After I'd found the metafora compass, I spent the

following five years hunting for anything that could help Lily. It was amazing how many Olympus artifacts had been hidden in the human world—just like me. Eventually, I'd followed the breadcrumbs of magical items to Oxford, England, and this book.

When I flipped open the leather cover, I saw the drawing that I'd hoped would be there. A map of Olympus.

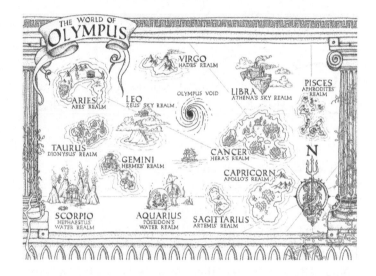

I recognized it from my own childhood. I hadn't been able to attend the Academy to learn to use my power or be educated in the ways of Olympus, but Lily had, and she'd shared a lot of what she'd learned with me, including this map.

Guilt twanged through me as I remembered what a brat I had been to my sister sometimes, bitter about my lack of magic - and jealous of hers. If Lily had ever resented having to take on the role of my mother and deal with my shit, she had never shown it.

I had always been too busy tinkering with artifacts and chemicals and things that I thought would cover up my being broken, to really appreciate what she did for me.

I refocused on the map before me, my finger moving of its own volition to touch the little representation of Aquarius. There was one other water realm - Hephaestus' underwater volcano world, Scorpio. There were two realms that floated in the sky, Athena's Libra, and Zeus' Leo, and the rest of the gods' realms were islands.

I scanned the map one more time to make sure I couldn't see what I was looking for.

A secret realm.

A realm that didn't appear on any map, but that the scriptures I had found in Germany suggested was the birthplace of my kind. And not just the Nereid. If the scriptures were to be believed, and I had no reason to doubt their authenticity, then the fabled realm was the birthplace of many of the creatures that lived in Olympus, and more importantly - the location of incredible healing magic.

The scriptures stated that the realm was hidden by the gods so it couldn't be abused by those with power. I didn't know what that meant, yet, but they had also said that the only way to find the realm was with a book devoted to navigating the world of the gods.

The book had I just stolen from a museum in Oxford.

"Please, please tell me how to cure my sister," I pleaded aloud, before turning the page and whistling a sigh of relief to see that the hand-scrawled text was in a language I could read.

"Knowledge is power, blah, blah, blah," I mumbled as I skimmed through the writing, eager to get to something useful.

"Ah!" I jammed my finger down on the fourth page, pulse quickening. "The Font of Zoi in the realm of Atlantis was the source of a great deal of life in Olympus and retains the power to heal all manner of ailments."

I kept reading. "If the font is used for ill purpose, then grave consequences shall befall those involved." I nodded. I had come across a writing two years ago that suggested that healing artifacts could backfire as often as they helped, often due to the intention of the user. Dark intentions equaled dark magic.

"A magic like this must be controlled, as with enough strength and commitment, new life could potentially be created, perhaps with disastrous consequences. The Font of Zoi should only ever be used to create life if a species is in mortal danger."

A little giddy with hope, I read on.

"This is a dangerous and involved magic, only possible in certain circumstances. See more in the book of mageía." I hissed out my disappointment. That was a book I had never heard of.

I flicked through the pages, looking for anything about Atlantis. There was a large group of pages about the four forbidden realms of Olympus, and then a long chapter about the colossal mountain that Zeus' sky realm ringed. After that I found an interesting but unhelpful few chapters on weather and seasonality in the various realms.

Next was the section on the two ocean realms. I found myself slowing down when I read the part about Aquarius, mumbling the words as I read.

"Aquarius is made up of undersea domes that most often glow faintly with gold. The bulk of the realm is made up of around two hundred of these domes connected by clear tunnels, but there are many parts of Aquarius that lie separate from the main body. Poseidon's Palace, for example, is in its own dome, and can only be reached by crossing clear ocean."

I scowled at the mention of the ocean god.

"Some domes have towers that rise up so high they penetrate the surface of the ocean, with stables at the top to house pegasi. Created by Poseidon, these winged horses prefer to live close to the waves, but need to be able to fly, so the stable towers allow them this."

There had been a pegasus tower near where Lily and I had lived, and Lily told me that they offered flying lessons at the academy once. She hadn't been interested in flying, but I couldn't recall ever being more jealous of her.

"There are also many creatures confined to the depths of the ocean, far beneath the dome cities. These creatures are giant, deadly, and some say, so horrific to lay eyes upon that they could send a weak mind mad. Poseidon is the only god who can keep them at bay. It is believed by this author that the ocean god has put these creatures to work to guard the realm of Atlantis."

For a second, I was sure my heart had stopped beating altogether.

I read the line again.

Poseidon's creatures of the depths were guarding the lost realm?

Excitement warred with fear. How in the name of all the gods was I going to get past Poseidon's sea monsters?

The irony was that Lily, with her fiercely strong water magic, might actually have had a chance. But me? I was barely even a decent swimmer, for god's sake. Where Lily could hold her breath for almost half an hour underwater, as a sea nymph *should* be able to, I struggled after five minutes. Anger and frustration welled up inside me, and I took a deep breath.

Focusing on the page, I read on.

"The reason for this belief is that Poseidon was witnessed on two occasions taking lesser beings far, far below his realm, to depths that should not be possible to survive, yet they returned safe and healthy. Poseidon undertook these ventures on his ship, the *okeánios ánemos*. Pulled by horses made of enchanted water, his is the only ship in Olympus that can move through water, and so, no one other than the god of the ocean himself can reach the pitch-dark depths below Aquarius. This makes for the perfect hiding place for the realm of Atlantis."

My eyes darted further down the page, but the author moved on to the subject of the rest of the ships in Olympus, which unlike human ships did not sail on the surface of water but flew through the sky to move between realms.

I went back and reread the relevant passage until my eyes blurred, my pulse racing.

"Lily, it looks like I'm going to have to up my game," I breathed eventually. "I've got a ship to steal."

I took a deep breath as I looked around my little trailer an hour later.

With any luck, this would be the last time I would see its drafty interior. It had been my home, though, and a small part of me would be sad not to see it again. A much larger part of me couldn't wait to get back to Olympus.

I had everything packed in my bag, and I was holding the metafora compass in my hand.

The little bronze object looked just like a normal compass, except instead of North, East, West, and South on the face, the needle could move between various Greek words. I didn't know the meaning of them all, but I knew the most important one.

Spíti. *Home.*

I had last been home six years ago, when I first found the compass. I hadn't been able to resist seeing Lily. I had only spent a few days there, and I'd been terrified of being caught by the merciless Poseidon the whole time.

I told nobody about my return, not even my best friend, who was keeping Lily's unconscious form safe in his home. Sneaking past him to see her had felt like a betrayal, but I hadn't known what Poseidon would do if he had caught me, and I didn't want to risk my friend's safety.

I'd used the compass to return to the human world, hellbent on finding a way to cure Lily before I used it to return to her.

And now I had one.

I was one-hundred-percent sure that I trusted the information that I had gleaned from the book. And if I was being honest, I had no other leads.

This was the final trip I would make with the compass.

And this time, I couldn't be scared of Poseidon.

I was going to steal his damned ship, sail it to the depths below Aquarius, and find Atlantis and its healing magic. I hadn't worked out how I would get past the sea monsters or use the healing magic yet - but first thing was first, I had to find the ship. And that meant getting into Poseidon's Palace.

That would be a feat for most people. But for me? Damn near impossible. The Palace was the home of the god who had banished me from Olympus, and the only person who knew who I really was. Poseidon's Palace was literally the last place in Olympus I should be going, but that was exactly what I was going to do.

Just as soon as I'd seen Lily.

"Thanks for everything, Betty Blue," I said, touching the Formica countertop fondly. I clutched the bronze compass, my stomach flipping over with excited trepidation. "Spíti," I said on a breath. *Take me home.*

I barely had time to finish the thought before the whole world disappeared around me.

# CHAPTER 5

*I* felt the bronze compass fall from my hand, then heard it clatter as the freezing wind that had just whipped around me vanished. My hair was a mess in front of my face, and I was vaguely aware I'd dropped to one knee. Chatter and loud voices filtered through to me as the spinning sensation lessened enough that I could stand and push my hair out of my eyes.

I wasn't in Betty Blue anymore.

In fact, I wasn't in the mortal realm anymore.

Slowly I tipped my head back, looking up. Praying, praying, praying that I wouldn't see sky above me, but that I would see-

"Water," I gasped.

*Aquarius.*

Far above my head was a faintly shimmering veil of gold, and beyond that, miles of blue ocean. The silhouette of a pod of whales was visible against the bright light of the surface, and closer to the gold shield overhead I could see dolphins playing as they sped along through the water.

I was in a gleaming, golden underwater dome of Aquarius.

I lowered my gaze, forcing myself to breathe deeply but my head dizzy with relief and excitement.

Buildings made from rusty-colored sand mixed with larger, shining white stone structures all the way up to the gleaming gold dome edge in the distance. Just in front of me was a large clearing filled with a bustling marketplace. People moved between the canvas stalls, and I stared. They weren't all human. Some had wings. Others had tails. Some were blue-skinned.

I turned slowly, looking for anything that would confirm that this was the market-town I had grown up in. The temperature was perfect, and despite being under-water there was a slight, salty breeze that I sucked in gratefully as I scanned my surroundings.

'Fyki Tanners' read a small wooden board outside a building with rails of leather hanging outside. Tears burned at the back of my eyes.

"I'm home," I breathed.

*For good, this time.*

"You dropped this, dearie," said a husky female voice, and I spun to see an older woman in a beautiful gold robe holding out the compass to me.

I blinked at her a few times, and she frowned. "Are you alright?"

"Yes," I answered, reaching for the compass. "Yes, thank you. Is this... Am I in Fyki?"

I knew I was. But I wanted to hear someone say it.

"Yes, dearie. Do you need somewhere to stay? There's a lovely taverna here, or a cheaper one in the next dome along." Her eyes scanned my crappy clothes as she mentioned the cheaper taverna, but I barely heard her.

"Is the bakery still here?"

She raised her eyebrow. "There are two bakeries in Fyki."

"Silos' bakery."

"Over there, beyond that row of stalls."

"Thank you," I breathed, and then my legs were moving. I'd broken into a run before I knew it.

I burst through the door of the bakery, heart pounding and mind racing.

I was back. I was in frigging Olympus.

"We're closed!" shouted a deep male voice. "Come back tomorrow." I moved to the counter, hardly seeing the empty shelves where the bread should be.

"Silos?" I called, directing my voice at the door that led to the kilns.

I heard banging and then a curse.

"I said we're closed," the man snapped.

"It's Almi."

There was another loud bang, then footsteps. A second later, a tall, dark man in a leather apron and scruffy hair appeared in the doorway.

His mouth fell open, then slowly formed a disbelieving smile. "Almi! Where in the name of the gods have you been?"

An almighty wave of emotion crashed over me as I smiled back at the boy who had been my best friend for my whole childhood.

"You have her safe, right?"

"Of course." He rushed forward, wiping his hands on his apron, and lifted a hinged part of the counter. As he pulled me into a hug, the burn of tears behind my eyes returned.

He may not look like the boy I had left behind anymore, but he smelled like the world I had been taken from. Familiar and safe.

"Take me to her," I said, pulling back from him.

"I can't believe you're back," he breathed, then nodded, his too-long hair falling over his forehead. "Come on."

Silos lead me through the back of the bakery and up a narrow flight of stairs. I held my breath as we passed two doors at the top, and he pushed open a third.

I didn't even try to stop the tears from spilling out when I saw Lily in the little bed.

I was at her side in a heartbeat, overwhelming emotions pulling me in different directions. Joy to be beside her. Devastation to see her as lifeless as my memory in the sketchbook.

Her skin was as ice-cold as I knew it would be when I ran my fingers down her face.

"Lily. Oh Lily, I'm going to fix this." I pressed my forehead to hers, my tears spilling onto her cheeks. "I'm back now. I got back to you. We're together again."

I wasn't sure how long I stayed with her, but eventually I heard Silos cough gently. I turned to him.

"I can't tell you how grateful I am to you, Silos. For taking care of her all these years."

He shrugged awkwardly. "I mean, she doesn't need much." His expression changed and he shook his hands vigorously, like he'd said something offensive. "Ah shit, I didn't mean, you know, just, she's..." He trailed off, wincing.

"It's okay. I know."

"There's, erm, something you might not know." His voice was grave, and he looked even more awkward as he stepped through the doorway and into the room. I was sitting on the floor by the raised pallet that functioned as Lily's bed, and he crouched down beside me.

He reached out and moved the blankets back. She was fully clothed under the sheets, and we both knew the blankets made no difference to her wellbeing, but it felt right to have them there.

"I'm sorry, Almi. But I noticed this a few months ago."

I tracked my eyes over her, looking for something wrong. "Her hands..."

I stared, my stomach dropping. Lily's skin used to shine like mother-of-pearl. But now... Now her skin was turning to stone.

Through fresh tears, I forced myself to look at her fingers, to touch them.

Cold, hard, stone.

"What's happening to her?"

"I don't know. Her feet are the same. I..." Silos swallowed. "I haven't checked anywhere else, I wasn't sure-"

I cut him off, laying a hand on his shoulder as hot tears

tracked down my face. He looked at me, dark eyes filled with sympathy.

"I didn't know if you'd ever come back, but if you did, this wasn't what I wanted you to come back to," he said quietly.

"I'm going to fix this," I said, forcing myself to my feet.

Silos stood with me. "Do you know how?"

I shook my head. "No. But I know where to start."

$\sim$

"Okay. First things first," Silos said as he placed two tankards down on the kitchen table, then sat down opposite me.

I took a swig of the drink, wincing with both shock and delight at the taste.

"Man, I'd forgotten how good this is," I said.

"Never mind the mead, tell me where you've been! All I know is that you show up with the fucking King of the Ocean one day, tell me your sister is in a magical sleep, ask me to take care of her, and then vanish!"

I gave him a look. "You were there. You know I didn't choose to vanish."

He took a swig of his own drink. "I have replayed the conversation you had with Poseidon over in my head so many times."

"You and me both," I growled. I'd watched it a hundred times since.

"Why did Poseidon send you away? Where did he send you? How did Lily end up like...*that*?"

34

I blew out a breath. "I can't tell you why he sent me away. As for where? The human world."

Silos' eyes widened. "No magic?"

I shook my head. "No magic." Silos didn't know I had no magic myself. Nobody except Lily knew that.

"Well, that explains whatever it is that you're wearing." He scowled at my outfit and I looked down. I guessed jeans and a Rolling Stones t-shirt weren't going to help me fit in in Aquarius.

"Do you have clothes I can borrow?"

"I can find something, sure," he said. "And Lily? How did she get like that?"

"I don't know." I glared at my drink, then downed a big gulp.

Silos took another deep swig of his drink too. "Almi, honestly, I'm so pleased to see you."

The truth of his words showed in his eyes, and I swallowed down my emotion. If I let it bubble up, it would overwhelm me. I was teetering on a precipice - utter joy that I was back in Olympus versus fierce focus and determination to save Lily.

I couldn't go to pieces. Not yet. Especially now she appeared to be turning to stone. I squashed my nausea at the thought and sipped more mead before answering him.

"I'm glad to be back. And I meant what I said, about you keeping her safe. It's kept me going, all these years. Thank you."

"That's what friends do." His eyes roamed over me, as though he still wasn't fully sure I was real. "You look different."

I laughed. "So do you."

His dark skin deepened in color. "Yeah. I got a bit taller."

"Just a bit."

"But you… Your hair isn't blue anymore."

"No. It turned fully dark when I entered the human world." Maybe it would turn back, now I was in Olympus again, but it had never been as vibrant as my sister's.

"Do you have somewhere to stay?"

I shook my head. "Could I stay here with Lily? Just until I get sorted."

"Sure."

I hesitated a moment, then asked a question of my own. "Where's your dad?"

Silos' eyes lit up. "He got a job in the palace."

"Huh. That's great." *Great if you wanted to be anywhere near the fuckwit that was Poseidon,* I added in my head.

"Yeah, he loves it. Best bread in Aquarius, fit for royalty," Silos beamed proudly.

I gave him a genuine smile back. "Your family always made the best bread."

"Yup. It was hard running this place on my own at first, but I'm good now."

"I'm sure you're doing great." And I meant it. Silos was as resourceful as I was. In fact, we'd met raiding the same trash for tossed out bits of junk that we could turn into something amazing.

"Thanks. Was it Poseidon who brought you back?"

"Hell no."

"Then how did you get here?"

"A metafora compass."

Silos stared at me. "How did you afford one of those?"

"I, erm , didn't."

Silos laughed. "Say no more."

I drained the rest of my mead, trying to work out how much to tell him. My brain was foggy, though, and I was starting to feel the first whack of fatigue hit me. The adrenaline buzzing through my body was wearing off, and it was getting harder to fight my emotions.

"Do you mind if I go upstairs?"

"Of course not. I'll get you some blankets and a pillow. Is there anything else you want?"

I gave him a grin. "You got any bread?"

# CHAPTER 6

"*A*lmi, you can't be serious. You want to steal from Poseidon?" Silos was working at the counter, kneading dough and throwing me disbelieving glances over his shoulder as he worked the next morning.

I'd slept, badly, on the floor of Lily's room, unable to keep checking her limbs, her stone fingers and toes making me feel unwell. *I had almost been too late.* I couldn't shift the awful thought that if I'd taken just a few months longer to come home, she could have been a freaking statue of herself.

Most of my wakeful moments had been spent wrangling my guilt into determination.

I was home now, and I was going to save her. Going to pieces, crying, or wallowing in remorse would do nothing for her. Stealing Poseidon's ship and finding the Font of Zoi would help her.

"I'm deadly serious," I answered Silos. "It's the only way to cure Lily."

I'd realized overnight that I would have to let Silos

into at least a little of my plan, as he knew far more about Aquarius and the palace than I did. I would be hindering myself by not asking for his help.

"Are you going to tell me what it is you want to steal?"

"No." I shook my head. "The less you know, the better. If your dad works at the Palace, then you must be able to get in to visit him?"

"No, I haven't ever been to see him at the Palace. Dad comes and visits here every three months. Almi, Poseidon sent you away - you shouldn't risk him finding out you're back, let alone getting caught stealing from him. He's merciless with criminals."

I shrugged, the movement far more casual than I felt. Poseidon was merciless, period. I knew that firsthand. "The Palace is huge. I'm sure Poseidon would never even know I was there."

Except, I had history with the god, and I was pretty sure he'd recognize me instantly, blue hair or not.

I would have to risk it, though. I needed to find out where he kept his ship. I knew I wouldn't be able to just walk in and take it - plans would have to be made.

"How can I get a job at the Palace?" I asked.

Silos looked over his shoulder at me, eyebrows raised. "You can't. I mean, short of entering the competition to be his personal guard." He snorted as he slapped more dough down on the countertop and began to beat it.

"What?"

"Nothing. It was a joke."

"Tell me."

"Every twenty years, he runs the Poseidon Trials, to

recruit members for his personal guard. The competition starts in a few days."

"A few days?"

Slowly, Silos turned to face me. "Almi, people die in the Poseidon Trials. We're too young to remember the last one, but my friend told me the other day that all but two of the entrants were killed."

When I didn't reply, he shook his head and wiped his brow, smearing flour across his face.

"Only the elite enter. The strongest of the strong, the most magic of the magic. *Heroes*."

I still just stared at him, my mind whirring. I didn't have magic. I was undernourished and out of shape. *Elite* was not a word I would use to describe myself. But I was smart. And I had a few days to arm myself with gadgets and artifacts to help me.

Besides, I didn't have to win. All I had to do was stay alive long enough to find a way to steal the ship. If nothing else, I was a tenacious sonofabitch - I could survive a few days, surely? If I was lucky, his magical ship was actually in the palace somewhere.

"Almi… They wouldn't even let you enter the competition. You have to have a reason. A connection to Poseidon, or crazy strong water magic, or be sponsored by another god."

"I do have a connection to Poseidon," I said quietly.

"Yeah, and I wish you'd tell me what it is," Silos said, his expression dark and serious now.

"How do I sign up?"

"You can't." Silos folded his arms across his chest.

I folded mine to match. "Watch me."

I left the bakery, rucksack over my shoulder and wearing an Aquarius-appropriate linen shirt. I couldn't help the ripples of excitement I felt as I reached the marketplace, the big blue ocean overhead and the dome edges gleaming gold in the distance.

I had spent the last eight years around human technology, which nobody could deny had a hell of a lot going for it, but here in Aquarius... The wares being sold at the stalls I was walking past were *magic*. And magic was just what I needed.

There was no question that swimming and water magic would be required to survive the Poseidon Trials. The truth was that even *getting* to Poseidon's palace was a pain in the ass for me. I could swim, but only as well as your average human. Which was *not* good enough to cross the expanse of freezing open water between the main city of domes and the one housing the underwater castle in which the asshole god lived.

Fortunately, Aquarius did have human - and non-swimming - inhabitants, so there were a variety of ways to help them maneuver between the domes that were not connected by tunnels. The problem was, I had to convince everyone that I was super-powerful, and that would be hard if I couldn't cross half a mile of water by myself.

If I wanted to make the right impression and hide my utter lack of magic, I would have to find a way to get to the palace in style. And that meant finding a way to breathe underwater and swim much better than I currently could.

. . .

I stopped at a stall on my right, scanning the bright powders and jars of fizzing liquids.

"All sorts of healing here, dearie," the man behind the stall said to me. I looked up at him and realized he wasn't a man at all, but some sort of griffin hybrid, with a beak for a nose and leathery looking wings behind him. I couldn't see his legs but knew they would look like they belonged on a lion.

"You got anything… destructive?" I asked hopefully.

He grinned at me, eyes crinkling above his beak. "Oh yes. What did you have in mind?"

It took me an hour to load up on all the supplies I needed. I had been relieved to find that some of my human gadgets were rare enough in Olympus that I was able to trade them for some of the more expensive magical items. A broken cellphone for two kilos of water-root was a damn good deal for me, given I had little in the way of drachma. I considered trading my now useless metafora compass, so that someone else could take their three turns with it, but I couldn't bring myself to part with it. I wasn't really sure why, but something made me want to hang onto the little bronze compass.

Plus, there was nothing in the market that matched it in value, so it would have been wasted financially.

I knew I had to get back to the bakery and start turning my haul into something useful, but I found myself heading toward the dome edge instead. The town I had grown up in was connected to six other domes, and there was a tunnel to each. As a child, I used to stand inside one of the tunnels as Lily zoomed around it in the water beyond, creating rings of bubbles that swirled around the clear tube like a watery tornado. I'd loved it.

I stopped when I reached the tunnel to the next dome. Either side of it were small pools of water that butted up against the dome edge. A woman lowered herself into one of the pools, and I watched wistfully as her legs morphed into a shining tail. I would have known she was a mermaid before I saw her legs change to a tail because of her blue skin and white hair. All merpeople had either jet black or snowy white hair. Her clothes vanished as her body changed, then she dove under the water of the pool. Seconds later, she emerged outside the dome, and a figure closed the distance, swimming toward her. A guy with his own gleaming tail. They grasped hands, then headed toward the bright surface.

Pools like this one existed next to every tunnel in Aquarius and they were the only way to get through the dome and into the ocean beyond - the places where water met water. I stared hard at the pool, willing some dormant power to lurch up inside me and make me want to immerse myself.

But nothing happened. Just like it had never happened as a child. I liked water well enough. I enjoyed the weight-lessness, I enjoyed the refreshing feel of moving through the liquid. But it didn't call to me like I knew it was supposed to. At best, I would describe my feeling for the ocean as an awed respect.

I blew out a sigh and moved to the tunnel. Once inside, I laid my hands on the glass and closed my eyes, trying to call up my image of Lily. I hadn't seen the vibrant depiction of her in my mind since I had seen the real-life version: the colorless girl turning to stone, lifeless in a lonely room.

Maybe I was avoiding her deliberately, unwilling to face the guilt I felt for leaving her alone so long.

"I wish you were here, now, making bubble rings," I told her.

My heart gave a relieved little swoop when her image materialized in my head, smiling.

*I will be, soon. If you can pull off this crazy plan of yours.*

"I will. I have to."

*How are you going to breathe underwater? That's going to be your biggest challenge.*

"I've got water-root. And a bunch of other stuff I can turn into something useful."

*Good. Get on with it then, instead of standing around in tunnels.*

I laughed out loud as she gave me her sternest look. "Yeah. Good idea."

"Almi, please don't do this."

"Silos, I have to."

My old friend stared beseechingly at me as I stood in the doorway of the bakery. I had set up a tiny workshop in Lily's room and had worked around the clock to fashion what I needed.

And now, I was ready.

I mean, I had tested nothing, and had about sixty percent confidence in my work, but that was as ready as I was going to be. I didn't have time to do any more.

"I don't even know why I'm worrying," the big man said, shaking his head. "It's not like they're actually going to let you compete. You've not even lived in Aquarius, hell *Olympus*, for eight years. It's not like you're just going to be able to just walk up and enter one of the most lethal water-magic competitions in all the realms."

His eyes were flinty as he spoke, and fear squirmed my stomach at his words. But I jutted my chin out and planted my hands on my hips. "I'll take that as you wishing me luck," I said. "And I'll say hi to your dad for you if I see him."

I spun on my heel, trying to ooze confident defiance as I strode out of the bakery.

"Almi." I felt Silos' hand on my shoulder and paused. He turned me slowly to face him, the hardness gone from his brown eyes. "If by some unholy cockup you actually get into the Trials, please, please, survive."

Impulsively, I hugged him. "Of course I will. Look after Lily for me." Leaving her, so soon after getting back to her, was the hardest thing. But I didn't have a choice. This was all I could do to save her.

"Always. Do you want me to walk with you?"

I shook my head as I stepped back. "No, you have to open the bakery. I remember the way."

"Good luck."

"Thanks. I might need it."

# CHAPTER 7

*I* underestimated how long it would take me to walk through the ten domes and tunnels I needed to reach my destination. The farther I got from my only friend, and Lily, the more my trepidation built. The enormous belt around my waist was comfortable, but heavy, and I could have done without using so much energy right before the swim I was going to have to make.

I'd had to make my belt myself because my old belt couldn't take the weight of so many pouches loaded on it. It would also hopefully keep Silos' shirt, which was much too big for me, from billowing up like a tent when I got in the water. Altogether, the oversized shirt, massive leather belt, shell necklace and blue scarf I'd used to tie my hair back made me look, and feel, a touch like a pirate. I decided to embrace the likeness.

"Let's go, me hearties," I muttered, as I walked along a paved path in a dome much wealthier than the market-town dome I had grown up in. The closer to the palace I got, the nicer the domes became, and this was the last one. The houses here were all made of the fancy white stone, instead of hard-packed sand, and some even had gardens. Grass was rare in Aquarius. The buildings were also more spread out, meaning that I could move between them. There, like a gleaming beacon in the big blue beyond, was Poseidon's palace. I was almost there.

The edge of the dome directly opposite the palace dome was lined with pools, every hundred meters or so. I walked to the one closest to me, and nerves made my stomach flutter as I looked between the pool and the palace in the distance. This pool was different from the smaller pools that flanked the tunnels in the other domes. It was three times as large, and white marble columns stood at the corners, vivid green ivy creeping up around them. Broad shiny tiles in matching marble edged the water.

Grateful that there was nobody else around, I took a deep breath, dug into one of my pouches, and took out one of the tiny capsules I'd made the night before. The water-root would serve two purposes—if I'd prepared it correctly. It should enable me to hold my breath for about fifteen minutes, and it should keep me from getting wet. I had been able to create a liquid that made anything I dipped into it waterproof, and that had been one thing that had been easy to test, so I was confident that my belongings would stay dry and safe. Hopefully, the water-root would do the same for my body.

I did one last inventory check of the pouches on my belt, knowing I was just procrastinating.

"Water-root capsules—check. Ink bombs—check." Those had been easy to make with the grenades the griffin had sold me. I had loaded half of them with magical ink that kept multiplying and acted like a glue underwater, and the other half with little pellets that zapped whatever they hit with a shock of electricity. Neither would make me look adept at water magic, or hurt anybody, but they were the best I could do.

"Elephant chip—check." It was my last one, and I hadn't had the heart to trade it at the market, although I couldn't imagine a use for it in Aquarius. "Book—check." A thin canvas bag I had spent a hefty chunk of my available funds on made everything that was put inside it weigh little more than a feather, and not much larger than one. I had nicknamed it the 'Tardis bag', and I had the book safely stowed inside it. "Sketchbook—check. Compass—check. Dagger—check." There was nothing magical about the little weapon, but when I'd seen it in the market stall, I had loved the tiny carvings of shells in the wooden handle, and it was priced low. A weapon of any sort seemed like a good idea.

I closed the last pouch, satisfied I had everything. Sadly, I had failed to find or create anything that would improve my ability to swim or move through the water. I would have to rely on my own pathetic athleticism to get me across the expanse to the palace. Hopefully before the water-root gave out. I closed my eyes and pulled my image of Lily up in my head. "I'm doing this," I told her. "Now."

*Yes, you are. And you're going to ace it,* she answered me, using one of my favorite American expressions and beaming at me.

"Damn straight I am."

I opened my eyes and stepped to the edge of the pool as I swallowed a water-root capsule. Before I could freak out, I lowered myself into the water.

The temperature was warm, and I was surprised how good it felt as I let go of the edge and let the liquid take my weight. I had avoided water in the human world. It reminded me too much of the world I had been snatched from.

I kicked my legs experimentally, pushing my arms wide. It felt good.

I took a breath, ducking my head underwater. I waited a moment, letting the initial wave of panic I felt at being submerged ebb away. I knew I wasn't supposed to feel panic at being underwater—I was a sea nymph. But I'd felt it my whole life, and today there was even more to be nervous of. I was going to Poseidon's palace. If he caught me, I would be sent straight back to the human world, or worse.

I halted the negative thoughts in their tracks, shaking my head a little under the water.

*Time to go,* Lily said in my head.

She was right.

I swam slowly to where the water met the edge of the dome and pushed my hand softly against the glass-like material. There was a tiny bit of resistance, then my fingers slipped through. Gathering my resolve, I kicked hard, and the rest of my body followed out into the ocean.

It was cooler than the pool. A lot cooler. I kicked my

legs and pushed with my arms, the shining palace fixed in my sights. It looked alarmingly far away.

I sang in my head, in an effort to stop my brain trying to convince me that it was too far to make in fifteen minutes. I wasn't even sure my fitness level could keep me moving for fifteen minutes. It was entirely possible that I would drown due to exhaustion before making it to the palace.

*You've eaten all the high energy food you could get your hands on, you'll be fine,* Lily told me, interrupting my song.

I sang louder in my head, trying to keep my pace steady. A claustrophobic feeling was nudging at my consciousness, the knowledge that I was under tons of water, with nothing but an endless black void beneath me terrifying if I let it get to me.

I didn't know how much time had passed but I knew I was starting to feel cold. I was vaguely aware of shapes moving in my peripheral vision, but it was all far in the distance, so I kept my focus squarely on the palace. *Count the towers,* Lily suggested. *It'll be a good distraction.*

The palace was massive. Truly huge. It looked like a castle had a baby with an ancient Greek temple. Spires and towers rose up from the main body of the structure, all at different heights and most topped with triangular, distinctly Grecian roofs. The towers themselves had columns running from the ground all the way up to the top, and I thought initially that the spaces between the columns were glass. But as I got closer, I could see that some were completely open. Others did have glass between them, making up the walls of circular rooms, but paintings moved across the glass. A tower near the back of the palace stretched so high that it penetrated the top of the dome and reached the surface of the ocean high above. The second highest tower was the central one, which was wider than the others and almost reached the dome roof. I was willing to be that was where Poseidon's throne room was.

As I got closer, I got a good view of the small cluster of buildings around the base of the palace, and I guessed they were guardhouses and workshops flanking massive gates made of glittering black stone. Courtyards with green lawns and neatly cropped trees and bushes filled the spaces between buildings.

A sharp burn in my chest snapped my attention inward.

The burn got stronger.

*Oh, shit.*

The water-root was wearing off.

I kicked harder, my leg muscles aching. I was only a few minutes away, but I was twenty feet too high. I angled down, the burn in my chest getting worse, and an irresistible urge to take a breath built inside me. I was only fifty feet from the dome. *I could make it.*

Something hard crashed into my side, and I cried out involuntarily as I went spinning through the water. I clutched wildly at my belt, my instincts forcing me to protect my trinkets.

When I was able to orient myself, I turned, treading water, trying to see what had hit me. It was taking all my effort not to take a breath in, my instincts all working against me.

Something was coming toward me through the water. Something a lot faster than me.

I dove toward the glowing gold of the dome but I was nowhere near the pool that would let me in. Trying to keep panic at bay, I swam as hard as my depleted energy would move me. The water around me plummeted in temperature, and I risked a look over my shoulder.

My mind blanked as fear engulfed me.

*Shark. Shark. Shark.*

The only word my mind was able to form echoed through my head as the predator powered through the ocean toward me.

The creature looked as though it were made from rotten liquid, black and deep red swirling together over the surface of its leathery skin, and its huge solid-black eyes fixed on me. It opened its mouth as it approached, revealing a second row of teeth even larger and sharper than the ones I'd first seen.

I scrabbled at my pouches, trying desperately to remember where the grenades were. Not that they would do anything against a beast this size.

My fingers fumbled, and I was unable to take my eyes from the shark.

I was going to die.

I was going to be eaten by a fucking demon shark.

*I'm sorry, Lily.*

There was a flash of something blue and white, moving through the water like lightning, and then the shark *exploded*. Red and black liquid cascaded through the water like some grotesque firework. My mouth opened involuntarily, and through my shock, I was dimly aware of my lungs betraying me. Cold water filled my mouth as I drew breath, then flowed down my throat.

Shit. The shark didn't get me, but I was going to drown.

A face appeared in front of me. A beautiful, fearsome face. A face I'd loathed for the last eight years.

The fury in Poseidon's intensely blue eyes was the last thing I saw before the world flashed white.

# CHAPTER 8

*M*y back slammed against something solid, and I felt rough hands turning me over. My chest heaved, and light blurred my vision completely as I was hauled up onto my hands and knees. Then I vomited.

I squeezed my stinging eyes closed as all the water I'd inhaled left my body, the disorientation and pain in my chest making it impossible to think straight. When I finally stopped retching, I sat back on my heels, wiping my eyes with the sleeve of my shirt and trying to make sense of what had just happened.

I looked around, my whole body shaking with exhaustion.

The palace. I was kneeling in front of the gates of the palace. Three guards stood along it, none of them human. In front of them was a woman dressed in a skin-tight blue leather bodysuit, her arms folded across her chest and about ten weapons strapped to various parts of herself. Her white hair was secured in a tight knot on top of her head, and she was staring down at me with what I thought was curiosity.

"What in the name of Zeus do you think you are doing?" growled a voice from behind me.

Slowly, I forced myself to my feet, before turning to face Poseidon. There was no way I was facing him on my knees.

Even if he had just saved my life.

*Was that what had happened?*

I swallowed as I saw him, my cocky bravado shriveling.

Holy hell, he was... *magnificent.*

The last time I'd seen him, I had been young and utterly uninterested in men or power.

Now though…. He was just as tall and broad, his white hair loose behind his shoulders. But he wasn't wearing the ocean-robe. He was shirtless. Leather straps and belts crisscrossed his muscular chest and held weapons similar to the woman's, and he had his own pair of tight blue leather pants. I forced my gaze to stay above his waist, angry with myself that I wanted to look at all. This was the person responsible for separating me from my sister for eight years. He was the reason I hadn't already found a cure for her.

Thinking of Lily focused me, and I finally found my voice. "Hello, husband."

"You are supposed to be in the mortal world," he snarled, as I heard the woman make a small noise of surprise.

My stomach constricted. He was going to send me back. One flick of his wrist, and I would be back there, unable to help Lily at all.

"I am *supposed* to be with my sister."

I thought I saw him flinch, but I was unsteady on my feet, and my vision was blurry. I couldn't trust much of what I saw.

He stepped closer, as if he knew I couldn't see him properly.

"Why are you here?"

I shrugged, the movement making me stumble. "Heard there was a competition on. I'm here to sign up."

His eyebrows raised, then his gaze intensified. "Why would you want to compete in the Poseidon Trials?"

I stared back at him, digging for an answer he might believe. "I thought if I could prove myself to you, that you might help me," I said eventually.

"I hid you for a reason," he said, his voice low as he stepped even closer to me. "I do not want proof of anything from you."

"You can't marry someone, and then hide them away!"

"So you're here to claim your rightful place as Queen of the Ocean?" he said, spreading his arms wide. "A mere girl who just *drowned*?"

"So you saved me, just to dump me in the mortal world again, where I can wait for my sister to die alone?" I loaded my words with as much venom as I could manage, but I was so weak now that my words were slurring slightly.

"You know why I saved you," he hissed, his voice low and quiet.

"The stupid fucking Oracle," I mumbled. I swayed on my feet, and the slight loss of balance gave me a jolt of shock. I straightened. "Don't send me back. Let me stay with Lily in Fyka."

I could find another way into the palace, to steal the ship. I *would* find another way.

Poseidon stared at me, and I stared back. The colors of the ocean swirled in his eyes, and a breeze carrying the scent of salt and ruffled past me. My vision rippled again, but this time, when it cleared, I gasped. All of the right side of his face was covered in pale gray stone, spreading across his jaw and down his neck.

"Your face..." I took a step toward him, reaching out with my hand without thinking. He moved back abruptly, his expression hardening.

"What about my face?" he barked.

"It's... turning to stone."

I heard another gasp, then the woman in the blue leather appeared, standing next to Poseidon. They looked at each other, before both pairs of eyes settled on me.

"Lily is turning to stone, too." My brain was fogging over, and frustration made me clench my fists. This was important. If both Poseidon and Lily were turning to stone...

"Take her into the palace," Poseidon said. "Before she collapses."

I blinked at the woman as she nodded. "The palace," I tried to repeat, but my mouth had stopped working properly, and a weird bubbly noise came out instead. My left knee gave out, and my other leg wasn't strong enough to take my weight. My ass hit the tiles beneath me with a painful thud, and everything went black for a moment when my torso followed.

"Too late," I heard the woman say, everything around me sounding tinny. "Sire, she shouldn't be able to see the stone."

"I know."

"Is... Is she truly your wife?"

"Take her inside, and make sure she is not recognizable for what she is."

"What is she?"

"The last of the Nereids."

# CHAPTER 9

*I* woke up in a bed. A much, much nicer bed than I'd ever slept in before.

My brain was slow as I blinked around myself, pain lancing through my head as I moved. I was in some sort of chamber, a round room furnished as a bedroom. I struggled into a sitting position and found myself patting my waist. My heart lurched as I realized my belt was missing.

All the fogginess vanished as I scooted up the bed, looking left and right around the room.

"Looking for this?" I spun, the woman in blue leather holding up my belt with one eyebrow raised.

"That's mine."

She tossed it onto the bed, and I groped for it. Just as I started to open the pouches it occurred to me that I might want to check my belongings when I didn't have company. I forced myself to lie back on the pillows.

"Who are you?"

"I'm Poseidon's general. Galatea."

"Oh." I eyed the myriad weapons about her person. I

had no doubt she could use every one of them. Her stern face was beautiful, and her gaze held a distinct 'don't fuck with me' edge. "Are you human?"

She snorted. "Of course not."

Eight years of living with humans caused a defensive flash of emotion inside me. "What's wrong with humans?" I scowled at her.

"Nothing, unless you live half a mile underwater and command the largest ocean army in Olympus."

I tilted my head in concession. She had a point. That would be tricky for a human. *Or a sea nymph with no damn power.* "What happened? Where am I?" I asked instead.

"I'm not sure what happened," she said quietly, her eyes appraising. "As for where you are, you're in the guest wing."

"Of the palace?"

"Yes."

I swallowed before asking my next question and noticed that my throat hurt like hell. "Where's Poseidon?"

"I have no idea. Now, this is not my usual job, but I have been tasked with making you look…" She trailed off and gave me another pointed once-over. "Different."

Snippets of the conversation I'd heard before I'd passed out came back to me. "He's turning to stone," I said, the memory of Poseidon's face smacking into me hard. I gripped the sheets as urgency took me. "So is my sister."

"Get out of bed. We need to find you clothes that fit."

"Why is he turning to stone? He must be able to stop it. He's a god!" If Poseidon, one of the three strongest and most important gods in Olympus, needed to find a cure, then surely one would be found?

Galatea looked at me, then let out a long sigh. "I can tell you're going to be a pain in my ass."

I nodded. "It's possible."

"Fine. Nobody except me knows about the stone affliction. It should have been invisible to you."

"How come you can see it then?"

"I can't. Poseidon told me about it."

"Oh. Then why can I see it?"

"I don't know. Nor does the king. That is why you are here, in the guest wing, irritating me."

"Does he know how to stop it?"

Galatea looked at me like I was stupid. "Don't you think he would have by now, if he did?"

I sat back, more pain gripping my skull. "Good point. My head hurts." I rubbed my forehead, trying to straighten my thoughts. My hope was fast fading, fear replacing it. If even Poseidon couldn't stop the stone...

I closed my eyes and called up my image of Lily. Slowly, she shimmered into being, blocking some of the pain of the headache. She smiled, and my thumping heart slowed a little. *Plan A, Almi. Nothing is different. Steal the ship, find Atlantis.*

I nodded.

"What are you doing? Maybe I should get a medic..." Galatea's worried voice made me open my eyes.

"No, I'm fine. Just a little slow."

That earned me another look that left me in no doubt of what she thought of my mental capacity. I sighed and swung my legs over the edge of the bed. "To clarify, I'm not being sent back to the human realm?"

"No. You are not."

Relief thwacked me in the gut. Poseidon knew I was here, and he wasn't sending me back. This was a good thing. "And how long am I staying here in the palace?"

"Until the Poseidon Trials are over, and the king can work out what to do with you."

The Trials! I'd totally forgotten. "I... I don't have to compete in the Trials?"

Galatea snorted. "Compete? You drowned after fifteen minutes in the ocean. You wouldn't survive five minutes in the Poseidon Trials."

"It wasn't like I drowned randomly," I protested, fisting a hand on my hip as I stood up. "There was a demon shark involved."

"That demon shark is called a *sápia aíma* and there's a lot worse than that in the Trials."

"It's called a what?"

"Rotblood."

"Well," I said. "You can tell Poseidon from me that these rotbloods shouldn't attack his visitors. It's rude."

I expected a sarcastic response, but her face tightened. "They should be nowhere near this close to the palace, or the city," she muttered. Her eyes found mine again, and she tilted her head. "You're really his wife," she said. It wasn't a question. More of a statement of disbelief.

"Yeah, if you can call a few words in front of Hera, then packing me off to another world to spend nearly a decade alone, a marriage."

Something in her eyes softened for a split second. "He tells me everything. But I didn't know about you."

I held my hands up. "Look, if you two are a thing-" She cut me off with a face that I didn't expect to see on one as stern as hers. It looked like she'd swallowed a slug.

"Poseidon is like a brother to me. I can't think of anything worse than engaging in... *sexual congress* with him."

"Huh. Well, I wouldn't know about *sexual congress* with him either."

"He never took you to his bed?"

"He took me to an altar, then to the Californian coast, and he left me there. Absolutely no beds involved." Something I had been grateful for. The man may have ruined my life and taken me away from my sister, but he never took anything more from me.

Galatea regarded me a moment longer. She had eyes that gave me the feeling that she knew exactly what I was thinking. They were such a pale blue they almost looked silver, and I found myself studying them so deeply that when she coughed, my cheeks flushed.

"Shall we?"

"Yes, right. Clothes, you said?" I replied in an embarrassed rush.

"Clothes. Are you wearing man's attire?"

"Yes. A friend gave them to me. My human clothes were drawing too much attention in Aquarius, and I have been away for eight years. I don't have anything here."

She rolled her eyes. "If you say 'eight years' again, there will be repercussions."

She shifted her weight, and a lethal-looking longsword skimmed her thigh in its scabbard.

I swallowed. "Well, I'm a touch bitter, but I'll do my best."

She left me alone to get ready, and the second she was gone I checked the contents of my pouches. Pulling out the Tardis-bag, I tipped out the book and my sketchbook, heaving a sigh of relief to see they were both safe and dry.

Flipping open the little book of memories, I ran my fingers over the pages as my mind tumbled through thoughts, one image dominating them all.

*Poseidon.*

I had seen him, fierce and furious, for the first time since that awful day.

My eyes focused on the sketches, my fingers turning the pages inexorably to the sketch I avoided the most.

I pressed my hand to the tear-stained drawing of my sister's bedroom, a shattered mug on the ground and a bad representation of me on my knees.

The image heated, and then I was back there, seeing the room as my eighteen-year-old self, taking my sister a coffee on the morning that was supposed to be her wedding day.

She was lying in her bed, her eyes closed, and I knew something was wrong instantly.

"Lily?" I dropped the mug and rushed to her, gasping as I touched her skin. It was ice cold.

"Lily!" My voice grew frantic. There was no breath coming from her lips. "Lily! Lily, please!" I dropped my head to her chest, desperate tears flooding from my eyes as I strained to hear a heartbeat.

Nothing. I could hear nothing. A wild sob burst from my chest as I clutched my sister, dizziness swamping me. This couldn't be happening. Lily couldn't be dead, she just *couldn't*.

A blinding flash of white light made me cry out, and the smell of the ocean crashed over me. I tried to turn, but my arms wouldn't release Lily.

I felt Poseidon's massive, godly presence, and then I was being pulled backwards, away from my sister. He cursed as he reached down, touching Lily's arm and recoiling.

"Leave her alone!" I yelled the command through my sobs, scrabbling back to her side. In my grief, I had no care at all for who I was shouting at. The almighty god could have done anything to me at that point, and I wouldn't have cared. Lily's lifeless form was all I could see, all I could think about.

Poseidon looked at me, his eyes filled with anger, then he clapped his hands. "Oracle! Explain yourself!" he bellowed.

A lyrical female voice filled the room. "The Nereid will sleep until the gods weep."

"What?" I stared up at Poseidon, and everything seeming to still around me, even my sobs. "Sleep?"

"Fucking deities," Poseidon hissed.

"She's asleep?" I said louder.

"Yes." Relief thumped through me so hard I felt my body sag.

*She was alive.* Lily was still alive.

Poseidon reached out, grabbing my elbow and I yelped, slapping at his hand.

"What are you doing?"

"We must marry. Now."

My relief that Lily was alive was momentarily halted as my mouth fell open. "What? Are you serious?"

"Deadly." He yanked me up to my feet and began to march me toward the door of my house.

"Let me go! We need to help my sister!"

"She is beyond your help."

A loud knock at the door pulled me from the memory, and I took a shuddering breath as the alien bedroom came back into focus around me.

A tear rolled down my cheek, and I brushed it away as Galatea's voice carried through the door to me.

"Are you nearly ready?"

"No!" I sucked in another shaky breath as I stared down at the book.

"I'm going to do this, Lily," I whispered. "He knows I'm here and hasn't sent me back."

*You've got this,* Lily answered in my head.

"I have. I'll let them reclothe me, and hopefully feed me, and then as soon as they leave me alone, I'll find out where he keeps his ship." Nodding firmly to myself, I closed the book and stood up. "I've fucking got this."

# CHAPTER 10

*I* followed Galatea down a corridor that had columns along each wall and beautiful gold patterns forming crashing waves between them. I reached out, running my hand along the wall to see if it was paint or magic. The gold waves moved as my fingers skimmed them, and the smell of the ocean washed over me. I couldn't help the grin that sprang to my lips.

My little cry-slash-pep-talk had helped, the emotion caused by seeing Poseidon's face for the first time since I thought I'd lost Lily forever, now forging into hardcore determination. *I was in the palace.* Which was exactly where I wanted to be.

When Galatea turned through an archway and pushed open a door, I risked asking her a question.

"So, what is Poseidon planning to do about the stone thing?"

She looked sharply over her shoulder at me as we entered a new room. "Do not speak of it when we are not in private chambers," she hissed. I looked around, seeing nobody. We were in a giant dressing room, mirrors and benches and marble countertops lining all sides of the room except one, which appeared to be a mammoth walk-in closet.

"There's nobody here-" I started to say, but she whirled to face me, her face fierce.

"You will not endanger the King's privacy," she spat. I did my best not to shrink back from her, but she emanated so much anger it was hard.

"Okay. I got it," I said, holding my hands up.

"You will have a chance to talk to him directly about it, in circumstances of his choosing. After the trials."

"Circumstances of his choosing," I repeated. Geez, he sounded high maintenance.

"He is the King. And a god. It is his way, or no way."

"Ideal husband material," I muttered under my breath sarcastically.

"As I am sure you are perfect wife material," she said, cocking an arched brow.

"I never wanted to be a wife!"

She rocked back on her heels, then pointed at one of the benches. "Sit. Wait. The nymphs will be in to attend to you shortly. Do not tell them who or what you are. You will have your skin altered to lose its shine, and your hair will need to change color."

"My skin?" I asked. My skin used to have a slight shine, nothing on my sister's mother-of-pearl glow, but it hadn't shone since I was in the human world. And my hair was brown.

She pointed again at the bench. "Sit. Wait. Don't speak to anyone."

I did as she told me, and my breath caught as I saw my reflection in the ornate dresser mirror.

My hair was the tiniest bit blue. Powder blue. And my skin did have a slight shine, like when I'd been a kid. I pulled at the neck of my shirt and looked down at my tattoo, almost scared to breathe.

*Please, please, let it have some color.*

Nothing. A black outline of a nautilus shell, nothing more.

When I looked back at my reflection, my face was screwed up in disappointment and Galatea was frowning at me, amusement in her eyes.

"Why did you just inspect your bosom?"

I snorted a laugh at the word 'bosom'. "That's my business, thank you very much," I told her.

"You are very odd. I can understand why Poseidon did not keep you in the palace."

Anger bubbled through me. "He sent me away because he's an asshole, not because I'm odd."

Her face blanched. "You blaspheme."

"It's the truth. He didn't know me for more than five minutes. He couldn't have known how odd I was. He married me because of my species and that stupid fucking prophecy, then dumped me where nobody knew about me, so that he could live the life of a single man. I may be odd, but I'm not taking the blame for him being a prick."

"You should watch your mouth." The dangerous glint was back in her eyes, and I was almost relieved when the tangy smell of the ocean washed through the room, and the god himself's voice rang out after it.

"Galatea, I need you in my throne room." The words boomed through the walls.

She glared at me a minute, then spun on her heel, slamming the door behind her.

I turned back to the mirror, seething. A ripple of fear that the god had magically heard me calling him a prick and an asshole assailed my gut.

*He didn't send you away because you're odd,* Lily's voice sounded in my head. Her vivid image sprang to life as self-doubt flooded me.

"I *am* odd, though."

She laughed. *Yes, you are. In all the best ways.*

"Why did he send me away?"

*So nobody could take you from him. Remember the prophecy? He who possesses the heart of a Nereid possesses the heart of the ocean.*

I'd been over this with Lily lots of times in my head and drew the same conclusion now that I always had. "It doesn't even make sense. Firstly, what is the heart of the ocean? And secondly, I'm not even a proper Nereid."

Lily frowned. *You are a proper Nereid.*

Before I could respond, the door behind me pushed open. Two nymphs came in, their skin the same powder blue as my hair and their robes gleaming white.

"Hello. We're here to make sure you fit in at court and look like a human," the smaller one said with a shy smile.

"Great," I replied. "Is there any chance this makeover comes with food?"

~

It turned out the makeover *did* come with food. A huge tray of fruit and pies and cold meat cuts followed swiftly after the nymphs. I devoured everything I could as they covered me in magical powders and did strange things to my hair. I gave up watching them in the mirror after a while, instead using the time to work out my plan.

I would go along with everything I was told to do, I decided. The less of a pain in the ass I was, the more likely it was they would leave me alone. I didn't know how long the Trials would take. I was guessing maybe a week? And they should keep both Poseidon and Galatea busy.

"Are all the competitors in the Trials staying in the palace?" I asked the nymph who was covering my hair in some sort of shiny goo.

They grinned back at me, nodding enthusiastically. "Yes. It's been so interesting working on so many different species."

That was good. If there were a number of strangers staying in the palace that would only make it easier to roam about. I decided to try my luck.

"Did any arrive on ships?"

"I'm sorry, I don't know. Please close your eyes, so we can do your make-up."

I did as they asked, sinking back into my thoughts. One doubt was starting to surface from the rest, and I was struggling to ignore it. If the book was to be believed, then Poseidon knew about Atlantis, and the Font of Zoi. And if that was the case, why hadn't he used it himself to cure his stone affliction?

He hadn't fallen into a magical coma before turning to

stone like Lily had. Were they the same sickness? Or did Lily now have two things I needed to fix?

If the Font of Zoi was as powerful as the book insinuated, then it should deal with both the sleep and stone. Which meant it wasn't worth waiting until after the Trials to see what Poseidon was planning to do about his own problem. I would be best off getting the hell out of the palace as soon as I could—before he could change his mind and send me away again.

"We've picked some outfits for you for the ceremony tonight, and your hair and make-up is all done," said the small nymph. I snapped my eyes open and saw the taller nymph standing in front of the closet, two dresses hanging on either side of the doors.

"Whoa," I breathed.

I had never owned a dress. Not because I didn't like them, but because they were impractical for somebody who rummaged through trash or stole things regularly.

But if I *were* to ever own a dress, then the two in front of me were beyond what I could have hoped for. They were utterly gorgeous.

One was an inky blue, with a huge, puffy bottom half and long drapey sleeves. The other was much slimmer fitting, a pale green satin with a plunging neckline, and an even lower back.

"Erm, which do you like best?" I asked, looking between the two nymphs.

"Your frame is very slight, and the paler dress may suit a more voluptuous silhouette," the smaller nymph answered thoughtfully.

A polite way of saying I needed to get some weight on my bones, I thought. "Let's go with the dark blue one."

"What's your name?" I asked, as they helped me into the surprisingly heavy dress. It had a corseted bodice, and it took both of the nymphs to help pull it tight.

"I'm Mov, and that's Roz."

"I'm Almi."

"We know. Are you ready to see yourself?"

"Sure."

My casual response didn't match my face when Roz slid a door across to reveal a full length mirror.

My jaw fell open.

I looked nothing like myself. I mean, my deep green eyes were the same, and my nose and mouth didn't look much different. But other than that... My once-pale skin was tanned, as though I'd spent a lot of time out in the sun. The make-up on my face made me look older, more distinguished. Perhaps even... Pretty. But the biggest difference was my hair. Mousy brown and shoulder-length, my hair usually spent its time tied out of my way in a knot on top of my head. But now, long strands fell in soft waves all about my face, the bulk of it in a complicated braided updo. The updo wasn't what was making me gape though. It was the color.

"My hair is purple."

"More of a lavender, I think," Mov said. "It is a very popular color in court right now. You look like a human wanting to be a part of Aquarius elite." They gave a satisfied nod of their head.

I turned to the side, trying to see more of it. There

were strands of blue and mauve and lavender, weaving all throughout.

"I love it."

"You do?" Mov looked pleased.

"I really do. I look like a movie star." I did a little twirl in the dress, making the full skirt poof out. A small panic shot through me though as I faced the mirror again.

*My tattoo.*

It should have been visible above the sweetheart neckline of the corset, but I couldn't see it in the reflection. I looked down at myself, relieved to see the shell outline below my sternum, the lines skimming my chest.

Not wanting to assume that the nymphs knew about my tattoo, or that it signified what I was, I said nothing. I would ask Galatea why I couldn't see it in the mirror when I next saw her. A scowl took my mouth as I thought of the stern general. I had to stop being so antagonistic to her. And to the almighty watery asshole.

As if on cue, the door to the dressing room banged open, and blue leather and white hair came into view.

Galatea gave me a quick look, then nodded. "You will fit in fine. Leave," she said to the nymphs. They both scurried off.

"Look, I just wanted to say sorry for being so-" I started to say, but she held up her hand.

"Poseidon has need of you."

"What? He's not needed me for..." I stopped speaking before saying *eight years*, dipping my eyes to her broadsword. I could have sworn she nearly smiled.

"You are to attend the Poseidon Trials ceremony tonight, under the guise of being a reporter."

"A reporter?"

"Yes. You have a large mouth and like asking questions. The persona should fit, and it is a valid reason for a human to be at such an event."

I deliberately kept my *large mouth* shut.

"Do not tell anybody who or what you really are. To everyone else, you are human. Poseidon has made sure your tattoo is invisible to all others. Nobody in the palace, other than the three of us, knows the truth. It must stay that way."

"You have made that abundantly clear," I said.

"Good."

"Can I keep my own name?"

"Yes."

"Can I call you Gala? Or Tea?"

She let out a long sigh. "No. You should not have to interact with Poseidon tonight, or indeed throughout the Trials. Stay out of trouble, and the next few days should pass uneventfully."

"Got it."

"Then we can find out why you can see the stone, when nobody else can. If you have designs on living as Poseidon's wife when this is over, with a crown and a place as Queen, then I'm afraid you may be disappointed." Her voice was surprisingly soft, and I got the impression she was telling me this not to be spiteful, but to manage my expectations.

It didn't stop the indignant defensiveness rising up through me like a firework. "You think I want to be a frigging Queen? Married to him?"

Her icy eyes bored into mine.

"Look, I don't need a man. When I cure my sister, I'll have all the company I need. I'm quite happy to stay well out of the way of his watery lordship." The truth was, he'd frightened the ever-living shit out of me the first time I'd seen him. The sooner I could get some distance between us, the better.

"I believe you," Galatea said eventually. "And I believe it must be difficult to be forced to marry against your will."

I froze, her words were so entirely unexpected. "Yes." Then I shrugged. "Well, being married to him is easy, actually. He's completely ignored me the entire time. What I objected to was being removed from my home." And Lily.

Galatea nodded. "Come. It is time to welcome the competitors."

I stepped forward, slightly off balance in the heavy dress. Again surprising me, she reached out an arm, steadying me.

"Thanks."

"Thank me by behaving yourself tonight," she said.

# CHAPTER 11

*I* followed Galatea down more corridors decorated with the enchanting gold wave paintings, my mind bouncing between thoughts like some sort of ping pong game. I couldn't help myself imagining what it would actually be like to be a Queen, living in this much luxury. Living in the shitty circumstances I had for years, I had poured all of my concentration on getting back, and I'd never given any thought to the fact that I was technically a queen. I was a business transaction to Poseidon, nothing more, and that had been easy for me to accept.

There had been a period when I'd been interested in men, times when I had been lonely and my body made demands my head wasn't sure it wanted. But I'd never acted on them. Not through loyalty to Poseidon, but because I couldn't see what the point would have been. If I had found a man, been with him, fallen for him, even, what could I have done about it? Hera was goddess of marriage in Olympus, and her rules were clear. One partner. No more. I might have been able to bring a human lover back with me, but then what? I couldn't marry them. And I didn't know the ocean god, *my husband,* well enough to know if he would have ignored his wife having a lover.

No, I had accepted a life without love not long after my forced wedding vows. But I had never, ever accepted a life without my sister.

The sound of hooves clacking on tiles drew my attention back to reality, and I looked over my shoulder.

A centaur was moving down the corridor behind us, catching us up fast. She was wearing body armor on her human torso, crossbows hanging from her hips and knives strapped to her amor-clad chest. Her brown hair hung around her severe face in tight braids, and her powerful horse body had symbols shaved into the chestnut-colored hair. She was magnificent.

"Galatea," she nodded at the general as she passed us. Her tail was braided in the same way as her hair. Galatea nodded in return, and a wave of excitement swept over me. I really was back. Years of no magic, and now... centaurs in the corridors.

We turned into a wider hallway, with nothing but air between the columns, and pedestals displaying busts of fierce looking fighters of all species lining it. Many were sea creatures. The hallway sloped upward, and I looked out as we moved along it. We were moving between two towers, I realized, and in the distance was the endless blue of the ocean. Shapes moved in the water, too far away to make out.

Ornate white double doors stood at the end of the

hallway, and Galatea strode toward them. They swung open as we reached them, and a voice rang out.

"Welcome, Galatea of Aquarius, General of Poseidon's Armies." There was a small ripple of applause as she stepped into the room. I took a breath and followed her.

"Christ on a cracker," I mumbled. The room was circular, and I assumed it was a whole floor of the tower we had entered. Like the hallway, it had columns ringing it, holding up the ceiling, with open spaces between each one. But unlike the hallway, the view was not looking out over the rest of the palace and the ocean beyond. Instead, there was some sort of enchanted coral reef encircling the room. Color and life blossomed everywhere. Hundreds and hundreds of fish in every color and pattern I could possibly imagine flitted between enormous fans of pastel coral, and tall green sea grasses waved in the gentle currents as neon eels slithered amongst them. Streams of bubbles glittering with golden particles corkscrewed through the water like shooting stars. It was mesmerizing. So mesmerizing that I stopped in the doorway.

"Oh, sorry," I muttered, as someone bumped into my back. The woman just tutted at me, moving on before I could get a glimpse of her face.

I shook off my awe of the space and moved further inside. A nymph like the two who had dressed me appeared out of nowhere, offering up a tray of delicate glasses. Pale liquid bubbled inside them, and I hoped it was alcoholic as I swiped one up gratefully.

I tried to keep my focus on the other guests in the room, instead of the incredible surroundings, as I sipped at the delightful drink.

The centaur who had passed us was there, and so were two minotaurs, the bull creatures hulking and dark in a room where most of the guests were brightly dressed or blue-skinned. My gaze was pulled to figures without my will, and I guessed that those with the most presence were the Olympian gods themselves. As a child, I'd visited events where the gods had been presiding, but I'd never been this close to one. Other than the watery asshole, of course.

Without a doubt, the most-presence-in-the-room award would go to the god with black robes, silver eyes, and tendrils of smoke dancing over his skin. *Hades.* But I'd never seen him in human form before—he had always presented himself as an ethereal smoke-being in public when I lived in Olympus. I raised my eyebrows as I watched him from across the room, his mouth quirking into a smile as he conversed with the largest Minotaur and Galatea. Since when did the god of death go to parties and smile? He moved to the right, and I saw that a woman on his other side was holding his arm. She was dressed in a green gown, her long white hair braided with golden flowers. She gazed at him as though he were water in a desert, and I suddenly understood why Hades was smiling.

He'd found love.

I dragged my eyes from the couple, looking for more gods. Specifically, Zeus and Poseidon. They should have been oozing as much power as Hades. But I could see, nor sense, either. There was no furniture in the room, but small pools with large golden fountains decorated with horses and dolphins were scattered around, and most guests were clustered around them. I recognized Dionysus—his iconic leather pants, open Hawaiian shirt, and half-naked forest dryads draped all over him giving him away immediately. He was a party god, which I supposed was fitting for a god of wine. I could also see Athena, the snowy owl on her shoulder looking as serious as she was as she talked to a small woman with a head-piece with a crescent moon on it. Hera and Aphrodite were absent, but Apollo and his twin sister Artemis were together, talking quietly at one of the fountains. They both wore white robes, and had gleaming honey-colored hair.

As if sensing I was looking, Apollo turned to me. Even from twenty meters across the room, I felt his power as his bright gold eyes met mine. He smiled, and my insides flipped. He was beautiful. Male model beautiful. I forced away my gaze, taking a few steps in the opposite direction. I didn't want the attention of any more damn Olympians, thank you very much. I supposed I'd gotten lucky that Poseidon had such little interest in me, beyond owning me in marriage.

I realized I was stamping slightly as my thoughts darkened, and I relaxed my shoulders and softened my pace.

*Take it all in. Learn what you can.* Lily's voice sounded in my head, and I took a deep swig from my glass, emptying it. She was right. I was here to pull off a heist, and all and any information would be helpful.

There were creatures in the room I'd never even seen before, and I found myself doing my best not to ogle as I moved as casually as I could through the crowd. Something I thought might be a harpy was darting a shriveled hand into one of the fountains, and I moved closer to see that she was trying to catch the carp that were swimming in the pool. She was short, with torn leathery wings jutting from her back and folding around her shriveled body. Her face was misshapen and angry, her eyes predatory. I moved on quickly.

There were a lot of sea species present, and whilst I'd at least heard of them all, it was my first time seeing some. Most interesting to me was a creature that seemed to be made entirely of gray sea-foam. When I got close to it, I had an intense urge to throw myself into the ocean, and never again see the surface, so I decided to give it a wide berth, swallowing down my curiosity. I wished Galatea had stuck with me, just so I could ask her questions. But she was engaged in conversation every time I spotted her, and I had vowed to not make a nuisance of myself, so I was forced to stick to making my assumptions.

Just as I got close to a group of merpeople, all boasting skin in various shades of green through blue, and full heads of white or black hair, the announcer's voice rang out.

"Presenting Poseidon, God of the Sea, and King of the Ocean!" The smell of salty brine filled the air and I turned to face the center of the room, where a white glow was building. Guests clapped loudly as the bright light faded to reveal Poseidon.

# CHAPTER 12

*H*e was wearing the robes I remembered from that fateful day on the platform, robes that looked like the ocean itself. His white hair was braided back from his face, his broad shoulders tanned. He looked like a Viking Adonis, and once again I cursed myself for noticing. He raised the hand holding his trident at the room in acknowledgement, but no smile came to his lips. Slowly, his eyes scanned the room. When they landed on me, they stopped.

My awareness of all the water in the room intensified, and I heard waves crashing in the far distance. Galatea strode up to him, causing him to look away from me, and the feeling vanished.

I shook my head, gulping down fizzy liquid from my refreshed glass. Why did he have such a damn effect on me?

*Seriously?* Lily replied in my head. *He's a god.*

"Hmmm," I mumbled. "I'm not sure he has this effect on everyone in the room."

"Why are you talking to yourself?"

I whirled at the deep voice, spilling my drink I was so startled.

Up close, Poseidon's presence was even more overwhelming, his eyes so intensely bright I couldn't look anywhere else. I dragged as much of my sass as I could muster to the forefront and jutted out my chin.

"Because I've been forced to live alone for years. There's been nobody else to talk to."

His expression tightened, and I found myself completely unable to imagine him wearing a smile. "So you talk to yourself?"

"I'm excellent company, thank you very much."

"Why are you here?"

"I already told you."

"You wished to prove yourself to me so that I might help you." His tone held no doubt that he didn't believe me.

I shifted uncomfortably. "This is your party—shouldn't you be talking to your guests?" I tore my eyes from his face and looked around us. Not another soul was looking our way. I cocked my head, surprised all eyes weren't on the host and the human nobody he was talking to, when I realized I was looking at everybody through a kind of shimmering film.

"We are in a bubble."

"A bubble?"

"Nobody can hear us. Or see us. So tell me. Why are you here?"

I didn't know if he was making a threat—his default

demeanor was so standoffish it was impossible to tell. "Galatea said to avoid you tonight."

Defying science, his mouth tightened even further. He looked like he was carved from stone. The thought made me realize something.

"I can't see the stone anymore," I half murmured.

"Never mind the stone. Why are you here? How did you get to Olympus?"

"Never mind the stone?" I repeated incredulously. "I thought that was the only reason you hadn't already sent me back to the human realm?"

"Gods, you anger me," he barked, and I took a step back as the rumble of thunder sounded. "Answer my question," he growled.

I folded my arms, trying to keep my rising fear at bay. His eyes flicked to my chest so briefly I almost missed it. Assuming he could see my tattoo, rather than assuming he was checking me out, I tried to weigh up my options.

I could either be meek and obedient and try to win his confidence. *Unlikely to work.* Meek wasn't really my go-to.

*Or* I could be so irritating he would get angry and leave me alone.

"You know, your trident is less impressive than I thought it would be," I said, as casually as I could. He looked at the trident, his eyebrows twitching.

I swear I saw actual waves in his eyes, silver foam speckling the bright blue. "You know, I could make you answer me," he hissed.

A true cold fear trickled through me at that. Could he force me to tell him the truth? Or worse, look inside my head?

"Yeah? Well, I could tell everyone who I really am. What would Olympus think of a king who married a woman against her will, then hid her from the world?"

"Olympus has low standards," he growled. "I highly doubt anyone would give a shit about who I marry."

"Do you?"

"Do I what?"

"Give a shit about who you married?"

The question tumbling from my lips surprised me as much as it did him. An awkward silence descended as he stared at me. The crashing waves in his irises had stopped, but his severe expression remained. "I must possess the heart of a Nereid," he said eventually.

An unexpected surge of emotion rose inside me. "And would you have dumped Lily in the human world, all alone, if you'd had the chance to marry her?"

"Yes."

"Why?"

"You are too valuable to be in this world, where anyone can see you," he snapped.

"Valuable? I'm not some fucking piece of jewelry!" I realized I was yelling and didn't have the self-control to stop. "What the hell is the heart of the ocean, anyway, and what the fuck does it have to do with me and Lily? Who the hell do you think you are, separating me from the only damn family I have left in the world, and leaving her to die alone!"

I hadn't even realized that I'd stepped forward until my finger jabbed hard into his solid chest. Pain lanced through my wrist, but it was too late. Nothing would stop the tirade of fury issuing from my mouth. The result of almost a decade of anger culminating in the discovery that if I'd got back any later, my sister might have been made of stone spewed forth, a tidal wave of hatred. "You're a monster! A goddamn asshole, with no compassion or kindness in a single bone in your body! You made me leave her!" I choked on the last words, heat burning at the back of my eyes and my whole body shaking. "You made me leave her." The sentence was a whisper this time, and a tear escaped, hot as it rolled down my cheek.

I jolted with shock as one of his hands gripped my shoulder. Fury burned in his eyes as he towered over me with a ferocity that made my entire body weak.

*I'd fucked up.*

I'd really fucked up. I'd taken my only chance at helping Lily and used it to yell and swear at the one person who would take me away from her again.

"You..." he said on a breath. His whole being seemed to swell, and more thunder rumbled in the distance. "You..." His grip tightened on my shoulder, and I sucked in a shuddery breath at the pain.

Letting go, he stepped back abruptly, and I stumbled. He whirled away, and the noise of the party slammed into me. I drew in deep breaths, dashing away the tears on my cheeks and not daring to take my eyes from the ocean god's back. He stopped striding across the room when he reached Galatea, snapping something at her. The smile vanished from her face as she turned to him.

"Are you okay? You look a bit... pale." I dragged my eyes from Poseidon to see the white-haired woman in the green gown who had been with Hades.

"I, erm…" I blinked at her. Adrenaline from losing my shit was coursing through me, and my legs felt wrong.

"Here," the woman said, and led me to a fountain. She sat down on the marble edge first, and I copied her, making sure Poseidon was still in my line of sight.

"I'm Persephone," the woman said. "Everyone here calls me Persy."

"Almi," I answered, flicking my eyes briefly to her.

"You know Poseidon, huh? Looks like he's giving Galatea a pretty rough dressing down." She had a knowing tone to her voice, and what I thought might have been a New York accent.

I finally focused on her. "Are you from the human world?"

"Yeah. Well, no. I was born here, banished for nearly thirty years, then came back." She shrugged and took a sip of her drink. "It worked out pretty well in the end though." She looked pointedly over at Hades. He looked like he was trying not to laugh at something a man with a red beard was saying.

"Thirty years?"

"Yup. I'm guessing you were not a spectator of the Hades Trials?"

I shook my head. She gave me a rueful smile. "Between you and me, these gods are messed up. But Poseidon? He's not as bad as everyone thinks he is."

My feelings must have been clear on my face, because she laughed. "Okay, so he *is* as grumpy as everyone says he is. But his heart is in the right place."

It was *my* damn heart Poseidon was interested in, I thought. *Possessing the heart of a nereid.*

His words came back to me. *You are too valuable.* The idea of me being or having anything of value to anyone was making my head spin.

I let out a long breath.

Why hadn't he sent me back? Why had he let me talk to him like that? I mean, everything I had said was true, and he totally deserved to be yelled at. But I couldn't believe I was still here, in the palace.

My eyes found his back again, and he stilled, as though he knew I was watching him.

"Are you from the human world?" Persephone asked gently.

"Yeah," I answered absently.

"Olympians, citizens, and all who are watching across Olympus!" Roared the announcer's voice.

All who were watching? So the Trials were being broadcast. That made sense, given that I was supposed to be masquerading as a reporter.

"Allow me to introduce you to your competitors!"

I couldn't see anyone that the voice seemed to belong to, but the double doors flew open. All the guests fell quiet and looked at the figures entering the room. Poseidon moved toward the door, Galatea flanking him.

A procession of four people strode in, coming to a stop in a line before the ocean god. I was unnervingly reminded of being one of the women lined up on the platform all those years ago.

Poseidon walked along the row of competitors, nodding at each of them. There was a good-looking older man with dark hair, pale skin, and leather armor, who could have been human by his appearance. Next to him

89

was a woman with dark navy-blue skin, black braids, and a skimpy black robe. A lethal-looking spear was clutched in her hand, and her lips had a slight sneer to them. Next to her was a tall, ugly man with green skin, no hair, and a vaguely angry, vacant look on his face. Finally, there was a woman who looked... wrong. There was no other way to describe her. It was as though she didn't fit in her body somehow, her limbs slightly too long or short. She had the blue skin and white hair of a mermaid, but her eyes were dark and her whole body was twitchy. Poseidon paused when he reached her, his eyes narrowing.

After a short moment, he turned to the room. "The Poseidon Trials will commence at first light. Enjoy." With a brief, but piercing, glance at me, he turned on his heel and strode through the doors, his beautiful robe swishing with waves as he left.

Galatea threw a look at me, then hurried after him. Was that a look to say I should go with them? Or a look to say 'you've done quite enough already'?

"Well, I guess that's Poseidon in a good mood," laughed Persephone as she stood up. "If you'll excuse me." She gave me a sincere smile. "Enjoy the party."

I watched her swish toward Hades, his eyes shining with light as he saw her approach. A flash of emotion sparked in me, and I closed my eyes a second.

"Lily, help me. I need to get a grip," I murmured.

*Yes, you do. I can't believe you yelled at him like that, Almi.*

"I know. But, for some reason, we're still here. And he made the stone go away."

I'd been so caught up in my anger, I'd forgotten. The stone hadn't been taking over his face. Did he have some kind of magic, or cure, that could keep the stone at bay? If so, I needed some. If I could buy Lily any time at all, I would take it.

I looked around the room. All the guests had surged forward now to talk to the competitors. Nobody was looking at me. I set my glass down on the edge of the fountain, scooped up my skirt, and moved as quickly as I could toward the double doors.

# CHAPTER 13

*I* hurried across the bridge-slash-corridor, not wanting to lose them, and almost shrieked in surprise when I reached the end and Galatea stepped out from behind one of the marble pillars.

"Jesus Christ on a cracker, what are you trying to do?" I gasped, clutching my chest.

"I could ask you the same question. Who is Jesus Christ?"

"A dude from the human world. I thought you wanted me to follow you," I lied.

"You're supposed to be a reporter. You should be interviewing the competitors."

"I don't want to. I want to know why I couldn't see the stone on Poseidon's face tonight."

Galatea sighed and rubbed a hand across her face. "Gods, give me strength."

I looked at her expectantly. "Does he know how to cure it?"

"No, or you wouldn't still be here," she half-growled.

"I'd tell you to ask him yourself, but given that you somehow managed to put him in the foulest mood I've seen him in for years during a five minute discussion, that might not be the best idea."

"Oh."

"What did you say to him?" she asked, then seemed to catch herself. "It's none of my business," she said, shaking her head and straightening.

"I don't mind you asking," I said, shrugging. "I told him his trident was underwhelming."

Galatea stared at me, and I couldn't tell if she was trying not to laugh, or trying to stop her eye twitch. "What the hell is wrong with you?"

"Nothing that couldn't be attributed to his royal highness," I smiled.

"You blame him for your apparent desire to anger everybody you come into contact with?"

"I blame him for a lot of things."

"Fine," she said. "I think it's probably best if I show you to your room."

I blinked. "But I want to talk to Poseidon about the stone."

"No. You're not talking to anyone else tonight."

I opened my mouth to protest, then closed it again. It might be wise not to push my luck with Poseidon tonight. He might even forget what I'd said to him and decide to be more helpful.

*Yeah, and maybe I'll wake up tomorrow and have magical powers,* I thought glumly. Fat chance of either of those things happening.

Still, going to my room was better. I would finally be left alone, and free to sneak out and explore the palace.

I followed Galatea, trying to keep track of the turns we were making. Eventually, we reached a plain white door, identical to most of the others we had passed, and she stopped.

"Here you are. I'll be back before first light to escort you to the Trials." She reached out and dropped something small into a hole in the door. Keys and locks in Olympus were usually orbs that fitted into holes. There was a click and the door opened to reveal the same bedroom that I had woken up in.

"Thanks," I said. She gestured toward the room. "Can I have the key?" I asked, holding out my hand.

My stomach sank as I saw her face tighten. "No."

"You can't lock me in."

"Yes, I can."

I felt like ice water was being poured over me. "So I'm a prisoner?"

"No, you are a guest. A guest who has no business being outside this room for the next six hours."

"I don't want to be trapped," I said through gritted teeth.

"You won't be. The palace is magical, if there is an emergency then the door will unlock."

I was certain I could hear reluctance in her voice, and I clung to it. "Galatea, please. I promise I won't leave the room, just please don't lock me in."

"I'm sorry, Almi." Gentle but firm, she gripped my shoulder and steered me into the bedroom. "I'll see you in a few hours."

The door closed behind her with a loud click.

The second she was gone, I tried pushing it. Unsurprisingly, it didn't move. "This is a fucking joke!" I bellowed at the door. It didn't make me feel any better.

"What the hell am I supposed to do now?" I threw myself down on the massive bed, trying not to notice how soft the sheets were.

*You could sleep?* Lily's voice was calm, quiet. The opposite of my raging brain.

"If I'd known they were going to lock me in, I would have stayed at the damn party," I snapped.

*You've got days. Get some rest.*

I snarled and got back to my feet. "I don't like being trapped in small spaces."

*This isn't a small space. Calm down. Take a look.*

She was right, I conceded, as I began to pace the room.

It was a massive bedroom. The ceiling glowed with a warm golden light that illuminated the whole space and made it cozy. The bed was in the center, under a window with blue and gold drapes drawn across it. My belt and all its pouches was exactly where I'd left it, on top of the excessive pile of pillows. A large bookcase with shelves full of books and trinkets stood against the wall on my right, and an even larger closet took up the rest of the wall. On the opposite wall was a door I assumed led to a bathroom and a dressing table, an ornate mirror perched atop it. I caught my reflection as I looked at it, startled by my elegant appearance.

I touched my purple hair, and felt my rage subside a little.

Maybe I did need a few hours to regroup. I could get

out of this crazy dress and take some time to think through everything that had happened.

I just needed some air. I glanced up at the window over the bed, then climbed up onto the mattress. Drawing back the drapes, I prayed it would open.

The view made my breath still for a beat. I could see the whole palace before me. The ocean around us was dark, making the golden glow of the dome even more beautiful. Spires and turrets and columns jutted up around the tower I was in, and I could see people moving along more walkway bridges like the one that had led to the party.

Remembering why I was at the window, I looked for a catch or handle. I didn't find one, but I did find a small depression in the center of the pane of glass. I pressed my hand to it curiously. With a small shimmer, the glass disappeared completely.

"Oh!" I pushed my arm warily out of the gap and felt a cool breeze blow across it. I leaned over, peering down, and vertigo made my gut swoop.

Climbing out the window was *not* an option. I was far too high up, and the tower wall below my window was sheer. That was probably why it wasn't locked. I retreated back into the room, leaving the drapes open.

With a deep breath, I moved to the dressing table, reaching up to pull free some of the pins that were keeping my hair back.

The purple strands tumbled around my shoulders as I sat down, and I realized I had been correct in thinking that I somehow had more hair than I did before. I couldn't help taking a moment to admire it. It was beautiful.

"Those nymphs know their shit," I mumbled, as I cast my eyes over the decorations on the grand mirror. The frame of the looking glass was made of the same marble that most of the palace seemed to be made from. Little sea creatures were carved into the stone, and I moved forward on the stool to see them better. There were ones I recognized from the human world, like turtles and dolphins, and the large starfish across the top corner. And there were more I recognized from Olympus, like the half-fish-half-horse hippocampus, and Charybdis the monstrous man-eating sea worm.

A breeze from the open window carried the smell of the sea into the room, and I inhaled deeply. I was home. I leaned forward, willing my connection to the sea to bring my magic to life like I had so many times before. I ran my fingers along the ocean creatures carved into the mirror.

"I am a creature of Aquarius, too," I whispered. "So why don't I feel like one?"

I felt something wet under my fingers and froze. Movement accompanied the moisture, and I snapped my hand back from the mirror.

"What the…"

My mouth fell open as the stone began to change color, the white marble turning a deep red where the starfish I had just touched was carved. Water dripped down the frame, pooling on the dresser below. I gasped as one of the arms of the starfish suddenly broke away from the frame. It wiggled a little, and then, with a squelching sound, the whole starfish came away, falling from the mirror.

# CHAPTER 14

"*O*uch!" said a voice as it landed on the dresser.

My heart pounded in my chest as I stared. None of the rest of the frame had changed, the other sea creatures still set in solid marble. But the red starfish...

There were more squelching sounds as it flopped about on the mahogany dresser.

"Did you just say ouch? Or have I finally lost it?" My voice came out a whisper, and the starfish froze.

"Erm..." The voice was high-pitched, and definitely coming from the starfish.

"Shit. You did! You just said ouch!"

"Well, you'd have said ouch if you fell on your face too."

I leaped to my feet, backing up from the dresser. The starfish continued to flop about, its suckers facing the ceiling.

"Could you at least turn me the right way up?" the high-pitched voice asked.

"What the hell is happening?" My legs were glued to

the ground as my mind raced through possibilities. Was the starfish a spy? Did all the ornaments in this palace come to freaking life?

"I don't know what's happening, because I'm upside-down," the voice replied. "I'd be much obliged if you'd turn me over."

Slowly, I moved back to the dresser and peered down at the beleaguered starfish. It was about the size of my palm. As quick as I could, I gripped the end of one of its arms and flipped it over. I heard its suckers grip the table as I snatched my hand back.

"That's better. Thanks."

"You're welcome. Who are you, and why are you in my room?"

"Ah, I was hoping you could tell me that. In fact, I have a number of questions."

I took a few deep breaths. "Shall we start with names? I'm Almi."

"I have no idea what my name is," the voice answered me. "I don't even know how I got here."

"You were on my mirror. Then all of a sudden you... came to life."

"How strange," the voice squeaked.

"Strange doesn't come close," I muttered. Although I had been away from magic long enough that I supposed I wasn't really qualified to judge. "What *do* you know about yourself?"

"I know that I am not a fearsome warrior." The voice sounded proud, and the starfish squished about on the wood of the dresser.

"Okay. Not a fearsome warrior." Given that he was

squishy and small, that was hardly a surprise. "Anything else?"

"I am male, and very clever."

"Clever, huh?"

"At hiding from my foes."

"Clever at hiding?" I frowned. "Were you maybe hiding on my mirror then? From your... foes?" I suggested.

"I have no idea. But that sounds likely." I moved closer, and he stilled. "You are large."

"I'm normal-sized," I protested.

"You are not human." It wasn't a question, and I raised my eyebrows.

"How do you know that?"

His middle raised a little, as though he was shrugging. "No idea. Can I touch you?"

"Ew, no!"

All of his arms bristled. "Rude," he said.

"Sorry, I just... you look slimy."

"I think, as I'm not underwater, I need the slime to breathe."

"Right. Why do you want to touch me?"

"I am compelled."

"By what?"

"My entire being."

I rubbed my hand across my forehead, staring down at the starfish. "I wish you had a face. I feel like I could trust you more if you had a face."

"Why wouldn't you trust me?"

"I'm the captive of a god, and I'm worried you're his spy," I admitted.

The starfish shuddered. "Captive of a god? That sounds dangerous. Perhaps we should hide."

I shook my head. "Any ideas, Lily?"

My sister's image formed in my head. *Let him touch you.*

"Why?"

*He's cute.*

"Who are you talking to?" the starfish asked me.

"Myself. Well, my sister. Except she's been asleep for a long time, so I'm pretty sure it's only my imagination really."

The starfish stilled, then his legs rippled again. "What is her advice?"

I closed my eyes, steeled myself, then laid my hand on the dresser, palm up. Opening my eyes, I spoke. "She says I should trust you. Because you're cute."

"Cute? I thought I was slimy."

"I guess you can be cute and slimy."

Slowly, the starfish moved, each of his suckers making a little pop as they came off the wood, then sucking back down on the surface.

I screwed my eyes up as the first of his cold, wet arms touched my finger. Almost instantly though, the cold vanished. He wasn't slimy at all, and as he kept moving, I felt his tiny suckers on my skin like soft little whispers. There was something weirdly comforting about his presence once he had settled fully onto my hand.

"So?" I asked him, when he'd been silent for too long.

"I like you," he said.

I cocked my head. "Most people don't."

"I am not people."

"No. I guess you're not." One of his arms curled up toward my wrist, and a smile came unbidden to my lips. He felt warm and right somehow. "You know, you need a name."

"You must name me for my skills."

"Which are?"

"I told you. Hiding from my foes."

"Who are these foes?"

"I don't know yet. But when I do, I am confident I will be able to hide from them."

"Good." I dug about in my brain, trying to remember the correct ancient Olympian word for 'hide'. "Kryvo," I said, as the word came to me.

A pulse of warmth came from the little starfish, and his red color deepened for a moment.

"I like that very much."

"I'm glad."

I moved backward, sitting down on the bed and lifting my hand to look at him more closely. "How exactly do you hide? You don't move very quickly."

As I watched, his skin changed color, blending seam-lessly with my own. Gaping, I lifted my hand, turning it cautiously upside-down. Kryvo clung to me, completely camouflaged. If a person didn't know he was there, there was no way he would have been spotted.

"Wow. That's really cool." He flushed red again as I lowered my hand.

"If cool means good, then yes. I am clever at hiding. Also at seeing things in other places."

"Huh?"

"I am seeing things that I believe are through another starfish's eyes."

I leaned forward, lifting him closer to my face. "Like what?" Maybe he was meant to be a spy, but he'd hit his head and forgotten who he worked for?

"I can show you, but you need to trust me," he said.

Nerves skittered through me. "I don't mean to be rude, but I literally just met you."

"We are bonded."

"What? How?"

"I don't know. But I am sure I can show you what I see. I just need access."

"Access?"

"Yes. With your permission. It may hurt a little."

I leaned my head back, alarmed. "Hurt? You're tiny, how could you-" I broke off as a sharp pain zipped through my palm. "Ouch!"

"That is the level of pain I am referring to. Do I have your permission?"

"Well there's not much point asking after you've hurt me!" I protested. "You got stingers in those suckers?"

"Yes."

I stilled my hand, looking at him more warily.

"Would you like to see what the other starfish are seeing?"

I was about to say no, but curiosity got the better of me. Curiosity *always* got the better of me.

"Yes," I said begrudgingly.

More pain spiked through my hand, but not so intense that I did much more than flinch a little. I felt a weird rushing sensation through my arm, and just as I was thinking that the little shit had injected me with poison, my vision clouded over.

It cleared almost instantly, and a room came into view. Not my room, but one I had seen before.

Poseidon's throne room.

It was another round room, columns ringing the space. But it was so high up above the rest of the palace I could see the whole city of Aquarius in the distance, the hundreds of golden domes looking magnificent against the blue. It was brighter too, I guessed as it was closer to the surface, and where the sharp rays of light fell on the white marble it changed color to a shimmering pale blue.

The ceiling was domed and painted with a breath-taking ocean scene. A reef covered in sea-life was depicted, all the creatures I'd seen on the reef yesterday, combined with shadowy beasts that would haunt a person's nightmares.

A throne stood in the center of the room, shaped like an enormous cresting wave, and sitting in it, leaning forward and tense, was Poseidon.

"My king, if she can see the stone, then she must be of use to you," Galatea was saying from where she was standing before him.

"It is too dangerous to keep her here!" Poseidon snapped back at her. He was no longer in his ocean robe with his hair braided back. In fact, he looked as though he'd just been swimming. He was wearing his leather strapping, but his hair was wet and loose, and water glistened on his hulking chest. The angry control on his face was gone, and a different, very real emotion played freely across his features.

"I wish you would tell me why, sire."

"I have," he growled. "If others know the last of Nereids is here, then they may try to take her. Whoever owns her, owns the heart of the ocean."

"But sire… You married her, and you do not appear to own the heart of the ocean. If you did, you would be able to stop this blight."

Poseidon stood up, swiping at a bowl of fruit on the pedestal to his side. It clattered to the ground. "The prophecy was clear! I only had to marry her. I don't understand."

"If she has anything to do with our problems, we need to find out what. The rotbloods are attacking every day now. Our defenses grow weaker. If we lose trust in the palace's ability to expel enemies…" She trailed off as Poseidon's eyes snapped to hers.

"You felt it too?"

She nodded. "The competitors. At least two of them."

Poseidon raised an arm, sweeping his wet hair back, bicep bulging. "I had hoped I was being paranoid. I believe there is something amiss about all four of them. But the palace has not identified them as enemies."

Galatea coughed. "The palace has not been able to alert us to the sharks. Or keep the blight that ails you at bay."

Poseidon said nothing for a moment, striding out of my view. I heard his voice as he replied. "Tomorrow, after the first Trial, I will talk to her. About the stone blight."

Galatea let out a sigh of relief. "Good. Thank you, my king. Aquarius needs you."

I didn't hear all of Poseidon's reply as the vision faded, but I was sure I caught the words 'fucking miracle'.

. . .

I blinked repeatedly as my bedroom came back into focus, Kryvo bright red on my palm.

"I..." Raising my hand to bring the creature close to my face, I squinted at him. "Was that real?"

"Yes. I think I can see through the eyes of the other starfish statues in the palace."

I tried to marshal my tumbling thoughts. The way Poseidon and Galatea had talked about the palace suggested it had a magic of its own. Perhaps that was where Kryvo had come from?

"Were they talking about you?" the starfish asked me.

"Yes."

"Correct me if I'm wrong, but it sounded like you are married to the king of the ocean."

"Yes."

"Then why are you a captive? And why are you not with your husband?"

I scoffed at the word husband. As succinctly as I could, I filled in the starfish on the prophecy, what had happened to my sister, and my subsequent wedding and banishment.

"So why did you come back to the palace?"

I paused before answering him. If he was a spy, I couldn't tell him I was here to steal Poseidon's ship to reach a fabled realm buried at the bottom of the sea that might be able to heal Lily. "I wanted Poseidon's help," I lied.

"Given that you are married to him, I think he *should* help you," Kryvo said indignantly.

I couldn't help smiling. "Exactly."

"It sounds like being married to you isn't giving him this heart of the ocean though. Are you really the last of the Nereids?"

His question stung more than he could possibly have known it would. I swallowed. "I think the prophecy was probably talking about my sister. Not me."

I couldn't admit to him that I had no power. But that stolen glimpse of Poseidon and Galatea's conversation had confirmed everything I had suspected. I wasn't a Nereid. Or if I was, I truly was broken.

# CHAPTER 15

*I* thought it would take me a long time to fall asleep, but I must have been more exhausted than I thought because I was out as soon as my head hit the overly fluffy pillows. Which I was thankful for when a loud knocking woke me up just four hours later.

I hauled myself out of bed, looking immediately for Kryvo. He was where I'd left him, on his own small pillow on the dresser. I moved to the door and opened it a crack. Galatea stood on the other side, hands on her hips.

"Get dressed," she said.

I gave her a salute, then slammed the door closed.

"Morning to you too," I grumbled, making my way to the closet and hoping there would be something suitable in there for me to wear.

"Good morning." The squeaky voice was Kryvo's, but it made me jump all the same.

"Hi."

I opened the closet doors and saw an array of clothing,

of two distinct types. Black, white, and brown utilitarian stuff, and ball gowns. I raised an eyebrow.

"Better not turn up to the first trial in a ballgown." Selecting black pants and a white shirt, I made my way into the bathroom.

"Where are we going?" asked Kryvo when I re-emerged clean and dressed.

"*We* aren't going anywhere. I have to go watch the start of the Trials." And then talk to Poseidon I thought, recalling the conversation I'd spied on him having.

I'd have been lying if I'd said I wasn't nervous to be around him. But any information at all on the stone ailment, or blight, as he had called it, could be important.

The fact that he must know about the healing font and hadn't used it nagged at me, but I was unwilling to give it ground in my mind. Mainly because, if I did, I had no plan at all, and I couldn't bear that.

"What are the Trials?"

"A deadly competition to see which of four powerful competitors is strong enough to be on Poseidon's personal guard."

"Oh yes, that doesn't sound appropriate for a starfish of my constitution," he said, arms rippling. "I'll stay here."

I cocked my head at him as I strapped on my belt. "You know, actually, you could be useful."

He stopped moving. "How so?"

"If I take you with me, you might be able to see things I can't. Or hear things I can't."

"No. I think I should hide. I mean, stay, here."

"Too late, buddy. You're coming with me. I'll clear you out a pouch."

He flushed a bright orange. "I am not getting in one of those pouches. If I am to go with you, I shall stay out in the open air, and hide using my superior skills."

"Okay," I shrugged. I stepped over to the dresser and tied my hair back from my face with my scarf. "Where do you want to go?"

I had left my shirt unbuttoned over my bandeau vest, and tucked into my belt. I rolled my sleeves up and showed him my forearms. "Left or right?"

"I will not feel safe on your fragile limbs." I frowned, but he carried on. "I will adhere myself to your collar."

"My collar?"

"Yes."

I looked down at my chest. He would fit between my shoulder and my collarbone, and still be able to see out. "Fine."

I picked him up, again getting a pleasant sense of rightness as I touched him. Carefully I placed him on my skin. I felt a tiny amount of pressure as he glued himself to me.

"You know how weird this is, right?"

"No."

I watched in the mirror as he rippled, then vanished. "I guess we're ready to go."


I half expected Galatea to look straight at the starfish and ask me what the hell it was doing there, but she just gave me a cursory glance when I opened the door and then strolled down the corridor. I hurried after her.

"I like your belt," she said.

I looked at her in surprise. "Oh. Thanks. I made it myself."

"Stay out of everyone's way, and Poseidon will see you after the Trial."

I remembered to look like I wasn't already aware of the sea god's plans. "He will?"

"Yes."

I followed Galatea all the way out of the palace to a grand courtyard stretching to the gated entrance.

I looked up, still in awe of the ocean above me after so long away from Aquarius. A pod of whales passed over the dome, their silhouettes dark against the bright light of the surface, and I grinned. We weaved our way through a maze of intricately pruned hedges and trees until people came into view, standing in front of the gates.

A row of Poseidon's guards, all with black or white hair and blue leather on, stood with spears at intervals along the entrance to the palace. In front of them stood the four competitors that had been introduced the night before. Along each side of the garden courtyard were the guests from the ball, Hades and Persephone included. Again, I scanned the faces for Zeus and Hera, or Aphrodite, but couldn't see them.

A crowd had gathered on the other side of the gates, clapping and whooping, presumably spectators from the rest of Aquarius and Olympus.

There was a flash of white light, and Poseidon appeared. He was dressed like his guards, and he held his trident aloft as everyone's gaze snapped to him.

"Welcome to the Poseidon Trials," he boomed. I scanned the four figures, looking for signs of cockiness or nerves. One of them would win this competition. Perhaps not all of them would survive it. I swallowed down the discomfort that made me feel.

Remembering what both Poseidon and Galatea had said during the conversation I wasn't supposed to have heard, I looked even harder at the competitors. The mermaid was the one that most made me agree with their suspicions that something was amiss about them. Something about her made me feel inexplicably uncomfortable.

"We shall start with a warm-up round. A short test of your abilities. The winner will gain an advantage over the other three," Poseidon said, pacing up and down the line of competitors.

The good-looking guy on the end stepped forward, and Poseidon paused.

"Your Majesty," the man said, bowing low.

An icy chill blew across my skin at his voice. It wasn't a normal voice. It rang with a deep, unmistakable power, though he hadn't spoken loudly.

Almost imperceptibly, Galatea drew her sword beside me.

"You dare interrupt me?" Poseidon said, facing the man.

"But I must interrupt you," he answered, straightening. He had a smile on his handsome face, and I saw something flicker in his eyes. "I'm afraid you are laboring under false pretenses, my king."

Poseidon took a step closer, fury dancing in his eyes.

Thunder rumbled in the distance. "Enlighten me," he growled.

"By all means. I must admit to a little... trickery." His eyes flashed again, and suddenly he was the same height as Poseidon. His dark leather armor vanished, replaced by gleaming silver straps that looked like liquid metal, tight over hulking muscle. His skin changed color, turning almost alabaster white, and his hair grew, changing to jet black as it fell down his back.

An emblem on the belt on his black pants surged with light. It was a globe, made up of interconnecting rings. I gasped, along with everyone else in the crowd. That emblem was famous. It was the emblem of the long-defeated Titan, Atlas.

Poseidon snarled and Hades appeared beside the ocean god in a flash of black smoke.

Atlas chuckled. "Ah, I see at least one of your brothers still stands by your side."

"Where have you been?" Hades said. "We presumed you dead after the Titanomachy."

Memories of my sister telling me all about the war Zeus and the Olympians waged against the ancient Titans skipped through my mind.

"You presumed wrong. I was merely asleep. Until I was awakened by a most unexpected god." Atlas looked between Poseidon and Hades. "Your wayward brother."

"Lies! Zeus would never wake a Titan," Poseidon barked. But Hades looked less convinced.

"Well, he did. And he gave me a gift. The perfect way to exact revenge on the one god I despise with every fiber of my immortal being." His eyes flashed again as they bore into Poseidon. "Zeus had his beautiful wife, Hera, with him. You are aware of Hera's powers over marriage, yes?"

Poseidon froze.

"Of course," said Hades.

"It is time to pay for your sins, Poseidon," Atlas said, stepping close to the sea god. "You killed my wife. And now, I shall return the favor."

# CHAPTER 16

Galatea stepped in front of me at the exact same time Poseidon's eyes flicked my way.

Atlas roared in triumph, and suddenly I was lifted from my feet, flying through the air. I bit back a shriek as I came to a halt, high above the crowd below.

"Your issue is with me, not her!" roared Poseidon. "Let her go!"

My heart was smashing against my chest, sweat instantly pouring from every damned cell in my body as I flailed in the air. *What the fuck was happening?*

"You want to save her?" I kicked and struggled as I floated toward the edge of the golden dome. My panicked mind faltered as I saw what was beyond the dome.

Six rotbloods, lined up, their onyx eyes fixed on me.

"Let her go!"

"I want control of the Trials. And the prize is no longer to be part of your pitiful army. The prize is your trident. Your realm. Your crown."

Bile rose in my throat as I got closer to the dome edge, fear making my skin feel like ice. I was vaguely aware of a pain in my shoulder, and the slight squeak of Kryvo's voice, but my blood was pounding too loud in my ears to concentrate.

The only words filtering through were those of the gods below me.

I was going to die.

There was no way in Olympus that Poseidon would give up his trident, realm, and crown to save me.

"Can I compete?" Poseidon's voice was granite, and I was so shocked that my limbs stopped flailing. I craned my neck, looking down.

"Of course. It would only be fair to give you a fighting chance at defending yourself." Atlas' voice was mocking, as though Poseidon didn't stand any such chance.

"I'll do it."

I could have sworn my heart actually stopped for a split second, then I was tumbling through clear air toward the marble. There was a flash of white, the strong smell of the ocean, and then I found myself on my ass at Galatea's feet. Fury lined every inch of her face, but I hardly saw her. My eyes went straight back to Poseidon.

"Excellent," beamed Atlas, rubbing his hands together. "Let me introduce you to your competition." He gestured at the three other competitors, and with a loud crack and shimmer, the woman transformed before my eyes.

I scrambled to my feet, feeling sick and dizzy as I tried to make sense of what was happening.

She looked nothing like she had just a few seconds ago.

About six feet tall, she was wearing a black gown that was a similar shape to the one I'd turned down due to my lack of curves. This woman had no such issues. She looked stunning in it, the fabric hanging from voluptuous hips and breasts, her dark skin glowing. But that wasn't what made her stand out. Her hair was made of water. I could see straight through it, and it moved when she stood still, swirling around her perfect face, her icy blue eyes seeming to glow the same hue.

"Kalypso, Titan goddess of water," Atlas boomed, gesturing to her. My stomach swooped. Kalypso? My sister had told me stories of the legendary water Titan. If they were to be believed, then she was as merciless as she was powerful. Looking at her cold eyes, I was inclined to believe.

The marble tiles rumbled beneath my feet, then the next man in the row shimmered and transformed.

"Polybotes, giant offspring of Gaia herself," Atlas grinned.

Twice the height of Kalypso and built like an oak tree, the giant stamped his feet, making the tiles rumble again. His face looked as though it had been beaten in times past and new, but his bright blue eyes were alert. And angry.

The shimmering started up again, and the mermaid began to change.

I held my breath as primal fear made me want to turn and run, far *far* away from the most terrifying creature I'd ever seen.

She had the torso of a woman, hulking with muscle, but the bottom half of an octopus. Tentacles slid across the courtyard tiles, covered not in suckers but thorny barbs. She was a deep red color, ripples of darker red and black moving constantly across the surface of her skin, making her look as though he was covered in liquid. Her eyes were like that of a shark, onyx black and unblinking, and she didn't have a hair on her skeletal head.

"Ceto, goddess of sea monsters."

*Holy shit.* Kids across the whole of Olympus had nightmares about this god. Hell, so did their parents. Just about every deadly creature in the ocean could call her their creator.

"And of course, for those who don't already know her, our final competitor, Almi! Last of the Nereids, and Poseidon's wife!"

My heart stuttered in my chest, and a new wave of dizziness stole my breath as every eye in the courtyard landed on me.

Every eye except Poseidon's. In a beat, he was at Atlas' throat, fingers wrapped around his neck. "We just made a deal," he snarled.

"Yes. I agreed not to feed her to the rotbloods. I never said anything else." Atlas' eyes were as hard as the sea god's. "I have thought about the woman you took from me every day for centuries. You will pay, Poseidon. You will feel the pain I have endured."

Poseidon bared his teeth and raised his trident. But it was as though his hand had got stuck in mud. He looked at his arm in confusion, then the trident floated up into the air. He let go of Atlas, reaching for his weapon, but it jerked out of his range.

Atlas laughed again. "Your prize!" he cried, pointing at

the trident and facing the row of hungry, lethal looking gods and monsters. "Control of everything Poseidon has. Yours for the taking."

# CHAPTER 17

"See you in one hour to find out which of you will have the advantage."

There was a flash of light and Atlas was gone, and the trident with him.

Poseidon gave a roar of rage, slammed his foot down and whirled to face the competitors.

"You dare challenge me for my blood-earned realm?"

Kalypso shrugged as she stepped forward. "Blood means nothing in Olympus, Poseidon. If you believe the realm should be yours, you can earn it. Prove you are strong enough." She tilted her chin, swished her water-hair over her shoulder, then strode past him, back toward the palace.

Polybotes bared his teeth before he spoke, his voice uncomfortably deep. "She's right, Poseidon. You and I have history, and I intend to see you crushed." He slammed one fist into his other open palm, then stamped after Kalypso.

"And you? After everything I have bestowed upon you

and your brother, and after serving me loyally for centuries?" the ocean god said, turning to Ceto.

"You expect us to give up the opportunity to rule?" Her voice was an awful hiss, making me flinch. "I have as much right to compete as the others," she said. "And, mighty king, I have as much chance at winning."

Without another word she melted into thin air, leaving a murky cloud in her wake.

Beside me, Galatea moved, and I caught her arm. "What is happening?"

She glared at me. "You're about to compete with Poseidon, a Titan, a giant, and a sea monster for control of Aquarius."

"Why did Poseidon agree to this?" My voice was a whisper.

Before she could reply, Poseidon's voice rang out loudly, making us both turn. "Citizens of Olympus! It seems you will have a better show than anticipated. Fear not. I will smash these unworthy opponents into the depths and beyond. Atlas and his champions will be no threat to Aquarius." The gathered crowd roared as Poseidon raised his fists, his fierce eyes alive with passion. "I shall emerge from the Poseidon Trials as the undisputed ruler of the oceans." There were more cheers and whoops. "See you all in one hour!"

He clapped his hands together, and everything flashed white.

When the light faded I found myself in his throne room. And not alone. Galatea was still standing next to me, but Hades, Persephone, Athena and Apollo were all in a ring around the throne.

"Brother, how did Atlas enter your palace?" Hades asked immediately.

"Zeus must have helped him," Poseidon snapped back. He wasn't sitting in the throne but pacing in front of it.

"If Zeus is befriending Titans, we need to be worried."

Apollo nodded, and Athena spoke softly. "It sounds as though he has finally brought Hera over to his way of thinking."

"There is only so long she could fight her husband," said Hades tightly.

I tried to follow what they were saying, but my mind was racing, both with information and emotion.

It sounded like Zeus was no longer on the same side as the other Olympians, but that was so far down my list of things to worry about at that moment that I couldn't care less. I just wanted the other gods gone, so I could talk to Poseidon.

Persephone glanced at me, then spoke. "We did not know you were married, Poseidon."

Everyone except the sea god looked at me.

"No," was all he said.

Persephone coughed. "What did you do to Atlas' wife that has made him seek this revenge?"

I focused on Poseidon's face, desperate to know the answer to that question myself. But his eyes were cold, and his mouth tight.

"That business is my own."

"Brother, it might help—" Hades started, but Poseidon cut him off.

"I will not look weak, and I will not bow to the command of an asshole like Atlas. I will beat the others."

"And Almi?" Persephone's voice was harder now. "Forgive me," she said, turning to me. "I don't know anything about Nereids, but are you powerful enough to compete with gods as strong as those entered in these Trials?"

My skin seemed to tighten over my bones, and my ears began to ring loudly.

*No*, I wanted to scream. *No. I will die in five fucking seconds flat.*

Surely others knowing my secret was less lethal than continuing to pretend?

I opened my mouth to admit I wasn't, but Poseidon spoke first. "She will survive."

Persephone frowned. "But not win?"

"I will win!" He hit himself in the chest, and my eyes widened.

The stone was back.

It crept across his face, down his shoulder, and along his arm. My insides coiled with fear and doubt.

Poseidon was sick. Nobody else knew, but he was sick.

What if he couldn't win?

Much as I hated him, did he really deserve to lose his trident and realm?

What if that terrifying monster Ceto won? Or the cruel Kalypso?

Athena spoke again. "You have been challenged in public, and accepted. I believe that there is nothing for us to do now but see this through."

Hades growled and the temperature in the throne room rose. "This is part of Zeus' plan. He is using Atlas. We should not let this go ahead."

"That is precisely why we *should* let this go ahead. For too long, the king of the gods has been silent. It is time he made his move."

"And you would let Poseidon take the risk?"

"If we back Atlas, rather than fight him, then we should be able to maintain a measure of involvement throughout. With the Olympians supporting the Trials there will be less chance of cheating and lawlessness."

"I am willing," Poseidon said. He stood straighter, and the stone spread down his hip, out of sight under his pants. How could the other gods not see it?

Hades reached forward, clasping his arm. "Win, brother. Aquarius is rightfully yours—it can belong to no other."

"What will Atlas do if Poseidon does win?" asked Apollo.

"With any luck, he will call in Zeus," answered Athena. "And then we will have a chance to reason with our wayward king. Farewell." She nodded at the other gods in turn. "Win, Poseidon. Or great danger could befall the whole of Olympus." Then she vanished.

"No pressure," grinned Apollo, then he too vanished.

"Good luck, brother." Hades nodded, and Persephone looked over at me.

"If you need anything, let me know," she said, then nodded at Poseidon before they both left in a flash of white.

"Sire," Galatea said. "What—?"

"Please leave us."

She froze. After a painfully long pause, she said, "Yes, Sire," and whirled away to leave the room.

My body was so tense my muscles shook as Poseidon turned slowly to face me. He locked his eyes on mine.

"Why did you do that?" I blurted out.

"You need to stay out of my way. Just survive and let me take care of the rest," he said, his voice calmer than his wild eyes.

"Why did you give up your trident to save me?"

"You would have preferred I let you be fed to the sharks?" His being flashed with power, and a wave of weakness washed over me. His eyes softened instantly. "You need to sit."

A scraping sounded behind me, and I saw that a chair had been conjured up out of nowhere. I thought about protesting, but my weak knees got the better of me. I slumped backward, letting the cushions take my weight.

Scrubbing my hand across my face, I tried again. "Why did you give up your trident to stop Atlas killing me?"

Poseidon moved closer, his scent filling my nostrils. It was the ocean personified, fresh and bright and powerful. He opened his mouth, indecision shining in his eyes. With a snap, he closed it again and held out his arm. "You see this?"

"Stone," I answered. The gray granite moved with him.

"Not even the Olympians can see this. Yet you can."

"Is that why you saved me?"

"Amongst other reasons," he growled. "When the Trials are over, we need to fix it."

I held my hand up. "Wait. Firstly, what do you think I can do that you, an Olympian god, can't?" Fear made my gut clench at his admission that he couldn't fix it himself. That was seriously bad news.

"That is what I intend to discover."

I let out a long breath. "Right. Secondly, why are we waiting until the Trials are over to fix it? Is it not going to..." I tried to work out how to word my question without making him angry. "Slow you down a bit?"

His expression turned stormy, and he pulled his arm back. "No. *You* will slow me down," he snapped.

I leaned back, folding my arms. "I didn't ask for any of this shit."

"You came back! If you'd stayed out of the way, where I left you-"

"Then my sister would have died alone!" I shouted over him.

He stepped even closer to me, his own temper clearly on the brink. "Your sister is not the most important thing in Olympus."

"She is to me," I answered, stabbing my thumb at my chest.

Something flickered in his eyes, something that wasn't his dark temper.

He took a long breath and a cool breeze washed over my skin from nowhere. "You can barely stand up. This is not conducive to surviving.

I blinked at the rapid change of subject.

"You are malnourished."

"And who's fault is that?"

He clapped his hands together, and when he drew them apart he was holding a vial. "Drink this. It will give you enough energy to stay the hell out of my way and let me win this thing."

"I guess losing your trident hasn't made you lose any

of your charm," I mumbled as I took the magicked vial from him.

"Not true."

I raised my eyebrows as I sniffed the liquid in the vial. It smelled like woodsmoke and salt. "You never had any charm to begin with?"

"The trident is my connection with the creatures of the ocean." The anger had gone from his voice, and a tense sadness had replaced it. "It is how I charm them."

I looked at him as he gazed up at the ceiling, his eyes skimming over all the sea-life depicted there. "So... You can't control sea animals anymore?"

He shook his head, strands of his white hair falling along his hard jaw. "I can't even communicate with them, let alone control them."

"Does that include sea monsters?"

"Yes."

"Shit."

He looked back down at me, eyes bright and wild. "I concur."

"Huh. Nice we can agree on something."

"Drink," he said.

I did. The liquid tasted freaking amazing, like rich smoky tea. Warmth flooded my body, and I felt my muscles twitch. The tiredness drained away, and even my mind seemed more alert.

"That's good," I muttered. "Thank you."

"Just don't die," he scowled.

"I still don't understand why you care about my life so much."

"I have told you, repeatedly. I need to possess your

heart, as the prophecy foretold, and I need to find out if you have any connection to this cursed fucking stone blight."

I stopped myself from pointing out that possessing my heart was achieving nothing. I only knew that because I spied on his conversation with Galatea, and I had no intention of admitting that.

"What is the heart of the ocean?"

"Stop asking inane questions and leave."

"No. I have so many more questions."

"I don't care. Galatea!" He roared his generals name, and she strode through the doors to the throne room in seconds.

"Sire."

"Escort Almi to her room."

She looked pissed, but she nodded.

I didn't bother arguing. It was clear Poseidon was done talking, and besides, I could do with a few moments alone. I had a lot to process and talking it through with my imaginary sister in public might raise the wrong eyebrows.


"I didn't know that was going to happen," I said, as I followed Galatea down the corridors of the palace. Even her back seemed angry.

She didn't answer me.

"Honestly, I didn't know anything about Atlas, or even Zeus, I've been away so long."

Still no answer.

"What happened with Zeus and Hades and Poseidon?" I asked hopefully.

"They fell out. Olympus is paying the price," she spat.

"Oh?"

"Hades and Persephone, then Ares and Bella... Now Poseidon." She shook her head, then looked at me over her shoulder. "I'm not sure I trust you."

Weirdly, I appreciated her honesty. And frankly, she *shouldn't* trust me. "I didn't know that would happen," I repeated. "I didn't ask Poseidon to give up his trident."

She glared at me some more, then turned back. "The palace should have kept enemies out. *Someone* let Atlas in."

I couldn't help my snort. "And you think that was me?" It wasn't like I could tell her that I had no magic, but the idea was absurd all the same.

"You expect me to believe it is coincidence that your return and this mutiny occurred two damned days apart?"

"It is coincidence," I snapped. "Atlas is crashing your Trials, and I didn't set the dates for those—that was your king. How is the palace supposed to keep enemies out? Is it alive?" I asked, thinking of Kryvo coming to life on the mirror. I knew he was still hidden on my shoulder, because I could just feel his presence when I moved. I hoped he was okay.

"I am telling you nothing you might use against the king." I sighed. "Fine."

We reached my room, and she opened the door with a little too much force.

"You locking me in again?"

"What do you think?"

# CHAPTER 18

*I* went straight to the dresser when the door closed behind me, sitting on the stool.

"You okay, Kryvo?"

Alarmingly slowly, the little starfish turned red and visible again. I held my hand to my chest, and he inched his way off my collarbone and onto my palm.

"Hiding did not help me," he said quietly.

"Of course it did. Nobody saw you," I said, a very fake cheerfulness to my voice.

"If you had been fed to the rotbloods, they would have eaten me too."

"You could have detached yourself from me and swam invisibly through the ocean?" I suggested.

He paused in his slow shuffle to my hand. "That is a possibility."

"Good."

"Are you okay?"

His question caught me by surprise. "Oh. Erm, no, not really."

"I don't blame you," he answered. "You must compete with a Titan, a giant, a monstrous ancient sea god, and Poseidon himself in a series of lethal Trials. Can I offer you some advice?"

"I reckon I can guess what it will be."

"You should hide."

I nodded. "Much as I'd love to, I'm not sure Atlas will give me that option. It looks like I'm key to his revenge." I screwed my face up. "Why couldn't that fucking Oracle have picked a different sea nymph species? Why the hell do I have to be married to that tosser?"

"Do you wish him to lose the Trials?"

Kryvo was on my hand fully, so I lowered him onto the dresser. "I don't know. I haven't thought that far ahead, to be honest."

"You clearly hate him. Losing his trident and Aquarius would be apt punishment for someone who has treated you and your family so badly."

I cocked my head, thinking. "Lily? What do you think?"

Her image appeared in my mind. *Aquarius belongs to Poseidon. It should not be any other way. He and his brothers are the core Olympus is built on.*

"But he's miserable, and mean, and selfish and, well, just an asshole."

*He is a fair ruler.*

"Fair? What the hell is fair about what he has done to us?"

*He separated us, but he never hurt us. Many gods would have done much worse.*

I let out an angry snort. But as I let the thought roll

around in my head a little more, I began to wonder if she was right.

Not about Poseidon not being an asshole—that was *not* up for dispute. But about him being the right ruler of Aquarius. Atlas had some bad vibes going on. I realized I had assumed that whoever won would rule alongside him, but that may not be the case. I made a mental note to find out why Atlas wasn't competing himself, and considered the others. Kalypso was strong and powerful. She might make a good ruler. But the stories about her were all of a being with no mercy and an explosive temper. Polybotes the giant was unknown to me, so I couldn't guess what he would do as a ruler. But Ceto... The goddess of sea monsters and her brother, Phorkys the god of the deep, had created most of the worst monsters of the ocean. They scared me just to look at. I didn't want to think about what they would turn Aquarius into if they ruled.

"Kalypso is very powerful," Kryvo said, surprising me.

"You know her?"

"No. But there are paintings in the palace that tell stories. Where there are statues, I can see them. I shall show you."

I moved back to the dresser and picked him up, carefully setting him back on my collarbone. "You comfy there?" I asked him.

"As comfortable as I can be. Although I'm not sure being able to see out is very pleasant, given what you are about to face."

"Don't remind me."

The more I thought about what I was actually going to have to do, the more I felt like I was going to throw up.

Compete with gods in lethal Trials. What would be involved? I remembered what Silos had told me about people dying in the last Trials, and images of underwater cages and enormous, vicious sea monsters floated through my mind. My stomach flipped and flopped, apparently doing everything possible to make me feel more unsettled.

"Ready?" Kryvo said.

"Yup."

His little stingers attached to my skin, causing a sharp sensation that faded quickly, then the vision came to me.

Like last time, I was looking out from what I guessed was a statue in the palace. But instead of looking at Poseidon's throne room, this time, I was looking at a mural on a wall. All in different hues of blue, except for the sweeping highlights of gold, the painting was breathtaking.

It showed Kalypso fighting Zeus. She looked furious, her watery hair a whirlpool of fury matched by her eyes as she raised her arms, tidal waves rising behind her in response. Zeus was above her, clouds swirling around him, eyes electric and lightning bolts streaming from his fingertips, lancing through Kalypso's defenses.

The vision faded and I let out a long breath. "I don't believe the other Olympians would let anything that bad happen," I said, false hope in my voice. "So let's not worry about that. I just need to concentrate on staying alive."

I stood up and began rummaging through my pouches. I got out my water-root, and reloaded my stash in the top of one pouch so that I could access it more quickly if I needed to.

The vial had indeed restored my energy, all the tired, shaky limb problems I'd had earlier gone. I was sure I could swim for fifteen or twenty minutes.

"This isn't an actual Trial," I told myself as I checked my little grenades for the hundredth time.

*Exactly. Just a test, Poseidon called it. A test you'll ace,* Lily said in my head.

"Just a test. I'll be fine."

I felt sick.

A male voice sounded in my head, making me cry out in surprise. "Be ready in one minute."

It was Atlas' voice, and he sounded like he could barely contain his glee. I hurried to my belt, strapping it tightly to myself as my pulse ramped up a few notches.

"You staying there, or do you want to wait here on the dresser?" I asked Kryvo, secretly praying he would come with me. I didn't know if he could help in any way, but trepidation was causing fresh sweat to run down between my shoulder blades, and not being completely alone was appealing.

He paused before answering. "Are you sure you can't hide?"

"Quite sure."

"Then I suppose I shall have to come with you."

"Thanks, Kryvo."

I barely got the words out before the world flashed white.

# CHAPTER 19

*I* found myself in a golden dome under the sea
dominated by a single structure. An arena.

Oval in shape, it reminded me of a coliseum, except
that in the middle, where there would usually be sand or a
stage, was a temple. Except...it wasn't a temple at all.
Greek style columns stood at each corner, and there was a
triangular style roof on top of the columns, but the sides
were clear glass, turning the whole thing into something
reminiscent of a giant fish-tank.

I squinted to make sure I was seeing correctly.

I was.

The thing was filled with water. A large, rocky cave
rose up from the bottom of one side of the tank, its
entrance angled up into the main body of water. Small,
black-and-white fish moved between tall swaying grasses,
but the greenery was sparse, and perhaps only for decora-
tion. Kryvo wouldn't like it, I thought as I stared. There
was nowhere to hide except the cave. And I got the

distinct feeling that was the last place anyone would want to go.

Rows of benches lined the sides of the arena, and the temple-tank was so huge I didn't think there was anywhere you could sit and not get a good view of what was happening inside it. And boy, were there a lot of people looking. The bleachers were filled with spectators. Hundreds and hundreds of Olympian citizens, all cheering and waving banners, had turned out for the spectacle.

I was standing on the top row of the seats, which appeared to have been reserved for the gods, and the competitors.

"Good day Olympus!" roared Atlas' voice. "Please find, in turn, your champions!"

I watched as a bright light shot up from opposite me on the other side of the stadium, like a laser-beam. Kalypso was illuminated, and she waved. The black gown was gone, replaced by tight black leather fighting garb.

Another beam of light went up to her right, illuminating Polybotes. I watched as the light ringed the stadium, lighting up Ceto, Poseidon, then myself.

Poseidon looked as angry as I'd ever seen him, weapons strapped to his chest and hips, and golden armor plating his shoulders. I couldn't help thinking he looked wrong somehow without his trident. The crowd roared for him though, a much bigger cheer than for any of the other competitors. Myself included. I'd barely received a smattering of applause.

"This is a game to win an advantage in the Trials. A warmup, if you will," boomed Atlas' voice. I looked around for him but could see no sign of the Titan. The Olympian gods, minus Zeus, Hera and Aphrodite, were sitting in a box of seats to my left, looking for all the world like they were attending a gladiator show. "Let me tell you more about the first Trial."

A flame the size of a building burst from the triangular tank roof, bright white and fierce. As it died down, an image appeared in the body of the flame. It was a shell. A nautilus shell, the geometric curves just like the one tattooed on my chest.

"The Poseidon Trials will be won by the contestant with the most of these at the end. The first Trial will be a race." The image shifted, and a ship with gleaming golden sails came into view. "To earn both your ship and your starting positions in the race, you will each now face a deadly sea creature. The time it takes to retrieve the ship's flag from the monster's lair is the time you will have to wait before starting the race."

I swallowed.

*I couldn't defeat a deadly sea creature.*

I had no weapons, no speed, no magic.

"Shit. Shit. Fuck, damn and shit." The cold sweat was back, and I shifted my weight between my feet, scrambling for a plan. "Any ideas, Kryvo?" I hissed.

"Hide?"

I gritted my teeth. Company, he may be, but the little starfish was not going to be useful in a fight.

Atlas's voice rang out again. "First up, Kalypso!"

There was a flash of light, then Kalypso was in the tank. She didn't even have to kick her legs to tread water, her body just hovered in the liquid like it was the most natural thing in the world.

I would have expected her hair to become invisible once she was underwater, given that it was made from water itself. But it didn't vanish at all. Instead, it turned bright violet purple, swishing up and around her face just like real hair.

"She will be facing a giant octopus!"

The water churned opposite her, then shimmered. A giant octopus appeared, with long muscular tentacles that whipped and churned at the water around it. Sticking out of its suckers were wicked dagger-sharp claws and its eyes were pitiless red orbs. I noticed one tentacle had a strange-shaped sucker on the end of it, with a bright red glowing spot, but then the creature attacked, and all my attention moved to Kalypso.

She easily dodged the first swipe, moving through the water like magic, no thrashing or kicking her limbs at all. She swooped and ducked under every lashing of the lethal tentacles, getting beneath the monster and closer to the cave entrance.

In the sand on the tank bottom, directly under the octopus was a glowing green flag, gently waving in the current. As Kalypso reached it the octopus made a screeching sound, flicking the tentacle with the glowing end toward her. She raised her hand, and I saw a short spear in it. Ignoring the green flag, she flicked the spear at the octopus above her. It landed directly in the glowing red spot, and the thing screeched even louder. Kalypso sped up and swam over a second flag just a foot from the entrance to the cave, this one yellow. The octopus moved fast, trying to get back to the entrance of what I was guessing was its lair, before Kalypso reached it.

The movement of the huge creature sent more currents pulsing through the water and I saw a bright blue flag rippling just inside the entrance.

Kalypso was moving so fast that she reached it just before the octopus did, but she didn't swipe up the blue flag. Instead, she kept moving, entering the cave. Dark liquid erupted from the octopus' suckers and one darted into the darkness after her.

I held my breath for a beat, then the octopus screeched a final time, shimmered and disappeared.

Kalypso swam back out of the cave, waving a red flag triumphantly.

"Kalypso reached the most difficult flag in one minute and four seconds," roared Atlas. "The red flag equates to her having a Whirlwind class ship for the race. Congratulations, Kalypso!"

She waved the flag some more, then she flashed white, disappearing from the tank and reappearing in the top row of benches where she'd started.

The crowd cheered loudly as I sat down hard on the bench behind me.

"I'm going to die."

"It is possible," Kryvo said.

Panic was setting in, making my fingertips feel weirdly numb. "What the hell am I going to do?"

"I would suggest not going for the flag that is inside the cave, but for one closer."

"No shit," I muttered. "What's a Whirlwind class ship anyway?"

"I don't know, but I can probably find out."

I rubbed my hand across my face, then back through my hair, pulling on my braid.

I tried to picture myself in the tank with the octopus. What would I have done?

"Next up, Polybotes!"

There was a flash and the giant appeared in the tank.

I stood back up, wringing my hands as I waited to see what the giant would be facing. "He must get past a rotblood!"

The demon shark shimmered into being opposite him. Icy chills rippled over my skin, but the giant had no such fear.

He beat his chest, and it looked as though he was laughing. How was he breathing underwater? I knew Poseidon was the creator of the giants, but I didn't know any of them had water magic.

Polybotes was almost as big as the shark, and it snapped at him, black soulless eyes fixed on his throat. Polybotes raised one massive fist. I frowned in disbelief as the rotblood darted forward and he drew back his arm.

"He's not going to-"

A gasp cut off my sentence as the giant landed a punch square on the end of the rotblood's snout. It spun backward through the water, and the giant kicked his legs, angling down toward the cave. The rotblood was fast though, wheeling and snapping at Polybotes heels. I bit down on my lip as the shark caught one of his massive leather boots. I half expected the giant's leg to come clean off as the shark shook its head from side to side, but Polybotes coiled up, landing punch after punch on the shark's face. Eventually, the thing let go of his boot.

"Remind me to find out what the fuck his footwear is made from," I muttered, as he kicked back down toward the flags.

I was equally surprised when the giant didn't go to the cave, instead swiping up the first green flag. Lifting it high, he gave the shark the finger before it vanished.

"Polybotes gets the Zephyr flag in two minutes and fifteen seconds!" bellowed Atlas' voice.

"Zephyr?"

I felt a little sting on my collarbone, and a vision descended over my own.

"I found something," said Kryvo.

I was about to tell him I needed my sight on the arena, but an image formed before me, and I couldn't help looking.

It was another painting, in gleaming color this time, and it showed four ships with cursive writing beneath.

The largest ship had Whirlwind written beneath it. It was completely clad in metal armoring and had three tall masts. Next to it was a ship labeled as a Typhoon, which looked like a Viking long ship to me. It had two masts and a pointy spike on the front. Next was a Zephyr, which was enormous compared to the others, and had an actual pool in the middle of the deck in the painting. Maybe that was why Polybotes went for the Zephyr, I thought. It was the only ship big enough for him. Lastly was a small ship, wooden and plain. A Crosswind, according to the script below.

"Next up, Ceto!" Atlas' voice reached my ears, and the

vision vanished, the temple-tank and arena coming back into focus.

"Thanks, Kryvo," I whispered.

"And she will be facing an enchelys!"

Poseidon's voice rang out around the arena dome, and I snapped my eyes to him. "Ceto is the mother of enchelys," he boomed. "This hardly seems fair."

"For the purposes of these Trials, Ceto and her brother have waived their powers over the creatures who call them their creators," Atlas replied. "Isn't that right, Ceto?"

The sea-goddess spoke, and it sounded like she was underwater, a gurgling sound to every syllable that instinctively made me think of drowning. "Indeed, Atlas. We wish for nothing but a fair win."

"Commence!"

With a flash, the half sea-monster woman was in the tank.

The water between her and the cave shimmered, and then a snake appeared in the water. And not just any snake. The meanest damn snake I'd ever seen.

It had a mane of spikes around its scaly face, and neon green flashes of color pulsed down its unfeasibly long length. Two probing tentacles jutting out from behind its jaws tested the water, flicking menacingly.

Unlike the last two sea creatures, this thing's bright green eyes seemed to hold a knowing gaze, and I wondered how intelligent it was.

I blinked and almost missed the two lunge for each other. Tail and tentacles swiped and splashed through the liquid, and then they coiled around each other, while the snake's mouth snapped at Ceto's human torso.

Dark red oozed around her, and I didn't know if it was inky liquid like an octopus had, or magic, but the snake's thrashing seemed to slow. She raised her hands high and began to twist, her tentacles still locked in a violent embrace with the snake's tail. She brought her hands together, and the dark red stuff expanded like a firework, filling the tank. The snake spasmed, then went limp, uncoiling itself as it floated down to the bottom of the tank.

Ceto moved through the water like a dart, swiping up the blue flag just inside the cave mouth.

"Ceto wins a Typhoon, in one minutes and forty seconds!"

I sat back down, sucking in air.

I couldn't punch a shark in the face or poison a sea snake. What the fuck was I going to do?

"Next up, your defending ruler, Poseidon!"

The crowd threw up a deafening roar as Poseidon was flashed into the tank. His white hair rose around him as he hovered in the water, muscles bulging under the leather strapping and his face fiercely confident. He held a spear in his right hand in place of his trident, and his left hand was glowing.

I stood up again, leaning forward involuntarily.

"He will be facing a xanosa!"

I shuddered as the creature appeared opposite him. Another monster reserved for kids' nightmares, xanosa were a type of siren. She was almost translucent, gray in color, like a watery wraith. Her bones and organs were visible, glowing red inside her mermaid-like body and wings on her back fluttered in the water as she flicked her tail. Her face was pretty until she slowly opened her mouth. Her jaw seemed to disconnect from the rest of her skull, and a dark, gaping hole appeared in her face. The water before her rippled, and I knew from the stories that she was sending lethal sound through the water toward Poseidon.

But the sea god's left hand rose high above his head, glowed brightly, then exploded with what looked like ropes made from water. They twisted and twirled toward the siren, wrapping her up in seconds, turning her over and over in the tank until she was surrounded by spirals of churning liquid. Poseidon moved through the water faster than any of the others had, and was inside the cave before the siren had stopped spinning.

A heartbeat later he emerged, a red flag in his hand. The siren vanished.

"Poseidon gets a Whirlwind in fifty-six seconds," said Atlas, his gleeful boom distinctly absent.

Bile rose in my throat as I realized I was the only contestant left. I rammed some water-root into my mouth as discreetly as I could, my hands shaking.

"Next up is our wildcard entry," he announced. "Almi, *wife* of Poseidon!" The glee was back in his voice. I barely had time to suck in a breath, before the world flashed white.

# CHAPTER 20

The water was warm, and though I had to kick my legs to tread water, I didn't notice any tiredness in my muscles. Poseidon's magic vial was working.

*I can do this. I can do this,* I chanted in my head, focusing below me, where the flags were. The closest flag. That's all I had to get to, and then I would be flashed back out of the tank.

"Please don't die," I heard Kryvo's terrified voice say.

"Almi will be facing a saraki!"

A what? I'd never even heard of a saraki. Kryvo clearly had though, because he let out a pained squeak.

The water before me shimmered, then revealed a creature I couldn't have dreamed up if I'd tried. Fear made my entire body seize as I tried to take it in.

The size of my shitty old car, it looked like a fish, but half of its whole frigging body was mouth. Hundreds of teeth as tall as me jutted out of its jaws at all angles, and I couldn't avoid seeing down its expansive gullet. It could swallow me whole.

A long arm came out of the top of its head, a glowing orb dangling on the end of it, in front of the monstrous mouth.

I had time to remember something about angler fish luring in prey with a light hanging in front of their mouths, when everything suddenly turned dark.

All I could see was the glowing orb. It seemed kind of far away, and a gentle fog clouded my mind.

Where was I? And why was it dark?

The light would help me. I just needed to reach the light, and I would be able to see what was happening.

I kicked my legs, moving toward the light.

A slight stabbing pain on my collarbone made me pause.

I could hear a distant squeaking, but the pull of the light and the muffled fogginess in my head made it impossible to work out what it was.

I shook my head, trying to clear it, but nothing happened.

The light pulsed, and I refocused on it. It was so pretty. A warm orange glow that promised safety.

I gave another kick of my legs. I needed to reach the light.

*Stop.*

A male voice boomed through the fog in my head. *Swim down. Now.*

I recognized the voice. Who's was it? My memory wasn't working properly. Nothing was working properly, I realized, a tiny trickle of alarm creeping into my calm.

*Swim down. Now. Look for a yellow flag.*

But... But the light. I needed to get to the light.

*The yellow flag! Now!*

Almost against my will, I changed my angle, tipping my head downward through the water. Some of the darkness receded as the orb left my line of sight. A faint glow of green was beneath me, and a little further on, yellow.

*Good. The yellow flag. Don't look at the light.*

Water churned around me, and more of the serenity that had overcome me leaked away.

Fear replaced it. As the green flag came into reach, the haze lifted completely, and awareness of my situation rushed me.

Christ on a fucking cracker, I'd nearly swum straight into the thing's mouth.

Instinctively, stupidly, I glanced up at the mammoth fish I was swimming under. As soon as the light came into focus, everything around me dimmed again.

*Almi!*

Wrenching my gaze away, I kicked my legs hard. I reached for the green flag.

*The yellow flag. You will not be able to sail a Zephyr,* the voice barked.

*Poseidon?*

It was Poseidon's voice, I realized now that the brain-fog had faded.

Hesitantly, I pulled my hand back from the green flag.

He was helping me. I would be fish-food if he hadn't spoken to me. I had no reason not to trust him.

I kicked my legs hard, heading for the yellow flag instead. The water around me churned suddenly, throwing me off course. I rolled in the water, the fish above me coming into view.

Apparently, it had given up trying to lure me in gently.

I swallowed back a scream as its disproportionately small fins whirred and it powered through the water toward me, its terrifying jaws snapping violently. The light swung before it, and everything around me dimmed and sharpened as my eyes betrayed my instructions and tried to follow it.

I used my arms to pull myself through the water, as low to the sand and out of the thing's reach as I could get.

The yellow flag was only a couple of feet away and I spurred myself forward as my chest hit the sandy bottom.

I lunged for the flag, and as I closed my fingers around it, pain screamed through my ankle. My lips parted as I saw stars, water rushing into my mouth and down my throat.

"Almi gets a Crosswind in four minutes and forty-seconds," I vaguely heard Atlas say, and then I was on the bleachers, gasping for air and choking on water as I crumpled to the floor.

I heaved, water clearing from my airways, my eyes streaming. The pain in my ankle was so intense I thought I might pass out.

"It bit you, oh gods, it bit you," Kryvo was squeaking repeatedly.

I wiped at my eyes and rolled over onto my side, before looking down at my ankle.

If I hadn't just spewed up a load of water, I probably would have thrown up. Blood poured from a gash low on my calf, the skin ragged from the thing's serrated tooth. I was pretty sure I could see bone, and my head swam. I looked away, leaning my head back on the bench and closing my eyes. A deep fatigue washed through me, the pain dulling. Somewhere in my head, I knew that was a very bad thing. But I couldn't fight the darkness pulling me down.

I heard footsteps, then a female voice.

"Fuck, that's nasty. Good job it only grazed you. Let me sort this out."

I forced open my eyes with an effort, and saw the white haired figure of Persephone sitting on the bench above me.

Vines flowed from her palms toward my legs. I was too out of it to respond, and when they wrapped around my thigh a pleasant warmth pulsed out from them. The darkness began to lift.

Then the pain came back full force, and I let out a hissing breath.

"It'll stop hurting in a minute," Persephone said apologetically. After a second, the pain faded, and I felt my shoulders sag in relief.

Atlas' voice echoed around the arena, making them tense again. "That's it for today! Tomorrow we will witness the first Trial of three, to decide who will win Poseidon's trident, and his realm."

"You can look now," Persephone said.

I did, screwing my face up in dread.

The gash was gone. A wide white scar was in its place, and the pool of blood still spread across the sandy ground, but the wound itself was no more.

"Woah." I scrambled into a sitting position and realized that my fatigue had disappeared too. "How did you do that?"

"I'm a goddess of life. I'm good at healing," she smiled at me, the vines unwrapping from my thigh and whooshing back into her palms. "Here. Let me help you up." She held out her hand to me and I took it, steadying myself on her as I stood up. Gingerly, I tested my ankle. It was a bit sore, like I'd twisted it or something, but that was all.

"I can't thank you enough," I said. "Why did you help me?"

"I had my own Trials, and I nearly died a bunch of times," she said, a rueful look on her face. "I won't be able to help you during the actual Trials as that's not allowed, but I'll do what I can otherwise."

Gratitude welled up through me, emotion making my eyes hot. Nobody had looked out for me since I lost Lily. "Thank you," I said, trying to project my sincerity.

"It's nothing," she said. "And well done. You made it through the first test."

"Shit, you're right." A smile sprang top my lips. "I survived!"

She laughed. "Yup. What magic do you have? I'd have guessed water, but the saraki has psychic magic and you resisted it. That's not easy."

She cocked her head at me and I swallowed. I could hardly tell her that I had no magic at all, and that I'd resisted the evil damned thing because Poseidon had helped me.

Why? Why had he helped me?

I looked over at where he had been standing, but there

was nobody there. In fact, the entire arena had almost emptied.

I looked back at Persephone, and an idea slammed into me. "Can you heal anything?"

She shook her head. "No. I'm pretty new to my powers, and I've only recently learned to do that with wounds. I'm pretty good at poisons now, but that's all so far."

I bit down on my lip. "Do you… Do you think you could take a look at my sister?"

Hope was rising inside me. A goddess healer. What wouldn't I have given to have access to a goddess healer before now?

"Is she sick?"

I opened my mouth to answer, but Poseidon's voice sounded behind me. "She is in a sleep induced by powerful magic. You will not be able to help her."

I whirled and saw Poseidon a few rows down on the benches. "You don't know that she can't help," I protested.

"I *do* know that she can't help."

His eyes were hard, his stance resolute.

Persephone touched my arm, drawing my attention back to her. "I must go. If you need me, use this." She passed me a tiny gold rose.

"Thank you," I said, and she vanished with a flash of light.

I turned back to Poseidon, but he spoke before I could. "Persephone can not know of the stone blight," he said.

"Why not? What if she can heal it?"

"She can't."

"You can't possibly know that without her trying."

Anger flashed on his face. "You forget who I am," he snarled. "I know a great deal."

"Then it's about fucking time you shared some of it!" I hadn't wanted to yell at him. I'd wanted to thank him, for saving my life a second time. But here he was, being an absolute prick again. "You can start with what powerful magic put Lily to sleep and why this stone thing has to be a secret."

I put my hands on my hips, then stumbled as he flashed himself to a foot in front of me.

I went from looking down at him on the lower bench, to having to tilt my head back to look up into his eyes.

His huge frame was dripping with water still, and he smelled like… *freedom*. The word popped into my head unbidden, and I didn't understand it. This man represented the opposite of my freedom, in every damned way.

His eyes were stormy with that wild look, and this close, I was sure I could see real waves crashing in them, sparks of silver ocean froth rolling across his irises.

"You test me," he growled. His voice even sounded like crashing waves this close.

"Just tell me. Tell me what you know about Lily." As I stared up at him, the memory of his stern, solid voice pulling me away from the saraki's light came back to me. "Please," I added softly.

His chest tensed, and his hard jaw ticked. "Not here."

"What?"

"I will tell you what you want to know. But not here."

"You will?"

"Yes." To my surprise, he held out his hand. I eyed it suspiciously and he bared his teeth at me. "If you want me to tell you secrets, then we need to be somewhere where they will not be overheard," he said through gritted teeth. "I can't flash you there without contact."

Frowning, I placed my hand in his. Electricity bolted up my arm, exploding in my chest and I gasped. It wasn't painful, it was… delicious. It was fast and powerful and fierce and free and-

"Are you ready?" Poseidon's voice was gruff, and I scanned his face for any hint that he'd felt whatever I just had, but he just wore his normal pissed expression. Wild, or pissed. Those were the only two looks I ever saw on his face. He was a furious force living on the edge of control.

"Yes. I'm ready," I said.

Narrowing his eyes at me, he grunted, then everything went white.

# CHAPTER 21

The first thing I was aware of when the light cleared was wind. Cool ocean air whipped across my face, blowing my hair free from its scarf.

"Where are we?" I breathed, turning in a slow circle. It was a space similar to Poseidon's throne room - in that it was round and had columns holding up the ceiling. But the view... We were outside. Not underwater in a golden dome, but above the surface of the ocean.

I stepped toward the edge to peer out. The ocean lapped at the sides of the tower, and birds called in the distance. All I could see for miles was the blue sea against a sky painted in pastel-colored clouds. Another gust of salty ocean air blew between the columns and I breathed in deeply.

"This is my private stables."

"Stables?" I turned to him in surprise, then scanned the space. I saw no animals, just the open area we were standing in, and nothing but a small spiral staircase leading into the plain ceiling.

"You wanted to know about the blight." His expression was tight and controlled. "And the sleep cast over your sister."

I instantly stopped wondering about the stables and stepped back toward the sea god. "Yes."

"The blight has been afflicting all of Aquarius. For some time. I have been keeping it from the citizens."

"Why?"

"I hoped to put an end to it before fear caused problems. I do not believe my people would behave favorably if they thought they might turn to stone."

"They deserve to know! What if they could help stop it?"

He ground his teeth. "I have tried many things to put an end to it. Things far more powerful than Persephone's healing magic. None have worked. And none will."

"How do you know? You can't just give up hope."

"I know because the Oracle of Delphi told me."

I scowled, hatred oozing through me. "Fucking Oracle."

Poseidon flinched. "Do not blame her."

"Why the hell not? She told you to marry me. Is she responsible for Lily's sickness?"

Poseidon faltered before answering. "No. But I am starting to suspect that she is somehow connected to everything that is happening." His gaze sharpened. "And that you are connected too."

I fisted my hands. "I'm just a revenge ticket for a god you pissed off," I snapped. "What does the blight do? You're living with it."

Even as I gestured at him, the stone crept across his

ELIZA RAINE & ROSE WILSON

skin, down one pec. I dragged my eyes up from his chest awkwardly.

"I was able to visit a healer powerful enough to keep it at bay, but their magic will wear off."

I raised my eyebrows. "And then?"

"And then it will not matter who wins these Trials to me. I will be as sentient as a statue."

"Shit."

He eyed me. "I concur."

"What did that jerk Oracle say when you saw her?"

His eyes moved from mine to look out over the ocean. "The heart of the ocean is the only thing that can save me and end the blight."

My stomach knotted itself up. So that's why he thought Lily and I were connected to the stone blight. "What *is* the heart of the ocean?" When he didn't reply, I coughed. "If it's a big sapphire and some little old lady threw it in the sea, it's got nothing to do with me."

He turned to me blinking. "What?"

"Guess you've not seen Titanic," I shrugged.

"You are…" He trailed off, and a flash of that wildness shone in his eyes, but it wasn't angry this time.

"Odd?" I offered. "That's what Galatea thinks. But she also thinks I'm plotting to bring you down so…"

"Are you?"

"I just want to cure Lily. That's it." *And steal your ship to do so.*

He cocked his head at me, his hair failing along his jaw. I was nearly overcome with the urge to brush it away and forced myself to step backward.

"Why did you help me today?"

"You would have died if I hadn't."

"You really care about my life, huh?"

His expression tightened. "We've been over this."

But I knew that being married to me hadn't given him his mythical heart of the ocean. So why hadn't he given up on me and tried to find a way to wake Lily up and marry her?

"Right," was all I said. "Well, based on today, I'll be lucky if I survive the next twenty-four hours. Any tips?"

I kept my voice casual, but the reality was that my confidence in surviving the race was zero.

I had no magic, no strength, no speed. I was running on empty, with nothing to back me up. If it weren't for Poseidon I would have swum straight into that freaking fish's jaws, and never even known what happened.

I had to take Kryvo's advice. I had to get the fuck out of the palace as soon as I could. If I couldn't find the ship before the first Trial, I would have to find another way to get to Atlantis.

"Have you sailed a ship before?"

I snapped my eyes to Poseidon's. "No. I spent my childhood underwater." My pulse raced a little as I added, "and ships fly through the sky. They don't work underwater." *Except yours.*

"No. They work via solar sails. The sails on the vessels absorb light, and that powers the ship's magic. They are steered and controlled by thought. The tighter your bond with the ship, the better your control."

"Do any ships work underwater?" I asked.

He frowned. "No. Not unless I make them. You won a Crosswind, and they are the smallest class of ship. It should be easier for you to manage." His face creased into a scowl as he studied my face. "You are planning to leave," he said slowly. There was certainty in his eyes as he moved closer to me.

How could he possibly have known that? "I…" I raised my hands. Was there any point lying to him? "I'm considering it," I said eventually.

"You will not get far."

"Is that a threat?"

He barked a humorless laugh. "If only. Atlas is a powerful, ancient Titan, and these are public Trials. Whether or not either of us like it, this race, and the following two Trials, are happening."

*Shit.*

"You're sure?"

His expression was grim as he lifted an arm, pushing his hair back out of his face. It seemed such a human gesture, rather than a godly one, and I found myself just a little less intimidated by him. "I am sure." His outrageously blue eyes left mine again, roaming over the ocean. "Atlas will stop at nothing to ensure your death."

A shudder rippled through me. "What did you do to his wife?"

I knew he wouldn't answer me, but I had to try.

"That is my business."

"Would it change things if Atlas knew you didn't care for me?"

When his eyes snapped back to mine, the wildness flared unmistakably, and power pulsed out from him, raw and barely controlled. For a second, I wanted to leap from the edge of the stables and immerse myself the sea, live forever in its unbridled, limitless world of sheer power. In the freedom the ocean offered. *And I wanted to do it with him.*

I blinked at him, and the feeling dissipated. I'd never, ever felt a connection to water like that. And... *And I'd never wanted a man like that.*

"You are weak."

"What?"

"You are weak," Poseidon repeated, matter-of-factly. "Physically," he added, as though that would help soften the insult. It didn't.

"Yeah. I guess. I haven't adjusted well." I shifted my weight.

"You should eat more."

I couldn't help laughing. "I would freaking *love* to eat more. Give me food, oh mighty king, and I will obey your terrible order." I gave him a mocking bow, then jumped in surprise when I straightened. He was inches from me, muscular frame looming over me.

"Do you know how many people mock me?"

I opened my mouth to say something smart, then closed it again. I shook my head, my heart beating hard against my ribs. A powerful gust of wind blew over us, and a whisper of that sense of freedom engulfed me.

"Very few who live afterward," he growled.

"You keep saving my life," I whispered. "Be a shame to kill me over a little light banter."

For a split second I could have sworn I saw amusement spark in his eyes. Then the waves crashed across his irises, the wild look returning. Wild and fierce like the ocean itself. He stepped back, and dammit, I almost reached my hand out to grab the straps of his armor and pull him back.

What the hell was wrong with me? *He's a god,* I told myself. He's supposed to have that effect on people.

"I have something for you." His sentence was clipped, and unexpected.

"Really?"

"To help keep you alive."

"So you're not going to kill me?"

His gaze bore into mine and I squirmed.

"Not today."

# CHAPTER 22

*I* followed Poseidon up the stairs, my heart beating a little too fast in my chest.

We emerged in a round space identical to the one below, except it was ringed with huge half-height stable doors between inset columns. Excitement made my steps quicken as I left the last step of the stairs.

"Is this where the animals are kept?"

"The pegasi. Yes."

I looked toward the nearest stall, hoping to get a glimpse one, but the bottom half of the door was too tall.

"I've never seen one," I breathed.

"You did not attend the academy, where you might have learned to ride one." He didn't word it has a question, and a zing of fear made my chest tighten.

"How do you know that?"

He ignored me, striding to one door and pulling it open, revealing the stall beyond. There was no animal in it, but I could see that the other side was completely open to the air, so the pegasus could come and go as it pleased.

A large amount of hay covered the floor, and ornate-looking iron troughs held both food and water.

"They cannot live in underwater domes as they need to be able to fly at will, so the tower extends high enough to break the surface of the ocean."

I nodded. "I read about them."

Poseidon took a deep breath. "For the duration of the Trials, you may borrow a palace pegasus." A small squeak escaped my lips. "These animals are my personal creations, and unlike most pegasi they can move under the water, as well as through the sky. I believe they will be able to help you both with flying ships and any tests beneath the surface."

I felt my mouth dropping open. "You... You'd really let me have a pegasus?"

"For the duration of the Trials only," he repeated, a strain in his voice. "And these animals are truly special. They have a will of their own. Without my trident, I can't force them to do anything. If they do not like you, they will do nothing to help you."

I nodded my head fervently. "Okay. How do I find one that likes me?"

"You must sense it. Close your eyes, reach out with your power, and go to the stall you are drawn to."

*Oh shit.* Use my power? Well, I was fucked.

Swallowing, I closed my eyes. *Lily? Kryvo? Any ideas?* I sent the thought out into the ether. Lily's image popped into my head.

*Just use your normal senses. You love animals. Feel for the pegasi and pick a stall.*

The little starfish remained silent.

A strong current of ocean air blew through the open stable door, and I inhaled deeply, trying to ground myself.

Pick a door, any door.

A tiny sound caught my attention. A whinny? I turned, eyes still closed. There it was again, followed by a distant huffing noise. I moved toward it. If I couldn't use magic, my ears would have to do.

I opened my eyes and found myself in front of three doors. Each had a symbol painted on the wood, but I recognized none of them. I strained to hear anything that would indicate which door had a pegasus behind it. The slight clopping of hooves reached me, and I reached out, moving quickly.

"This one," I said, laying my hand on the wood. A loud whinny went up from the other side, and I snatched my hand back.

To my astonishment, Poseidon smiled. And hell, *was it a smile.* His whole face changed, the constantly angry or out-of-control energy replaced with that of a man who had no worries in the world. He looked like the carefree, sun-kissed surfer every girl would give anything to spend Saturday night with, eyes alive with the promise of endless fun.

I stared at him and his smile faded, as though he'd realized what he'd done but was reluctant to retract it. "That is *galázies apochróseis tou okeanoú.* My wildest animal."

"Oh. That's quite a wild name."

"It means *blue shades of the ocean.*"

He strode over and pulled up the latch. A slight panic

took me. "Wait! Do I need to know anything? How do you talk to a pegasus?"

Poseidon just eased open the door and stood back.

Two eyes, shining like cobalt stars, fixed on mine, and my breath caught.

I'd never seen anything so magnificent as the creature moving slowly out of the stall toward me.

He was the size of a large horse and although his coat was chalky white, his mane and tail were just like Poseidon's eyes. Silver froth and an ombre of ocean blues were running through the hair, making it look as though it was covered in waves as the pegasus moved.

With a loud whinny, the creature snapped its wings out taut, and I gasped in delight. Light rippled across them, a sheen of gold swooshing over every feather as though a layer of liquid metal coated them. He raised his head, nostrils flaring as I stood before him.

"Hi," I said nervously, as I heard Kryvo give a barely audible squeak. *Please don't eat starfish,* I thought as I took a tentative step toward the Pegasus. I was aware of Poseidon's eyes on me as I slowly reached out a hand to the creature. His head was a foot above mine, so I lifted my arm high.

He snorted, making me jump, then stamped his feet. I stood my ground and tried to keep my hand steady.

"I don't have anything to give you, like an apple or... whatever pegasi eat," I said. "But I can tell you that you are the most gorgeous thing I've ever laid eyes on."

The pegasus paused in his stamping and turned his head a little so that he could fix one eye on me.

Hoping it could understand me and was susceptible to

flattery, I continued. "Your wings are just beyond beautiful. And Poseidon here tells me that you can fly through water as well as the sky? That is epic."

The pegasus rustled his wings in what I hoped was appreciation of my words.

"I'm, erm..." I glanced at Poseidon, but his face gave away nothing. "Weak, apparently. And I need a little help with some situations that, well, will probably kill me." I lifted my hands in a what-can-you-do kind of way, and the creature's nostrils flared again. Then he dipped his head and moved a couple of steps closer. My pulse quickened.

"I was kind of hoping, if you've nothing else planned, that you might help me out for a few days?"

The pegasus froze, then snorted, shaking its head.

"Obviously, I wouldn't want to put you in any danger," I said quickly. He lifted his snout and turned to Poseidon. I watched as the god stared into the creature's shining eyes for a long moment.

Eventually, he spoke. "I am sorry, my friend. I can't communicate with you."

There was so much sadness in Poseidon's voice, and the pegasus gave an equally sad whinny. Compassion for the god's loss surged through me, unbidden.

*You don't like him, remember!* I chided myself silently. *He's made your life hell! Who cares if he can't talk to his animal friends anymore?*

But as Poseidon dropped his head respectfully at the Pegasus, and the creature did the same, I knew I did care. I could feel his connection to the amazing creature, and his sorrow was tangible.

He may treat Nereids like crap, but the man clearly looked after his animals.

With another stamp, the pegasus turned back to me.

"Oh. Hello again," I said, giving a lame little wave. I suppressed a yelp as the thing moved faster than I expected and bumped his cold nose against my hand.

An impression of rushing wind, tangy, cool, ocean spray and roaring waves filled my mind, and laughter bubbled out of my mouth unbidden.

"Blue," I said, the word ringing out in my head.

"He has told you his chosen name. He has accepted you." Poseidon's voice remained soft, but I didn't turn to him.

Blue had backed up, raising and dropping his beautiful wings in some sort of show, and my delighted attention was riveted on him.

"Blue, huh? That's a lot easier to say than your real name." He pranced up and down, flicking his tail and neighing, and I clapped my hands. "You're amazing!"

"Wait until you see the ocean from his point of view."

This time I did turn to Poseidon, the wistful tone of his voice almost painful to hear. I frowned at him. "Why do you say that like you can't?"

"My duties keep me in the palace. Containing this blight and the people it is affecting is a time-consuming job."

"You're the king—surely you can get out for the odd pegasus ride?"

"I do not want to risk passing the blight on," he said, after a long pause.

I stilled, as did Blue. "Is that how it is contracted?"

"We don't know. There is no evidence that it is passed on through physical contact, but I can't risk the life or health of these creatures."

More unwelcome respect for him crept into me. "My friend who has been taking care of Lily has not got it. And I am sure he has been in some contact with her." The thought of her alone in the Silos' bakery made some of the softer feelings I appeared to be having toward Poseidon recede a little.

He nodded. "Those in the city who have fallen ill do not seem to have any link to one another."

"What have you done with them?"

His expression turned sour, and angry. "They are in the palace."

"And their families?"

"We have had to use magic," he said.

I cocked my head at him, unease washing over me. "What do you mean?"

"Until we know how to cure the sick, the families of those afflicted must be kept unaware."

"Define 'unaware'." I heard my own tone turn sour.

"I had a choice," the god snapped. "Isolate those who know about the blight or remove it from their memory. I took what I believe is the fairest option. I removed their memories."

"Of the blight?"

"Of the person afflicted."

Horror coursed through me. "You made people forget about their loved ones?"

"Only temporarily. Even gods can't remove memories permanently, not without drinking from the river Styx."

His tone was granite now, and I knew he would not tolerate my insolence much longer, but I couldn't help my outrage.

"You have no right to do that!" I'd lived with the memory of my sister as my only companion for so long that the thought of not even knowing she existed made me feel sick.

"It is temporary," he growled. "They feel no sadness, and their lives are not impacted in any way."

"Just because they don't know it, doesn't mean they are not impacted!"

"You would prefer I told them their loved ones were dead?" he roared, making me flinch with the sudden loss of temper. "To tell them they are nothing but lifeless statues that I failed to save!"

Blue whinnied and backed into the stall as Poseidon advanced on me. His words rang through my head. *Failed to save.* He was angry that he had failed to save his people.

"Why do you have to keep the blight a secret? Why not just tell the citizens and make them aware you are trying to fix it?"

"Because." He snarled, coming to stop a foot from me and towering over my smaller frame. "If the world knew I couldn't heal it I would be challenged. It is not possible to show weakness when you are the king of the ocean, and Zeus' brother." His voice was venom, and it took all my courage to stand my ground. The whole tower rumbled with distant thunder and rain had begun to lash down into the sea beyond, making it churn. I took a shaking breath as he continued. "I thought my brother would challenge me if he discovered I, or my realm, was sick. I didn't not expect Atlas." Emotion was sparking in his eyes. Emotion that wasn't anger, it was something deeper, something intense, something raw. "You were not supposed to be a part of this."

My own emotions were reflecting his, growing inside me, fueled by his fierceness. "Why do you care?" I could see in his eyes and hear in his words, that he did.

And I didn't understand.

The fury of the building storm coursed through me. "Marrying me hasn't given you your stupid heart of the ocean. I'm nothing to you!"

Thunder cracked and the wind whipped up, beating at us where we stood, face to face and inexplicably furious.

"You!" Poseidon shouted, then tore his eyes from mine, flinging an arm out. Waves surged up behind him, so high they blocked out the sky.

"I what? For the love of the gods, what?"

He raised another hand, and a tidal wave the size of a skyscraper crashed down over the stables. I sucked in a breath, my whole body tense, ready to be washed away. But not a drop of water entered the stables.

"You make me fucking crazy!" Poseidon bellowed, then with a flash of white light, he was gone.

My limbs were shaking as I stared at the spot he had vanished from. The ocean still churned around me, rain pelting down to be instantly absorbed by the endless sea.

"Is this what happens when the king of the ocean throws a temper tantrum?" I muttered, staring out at the storm and trying to calm my racing heart.

A quiet snicker answered me, and I turned slowly to Blue's stall. Hoof by cautious hoof, he moved toward me.

"You've seen him lose his shit before?" I asked the pegasus gently. Blue shook his stunning mane. "I'm gonna take that as a yes." I stepped closer and felt a tiny sting on my collarbone.

"Shit, Kryvo, I'm sorry," I said, lifting my hand to my shoulder. I'd totally forgotten about him. "You okay?"

"No." The little starfish's voice was as wobbly as I felt. "No, I am not okay. I don't know what's worse, that saraki or Poseidon."

"Yeah," I said, but I didn't mean it. I stared out over the tumultuous sea as the starfish suckered his way slowly onto my palm. Whatever the hell had just happened had irrevocably shifted my opinion of the sea god.

He cared about his people. He was doing the wrong thing, for sure, but not for the wrong reasons. He cared for his animals too, and I didn't think he mourned the loss of his trident for the power it had cost him, but for the removal of his ability to talk to the creatures of his realm.

And... I was truly starting to believe that he cared for me. His smile sang in my mind, an image, so utterly at odds with his normal persona, but so perfectly right somehow.

"He can't care for me," I said aloud, as Kryvo settled in my palm, bright red again.

"Poseidon?"

"Yeah. He doesn't even know me. How could he possibly care for me?"

"He sure gets mad with you for someone who doesn't know you," he said, giving a little shudder.

Blue whinnied, and I looked up at him. "Do you eat starfish?" I asked him. The pegasus stamped his feet, ducking his head low. "Hmmm. I think that's a no. But just in case, please don't eat this one. He's my only friend."

Kryvo heated in my hand as I moved closer to the Pegasus. "I'm your friend?"

"You just faced a lethal sea monster with me. Of course you're my friend."

"I didn't do anything. I tried, though. I was telling you to stay away from the light, but I was too quiet." He sounded so dejected that my heart warmed with sympathy for him. I knew what it was like to feel useless.

"We survived. And I appreciate you trying, so much."

"This is true. We did survive." He sounded a touch more cheerful.

"And now, we have a new friend. This is Blue."

I held him up to the Pegasus, who flared his nostrils and snorted. "He smells," Kryvo announced.

Blue stamped his hooves, and I pulled Kryvo back into my chest. "Maybe don't insult him," I whispered to the starfish, before telling Blue loudly, "You smell amazing." I reached out my empty hand, hoping he would nudge it again. After a small hesitation, he did.

"Blue usually hates everyone." I whirled at Galatea's voice.

"Huh. We're a good match then," I snapped back at her. I wasn't in the mood for her shit.

"You did well today."

"What?"

"Honestly, I didn't think you'd survive. So far, I've seen no evidence that you even have any power. If it weren't for Poseidon's insistence that you do–"

"Why are you here?" I interrupted her. I glanced down

at my palm to see that Kryvo had camouflaged himself perfectly, but I didn't know how long she'd been watching me.

"Poseidon sent me to take you back. Unless you'd like to try yourself?"

I considered her words, it only taking me a second to realize that I was totally trapped on the platform out on the ocean.

"Fine." I turned back to Blue. "If you could help me out tomorrow, I'd be super grateful." He locked his shining, intelligent eyes on mine and snorted. "Thanks," I beamed at him, and prayed to anyone who was listening that the beautiful flying horse would show up if I needed him.

## CHAPTER 23

There was a frigging feast waiting for me when Galatea deposited me back in my room. "Is this all for me?" I gaped at her.

"Yes. And Poseidon has decided that you don't need to be locked in." She looked as though she thought that was a terrible idea, but I knew why. He'd made it crystal clear that there was no point in running. "The Trial is at dawn tomorrow, so you can spend the rest of this evening in the palace as you wish."

A childish excitement whipped up inside me at the thought of exploring the epic building. *And maybe finding the ship.* "Okay. Thanks."

With one last suspicious look, she left me alone with my ridiculously large, but well earned, feast.

When my stomach was full of pastry and beef, followed by liberal helpings of chocolate, I strapped my belt back on and headed out to explore the palace. And hopefully get an idea of where Poseidon kept his ship.

Just thinking about the sea god made my head spin, and an annoying mixture of emotions churn up in my stomach.

"Kryvo," I said firmly, trying not to think about Poseidon and focus on the task at hand. "Any of your statue friends know where one might keep a ship in this palace?"

The starfish was back on my collarbone. His tiny squeak reached me. "No. I can see some nice gardens though."

"Okay. How do I get there?"

I walked down the corridor until I reached a grand staircase lined with statues. It curved gently downward, and more gold paintings delicately adorned the walls. As I descended I noticed little stone starfish on lots of the statues, whether they were busts of people or depictions of sea creatures.

"Are these what you can see through?" I asked Kryvo, reaching out and touching one that was riding on the back of a leaping dolphin.

"Yes."

I carried on down the staircase until it leveled out in an enormous round hall. There were bridge-corridors leading off it on all sides and I guessed I must have been in a pretty central tower. In the center of the atrium was a fountain, a likeness of Poseidon holding his trident high standing twenty feet tall, as water leaped and played around his legs in a kind of dance.

I walked up to it, frowning. "Bit full of himself," I muttered. "How do I get outside?"

"There's another staircase, along the corridor with the manta ray statue," answered Kryvo. I followed his instructions, finding a staircase leading down at the end of a short bridge-corridor. At the bottom was a set of doors, and when I pushed through them, I found myself at the start of a path with tall green hedges on either side of me. I looked up, seeing the towering white spires of the palace all around me, and the gold of the dome ceiling shining against the blue ocean overhead.

I made my way down the path, which curved gently left and right, the high hedges blocking my view of anything on ground level until I reached an archway.

"Wow," I breathed, as I stepped through. Garden was too polite a word for the space. It was stunning. I was standing at the top of a tiered area, leading down to a massive pool. Rather than meet the edge of the dome to willow people out, this pool appeared to be for actually swimming in. Surrounded by golden tiles, the water was an unnaturally bright blue.

Arches made of twisted wood and draped in purple flowers framed steps that weaved down through the tiers. Flower beds displayed almost exclusively purple and yellow flowers, many of them creepers that wound their way around benches and statues of water creatures.

Green turf covered the ground everywhere, and the color was somehow energizing when I was getting so used to seeing the blue backdrop of the ocean.

I strolled along the paths, trying to work out what I could do next.

I drew on Lily's image, and she materialized in my mind. "I don't know where to look for the ship," I told her.

*If the ship is as special as the book says it is, then he is likely to keep it hidden.*

"But this is his palace, why would he need to hide it here?"

*Hundreds of people live and work here. Including Silos' dad,* she reminded me.

"Hmmm."

*Have you considered telling him what you know about Atlantis? He may willingly take you.*

"The thought had occurred to me." Poseidon believed I had something to do with all this, and he'd said we would 'fix it' after the Trials. Asking him about the healing font may be a lot easier than trying to find it on my own. "If it was likely to work, then he would have tried already," I said. "He said he'd tried lots of powerful things to cure the blight."

*There must be a reason he hasn't.*

"Or he has, and it didn't work," I said glumly. "Or maybe the book is fiction, and Atlantis doesn't exist." I kicked at a stray tuft of grass creeping up between the slabs under my feet. "Making all of this for nothing."

*Dear sister, I believe you would have ended up here eventually, regardless.*

"Why?"

*Atlas. He wants revenge. He would have found you, just to hurt Poseidon. Revenge is a most powerful motive.*

I scowled. "I wonder what Poseidon did to his wife? Killed her? Slept with her? Left her in the human world for years by herself?"

*It doesn't matter now. What matters is surviving these Trials. Then, you can work together to find a cure and save Aquarius.*

"Save Aquarius? I'm saving you, not the whole damn realm."

*I rather think that they're one and the same goal now.*

"Shit." I hadn't thought about it like that. But she was right. I groaned. "You know Lily, the fates really fucked this up. It should be you doing all this. I bet you could defeat a demon angler fish, and fly a ship, and breathe underwater, and-"

*Enough, Almi. You have what you need to get through this. And now you have a cowardly but smart starfish and a slightly scary pegasus to help you.* Her mental image smiled at me, and a tiny bit of confidence snuck through the swamp of self-doubt.

"This is true."

"Who are you speaking to?" The deep voice startled me, and I whirled as I recognized it.

"Atlas."

He was standing beside a statue of a naked mermaid, her arms raised above her head and her eyes closed.

"Almi. Wife of Poseidon." He took a step closer to me, and my pulse quickened. He was wearing robes, formal and black and clasped with his sigil. His skin was so pale he looked like a statue himself, and he oozed a tingling power that felt nothing like the sea.

"Does Poseidon know you are here?"

He spread his hands wide. "We are all here now. Every contestant is residing within this dome." His smile didn't

177

reach his eyes, which were hard. The dark irises were ringed in red, I realized as he moved even closer.

"Why aren't you competing?"

He snorted. "I don't want control of this shitty, water-logged realm."

Defensiveness flashed through me. "Aquarius is too good for you," I spat.

His smile widened, even as his eyes hardened. "Poseidon is responsible for pain you can't even imagine. He will feel it himself, I swear."

"What did he do?" I took a step back as he tried to close the gap between us.

"Ask him yourself." He raised his eyebrows. "Unless you already have and he's refused to tell you?"

I opened my mouth but the truth must have been written on my face.

Atlas laughed. "Good luck tomorrow, little Almi. You're going to need it." A blanket of heat engulfed me, a warning hum of power laced through it, and I felt my knees start to bend.

"You will honor the right gods soon," he hissed, as my kneecaps met marble, and the rest of my body folded into an unwilling bow. "For as long as you are alive, at least." His power was massive, his presence becoming painful, and I screwed my face up as I tried to resist him. His message was crystal clear. He was just as powerful as Poseidon. Possibly even more.

The pressure on my body and the oppressive electric heat vanished, and I raised my head with relief. He gave me one last hatred-filled look, and then he was gone, striding away through the courtyard.

"What the hell was that about?" I whispered.

"I don't like him," squeaked Kryvo.

"That makes two of us."

What had Poseidon done to his wife?

# CHAPTER 24

*I* woke with a start, the heavy book across my chest making me panic.

A knocking sounded at my door, loud and insistent, and I blinked around myself.

I'd fallen asleep reading about flying ships, I realized. Was it dawn already?

"Who is it?"

I expected Galatea to answer, but Poseidon's gruff voice barked, "Open the door."

I shuffled my legs off the bed, my muscles stiff from falling asleep in such an awkward position. Nerves blasted my sleepiness away though as I pulled open the door.

"Why knock? Surely you can just barge your way in?" I scowled at him. He was dressed in his leather fighting garb, and droplets of water glistened on his bare chest. I forced myself to remember that we didn't get on. "It's your palace after all, and you're good at taking what you want without asking."

He bared his teeth at me. "We have an hour before the Trial begins. I came here to show you what to do with the ship, but if you're going to be difficult—"

I held my hands up, cutting him off. "I may be difficult, but I'm not stupid. Give me ten minutes to get ready."

He just grunted and folded his arms. Trying not to notice what that did to his biceps, I slammed the door shut.

As fast as I could, I showered and dressed in identical, but clean clothes from the closet. "Kryvo, I know you're not going to want to come, but you helped me out last time, and honestly? I would appreciate the company." The starfish rippled red on his cushion on the dresser.

"I thought you might say that. Are you absolutely sure we can't hide?"

"One hundred percent, little friend."

He let out a squeaky sigh. "I will do what I can to help us survive. Although I sort of wish I'd never met you."

"Charming." I let him squish his way onto my palm, then lifted him to my shoulder. Strapping on my belt, I looked at my reflection in the mirror.

"Oh Lily. This really should be you," I sighed, my stomach knotting with trepidation.

There was another bang on the door, and I clenched my jaw tight and shook my head.

*But it was me.* I had to do it, for both of us.

Poseidon gave me a cursory look as I stepped out of my bedroom door, then, with no warning everything flashed white.

"Hey!" I spluttered as the light faded and I stumbled. "You could have told me you were about to do that!"

"Be quiet."

I bristled, but my surroundings caught my attention before I could reply.

We were standing on a pier, and there were real ships in front of me. Real big-ass ships.

We were outside too, above the surface of the ocean, and the breeze was warm as it blew across us.

"Where are we?"

"That is Sagittarius." He pointed behind me and I turned to see that the pier we standing on was attached to an island.

"Artemis' realm? Isn't Sagittarius a forbidden realm?"

"Nowhere is forbidden for one as powerful as me."

I pulled a face. "Right. Of course not, oh mighty one." He growled low in his throat, and I tried to look vaguely meek. "Why are we here?"

"This is where the race will commence. It is the nearest coastline to Aquarius."

"How do you know this is where the race will start?"

"It is where I would start it. And I originally designed these Trials. Although I am sure Atlas will make some alterations."

"Oh."

"This is a Crosswind." He turned back to the pier and pointed at the smallest ship.

The wooden hull loomed over me, and I stared up at it.

Something stirred in my gut, something fluttery and just beyond my reach. Putting it down to fear that this was all getting very real, and I would be about to face a Trial that would likely kill me, I looked at Poseidon.

"I can't see anything except the hull," I said.

Everything flashed white again, but this time, I didn't trip as we materialized on wooden planks.

"Thanks for the heads up," I ground out sarcastically.

To my surprise, he flicked a look at me that was definitely an equally sarcastic 'you're welcome'.

"This is the main mast."

I looked where he was gesturing, and the fluttering in my stomach intensified. The sails were *glorious*.

Glorious.

There was no other word for them. They were like fabric made of metal, gleaming with silvers and golds as they rippled in the wind, the light moving over them almost like liquid flames.

Following my gaze, Poseidon spoke softly. "They absorb and use light. They are quite something to look at."

"They're fucking ace," I breathed.

"I don't know what that means, but I shall take your look of awe as a positive reaction."

I nodded my head in agreement.

"The bridge is here, and that is where the ship's wheel is."

I dragged my eyes from the sails to where he was pointing. But my gaze didn't skim past him as I intended it to. My breath caught, my stomach almost flipping in its jittery ferocity.

He looked as he had most of the previous times I had seen him; leather boots and pants, weapon straps crisscrossing his powerful body, his hair blowing around his hard, fierce face. But on the ship, framed as he was by the rich-colored wood of the planks, the light reflecting from the sails, and the rolling waves of the ocean beyond…

He looked *right*. So damned right, I couldn't take my eyes off him.

"You belong here," I said, without meaning to.

He faltered, emotion flaring in his eyes. "What?" The word was soft, wary even.

"You just… You just look right here. On the deck."

Every hard plane on his body drew me in, the tanned skin of his abs disappearing into his waistband so suddenly, glaringly, deliciously. Images of us together on the ship, the roaring wind and fierce ocean around us nothing compared to the passion in his stormy eyes as his mouth took mine-

"No. I belong in Aquarius, under the sea, with my brethren."

"Then why…" I didn't know how to finish my question. Why did he look so utterly perfect here, out in the open?

*Where in the hell were these thoughts coming from?*

I felt my face flush, and I dropped my eyes to the planks.

"Ship's wheel," he said, slowly.

"Ship's wheel," I repeated, looking over at the bridge.

"It is easier for most to guide the ship with the wheel. If you are bonded with the ship, you can just touch the wood of the mast. But bonding takes time. Time we don't have."

"Right," I said, though I was barely listening. I was too busy scolding my ridiculous, apparently romance-starved brain.

"To steer, just think where you want to go."

"Sounds easy," I said, forcing a fake cheeriness into my voice.

"It is not easy," he said. "We will, no doubt, have to do more than just steer the ship. You will have to concentrate on both that and whatever Atlas throws at us." He paused. "Why are you not looking at me?"

*Because my brain keeps threatening to mentally remove your pants ever since we got on this stupid ship?* "I'm just nervous."

"You should be. Come." He strode to the small set of steps leading up to the bridge, and I followed him. When he started to climb, I made sure my eyes were fully averted from his ass in the tight leather, staring out absently at the island of Sagittarius. It mostly looked like scrubland, nothing more than hardy weeds peeking out of the sand on the narrow shore.

"I said come."

"Right." Snapping my eyes back I saw that Poseidon had ascended the steps.

I moved up them quickly and took a second to study the ship properly.

The deck stretched in front of me, the solar sails dominating my view. The masts and sails apparently needed no rigging, as I could see no ropes. The ship narrowed at the front, which I was sure was called the prow, and I saw one single weapon mounted there, possibly a harpoon.

At the back of the raised bridge was a large wooden chair, bolted to the deck, and some sort of contraption on wires - a large box. The whole ship was made of a deep, rich-colored wood, and the railings that wrapped around the entire deck were waist high and quite intricately carved in the shape of waves.

"Touch the wheel."

I lifted my hand to my temple in a salute. "Yes, sir."

I moved to the huge ship's wheel. I couldn't count the spokes, it had so many. When I laid my fingers on it, the wood was warm and welcoming. I closed my fingers around two handle-ended spokes.

"Imagine the ship lifting."

I closed my eyes and did as he told me. I felt a slight lurch, then became aware of a smooth movement under my feet. I opened my eyes, and a grin leaped to my face. We were moving, lifting higher in a vertical motion.

"Good. Now stop."

I willed the ship to stop, and it did. "No way."

Poseidon walked to the rails and looked over. Unable to contain my curiosity about how high I'd taken the ship, I let go of the wheel and joined him.

Peering over the edge, my grin widened. We were a hundred feet over the pier now, and the other ships there looked small. I looked toward the island and saw that the scrubby shore was misleading, as just a few feet further inland was a rich green meadow.

"Can I make it go fast?"

Poseidon looked at me, one eyebrow raised and a hint of *something* in his eyes.

"Yes, I think you probably can. It is unusual for control to come to beginners that easily."

I shrugged nonchalantly, while fireworks of excitement went off in my head. "Maybe it's because I'm a

Nereid," I said, taking the opportunity to reinforce my make-believe powers.

"I doubt it."

I scowled at him. "Why?" I instantly wished I hadn't asked.

He sighed and leaned his elbows on the railings. "I know you have no magic."

Ice cold fear doused me. "What? No."

"That's why I thought you'd have trouble with the ship. I am pleased to see that's not the case. You might actually survive this." He was staring out at the sea, not meeting my flustered face.

"I..." I scrambled for any reason I might not have my magic, any lie I could tell. Lily's voice telling me all my life that I must keep my broken powers a secret rang in my head.

Slowly, Poseidon straightened, turning to me. "I am the king of the ocean. I sense water magic in places you wouldn't even know existed. Did you really think I wouldn't know you were without power?" His voice wasn't hard or angry. It was matter of fact.

"Why didn't you say so before? Why did you let me pretend?"

He stared at me. "It's not important. Your tattoo," he said abruptly, pointing to my chest. My shirt was open over my bandeau vest, the shell clear.

"What about it?"

"Nereid's tattoos are supposed to be vibrant in color."

"Mine's broken." I couldn't keep the bitterness from my voice.

"If I know this, so will Atlas. So will Kalypso. They are

both powerful gods." He glanced at my belt. "Water-root and gadgets will not get you past them."

Embarrassment and shame made my cheeks flame and anger take over my thoughts. "Making me feel stupid and weak isn't going to help me survive," I said through gritted teeth.

"Almi, that is not my intention." Sincerity laced his tone, measured control still governing his expression. "I am trying to prepare you."

"I'm as good as human. How the fuck am I supposed to prepare for this?"

Somehow, not having to keep it a secret anymore made it more real, and tears pricked my eyes as my stomach continued to knot itself.

Poseidon held out his hand, a vial appearing in it. "This will help. And you are a natural with the ship. That might well be enough."

"This is what gave me strength yesterday?" I said, taking the vial from him.

"Yes. It is the best I can do. That and hope Blue comes."

"Why are you helping me?"

"Why do you keep asking me that?"

"I'm broken. You married the wrong Nereid. So why do you care if I live?"

Finally, some of the control slipped from his face. His shoulders tensed as his jaw worked. "Do you want to die?"

"No."

"Then stop questioning me, and just do as you're damned well told." I opened my mouth to respond but he spoke again, "Practice with the ship," he barked, then flashed away.

# CHAPTER 25

"*H*e knows, Lily. He's known all the time." I gripped the ship's wheel, staring at the spot Poseidon had vanished.

*That's a good thing. I should have known he would be aware.*

A gust of wind blew over me as I tried to control my roiling emotions.

Kryvo's squeaky voice carried to me. "You thought he didn't know you were without magic?"

I closed my eyes. "You knew too, huh?"

"Well, yes."

*It's one less thing to worry about. Practice with the ship.*

I opened my eyes. "Why didn't he tell me?"

*I don't think you'll believe me, but I think he didn't want to embarrass you.*

"What?"

*I can think of no other reason than for him to play along with your lie.*

I shook my head, and the scarf keeping my hair back

came loose. Wind picked up strands of my hair, the purple color whipping in front of my eyes making me stare.

Of course he knew. I didn't even look like a proper Nereid.

*Practice with the ship.*

"Can't I have five fucking minutes to feel sorry for myself?" I snapped.

*Absolutely not.*

"Fine!"

I tied my hair back angrily, then squeezed the wood of the wheel. I willed the ship forward. My anger must have spilled into the command, because we lurched forward so fast I immediately fell over. I landed sideways, my knee taking the brunt of the impact, and I swore loudly.

*Concentrate,* said Lily.

"Or hide," offered Kryvo.

With a deep breath of clear ocean air, I tried to focus. All this shit with Poseidon would have to wait. Lily was right. I needed to concentrate on surviving the race. And if I did, I could reward myself by yelling at the baffling watery ass all I liked.


I had ten minutes to practice with the ship before Poseidon appeared on the deck beside me.

"It's time," he said, and gave me no chance to respond.

With the next flash of light, we were back on the pier.

Kalypso, Polybotes and Ceto were there too. The scrubby shore was now filled with a crowd of spectators, and to my complete astonishment, I saw Silos among them, standing beside his father. When he caught my eye, he beamed and called out with the rest of the crowd, lifting a banner high.

"Almi to win," it read.

He yelled something that to my average lip-reading skills looked like, "You're doing amazing," and I waved gratefully at him.

There was a resounding boom, and the crowd's cheering fell silent. All the ships at the dock had vanished. With a flurry of glittery swirls, five new ones appeared, hovering a few feet above the surface of the water.

"Kalypso and her Whirlwind!" roared Atlas' voice, and fireworks erupted from the deck of something that looked like it could survive a nuclear holocaust, never mind a race. The hull was clad in gleaming silver armor, and hundreds of cannon tips peeked out of portholes lining both sides. Three masts held gargantuan solar sails, and a harpoon was mounted on the high bridge.

Kalypso waved at the crowd, then a jet of water burst up from under the pier. She stepped gracefully onto it, and it shot upward to deposit her on the deck of the warship.

Acid burned in my chest, nerves making me wring my hands together.

"Poseidon and his Whirlwind!" With a glance at me that was so brief I might have missed it, Poseidon flashed onto the deck of his ship.

"Polybotes and his Zephyr!"

The giant's ship was so big that it appeared to have a bridge at both ends, raised high and sporting wheels as big as cars. The giant stamped along the pier, crouched low, then launched himself up into the air. I would never have guessed a being so large could jump so high. My mouth fell open as he caught hold of a porthole halfway up the hull, then swung himself up to the next one. In seconds, he was pulling himself over the railings. The crowd hooted and cheered as he waved.

"Ceto and her Typhoon!"

The sea goddess immediately dove off the side of the pier. A beat later, I saw her form slithering up the side of the hull of the only ship that looked like a longboat, with a small extra sail and an enormous spike adorning the front.

How the hell was I going to get onto the deck of the last ship; the small, unassuming Crosswind?

I felt dizzy with nerves as Atlas' voice rang out.

"And Almi and her Crosswind!"

I lifted a foot, desperately trying to think of a way onto the ship, when I heard Poseidon's voice in my head.

*The box at the back.*

I sped up, jogging past the huge hulls of the other ships, their occupants gazing down at me as I passed. When I reached the Crosswind, I saw the crate on wires at the back, only this time it was lowered over the edge of the railings instead of sitting on the bridge. Was it like some sort of elevator?

*It's called a hauler. Get in it.*

I saw that one of the sides was actually a door and stepped into the box. When nothing happened, I laid my hand on the wood of the box, and willed myself to rise. With an ominous creak, the crate rose.

When it came to a stop, I pushed the door open

nervously. The bridge of the Crosswind came into view, the wheel standing proud in the middle

"Thank fuck for that," I muttered as I hurried to it. I gripped the spokes. "Hi, ship. I'm Almi, and I really, really hope you're going to help me out today."

The wood heated under my hands, and a tendril of confidence snaked through me.

I could do this.

*You can do this,* Lily agreed.

"It's too late to hide now, right?" said Kryvo.

"Citizens of Olympus!" There was another firework of red light, high in the sky, then Atlas's face formed in the sparks.

"Let me tell you, and the competitors, the rules of the race. You will see rings like this,"—a shining red hoop appeared in the sky next to his face—"along the course. Each one you fly your ship through will reveal more of a map to the finish line. Only once you have flown through all nine rings, will you know where to end the race. You will find the rings in sets of three. The first to cross the finish will receive five shells. The competitor who comes second will get four, the third three, fourth will receive two, and the last will receive one." The image of his handsome face smiled, and his hand appeared, holding a gleaming nautilus shell. Malice sparkled in his eyes. "And trust me when I tell you, you need these shells."

The number of shells didn't matter to me. All I had to do was stay alive.

"If your ship leaves the boundary of the Trial, you will be alerted." His eyes glinted even more wickedly, and I assumed it would be a painful alert. "I'll help you all out to start. The first ring is a mile to the west of Sagittarius. Poseidon, you won the last test, so you start. Three, two, one, go!"

The Whirlwind launched high into the air, and my stomach twisted as I watched him speed away, toward the west of the island. After a moment, Atlas spoke again. "Time's up. Kalypso, you may go!" Her Whirlwind sped after Poseidon's.

Polybotes went next, then Ceto. By the time my four-and-a-half-minute deficit was up, my hands were sweating on the spokes.

"Lastly, Almi!" His image disappeared from the sky as I willed the Crosswind into the air.

# CHAPTER 26

*R*elief powered through me as the vessel lifted, the gleaming sails shining bright. As I spurred the ship in the direction the others had gone, an unexpected rush of exhilaration blasted through me. The wind was warm as we soared through the sky, and I could still smell the tang of the ocean below.

Maybe it wasn't Poseidon that had felt right on the ship, I thought as the Crosswind sped through the clouds. Maybe it was me.

The other ships were too far ahead for me to see anything of them, but it wasn't long before I could see something else, gleaming red high above the water.

Giant, flaming hoops.

"Let's do this," I said. Agility was something I might even be better at than some of the others, given the ship's apparent willingness to follow my mental commands.

The ship powered toward the first ring.

A jet of water burst from the ocean below, clipping the side of my ship as we sailed through the air.

I suppressed a shriek of surprise and angled the ship the other way. If I hadn't looked over, I would have missed the second jet, blasting up on my other side. Swearing, I weaved the ship between them, wishing I had more eyes.

"Kryvo! Can you watch my left?"

"Put me on the wheel!"

One handed, I plucked the little starfish from my collarbone, and set him down on the wheel, all while trying to avoid the jets of water. Over half of them were hitting me, taking all the speed out of the ship as it rocked left and right.

"I'm on it! In thirty feet, you got a big one!" His squeaky voice only just carried to me, but it was enough.

With his help, I reduced the hit rate of the jets to well under half, and none of them were square on.

We were fast approaching the first ring when a jet shot up on our right, and I realized something was different about it. It was red.

"What-" I started, then froze in horror.

Crabs. In the jets. Giant, beady-eyed, vicious looking crabs.

"Ooh crap," I hissed, as they began to leap from the jet of water onto the deck of the ship. One landed on the bridge, and began to scuttle toward me. I kicked out at it, the movement making me let go of the wheel. I felt the ship lurch to a stop as my boot connected with the knee-high, bright scarlet crab. The thing went flying backward as I sprang back to the wheel.

"To the hoop!" I urged the ship, as two more crabs ran

at me. The ones on the deck had yet to figure out how to get up the steps, thank the gods.

I kicked away the crabs as they came at me, but I didn't have enough power to get them over the railings, so they just straightened themselves out and came back. Another jet of water burst up on the left, Kryvo yelling something about listening to him and not getting us killed. More crabs flooded onto my ship, and another four of them made it onto the bridge.

Fuck. I couldn't deal with seven *and* control the ship.

I became aware of a change in the light, and glanced up from the claw clacking crabs just in time to see the ship swoop through one of the rings.

"Yes!" I swung my head round, looking for a map.

"The sail!" squeaked Kryvo.

There, on the main sail, a dark ink drawing was appearing. I didn't have time to inspect it though. Pain lanced through my foot, and I looked down to see a crab right in front of me, nipping at my boots. I punted it as hard as I could, and it went flying at another two. Almost like skittles, they collided and skidded across the deck.

"To the next hoop!" I yelled at the ship. I didn't know if commanding it vocally made any difference, but the words came anyway.

I dipped my hand into a pouch on my belt, and pulled out the same little box that had saved my ass in Oxford. With a small prayer, I pressed the button and threw it down on the planks. The hologram elephant sprang to life, the light flickering as it raised its trunk.

All the crabs froze. I watched them just long enough to

ensure they were distracted by the hologram, and then turned back to the sail. Mercifully, the jets had abated.

The corner of a map had appeared on the main mast, the blackness of it stark against the gleaming metallic surface.

I tried to make sense of it, but there wasn't enough to work anything out.

Instead, I focused on the next hoop as the Crosswind powered toward it.

I was ready this time, when a jet shot up as we approached. This one though, was green.

Expecting green crabs to be waiting in the jet of water, I veered hard out of the way. The crabs already on the deck chittered angrily as they slid, and I had an idea.

Kneeling and scooping up the hologram chip, I gripped the wheel hard.

"Hold on, Kryvo," I said, then mentally asked the ship to tilt. It obliged, and the crab chitters turned to tiny clattery shrieks as the deck moved to a ninety-degree angle. I wrapped my arms around the wheel and clung on, grateful for the strength Poseidon's vial had given me. There was no way I could have held on otherwise.

When all the crabs were scrabbling around on the now horizontal railings, I held my breath, clutched the wheel, and willed the ship to tip them over the edge as quickly as possible.

With a jerk, the ship did just that. My feet slipped on the deck and for a terrifying moment I was hanging on with just my arms, but it righted itself fast, leaving me panting as I dropped to my knees.

"Good job," I gasped, stroking the wood. "Clever ship."

Another green jet burst up on my left, and I was so wrapped up in recovering from turning the ship sideways that I didn't have time to react.

I leapt to my feet as animals jumped from the water to my ship.

And they weren't crabs this time.

They were lobsters. Huge green things, with even snappier claws, and tails that curled up over their backs like a scorpions.

"Oh man. Kryvo, you got a good grip there?" I asked him as I kicked out at a fast-approaching lobster-scorpion-thing.

"Yes!" he squeaked.

"Here we go again, then."

By the time we got through the next hoop, I felt sick from all the rolling. The muscles in my arms were beginning to ache every time I held on, but it was working. The ship tipped the vile little creatures off the deck every time I willed her to.

I wasn't sure when I'd decided that the ship was a she, but I was positive she was.

"Last one," I gasped, willing the ship toward the last gleaming red ring. As the ship got closer, I realized with a bolt of hope that I could see another ship. Had I really caught someone up?

As the Crosswind zoomed closer, I could see the other ship wasn't moving. It was the Zephyr, and one of its bridges was drowning in giant red and green shellfish.

As we whizzed past, I saw a massive fist fly up out of

the sea of snapping claws, and crabs and lobster-scorpion-things went flying through the air. I felt a stab of pity for the giant, natural instinct making me want to stop and help before the man was hurt.

But my goal was to stay alive, and it wasn't like there was anything I could really do to improve his situation.

We sped on, and I kept my eyes wide and alert, ready for the next jets to erupt from the ocean. Nothing came, though. The surface of the sea was deceptively calm, the sky clear and bright, drifting with coral-colored clouds.

We soared through the ring with no problem, and new inky lines spread across the beautiful sails, filling in more of the map. It could have been the bottom third of an island. I tried to remember the map of Olympus, to see if it was Sagittarius. Surely we wouldn't be going too far from where we had started?

I felt the ship slow down, and I frowned in alarm.

Shit. I didn't know where to go. That was the next hurdle, I realized. Looking left and right, I tried to make out any sign of ships in the distance. All I could see was the green of Sagittarius on my right, and the wide-open ocean on my left.

Shrugging, I steered the ship left. These were the Poseidon Trials after all, so the ocean was as good a call as any.

I risked taking my hands from the wheel, darting to the railings to look over. Nothing but bright blue sea, frothy waves dancing across the surface. I moved back to the wheel and kept my guard up, looking for any signs of rings.

I was just starting to worry that I'd gone in the wrong direction when pain lanced through my entire body. Kryvo began squealing and I whirled, trying to work out what was happening. The whole ship vibrated, and Atlas's warning came back to me: *If you leave the bounds of the race, you'll be alerted.*

I barely had the sentience to steer the ship in the opposite direction, the pressure in my skull was so bad. As soon as we started back toward the island though, the pain lessened, and eventually faded.

"You okay, Kryvo?"

"N-n-n-o."

"I'm sorry."

"This is a very stressful morning." His voice was tiny, and I felt bad for putting him through this. In an effort to make him feel better, or at least distract him, I pointed to the sail.

"Any ideas on that map?"

"I'll have a look," he said shakily.

"Thank you."

I didn't know how much time I'd lost sailing out in the wrong direction, but coming last wasn't really an issue, so I tried not to let it bother me. Keeping my eyes peeled for red rings, I willed the ship to soar over the ocean. My eyes caught on a dark patch of sky toward the north of Sagittarius. It stood out from the rest of the bright vista, and I angled the ship toward it. It was a storm, I realized as we got closer. A small, isolated storm that was churning a chunk of the ocean up into a heaving, roiling mass of power.

But sparking and catching the light every now and then, were flashes of red. The rings.

With a near debilitating bout of trepidation, I commanded the ship to fly into the storm.

# CHAPTER 27

$\mathcal{A}$s soon as the ship moved into the rain, I knew I was in trouble. Wind as strong as a battering ram slammed into the hull, and the vessel lurched.

"Almi?" Kryvo's unsure voice was barely audible over the sound of the rain pelting the deck. "This is not good!"

"We'll just get through the rings and get out of here!" I called back. But I could barely steer the ship, the rain and the wind were so powerful. The sea was half frigging whirlpool below me, it was so wild. I wanted to will the ship higher, in order to keep clear of the turbulent waves, but the rings were dangerously close to the surface.

Of course they were, I thought, snarling.

I couldn't keep the rain from lashing my face, making it hard to see without constantly wiping the water out of my eyes.

What felt like painfully slowly, we made our way closer to the first ring. The bottom of the hoop was practically skimming the churning waves.

"Nearly there!" I called to Kryvo, as much for my own encouragement as his.

I blinked through the hammering rain as a flash of lightning lit up my surroundings. There, in front of me and moving through the farthest ring, was a ship. A ship with a metal hull.

Was it Poseidon or Kalypso?

Either way, I couldn't believe I'd caught one of them up. The two Whirlwinds started the race first.

Spurred on by the revelation that I possibly wasn't as shit as I thought I was, I guided the ship through the first ring. Something thudded against the hull, and we rocked to the side.

"What was that?" Kryvo's terrified squeak reached me.

"I don't know, and I don't want to."

I tried to get the ship to rise, to put some distance between us and the surface of the sea before we got to the next ring, which was easily another half mile away, but it was getting so hard to control. It was as though the storm was quicksand, and it was taking all my concentration to get the Crosswind to move through it. The second I got distracted by something, the ship slowed to a crawl, dropping slowly back toward the water.

The thudding against the hull sounded again, and I begged the ship to move higher over the sea.

"Come on! You fly, and you fly so well! Up you go!"

My urgent bidding seemed to work, and we lifted higher, the pull of the sea lessening.

I gave a small sigh of relief as we moved more freely toward the next ring, but my relief was short lived. We had risen high enough that I could see what was leaping out of the waves below us, and my stomach clenched.

Rotbloods. That's what had been butting the side of the ship. Their evil eyes fixed on the ship as they dove in and out of the water, snapping their huge jaws. At least three of them were visible in the waves, keeping pace with us.

"Oh shit. We do not want to risk being near the water for long."

More rain lashed down, and I was starting to feel cold. My hands were numb around the spokes of the wheel, and my teeth were chattering as I swore aloud.

Reluctantly, I willed the ship lower as we approached the next ring. The thudding started instantly. As the sharks battered the sides of the hull, frenzied wind pulled at the sail, forcing me to give everything I had to keeping the ship steady with my mind.

With a surge, the rain thickened, a torrent of water gushing down over us as we moved through the gleaming red ring, barely visible in the storm now.

More lightning lit the horizon, and I looked out for the Whirlwind, but I couldn't even see the next ring any more.

Fearful of losing my bearings and flying through one we'd already completed, I wiped my face angrily, wishing my eyesight was better.

"Kryvo! Do you know where the next ring is?"

"No!"

A flash of blue and gold caught my eye in the gray, and I locked onto it. "Blue!"

The rain was lashing the pegasus as his wings beat

wildly. His eyes locked on mine and I knew instantly that he couldn't stay in the storm long. He turned in the air and flew fast.

"Follow Blue!" I commanded the ship.

My burst of grateful energy must have poured into the ship, because this time it was easier to rise from the magnet-like waves and force our way through the storm.

When the last ring came into view, I was numb from the cold. The final hoop was actually touching the surface of the sea, the angry waves sloshing over the curved bottom. The red of the rotbloods flashed and I saw that they were jumping through the hoop themselves, almost in a mockery of our task.

Screwing my face up, I willed the ship lower, aiming for the ring.

I expected the hammering of the rotbloods against the ship but there was nothing. As we dipped I lost sight of the sea beneath us, and focused on the glowing ring through the rain.

A furious gust of wind slammed into the ship, and the sail billowed out, dragging us off course. The whole ship tipped alarmingly, and I dug deep, desperately trying to keep her upright.

I watched almost in slow motion as we rocked the other way, and a wave came crashing toward us, higher than the hull. It was too late to veer out of the way, and besides—we'd reached the ring.

"Hang on Kryvo," I yelled, as the wave crashed over the deck.

The water was icy cold as it doused me head to foot, trying to rip me from the wheel. I gasped for breath as the wave drained away, my concentration severed, and the ship slowing. Another gust of vicious wind took us, and we rocked hard. I barely had time to see the mast tipping toward the edge of the red ring before a second wave crested over us. The power behind the second wave was so great it dragged the whole ship over, low enough for me to see the waiting forms of the demon sharks. That's why they weren't battering the ship. They didn't need to. They were waiting for me to be washed off the deck and into the deadly ocean.

And they were about to get their wish.

I was vaguely aware of the top of the mast snagging on the ring, and then I was thrown from the wheel as another wave slammed into the Crosswind.

My numb fingers screamed in protest as they were prized from the spokes, and I didn't have time to cry out before I was rolling down the now vertical deck. I slammed into the railings, and for a second, I thought I might be saved, but then freezing water rose up around me, and I realized the railings were sinking. The ship was capsizing.

# CHAPTER 28

I tried to get to my feet on the sideways railings, but the lashing rain made getting a purchase on anything impossible.

"Kryvo!" I screamed, but I was too far from him to hear anything, and the wind was howling.

Flashes of red caught my eye, and I knew it wasn't the ring. I scrambled along the railing as it sank, trying to pull myself up the deck but it was impossibly sheer. If I didn't get out of the way, I'd be dragged fully under the ship. But throwing myself into the ocean with the sharks was as sure a death as drowning.

*Control the ship!*

Poseidon's voice bellowed into my mind, so loud it hurt.

Control the ship? Could I will it to obey me like this?

Gripping the wooden slats of the rails I begged the vessel to rise.

"Up! Go up! Take the fucking ring with you if it's stuck!" I screamed at the ship.

A wave crashed over my head, submerging me completely, and I clung to the rails as my body was lifted from them. The deck was vertical behind me, trapping me, and I saw the rotbloods speeding through the water toward me.

I had less than a second before it reached me.

The water swirled between me and the shark and then Poseidon was there, his back to me and facing the predator. He raised a spear and launched it at the shark. Turning, he moved through the water like lightning, his eyes electric blue in the gray water. He grabbed my arm, pulling me from the railing as a current of water began to push us from beneath. We burst through the surface together, riding the wave as though it were some sort of surfboard. Pulling me tight against his body we continued to fly through the air, and over his shoulder I could see a second wave rise up under the Crosswind and lift it from the ocean. With a surge, it was wrenched free from the hoop, and then it was speeding after us on its own wave. We broke through the edge of the storm and I gasped for breath as the rain vanished, bright pastel skies calm above us.

The wave we were riding swerved, depositing us on the deck of the now righted Crosswind.

Poseidon moved, gripping my shoulders and holding me at arm's length, checking every inch of my body.

"Th-th-thanks," I gasped. I was so cold I could hardly move my limbs, and I was pretty sure shock was setting in.

"You nearly died," Poseidon growled. I'd never seen his eyes so wild, a vivid version of the storm he had just rescued me from. I stared up at him. Warmth was starting to seep into me from where he was gripping me, and now we were out of the storm I could feel my strength slowly returning.

"You saved me. Again."

"Almi." Emotion was choking his words and I blinked at him. He looked every inch a god, fierce and solid and oozing blinding, lethal power. Yet at the same time, he looked utterly helpless. "I will always save you."

Before I could even process his words he pulled me to him, taking my lips with his. Desire exploded through me as he kissed me like a man with nothing to lose, a man starved. A man who had never wanted anything so much.

And I kissed him back, my own ferocity matching his. I pressed myself against him, desperate to feel every part of his body, for him to be as close to me as was physically possible.

He was right. Right in every way, and I didn't know how I'd ever not known this feeling was possible.

With a wrench he stepped back, breaking the kiss. My lips tingled, and I gaped at him, flushed and dizzy, desire pounding through my body and pooling between my legs in the most alien and incredible, way.

"No, this can't… I thought I was going to lose you. I'm sorry. I'm sorry, Almi."

"Wait—!" But I was too late. With a flash of white light, he was gone.

"What the fuck!"

The expletive burst from my lips, and I lifted my hands to my head in frustration, my limbs shaking.

A squeak caught my attention, and I looked at the bridge. "Shit, Kryvo!"

I took the steps two at a time, astounded I had the energy to do so, and saw the red starfish still clinging to the wheel.

"Kryvo, jeez, I'm sorry."

"W-w-w-e s-s-survived?"

"We did. Poseidon saved us." I shook my head. "Then he kissed me like I was his actual wife and he'd never wanted anyone so much in his life, and then he fucked off."

The starfish paused in his shivering. "He did?"

"Yeah."

I slumped down to the planks, needing a second to sit.

"Are we still in the race?"

"Yes. But we nearly drowned and got eaten." *And was kissed by a man I thought I hated and who hated me.* "I don't care if we come last. I need a moment."

I heard the sound of wings beating, then Blue landed on the bridge beside me. He tossed his mane as I looked up at him. "Hey, Blue. Thanks for your help in there."

He whinnied.

"Do you get whiplash from Poseidon's mood swings?" I asked the pegasus.

He stamped his feet.

"Yeah, maybe just me. That man is complicated."

I didn't know what it said about me that I seemed to be more shaken by the kiss than the ship capsizing in the storm and delivering me to the rotbloods.

"We should get this over with," I said, trying to pull myself together. I was distinctly aware that I was avoiding bringing Lily's image into my mind, almost as though I wasn't ready for her opinion on what had just happened. I needed my emotions to stay private, to belong to just me, a little longer. Just until I could make sense of them. And I couldn't do that out here, knowing I had to survive this stupid trial.

I stood up, dragging my shaking, confused ass up off the planks. Need was still pulsing through me, and I could feel the god's presence on my lips, his wild gaze burned into my brain.

I shook my head, clenching my jaw hard.

"Later," I told myself aloud. "Deal with this later. Right now, you need to focus."

I looked around me at the clear skies. Blue stamped his hooves and snorted.

"You know where we're going next, Blue?"

He ran a few steps along the planks, then launched himself into the air, his gold wings stunning in the light. "Follow the pegasus," I told the ship, as I retook my position at the wheel, trying to lock my spiraling thoughts about Poseidon away where they couldn't distract me from the lethal task at hand.

# CHAPTER 29

After a couple of minutes, we were flying over the west coast of Sagittarius, a mountain range consisting of only three mountains to my right. But boy were they big. Conjoined lower down, they spread out like a huge ridge on the landscape, and I would have expected them to be covered in snow in the human world, but here they were covered in a sheet of green.

Blue dipped ahead of us, and I commanded the ship to move lower, and increase her speed as we chased after him. She responded immediately, and the wind stung my eyes as we went faster. Sailing over land didn't have the same feeling, the same scents or openness, that sailing over the water did.

The pegasus made a sudden dive, his golden wings catching the light of the sky as he dropped from view.

I let go of the wheel and moved to the railing, the ship slowing down as I did so. There was Blue, kicking his hooves in the sand on the beach below us. Nestled in the sand also were three massive treasure chests, separated by tall palm trees. A sense of trepidation filled me at the quiet calm of the scene below.

"Have I gotta go down to the beach, Blue?" I called as the ship came to a gentle stop.

I couldn't hear the Pegasus, but he flicked his head, mane waving, and stamped on the sand.

"Oh boy." I really, really didn't want to get off the ship. But if that's what the Trial called for, then that's what I would have to do. "Let's go, Kryvo," I said, picking up the little starfish.

"I'd rather stay here," he squeaked.

I lifted him to my face. "What if I need your help?"

He gave a rippling squeaky noise that I thought was his equivalent of a sigh. "I shall accompany you," he said reluctantly.

"Thanks, buddy."

I set him on my collarbone and headed for the hauler at the back of the bridge. I stepped into the rickety wooden crate, pulled the shutter across it and willed it to lower. It did so immediately.

The sand was a few feet below me when it stopped moving, the Crosswind hovering a person's height above the ground and the hauler dropping just lower than its hull.

Carefully, I jumped down. The powdery-soft sand took the thump out of my landing, and I straightened. Blue trotted toward me, then turned pointedly to face the chests.

Now I was down here, they looked even larger. They also looked deliberately placed, palm trees between them, and large rocky boulders poking out of what looked like jungle behind them. Wind blew across my face, carrying the scent of the sea, and I turned instinctively to check for demon crabs or sharks or anything else crawling out of the water to eat me.

There was nothing but gentle waves lapping at the sandy shore.

I turned back to the enormous treasure chests and walked cautiously toward one. My foot hit something hard in the sand, and I looked down.

Bone. It was a long bone, picked clean and gleaming ivory.

"Huh. Please don't let that belong to any of the other contestants," I muttered. "Except maybe Ceto."

"I'm not sure she even has bones," said Kryvo.

I glanced up at the sky, checking for other ships, though I was positive that I was well behind everyone else after the storm. Unless, of course, Polybotes never escaped the crabs.

Blue whinnied, drawing my gaze back down.

I steeled myself and moved purposefully toward the first chest, eying it warily.

It was almost as tall as I was and made of a rich, shining wood. It didn't appear to have any age to it at all. When I moved, the light caught on the wood, and I saw a faint greeny-blue shimmer. Iron bands lined the rounded top, and it looked for all the world like it could have come from the set of a pirate movie.

Except for where the padlock should have been. There, there was just a shining bronze plate with one word etched into it. "Stingray."

I frowned, then moved backward, careful not to touch

anything. The second one shimmered red in the light, and the plate on the front said 'Seagrass'. The last chest shimmered purple and had 'Seashell' written on it.

"Right," I said out loud, chewing on my lip as I clasped my chin. "What the fuck are we supposed to do now?"

"Is there anything else here?" squeaked Kryvo.

I turned in a slow circle, eyes sharp.

"Yes!" There, pinned on a palm tree, was a sheet of paper, its slight fluttering in the breeze catching my attention. I hurried over to it, tearing it from the pin.

*See here before you, chests numbering three*
    *Each is different, and only one will set you free*
    *All the other two hold is certain death*
    *Get it wrong and you will draw your last breath*
    *Rage and fire lie within the wrong box*
    *Avoid your body burning on the rocks*
    *Select with care the chest that holds no doom*
    *Surely that will keep you from an early tomb*

I blinked as I read the words, then read them aloud for Kryvo.

"So, we have to open one of the chests?"

"Yes. The one that won't kill us."

"And… How the hell are we supposed to know which one that is?"

The starfish made his sighing noise again. "We can work this out. It says each is different, right?"

I nodded. "Yup."

"What's different about them?"

"They all shimmer a different color, and they have different words written on them. Seashell, stingray and seagrass."

I peered at the riddle in my hands, looking for something I'd missed.

"Rage and fire. That sounds..."

"Like something we want to avoid at all costs?" offered Kryvo.

"Yeah." A slight panic was starting to make me twitchy. This wasn't something we could walk away from. There was a one in three chance we would get this wrong, and die. And unlike the geysers and the storm, I couldn't just strap on my big girl pants and fly straight into it, hoping for the best. This challenge gave me time to think, time to question. Time for fear to settle in.

"Read it one more time," said Kryvo.

I did, staring at the words, willing them to give us more.

"I like seashells," I said, unhelpfully.

"I like stingrays," the starfish responded, equally unhelpfully.

I blew out a breath, looking again between the three chests. I used to do puzzles on my phone when I was bored in my trailer. Surely I could work this one out?

"Maybe it's a word game," I murmured, looking back at the riddle, trying something new.

*See here before you, chests numbering three*
*Each is different and only one will set you free*

*All the other two hold is certain death*
*Get it wrong, and you will draw your last breath*
*Rage and fire lie within the wrong box*
*Avoid your body burning on the rocks*
*Select with care the chest that holds no doom*
*Surely that will keep you from an early tomb*

I saw it in an instant, letting out a whoop of triumph.

Kryvo squeaked in surprise.

"Don't do that!" he admonished.

"But Kryvo, look!" I held up the paper. "It *is* a word game. Look at the first letter of each line!"

The starfish slowly read out each letter. "It spells seagrass."

Grinning like an idiot, I strode toward the chest that had the plate that read seagrass. "Who needs saving now?" I beamed.

I laid my hand on the chest, and looked around, unsure how to make my selection. "This one," I said loudly. I had no idea if that was how I was supposed to do it, but it was worth a try.

There was a loud clicking sound, and painfully slowly, the chest creaked open. Just when I thought nothing was going to happen, red sparks flew into the air, rushing from the open chest. They danced in the sky a moment, then zoomed higher, forming three large hoops.

"Yes!" I turned to Blue, grinning, and a loud rumble sounded. The pegasus neighed, then took flight, wings beating hard to make up for his lack of run up.

A heartbeat later I wished I could fly too.

The sand beneath my feet was moving. Sinking.

"Shit." I ran, powering my arms and willing my legs to be strong. Every step felt like I was fighting a battle though, the sand trying to suck my body down. I threw a glance over my shoulder, fear pounding through me as I saw the chests were half submerged in the quicksand.

I'd begun moving just early enough that my momentum was carrying me, but my ship seemed a frigging mile away as the suck of the sand increased.

Blue swooped down in front of me, flicking his tail, and I didn't question his intention.

I reached out and grabbed it and he beat his wings, his strength helping to move me faster across the sand.

"You're a fucking legend, Blue!" I yelled at him, furiously working my legs as we closed in on the hauler dangling from the back of the Crosswind. With a desperate leap, I let go of Blue's tail and threw myself into the crate. Landing hard on my shoulder, I heard the snapping of wood and thought the bottom might give out under my weight. Breath held, I waited to fall into the deadly sand below.

"Almi?" squeaked Kryvo when nothing happened. "P-p-p-p-please take us up to the bridge."

"Good plan," I said exhaling hard, my heart pounding so fast I thought it might escape my ribcage. "I'm not built to run that fast."

I felt sick as I willed the hauler to take us up, but my nausea was fast replaced by relief when I stepped shakily out onto the sturdy planks of the ship.

I moved to the ship's wheel and closed my fingers around the spokes, feeling my hands shake a little less at the now familiar warmth the ship gave me. "Take us through the rings, please," I whispered to the ship. We swung around as we rose, then she sailed through the gleaming rings, one by one. I was tense as we flew, waiting for the next curveball to come our way, but it appeared that the quicksand had been deemed enough of a challenge for the time being. We were unhindered as we passed through the rings.

I watched the spidery ink on the solar sails spread out further, tilting my head as the last three sections of the map appeared, then coalesced into something readable.

"Any ideas Kryvo?"

"Yes. You see those three shapes around the cross?"

I looked at the map as the sail snapped taut, as though it was trying to help me. The map looked like someone had zoomed in very close to a single part of Olympus, and there was a giant cross in the middle of three roughly round shapes. Something moved under the cross, the ink swirling across the glittering fabric of the sail.

"Yes."

"I believe those are three small volcanoes on the other side of Aquarius, the north-easterly part of Scorpio."

"Yeah?"

"Do you want me to show you the map of Olympus I am seeing in the palace through my starfish friends?"

I shook my head. "No, I trust you." Blue had been with us too long now to have seen where anyone had gone before us, so I assumed he couldn't help us. But the little starfish had got everything right so far, and I had no reason to hold us up any longer.

I willed the ship to move west. The ink moved again

on the map, as though it were zooming in further on the cross. Did that mean we were going in the right direction?

Whatever kept moving under the cross was getting larger.

The further we flew, the more the cool gusts of ocean air calmed my fried nerves. I refused to let myself think about the kiss or anything else Poseidon-related, just focusing on getting to our destination. A couple of times the map started to zoom out instead of in, until I adjusted our course. The closer to the cross we got though, the more the thing under it came into focus.

It was a skull, I realized, once most of the map was dominated by the cross and the three representations of the volcanos.

"What do you think the skull means?"

Kryvo chittered. "What do you *think* it means? There's something there that will try to kill us."

# CHAPTER 30

*J*ust a few moments later, shining in the distance, we saw the finish-line. It was a long shining line made of the same sparks as all the hoops were, the tips of three volcanoes visible in the distance.

Squinting, I could make out three small dots hovering the other side of the red line. Ships that had already finished the race, I presumed. And there were only three, which meant someone was behind me. *Or dead.* I found myself willing one of the ships on the other side to be Poseidon's Whirlwind.

I resisted the urge to propel the Crosswind forward, taking my time to scan the sea below me for any sign whatever Kryvo believed might be stalking these waters. I was in no rush. And frankly, I was astonished not to be last.

Though I wouldn't even have survived if it weren't for Poseidon's interventions. *Again.*

"I need to learn to rescue my own damned ass," I muttered.

"Or hide."

I rolled my eyes at the starfish. A deep growling sound reached my ears, and Blue swooped above us.

"What was that?" Kryvo asked hesitantly.

I willed the ship to move a bit higher, and a bit faster. "I don't know," I answered, as the growl grew louder. Thunder clapped suddenly, and then something burst up from the water before us. Wooden planks, I realized, as I swerved the Crosswind instinctively.

My mouth fell open as I watched the shattered pieces of a ship shower up in an arc before us, before falling back down to the waves below.

"Oh my god," I breathed, trying to resist the urge to run and look over the edge of the ship. "Whose ship was destroyed?"

"And by what?" Kryvo's voice was wobbly with fear, and I jumped in fright as Blue's hooves landed noisily on the deck.

I turned to him and saw that he was skittering his feet uneasily, shaking his head and snorting continuously.

A deep sense of unease gripped me.

"What's wrong, Blue?" He whinnied loudly, the sound pained.

I couldn't tell how I knew what he was trying to tell me, but I did.

*Poseidon. It's Poseidon's ship.*

Letting go of the wheel, I ran to the edge of the railings and looked over.

. . .

Just a few feet below the crystal-clear water was the god of the sea. And wrapped around him was the tail of something that looked like it had come straight out of a Jurassic Park film.

Terror made my muscles freeze, and I watched in horror as Poseidon was lifted clear above the surface of the sea, then slammed back down with a force that would have killed a human.

The creature was larger than my ship, and shaped like a crocodile at its bottom half, its barbed tail wrapped tight around Poseidon. Its top half was dinosaur-like, its long reptilian snout filled with enormous teeth, and its beady eyes fiercely intelligent. Six arms like crabs' legs, jointed and ending in fierce looking spikes, jutted out of its body, flailing toward Poseidon, and blue tendrils that almost looked like feathers lined its neck and back, glowing.

"What do we do?" I half-shrieked, digging in my pouches.

I threw in a grenade, watching as it gave a little poof and sent ink spreading through the water utterly ineffectually.

Blue galloped to my side, shaking his mane and neighing. I looked at the Pegasus, my mind racing.

The finish line was a hundred meters away. The monster guarding it was not at all interested in me. I knew what I was supposed to do.

The monster lifted Poseidon again, this time pulling him into his torso, the spiked arms bending in to stab at him. Light blasted from Poseidon's body, blasting back the spikes, but only for a moment.

With an agonizing screech, the creature moved faster

than I thought it would be able to, rushing through the ocean. I lost sight of it as it moved under the ship, and I ran to the other side of the ship just as it leapt out of the water. It arched high as it jumped, a grotesque parody of dolphins playing, its prey clutched in its tail.

My heart thudded, my chest constricting, as I saw Poseidon's face. Half of it was the color of granite.

"No," I whispered, fear coiling in my gut inexplicably. Poseidon's eyes met mine for a fraction of a second, before he was dragged back under the surface.

I leaned over, looking for them under the water. There was an almighty splash and then Poseidon's voice rang through the air.

"Go back to the depths you came from!"

And then he was there, three times his normal size, fierce and strong and unstoppable, a tidal wave lifting him from the ocean as a whirlpool of water formed before his towering form. The creature thrashed and flailed in the churning water, and Poseidon raised both his hands, his eyes closing.

Glowing such an intense turquoise that I could barely see, he roared. The light rushed the monster, and it spasmed as the magic flooded its body. With a jerk, it exploded in a mass of light and scales.

Relief rushed from me, my whole body sagging against the rails. "Thank fuck for that."

Poseidon turned on his wave, his eyes locking on mine, and all my relief vanished.

The light was leaving his body, replaced entirely by stone. Horror took me as sadness filled his expression, before the light left his eyes. Slowly, terrifyingly slowly, his stone form tipped and fell from the collapsing wave.

"Poseidon!" I screamed his name as I watched his granite form sink below the surface.

A hundred emotions rushed me. Lily's face filled my mind. I felt myself reach for the frantic pegasus beside me.

"I'm sorry, Lily," I half sobbed, as I pulled myself clumsily onto the winged horse's back. "I'm sorry, I have to. I don't know why." All I knew was that I couldn't let him sink to the bottom of the sea.

I had to save him.

*Go.*

A gust of ocean wind lifted me as Blue snapped his wings out and sprang into the air.

I had time for one big breath before we dove into the ocean after Poseidon.

THE STORY CONTINUES IN SURRENDER OF THE
BRUTAL KING

# SURRENDER OF THE
# BRUTAL KING

# ALMI

Freezing water engulfed me before it even occurred to me to swallow some water-root. If I was being honest, *nothing* had fully occurred to me before leaping on the pegasus' back and diving in after Poseidon's sinking form.

Blue beat his wings on either side of me, and we powered through the water faster than I ever could have managed on my own. But Poseidon's stone body was sinking faster.

I gripped Blue's mane, panic and fear flooding my system, and no idea at all what I would even do if I could reach him before I ran out of air.

Blue must have sensed my thoughts because he surged forward suddenly, spurring us farther into the darkening depths. Poseidon's armor glinted in the now dusky light, and a bolt of hope made my muscles tighten as I realized we were now moving faster than he was. Barely ten seconds later, the pegasus had caught him up, his golden wings cutting through the ocean currents as he swooped beneath the sinking god. I shifted on Blue's back and clung on as Poseidon's heavy form landed hard across the winged horse's shoulders. He began to slide, and I wrapped one arm tight around him as I tried to grip Blue harder with my thighs.

The pegasus kicked his way up, his load now significantly heavier and his pace reflecting it. I tried not to notice the burn in my lungs, or the ice cold feel of Poseidon's chest under my unsteady grip.

*What the hell had happened?* Had the healer's magic worn off? Had killing that insane creature weakened him enough the stone took over?

And what the hell would I do with him when we got to the surface?

*If* we got to the surface.

Blue's wings beat even harder as he struggled, and the exertion required for me to keep the statue of Poseidon on the pegasus's back and hang on myself was exhausting. I would run out of air soon, I knew.

A voice rang through my mind, tense and urgent. *Just get him to the finish line. We can't interfere until the Trial is over, but we can help as soon as you're back.*

Persephone?

Had she and the other gods seen what had happened? Could they see us now?

Willing the pegasus to move faster, I craned my neck to look up. Light shone above the surface of the water, and blessed air was so close now. My lips parted, and I clamped them closed again.

*Come on, come on, come on, please. Please, let me hold my breath a little longer.*

It wasn't just my life dependent on my ability to survive. It was Lily's and Poseidon's, too.

A tiny stream of bubbles corkscrewed through the water toward me, growing larger as it got closer, and I tensed. Poseidon slipped in my grasp, and I was forced to let go of Blue's mane to grab him, lifting him tighter between my body and the pegasus' neck. The motion was too much, and my lungs burned like they were filled with acid. My mouth opened, my nostrils filling with water as instinct forced me to try to suck in air.

The ribbon of bubbles rushed me, zooming around my head and pouring into my mouth. Air, cool and crisp, filled my throat and lungs, and I gasped. Relief slammed through me as the bubbles kept whizzing, lifting my hair from my stinging eyes and making my vision clearer as they delivered blessed air into my body.

I had no idea where the air was coming from, but I sent a prayer of thanks to whoever had heard my plea as I gulped it down.

The bubbles rushed around my head, so fast that they blurred together, making a layer of clear air all around my face, as though I was wearing a helmet of air. I adjusted my grip on Blue, rubbing his shoulder encouragingly, and I heard a faint whinny through the water. I tried speaking, my thoughts singular, exhaustion and desperation forcing adrenaline through my body.

"You're doing fucking amazing, Blue. You're saving his life." My voice came out clearly. I blinked incredulously as the pegasus whinnied louder, and I was sure he moved a little faster.

Seconds later, my head broke through the surface. The

bubbles vanished, and I twisted in my awkward position to see the Crosswind right next to us.

*Finish the race,* I told myself urgently.

I had to finish the race.

Blue kept beating his wings, and it pained me to see how tired he was. "Can you get us to the ship?" He gave a small, exhausted whinny, then he lifted us from the sea.

I suppressed a shriek as Poseidon's stone body began to slip again, but Blue moved fast, and within another few seconds we were hovering next to the box that moved up and down to the bridge. Scrambling, I tipped the Poseidon statue into the crate and climbed in after him. Free of his heavy burden, Blue shook his wings, his legs kicking in the air.

"Thank you," I breathed. "See you on deck."

I willed the box to rise, unable to pull the door shut with Poseidon lying there, limbs unmovable. I looked at the expression etched into his beautiful face as I slumped against the wood, panting.

Sadness. His expression was one of almost unbearable sadness.

*Why in the name of all the gods had I gone in after him?*

What the frigging hell had I been thinking?

I hadn't, I realized. Rational thought had abandoned me utterly, instinct as deep as my soul sending me into the sea.

Had he made me do it, before he had turned to stone? Had he compelled me to save him with magic? I was the only one who could have helped him; only the competitors could be involved in the Trial.

The box clacked as it reached the deck, and I dragged

myself to my feet as fast as I could, pulling Poseidon's insanely heavy stone body with me as I moved onto the deck. His stone boots left scratches on the planks.

"I'm sorry, ship," I told her as I let go of him and jogged to the wheel. "Take me to the finish line, please."

Blue touched down on the deck as Kryvo squeaked, and the ship lurched forward.

"Almi! Almi, I thought you were dead! You can't be dead, you're my only friend!"

"I'm not dead," I assured him, pushing my wet hair back from my face and gratefully breathing in the ocean air in long breaths.

"Is Poseidon?"

I glanced over my shoulder at his solid granite body. "No. Not yet."

# ALMI

The second the Crosswind sailed over the gleaming finish line, there was a flash of white light, and Hades and Persephone appeared on the deck beside me. Persephone moved to Poseidon's side in an instant, vines shooting from her palms and wrapping around Poseidon's limbs before she even reached him.

"What happened to him?" Hades asked, turning to me. An overwhelming urge to bow to the god of the dead took me, and his silver eyes swirled as his gaze bore into mine.

Atlas' voice boomed through the sky before I could answer, glee in his voice.

"It seems we may have suffered a casualty in the Poseidon Trials already!"

Hades' face twisted into a snarl and tendrils of smoke leaked from his body, obscuring his black clothing.

"Hades, I can't wake him, but he's alive in there."

We both turned at Persephone's voice.

Somehow, I had already known he was still alive, but

that didn't stop the relief I felt at having my instincts confirmed.

Hades turned back to me. "What happened?" he repeated.

"I don't know. I mean, I know he has been fighting an affliction that turns people to stone." There was no point hiding that from them anymore. "But I don't know why it happened now. Were you watching?"

Hades nodded slowly, looking between me and the stone god. "Yes. The whole thing is being broadcast in the flame dishes." Flame dishes were like TVs in Olympus. Most households had large iron bowls to keep burning embers in, so they could gather round and watch whatever the gods wanted to show the world.

"Why was he fighting that monster?"

"Atlas," Hades growled. "The creature was waiting for Poseidon. It let Kalypso and Ceto straight over the finish line without even surfacing. As soon as Poseidon got there, it rose up, dragging him and his ship under. Polybotes crossed just before you reached the finish-line and had no attention from the beast whatsoever. It was only after my brother."

"We need to find someone who can help him," Persephone said, standing up from where she was crouched over Poseidon.

"He said a healer had been helping him keep it at bay, but they couldn't cure it."

"What healer?"

I frowned as I answered. "He didn't say, but Galatea is the only other person who knew about this."

"Then we'll ask her. Are you ready to go?" Hades

looked at me, and I was so unaccustomed to being asked if I was ready for something, that I just blinked at him.

Persephone spoke softly. "I can understand you might be in shock, Almi. But we must go now."

I shook my head. "Wait!" I turned back to the ship's wheel. Kryvo flashed red just long enough that I could see where he was hiding. "Thank you, ship," I said loudly, trying to mask the fact I was lifting the little starfish into my palm. "Okay. I'm ready."

We flashed into the courtyard of the palace, where Galatea and a dozen palace staff and guards were standing before an enormous flame dish, an image of the finish line and the four surviving ships hovering in the orange flames.

"Sire." She rushed forward, her face a mask of horror.

"Galatea, who was the healer who helped him before?"

She turned to me, and instead of anger or suspicion, I was shocked to see her expression was one of pure gratitude. "You saved him. He would be lying on the ocean floor right now, if it weren't for you."

"I, erm…" I ran one hand through my tangled hair awkwardly. "Blue helped, too," I said.

She reached out, clasping my other hand. "Thank you."

Hades sighed. "The healer," he commanded. "Now."

Galatea turned to him, her face flushing and her head bowing low. "Of course, mighty one."

Shit, should I have been calling him that? I glanced at Persephone, and she gave me a tiny smile of reassurance.

"It was a dragon, on the realm of Pisces. She does not take visitors lightly."

*A dragon?* I gaped at Galatea.

Hades nodded. "Erimítis?"

"Yes," confirmed Galatea. "She will only entertain one as strong as you or your brothers."

"Fine. I will take Poseidon to her myself." Hades turned to Persephone, kissing her with an intensity I didn't know was possible in such a brief embrace. "I will see you as soon as I can, my love."

"Be safe," she said, touching his cheek. There was a flash, and the two brothers were gone.

Persephone looked at me as I blinked around dazedly.

"You look like you could do with a sit down," she said. "And maybe a stiff drink."

When I looked at her, the feeling of warmth she generated in me was so unfamiliar that I was tempted to distrust it. But she was a healer, and she appeared to harbor no animosity toward me. Maybe she was just... being nice.

I felt a flash of desire to call up Lily's image, to be alone with her so I could go through everything that had just happened. But then I would have to face up to a whole load of questions. *Like why the hell I had risked my life and hers to save Poseidon's.*

"A drink sounds good." Putting those questions off a while longer suited me just fine. "If there are donuts, that would be even better."

"If you need donuts, I can find donuts," said Galatea, still looking at me like I was some sort of hero.

"Seriously? You can get me donuts?"

"I will get you whatever you want. You saved the king."

Her words rolled around in my head as I followed her and Persephone into the palace, discreetly lifting

Kryvo to my collarbone when the women's backs were turned.

*You saved the king.*

Why? Why had I saved him?

I couldn't avoid the damned question.

And deep down, I knew I couldn't avoid the answer, either.

I could have told myself that it was because Poseidon had spent the entire time I'd been caught up in this obscene mess saving my life. I owed him.

I could have told myself it was because I believed him to be the right person to rule Aquarius, and that ancient angry Titans were the bad guys and I was obligated to keep the true king on the throne.

I could have told myself that it was because I was the only one who could have helped him at that point, and I wasn't wired to let a person die when I could stop it from happening.

The truth, though?

I couldn't *not* have gone in after him. It wasn't something I had carefully thought through and come to a sensible decision on. Leaping into the ocean after him had been as instinctive as walking, or even breathing.

I may have barely known the man, but I was connected to him somehow. His fiery temper and miserable attitude were the antithesis of the light and bright Lily, and he represented everything I didn't want in my life — control, rules, and sullen silence.

Yet, when I looked into those stormy eyes, I could feel the passion he was suppressing. I didn't know what the passion was for; perhaps that endless sense of freedom I had felt from him more than once, or the bond he had with the creatures of his realm? But whatever it was, I knew there was more to the fierce and controlled god of the sea than what he was presenting to the world.

And if I hadn't been certain?

Then that smile… *Fuck, that smile.*

I wished I'd never seen it. So brief, and yet I needed to see it again.

And I hadn't needed anything other than my sister, my whole life.

# ALMI

*T*he emotions and thoughts fighting for attention inside me were bordering on over-whelming. I rubbed my hand across my face.

"Shit, sorry!" I'd been so distracted I'd walked straight into Persephone.

"You okay?" She steadied me as Galatea pulled open the large double doors on our left.

"Sure. A bit... overwhelmed," I said.

"I know the feeling."

Persephone ushered me into the room after Galatea, and a weird calm came over me as I entered the space.

Not a foggy calm, like the demon jackass angler fish had caused, but a serene, relaxing vibe that made me want to curl up with a good book and doze peacefully.

"We call this the drawing-room," said Galatea. "I'm sure Poseidon won't mind us using it while you recover."

I associated the idea of a drawing-room with English period dramas, and in some ways, I could kind of make the connection. It looked like the room was half of one tower, a semi-circle in shape. There were walls between the columns ringing the edge of the room, but huge drapes lined them, almost like tapestries. The fabric was exactly like the stuff Poseidon's robe was made from, and though the material didn't move, the colors of the ocean swirled and played across the surface.

The floor wasn't covered in marble tiles like everywhere else I'd seen in the palace, but a rich, soft, black carpet instead. Huge squishy couches were dotted around the room in various shades of navy, and rosewood side tables covered in books and trinkets stood beside the chairs. Tall potted plants at random intervals along the walls gave it a slightly exotic air, and I was sure I could hear the gentle lapping of waves.

"It's lovely," Persephone said, running her fingers through the leaves of a ten-foot-tall bamboo plant as she walked along the edge of the room.

"It is," I nodded. "Very relaxed."

Persephone glanced at me. "Unlike your husband."

I snorted, and she smiled as she picked a couch big enough for three and sat down. She was wearing jeans and a green wraparound top, her long white hair tied back in a complicated braid. Her bottom half said human world, and her top half said Olympus. She patted the cushion beside her, and I made my decision.

I was going to trust her.

"So, donuts, and what do you want to drink?" Galatea asked as I moved to the couch.

"I'll have red wine, please," said Persephone. "Dionysus knows his shit," she added to me.

"Then I'll join you."

I didn't really drink red wine, ever. I was more of a beer-if-I-could-afford-it kind of girl. But who was I to turn down wine made by a god?

"Be right back." Galatea strode from the room.

"You must be worried," Persephone said. I shifted on the couch so I could see her face.

"Okay. Here's the thing. No. But yes. And I shouldn't be."

Her pretty brows drew together. "I don't follow you."

I blew out a sigh. "That makes two of us."

Galatea came back into the room and sat down in an armchair facing our couch. "This dragon," she said. "She will help the king. She did before, and she will again, I am sure." Tense concern was etched into Galatea's face.

"Poseidon will be fine," I said.

"How do you know?"

"Because… I do."

"Your marriage bond," said Persephone, knowingly. "I always know if Hades is in trouble."

"Erm, about that. You see, I am technically Poseidon's wife, but it was a very quick wedding, and then he hid me in the human world where nobody could find me for-" I glanced at Galatea apologetically. "Eight years."

Persephone's lips parted in surprise. "What made you return?"

Galatea moved forward in her seat, and I realized she would be keen to know the true answer to this question too.

"My sister," I said. It was the truth, and I had no intention of giving either woman details of how I got back, or my plan to find Atlantis.

"You said she was sick?"

"Yes. Eight years ago, she fell unconscious. Since I returned, I discovered that she has an ailment that is turning her to stone."

Persephone frowned. "Is she connected to Poseidon and his ailment?"

I shrugged. "I don't know." I looked at Galatea, unsure how much to say about the blight that was spreading through Aquarius. "Atlas referred to me as the last of the Nereids, but he's wrong. Lily lives."

"What has that got to do with the stone?"

I sighed again. There was a knock on the door, and a nymph entered with a tray laden with three glasses of ruby-red wine and a huge plate of donuts.

When we each had a drink and I'd practically inhaled a salted caramel delight, I continued.

"The Oracle at Delphi told Poseidon that something called the heart of the ocean is the only way to cure the blight. And... The only way to possess the heart of the ocean is to possess the heart of a Nereid."

Persephone looked at me a long moment, then took a deep drink of her wine.

I decided to do the same. "Fuck, that's tasty," I muttered.

"So Poseidon married you for this heart of the ocean?"

"Yeah. Then he hid me, so nobody could steal me from him."

"What a prick," she murmured.

"Yes!" I exclaimed, as Galatea tutted loudly. "But anyway, it didn't work. He doesn't have his heart of the ocean." I took one more massive breath and turned square

243

on to Galatea. "I may as well tell you this. Poseidon knows already, and... Well it's probably just easier that you know."

She looked at me warily. "What?"

"I'm broken." I swallowed, then took another big gulp of delicious wine. "I have no power. The nautilus shell tattoo of a Nereid should be filled with color, like my sister's. My hair should be bright blue and my skin shiny like pearls."

I took another swig of wine, and realized I had never said those words out loud before.

"I should be able to control water, to long to be in it, to have an affinity with the ocean. I don't. I can't do anything with it. I can't even hold my breath longer than a human."

It was as though I was letting out over two decades of a dirty secret, and I couldn't stop.

"My sister went to the academy, and she was amazing. Her water magic rivaled a god's. That's who Poseidon was supposed to marry to get his heart of the ocean." I let out a long breath. "He married the wrong sister."

Galatea blinked at me, then drained her own glass. "You have no magic," she repeated.

"Uh-uh."

"And you survived the first Trial?"

That wasn't what I had expected her to say. I nodded. "Yeah. With help. Poseidon spoke to me when that fish lured me in, and he saved me from the storm."

"Almi, the fact that you even showed up with no magic is insane!"

"It's not like I had much choice," I mumbled.

"I admire your bravery. Both in the Trials and in telling us this now."

"You... You do?" I had never been admired before.

"Yes. But we do now have a massive problem."

"Yes, we do," said Persephone. "If the only way to wake your sister up is with the heart of the ocean, and the only way to get it is for Poseidon to marry her..."

"Can you marry an unconscious person?"

"No. I'm pretty sure that's not a thing."

"Shit."

Galatea stood and topped up our wine glasses from a tall bottle that looked no emptier than when she had started.

"Can we awaken your powers somehow?" Persephone asked hopefully.

"I can't tell you how much I would love that. But I wouldn't know where to start. Lily could never get them to show."

"What is the heart of the ocean anyway? Didn't the little old lady throw it into the sea at the end?"

The explosion of warmth I felt for the woman sitting beside me caused me to grip her arm. "You should have seen the look on Poseidon's face when I said the same thing to him," I said.

Persephone snorted as she laughed, then gave a small squeal as she nearly spilled her wine. I couldn't help laughing with her.

"What is funny?" asked Galatea.

Through giggles, we tried to explain the movie Titanic to Galatea. "That sounds like a very sad way to spend three hours," she said.

I nodded. "Yeah. Totally worth it though."

Persephone nodded. "Die-hard romantics don't get it much better."

"I do not have time for romance," Galatea said, a little sadly.

There was a flash of white light that made all of us jump in surprise, then Hades was standing beside the couch.

"Poseidon is resting. He will be fully recovered in a few hours," he said.

"By fully recovered, do you mean-"

Hades shook his head, ending my question before I finished it. "She is not able to cure the blight. As she did before, she can keep it from taking his whole body, but only as long as he does not exert so much power again."

"How is he supposed to win the Trials without exerting power?" asked Galatea, a new expression of concern covering her stern face.

"A very good question. And one I have no answer for."

"When is the next Trial?" asked Persephone.

Hades scowled. "If he knows Poseidon is injured, then Atlas will start it soon, so he has less time to recover."

Nerves fluttered through my gut, and I reached for another donut in an effort to settle my stomach. The thought of facing another Trial...

"Almi."

I turned to Hades as he said my name.

"He asked to see you."

# ALMI

*P*oseidon was lying in a bed much like the one in my guest room. In fact, the whole room looked very similar to the one I was staying in. But I didn't take much time to check out the decor. My focus was entirely on the god of the ocean.

I found myself moving fast to his bedside, gaze locked on his face. His eyes fluttered open as I reached him, and he moved, sitting up. The sheets fell away from his completely bare chest, and I paused, suddenly awkward.

"Hi," I said, raising a hand, then feeling really stupid.

"You saved me." His serious face burned with rigid control.

"Yeah, I guess. Couldn't have done it without Blue."

"Why?"

I couldn't help a small laugh at the irony of his question. "Now you know how I feel," I said.

His fierce blue eyes softened. "I mean it. I thought nothing was more important than your sister. If you had died trying to save me, then your sister would not be saved either."

A ripple of fear moved through my whole body at the truth of his words.

"You saved me a bunch of times," I said quietly. "I was just returning the favor."

Energy seemed to thrum around the room, and I couldn't help drinking in the rich, tanned tone of his skin, savoring the lack of granite stone. Last time I'd seen him… "I knew you weren't dead," I blurted out. "I don't know how, but I knew you were alive inside the stone."

"I was not conscious," he replied, his lips barely moving.

"How do you know I saved you then?"

"Hades told me. Almi, you are connected to this blight somehow."

"I don't know about that, but I know…" I bit my lip, trying to work out how to say what I was thinking. "I know I am connected to *you* somehow, and you to me. Why else would you have agreed to the Trials to save my life in the first place? And why risk your success in the first Trial to save me from the storm? It's for the same reason I went in after you, isn't it?"

He took a slow breath, chest expanding. I kept my eyes on his. "We have a bond, yes."

"What kind of bond?"

He frowned at me. "I know it was almost a decade ago, but I assume you haven't forgotten us being married in front of Hera?"

I gave him my best scowl back. "Yeah, women forget their wedding days often," I replied sarcastically, fisting my hand on my hip. "You're saying the marriage is what's causing us to want to save each other?" I emphasized the word *save* and hoped it wasn't obvious that, on my part, it could easily have been substituted with a number of other words. Especially when he was shirtless.

"Yes." Emotion flickered in his eyes, too fast for me to decipher.

I was tired, I realized, emotionally and physically, and I decided to change the subject, unwilling and unable to process the notion of marriage bonds. "Can I have some more of those vials before the next Trial, please?"

"Yes. I can't conjure them now. I need to wait for my strength to return."

"Thanks." I bit my lip again.

"Thank you," he said, his voice deep and sincere.

I raised my eyebrows. "You're, erm, welcome."

"Why do you have a starfish on your shoulder?"

I froze. "I don't know what you're talking about." He gave me a look, and I sighed resignedly. "He's my friend." I looked down at my chest. "Kryvo, you've been busted." The starfish remained silent, and camouflaged, but I could feel his warmth on my skin. "I think he's too shy to say hello," I told Poseidon.

"Hades said you were seen talking to someone the whole Trial. Was it the starfish?"

I flushed. It hadn't occurred to me that I was being broadcast. "Yeah."

"Does he talk back?" Poseidon was speaking to me like I was some sort of crazy person, which led me to believe that he didn't know the starfish was part of his own palace. Did that mean he didn't know the starfish could spy on him through the other statues?

Thinking fast, I decided on a partially true answer. "Yes. But he doesn't say much. He's sort of an emotional support starfish."

Poseidon frowned at me. "You are odd. Very, very odd."

"Gotta be odd to be number one," I grinned at him, reciting a favorite mantra.

He shook his head, but I was certain the corner of his mouth quirked up a tiny bit. "I think there is little chance of either of us being number one right now. I am unable to use my full power due to this accursed blight and the loss of my trident. We must come up with a new plan to win these Trials."

"I'm not here to win," I said, shaking my head.

He stared at me a long moment before speaking, and I concentrated on not looking at his nipples. "Then perhaps we can try something different for the next Trial."

"What did you have in mind?"

"If you stay where I can see you, I will not have to worry about rescuing you all the time."

I opened my mouth to defend my sorry ass but closed it again. There was no point. I was so far out of my depth it was laughable. "You're suggesting we work together?"

He nodded. "Under the proviso that you are not in this to steal my trident and realm." A hard glint shone in his eyes, the crashing waves simmering dangerously.

I snorted. "Fuck no. I just want to wake my sister up."

"Then we tackle the next Trial together. Hopefully I will lose less ground, not having to keep an eye on you."

I folded my arms over my chest, unable to take being patronized any more. "Maybe I'll be the one saving you next time."

*As if.* But I had done it once—I'd milk that for everything it was worth.

One of his brows rose, and he folded his own arms, making his pecs tense. "Stay out of trouble, don't slow me down, and we might stand a chance of you surviving, and me winning," he growled.

# POSEIDON

*I* watched Almi leave, my jaw working as she cast a small glance back over her shoulder at me.

"Fuck," I swore, once she had closed the door behind her.

She was getting too close to the truth. Too close to the real reason I'd had to leave her alone in the human realm for all that time.

But I couldn't beat the blight without her.

I needed her close to me.

# ALMI

*I*t was both a relief, and a burden, to be alone in my room at last. I climbed up onto the bed to open the window as soon as I'd set Kryvo on his little cushion.

Slumping onto the pillows, I let out a long breath.

I'd survived.

And now, I had to talk to Lily.

I couldn't escape the fact that something had changed. It wasn't just me and her anymore. Poseidon was linked to me, and I him.

"Lily?" I closed my eyes and sank as far as I could into the pillows behind me.

*Almi.* Kindness laced the single word as her image appeared in my mind.

"I'm sorry. I risked your life today."

*You've been risking your life for me forever. Today you did something for you. I'm pleased.*

"Really? In what way was that doing something for me?"

She laughed, the sound tinkling. It made me feel warmer, safer. *You know, you are odd. You faced some of the most terrifying things in this realm today, and you were incredible. You were brave, resourceful, smart... You survived a Trial meant for gods.*

"I guess."

*And here you are, only thinking about one thing.*

"Poseidon," I said on a sigh.

*He is your husband,* she said, a playful smile on her lips.

"This doesn't worry you? This weird freaking need we both have to look out for each other?"

Her image in my mind frowned. *You think I'm worried that one of the three most powerful Olympians in the world feels compelled to keep saving my little sister's life?*

"Huh. Well, when you put it that way, it doesn't sound so bad. Except I did it, too. Plus, he's not that powerful right now. He's sick. Like you."

Her expression softened. *You need to ask him about Atlantis. Together, I think you can both do a lot more.*

I nodded. I knew she was right. "Do you think his dragon would see you?"

*No. Dragons are crazy rare, and crazy dangerous. Hades made it clear you had to be Olympian royalty to see her. And besides, she has no cure.*

I nodded again, already knowing that was true. Opening my eyes, I pulled out the little sketchbook. "I'm going to draw the last few days," I told her. "Just in case."

*Just in case what?*

"I need to see it again."

*Good idea,* she said, the playful smile back. *Make sure you include that kiss.*

"Lily!"

She shrugged. *It might be important.*

It *was* important. I already knew that. My whole freaking body knew that.

We were both quiet as I made bad pencil sketches in the little book of everything that had happened since I'd arrived back in Aquarius.

When I was done, I stretched, tiredness from the day coursing over me.

"I wonder what the next Trial will be?" I mused aloud as I undressed for bed.

Kryvo's squeaky voice answered. "Hopefully something you can do alongside Poseidon."

"Do you like him?" I asked the starfish, sitting down at the dresser and loosening my tight braid.

"He scares me. But I think he can offer a good alternative to hiding."

I smiled at him. "Good summary. I feel similarly."

I looked at the mirror to check how much of my braid was undone, and my breath caught as my eyes snagged on color.

Not the purple streaks in my hair, but color *on my skin*.

My tattoo was clear on my chest above my bandeau vest, and the very center of the spiral of the shell was blue, the color leaking into turquoise before fading away like a watercolor painting.

"Lily! Lily, my shell!"

*The center has color.* My sister's voice was tight with what I hoped was excitement.

255

"Yes! Does this mean I have magic?"

*I don't know. I think the whole shell needs color for your power to be present.*

"Is something waking it up? Being in Aquarius?"

*That is the most likely reason. Or perhaps the magic of the palace is so strong it's waking it up? I don't know.*

I scrambled up from the dresser stool and rushed to the window. Looking out at the ocean, I willed myself to feel the pull of the water, that sense of freedom and excitement I had felt on the deck of the ship with Poseidon.

Nothing happened. I just saw masses of blue, raw with power and weight.

"Maybe you're right; the whole thing needs to be filled with color," I conceded.

*I'm always right,* she answered. I stuck my tongue out as I moved back from the window, excitement still whirring through me.

"Do you think I can speed it up?"

*Not without knowing what's caused it,* Lily said.

"Good point. Kryvo, can you sense magic?"

"No," answered the starfish. "Poseidon said he can, though."

"He didn't say anything about me having new magic when I saw him earlier." My shoulders slumped a little. "Well, hopefully it keeps filling with color, and then..." And then what? I would be able to do what Lily could? Hold my breath for hours, make water move, swim like I was born of the ocean?

Gods, I hoped so.

I thought my excitement about my tattoo might keep me awake, but my concerns were unfounded. The physicality of the Trial won out over my churning brain, and I slept like the dead.

When I finally roused myself from the peace of sleep, all the thoughts from the previous day crashed back over me. I leaped from the bed to stand in front of the mirror, staring at the tiny splurge of color in the middle of my shell.

"It may be little," I murmured, running my fingers over it, "but it is bright."

And it was. The shade of blue was deep and vivid, and the turquoise ombre a beautiful bright color.

"You slept a long time," squeaked Kryvo. "I was beginning to worry."

"Really?"

"Yes. It is long past midday."

"Huh." I wasn't surprised. I had massively exerted myself the previous day, both physically and mentally.

I made my way into my bathroom, noting that I felt surprisingly good. I expected to have aches and pains from the exertion of being thrown around on the ship, but as I stretched my limbs in the shower, I only felt stronger.

I washed my vest in the large sink, and once it was dry, I dressed in more of the identical clothes from the closet: dark pants and a white shirt over the vest. I couldn't stop staring at the tattoo as I braided my hair.

"Please, please, please let this mean I am a real Nereid."

If my power came to life and my shell colored, maybe that would mean Poseidon would get his heart of the ocean? And then we could heal Lily.

Once I was ready, I realized just how hungry I was. All my mornings in the palace had begun with somebody collecting me from my room, to deliver me to whatever stressful activity was happening next. But today, I had no idea what was coming next.

Putting Kryvo on my collarbone, I cautiously pushed open my bedroom door.

"Holy shit!"

Poseidon was standing in the hall, right outside my room. I clutched the doorframe, my hand on my chest, trying to slow my startled heart rate.

"Are you trying to scare me to death?"

"I was about to knock," he said drily.

I looked at him. He was wearing his fighting garb, and he looked healthy again. No stone was visible on his face. "What do you want?"

He pointed to the wall behind him. The gold paintings of waves were gone, words in their place.

*Gather in the ballroom when the sun sets for the second Trial.*

I frowned. "Is that from Atlas?"

"Yes."

"How can he make stuff like that happen inside your palace?"

Poseidon scowled. "I don't know. I believe he might have been infiltrating my palace for some time."

"He spoke to me here. In the courtyard," I said.

Fury flashed on Poseidon's face, the smell of the ocean

and the sound of waves crashing over me in a rush. "When?"

"Before the first Trial."

"What did he say?"

"Not a lot. Just wanted to psych me out, I think." I shrugged. "Don't worry about it."

A rumbling sounded in his chest. "Don't worry about it?" he repeated. "My oldest enemy, an ancient, all-powerful Titan is able to roam around my personal palace and intimidate my—" he paused, eyes flicking over me, "*Guests*, and you're telling me not to worry about it?"

"Once you beat him in the Trials, he'll be gone," I said.

Poseidon snarled. "I do not trust the bastard to return my trident, even if I do win."

"Really? Then why compete?"

"For my people." He stood straighter, his jaw clenched. Sweet baby Jesus, he was a fine example of a man.

"Right," I said, trying not to show my thoughts on my face.

"And if I win fairly, my Olympian brethren can back me."

"Of course. Olympian brethren. Known for their fair-ness." If there was anything most of the Olympian gods were, it was *not* fair. Bored, petty, over-indulged children would be closer to the truth. Poseidon's eyes darkened, but before he could respond to my sarcasm, I stepped out of my room, closing the door behind me. "Where can I get breakfast?"

# ALMI

"You can eat shortly. First, I want to show you something."

He held his hand out, and I took it without question. Last time I had taken his hand he had taken me to the pegasus stables and Blue. If whatever he was showing me this time was even half as good, I wanted in.

To my surprise, he flashed us to the deck of a ship.

I looked around at the shiny planks, gleaming sails, and impressive gold-embellished wheel. "This is a Typhoon," I said, turning in a slow circle.

"I'm impressed," said Poseidon. "You have been studying."

"I have a good memory," I murmured, staring around me as my heart skipped in my chest. "Is this your ship?" *The freaking ship I'd come here for in the first place?*

Poseidon eyed me a moment, then shrugged. "It is one of many ships. But for our purposes, it is an escape plan."

"An escape plan?"

"Atlas is unpredictable, and he hates me. Should anything happen, I want you to come to this ship. It will be here over the palace, at all times, and if you are riding Blue, you will be able to access it."

I stared at him, mouth opening and closing like a goldfish as I tried to pick a question.

"What could happen?" was the question that emerged from my lips first.

"I die."

"You're an immortal god! How the hell would you die?"

"Titans ruled Olympus long before us. And the Olympians only won the war because a few Titans defected and joined us against their own kind."

Fear squished about in my stomach, making me feel a little ill. "He doesn't look as dangerous as you," I said.

Poseidon's chest expanded a little, almost proudly, then his face turned even more serious. "Do not underestimate him. If anything happens to me, you come to this ship on Blue."

"Then what?"

"Then the ship will take you somewhere safe."

"Can you control it if you're..." I didn't want to say dead. My mind was revolting at the idea of Poseidon dying more than it was celebrating the fact that I may have found the ship that could help Lily.

"She'll know what to do." He touched the wood of the railings almost intimately, and I knew then that it was his own ship, not just part of a fleet or something.

"What is she called?"

He looked into my eyes a long moment, and I tried not to squirm. "*Okeános ánemos.*"

My pulse quickened. It *was* his ship. The only ship that could move underwater as well as through the sky. "She's lovely," I said.

He held my eyes a moment longer, the wildness burning behind that constant stoic control. "There is some color in your shell," he said.

I forgot about the ship completely and looked down at my chest. "Yes! Can you feel if I have any water magic?"

He shook his head. "I can sense no power from you." He held his hands up, clapped, and parted them to reveal two of the vials he had given me before. I took them from him, and as my fingers brushed his palm, that intoxicating sense of freedom powered over me. *My hair whipping around me as I moved fast, no constraints, no rules, no end to the possibilities...*

It wasn't an image so much as a feeling, and it was nothing like anything I had ever felt before coming to the palace.

My whole adult life had been about one singular, all-consuming focus: Lily. The possibility of not having to worry for her life all the time, to be able to just live free...

I wanted it. I wanted it bad.

I realized that Poseidon had tensed, and I was still resting my hand in his, fingers clutching the vials in his palm.

"Oh, sorry," I stuttered, whipping my hand back.

Did he feel something, too?

I risked looking up into his eyes. The froth-tipped waves were crashing in his piercing irises, his jaw clenched tightly. His other hand shot out as mine retracted, and he gripped my shoulder, dropped his head and pulled me toward him. Heat coursed through my body, making my cheeks flush, and a need that was utterly unfamiliar to me pound through my torso, pooling between my legs.

The smell of the ocean surrounded me as I lifted my other hand, unable to stop myself touching his hard, beautiful face. His skin was smooth and hot as I brushed my knuckles down his jaw, and I felt his whole body harden.

"Poseidon," I whispered, as he ducked his head further, his warm breath feathering over my lips as his mouth almost touched mine.

He stopped still.

For a split second, all I could hear was the sound of my own heart trying to pound its way out of my ribcage, then everything flashed white.

I found myself back in front of my bedroom door, and Poseidon stepped back into the corridor, releasing his grip on me. "The ballroom, in a few hours," he barked, and I barely got a glimpse of the wildness in his eyes before he flashed away.

"I don't want to be on you when you and him do that." Kryvo's tiny voice cut through my stunned silence.

"Do what?" I whispered. "What even was that?"

The first kiss I could have put down to adrenaline, or overexcitement. But that? That had come out of nowhere.

No. Not nowhere. If he had felt even a fraction of that blissful feeling I had when our skin had touched, then he could easily have translated that into desire for me.

Is that what I had done? Misread my desperation for a life free of worry as a desperation for him? Maybe I was mixing them up.

Maybe *he* was mixing them up.

I took a deep breath. "Marriage bonds are stupid," I said.

"You seem to quite enjoy it."

I frowned, unable to respond. Did I enjoy it?

*Hell yes.*

Did I need or understand it?

*Fuck no.*

I had been on the ship. More than that, Poseidon had told me how to get to it. He had as good as given me a damn key. Blue could take me straight there.

I could go to the stables, get on the pegasus' back, and steal the ship I had come to get that very second.

Except… I couldn't.

Atlas had held me up in front of the whole world of Olympus, and I was as bound to these asshole Trials as much as I was to the king of confusing-emotional-shit, Poseidon.

My ridiculous *husband* had given up his damn trident and realm to save me. I couldn't run. Could I?

"Ohhhh, what a fucking mess." I sagged against the door behind me.

"What's wrong?" Kryvo squeaked.

I hadn't told him about my plan to get the ship and find Atlantis and the legendary healing font. Mostly because I had been suspicious that he was a spy. But that suspicion had leaked away a while back, I realized.

"Let's get some food, and I'll tell you all about it," I said.

# ALMI

*I* followed the starfish's directions to a hall that made every other canteen I'd ever seen look, well frankly, shit.

It was a cathedral-like space, with a huge arched ceiling painted with golden waves, and long tables with bench seats lining the hall like pews. All of the tables were covered in food and I walked along them with a plate, loading up with pastries, bread and cold meat cuts.

There were other diners in the room, but not many. I supposed I was too late for the lunch rush. Lots of folk were wearing the blue leather of Poseidon's guard, and I found myself wondering where Galatea was.

"I thought you would die yesterday."

A crisp, clear female voice spoke behind me, and I whirled, nearly dropping my overloaded plate.

Kalypso raised one perfect brow at my food. "That lot might kill you instead," she smiled. Her liquid hair moved around her face, and I tried to shake off my awe. She was regal in her beauty, her rich dark skin glowing with power.

"Did you win?" I asked her. I hadn't thought to ask who came first in the Trial.

She pursed her lips, and her eyes moved from me to somewhere behind me. I glanced over my shoulder but could see nothing.

"No. Ceto won."

"Oh."

Ceto terrified me. Of all the contestants, she was the one I could least imagine ruling a realm. She was a literal monster.

"Oh, indeed. So, how does your husband fare?"

I frowned at her, both at hearing Poseidon described as my husband, but also at her questions. "Good. Why are you talking to me?"

"You are one of us," she said, her eyes a bright icy blue. "One of the five competitors for a place as a ruling god."

Desire burned in her tone, and a true sense of danger started to trickle through me. She wanted the trident and Aquarius. *Bad.*

"Atlas is forcing me to do this. I don't want to rule anything." I decided to seize my opportunity to ask something I'd been wondering about. "Do you have to share Aquarius with him if you win?"

Her features hardened, and my sense of danger heightened. "I share what I want, with who I want," she hissed.

I held my empty hand up in submission. "Okay, I get it. I'm a fan of consent too."

Her eyes narrowed suspiciously, but she relaxed a

little, the power rolling from her lessening a touch. "What are your powers?"

"I'd love to chat, but I have to take this,"—I held up my stacked plate—"to meet a friend."

She stared at me a moment, then shrugged. "Fine. See you at sundown."

"Yeah, see you."

I made my way out of the dining hall as quickly as I could. I hadn't intended to take my food back to my room, and I certainly wasn't going to tell her that the friend I was meeting was a tiny magic starfish, but I didn't want to spend any more time with Kalypso than I had to. Being in her company felt like being with a ticking timebomb, a weird pressure pushing at my mind the whole time her eyes were on me.

Maybe that was a god thing. I shook my head as I hurried along the corridors.

"You missed a turn," squeaked Kryvo.

"Good thing I've got you with me," I muttered to him, backing up.

Eventually I found my room and I wolfed down everything I'd put on my plate, using my dresser as a table. As I ate, I told Kryvo what I had read in the book and about the Font of Zoi.

"So, I'm thinking that if I can get to the font, then I can cure Lily of both the sleeping sickness and the stone blight," I finished, stuffing the last of a small meat pie into my mouth.

"There are a few problems with your plan," said Kryvo, his little suckers squelching on the dresser surface.

"Just a few?" I muttered.

"Firstly, and most importantly, if Poseidon knows about this font, he would have visited it and used it himself already."

I nodded slowly. "Yes. I know, I... I have to ask him about it, I guess."

"You do not want to?"

"I don't want him to say it won't work," I said, realizing the truth of the words as I said them. "Atlantis is my only hope. If Poseidon tells me it won't work, then I have nothing."

"That's not true. Poseidon said that the Oracle told him the stone blight can be cured by the heart of the ocean, correct?"

"Yes."

"If your power awakens then you might make the prophecy possible."

"Maybe." I looked at the starfish. "I don't think pinning my hopes on my absent magic is a very solid plan though."

"I don't like to upset you, Almi, but if the Oracle said that the heart of the ocean is the only way to cure the blight then..."

"Then my font won't work," I said on a sigh.

"It looks that way. I think you should reset your focus on finding out more about this heart."

I stared at him, not really seeing anything. My glum acknowledgment of his words was working its way through me, and I was trying to keep my anger at bay. It wasn't fair that this had happened to Lily. She was a good person and had been her whole life. Selfless and kind. Why should she, and all the other families in Aquarius, be affected by this blight? *Poseidon included.*

I didn't have the emotional capacity to work out why I felt a surge of panic when I thought about him turning to stone again and was relieved when Kryvo spoke. "Do you want me to see if there is anything in the palace about the heart of the ocean?"

"Could you? That's a great idea."

The starfish wiggled his arms. "Of course. I am your friend."

I smiled at him. "Yes. You are. Thank you."

He was right. I should move my focus to finding out about the heart. If Poseidon and the Oracle were right, then Lily and I were connected to it somehow. And I couldn't steal the damn ship and get to Atlantis anyway, not while I was bound to the Trials. I needed to set aside the certainty I felt that there were answers there and concentrate on the heart of the ocean.

A knock on my door a short while later turned out to be the two nymphs who had dressed me for the start of the Trials.

"Hello. Please come with us to the dressing rooms to be prepared," the small one said.

I followed them dutifully, taking Kryvo with me. He didn't camouflage himself, and both nymphs kept giving him small, disapproving glances.

"You've decided not to hide anymore?" I asked him.

"Poseidon knows I am here, and they all saw you talking to me in the Trials. If you insist on me accompanying you, then I may as well save my energy."

I was sure I heard a hint of pride in his voice. Maybe my cowardly little starfish was getting a teensy bit braver.

"Good. Be proud, Kryvo," I told him.

We reached the dressing rooms and I looked at the nymph next to me. "This is my friend, and I'm going to need an outfit that he looks good with." I was joking, but I felt Kryvo warm a little. The nymph raised their eyebrows, then raised a hand to their chin thoughtfully.

"We can make that work."

# ALMI

Somewhat to my surprise, the nymphs dressed me perfectly to match Kryvo. They put me in a corset dress, the top half the same shape as my vest, leaving everything above my breasts and my shoulders completely bare. At first, I felt uncomfortable with so much skin on show, but when I swished around in front of the mirror, the full bottom of the dress weighing nothing and moving like liquid, I decided I liked it. The dress was jet-black, a color I hadn't expected to suit me. But with my bright red starfish accessory, it looked good. And there was another splash of color showing in the mirror.

"Can you see the tattoo on my chest?" I asked the nymph.

"Yes. It was not there last time."

"Huh."

Poseidon must have lifted the glamor hiding it. The vivid blue and turquoise center caught my eye, the black gown only enhancing it.

The nymphs put my hair up in an elaborate knot, much of it curled and falling in tendrils that looked effortless, but that they had actually carefully arranged. More streaks of blue had joined the purple, I noticed.

My makeup was done the same as it had been last time, subtly, but making me look older in a way that I liked.

"You guys are really good at this," I said when they were finished.

They both nodded. "Yes."

I smiled. "Thanks."

With more nods, they bowed their heads and left the room, just as Galatea appeared in the doorway.

"Hi," I said.

"Good evening."

"You coming to the ballroom too?"

"Yes. Why is there a starfish on you? Is that jewelry?"

"He's my emotional support starfish."

Galatea just shook her head and held the door open for me. I heard her muttering the word odd as I walked past her.

"Any ideas what the next Trial will be about?" I asked her.

"No. But Poseidon told me he has shown you the *Okeános ánemos*."

"Yes."

"Good. I will meet you aboard if anything happens."

"Would you not have to take Poseidon's place if anything happens to him?"

Her pace slowed as she threw a surprised look at me. "No. Aquarius must be ruled by a god."

"What are you?"

She paused before answering me, her pace quickening along the corridors again. "A nymph".

"You must be a very powerful nymph, to be Poseidon's General."

"Yes," was all she said.

Sensing her reluctance to talk about it anymore, I changed the subject. "Kalypso spoke to me earlier. She wants to win."

Galatea pulled a face. "I've no doubt. She is the strongest in the competition. Apart from the king, of course."

If Poseidon was at full strength that might have been true, but I refrained from correcting her. "Ceto scares me," I said instead.

"Ceto has been under Poseidon's control for all of time. This will be a hard rift to heal, once the Trials are over."

"Was she under his control voluntarily?"

"It was a mutual arrangement. Poseidon let her and her brother create all manner of hellish creatures, in return for allegiance. For the most part, they had free run of the deep. He was not abusing his position," she said, with a severe look.

"I wasn't suggesting that he was. Just trying to understand how she might see it."

"She has betrayed his allegiance. There is no more to it than that."

Galatea's unending loyalty to her king was admirable, but I wasn't surprised it wasn't echoed by Ceto. In fact, there were likely a number of Poseidon's subjects who resented being controlled by a god their whole lives, especially if like Ceto, they had so much power of their own. "I heard she won the last Trial," I said.

"Yes. She has the most shells now. But that will change," Galatea replied fiercely.

We reached the large, familiar double doors to the ballroom, and she pushed them open.

The room looked the same as the last time I'd been there, except there was now a large chair in the middle of the room. It was made from hundreds of interlocking rings that made up globes, and there was no question it was representative of Atlas' sigil.

Atlas himself was lounging in the throne, the light from the beautiful coral reef surrounding the ballroom playing across his face as his eyes found mine. A cruel smile twisted the corners of his mouth.

Galatea growled low in her throat. "That bastard sits on a throne in the true King's own palace?"

I looked around for Poseidon, and found him instantly. He was standing with Hades, the two of them talking quietly. He was wearing the ocean robe, waves washing over the fabric and drawing everyone who passed him's gaze.

I scanned the rest of the room quickly, noting that the audience was mostly the same as last time, the same Olympian gods—and the same three missing.

I started to move toward Poseidon, but before I took one step, Atlas rose.

"You're here, *Queen* Almi!"

I stalled in both movement and thought.

*Queen.*

Well, that was new.

I glanced at Poseidon, but his angry eyes were fixed on Atlas.

"We have been awaiting your arrival so that we may begin the festivities. And may I say how lovely you look?"

I gave him a sarcastic smile, then flipped him the finger.

My knees buckled beneath me, and I cried out in shock as my body folded itself over into a groveling bow.

"Atlas!" roared Poseidon's voice, and the compulsion controlling my body vanished.

"She must learn to respect those more powerful than her, Poseidon," Atlas said, voice silky sweet. "Which, I believe, is everybody."

Fury coursed through my veins as I got to my feet. "Prick," I hissed through my teeth. I knew he heard me, because his eyes narrowed, and a fizz of pain jolted through my body. It was gone before I could suck in a breath, though, and he turned back to the rest of the room.

"Citizens of Olympus, honored Olympians," he called, spreading his arms wide. "Welcome. As it stands, Ceto has four shells, Kalypso three, Polybotes two, Almi one, and Poseidon,"—he turned to the sea god. "None."

Thunder cracked in the distance, and the coral reef's bright pastel glow flickered dark for a split second.

I had more shells than Poseidon? Shit. That must be because it was my ship that had flown over the finish-line. His had never made it.

"The next three Trials will be a feast for your senses, good people!"

He clapped his hands and a massive flame dish appeared in place of his throne. Flames leaped high in it, flashed a white-hot color, then an image appeared in them.

"Apollo has graciously agreed to host the first of three elemental themed Trials. As his realm has the most extreme temperatures, it seemed fitting to hold the ice Trial there."

The image of a cliff made from solid ice moved as though a drone was panning, and I felt my muscles tense as I saw something huge and dark moving inside the ice. The image swooped to show a sheet of ice that seemed to go on forever at the foot of the cliff, with more dark shapes moving beneath it in the sea below.

Atlas' eyes glinted with cruel excitement as he spoke. "You must collect as many shells as you can in one hour. But be warned, the only way to leave the Trial is to find the red shell. Without it, you cannot return."

Fear gripped my gut, and I felt hot at just the thought of being trapped.

"The second of the elements will be earth, hosted in Aphrodite's deadly tropical seagardens."

The image changed to a panning view of a series of tropical islands. As the view swooped closer to the water, I could see green beneath the surface, then red liquid began to seep like blood through the water, obliterating the green below.

"The last will be fire, held where the volcanoes of Hephaestus' Scorpio meet the depths of Aquarius."

Once more, the image changed, this time to a scene below the surface of the water. Everything was dark and gloomy, except for a searing river of molten lava carving its way through jagged black rock.

"Do we take it in turns or all do it together?" Polybotes' deep voice rumbled from where he stood on the other side of the room, towering over everyone else.

"No. You will decide what order you take on the Trials, now."

My heart was beating too quickly as I looked at Poseidon. His eyes met mine, and I knew we were thinking the same thing. If we were going to work together, we had to choose the same order as each other.

# ALMI

*J* began to move toward Poseidon, but after one step, my feet froze. I tried to pick them up off the ground, but they wouldn't obey me. More anger surged through me as I looked at Atlas.

"You will be choosing in private," he smiled.

"Choose the—" Poseidon's voice in my head was abruptly cut off.

"There will be no mental communication, either." Atlas looked at Poseidon, and I thought for a minute the sea god would throw himself at the smug Titan.

Hades laid a hand on Poseidon's shoulder, and he flinched.

Atlas gave a small chuckle. "Ceto, as the leader, you will choose first." He clapped his hands again and the flame dish vanished, replaced by a table with three small, identical urns on it.

"He shouldn't have this much power in the palace," hissed Galatea quietly. "I will find out how he is doing this if it kills me."

"Can you speak to Poseidon in your head?" I whispered to her.

She concentrated a moment, then shook her head. "No."

"Shit."

Ceto emerged from the crowd, and she slithered on her many creepy, rotten looking octopus legs up to the table. Silently, she leaned over the urns, then moved two of them so that they were in a different order. I watched carefully, but I could see no indication that there was anything on them that determined which was which, or even that they were different from each other.

"Kalypso?" Atlas said when Ceto moved back from the table.

The beautiful Titan was wearing scarlet red and looked as fierce as a lion as she stepped forward. As fierce as a loin-fish, I corrected myself mentally as she made her way to the table, her water-hair swishing. She reordered all of the urns before stepping back with a nod.

My stomach felt uncomfortably jumpy as I watched Polybotes stomp over next.

Poseidon's plan for us to stick together had clearly been anticipated by Atlas.

I looked at the Titan I had been repeatedly told not to underestimate. He looked like a man. A normal, if a little hotter than usual, middle-aged human. Tanned skin, symmetrical, good-looking face, and the build of someone who went to the gym a lot.

Sensing me looking, he fixed his dark eyes on mine. I swallowed, about to look away, when his whole appearance changed. It was only for a split second, but for that second, he was made of freaking fire. Everything other than his eyes were flame-red, sparks of deadly power running in rivers across his whole body. Those eyes, though… Black pits of nothingness, a promise of an eternity of soulless, lifeless *nothing*.

His human image flashed back into place, a cold smile on his handsome face, and gooseflesh erupted over my skin.

"Can he read my mind?" I asked Galatea out of the side of my mouth. It was too much of a coincidence that I had been thinking about his appearance for him to give me a flash of himself looking so terrifying.

"The palace forbids mind-reading as part of its magic, but Atlas has been thwarting its magic since he got here, so fuck knows."

It was the first time I'd heard her swear, and I turned a little to her. Her sternness had amplified tenfold, and I felt a bolt of sympathy for her. She loved Poseidon and Aquarius; that much was clear. And that meant everything she loved was under very serious threat. Hatred for Atlas oozed from her every pore.

"Can I stop it?"

She glanced at me. "Not with no magic. But I can try to shield your thoughts."

"You can do that?"

"I can try. Take my staff."

"Thank you," I said, as she passed me her staff as subtly as possible.

Polybotes had finished rearranging the urns, and Atlas looked at me.

"Almi's turn," he said, gesturing at the table.

I strode up, keeping the staff by my side and gripping it hard. I had a plan, but I had no idea if I could pull it off.

When I reached the urns, they all flared to life with a deep red glow, and writing in a messy scrawl burned in the ceramic: Fire, Ice, Earth. One label on each urn.

Shrugging, I put them in the order Atlas had introduced them, in the hope that Poseidon might instinctively do the same if my plan failed.

I moved the pot that read ice to the left, put the earth one in the middle, and the fire one last.

When I turned away from the table, just as I had hoped, Poseidon was waiting a few feet behind me.

"Kryvo," I said as quietly as I could, without moving my lips. "Tell Poseidon what order I put the urns in." As swiftly as I could, I moved my hand to my collar and lifted the starfish from my skin as I walked toward Poseidon, my back to Atlas.

Poseidon's eyebrows rose as I walked straight at him, holding his gaze and trying to send my best 'just-go-with-it' vibes.

"Good luck, husband," I said loudly, and pressed my lips to his in the most over-the-top manner I could, whilst also pressing Kryvo to the shoulder his toga left exposed. The starfish gave a tiny, startled squeak, and it felt like Poseidon had turned to stone again, he was so still. He flared to life suddenly, gripping my waist and pulling me into him, his lips moving beneath mine. Heat rushed me, my stomach swooping, and I heard Atlas bark.

"Enough of this nonsense. Poseidon, choose your urns."

Poseidon stepped back, and I dragged my eyes from

his to glance at his shoulder. Kryvo had camouflaged himself completely.

I walked slowly back to Galatea. "I think it worked," I whispered to her. Atlas had said nothing, and Poseidon was moving the urns with a sense of purpose.

"What did you do? Where is your ornamental starfish?"

"Hopefully saving my ass. Again."

Poseidon moved back from the table, and Atlas waved his hands. The table vanished and the throne reappeared as he began to read the order the first three competitors had chosen. I barely heard what he said until he said my name. My pulse quickened and I fixed my eyes on Poseidon. He stared straight back at me.

It was him who had suggested us working together, but now it seemed I had been keener on the idea than I had realized. More than anything in the world, I wanted the moody ocean god by my side when we faced the Trials we had just been given a glimpse of.

"Almi chose Ice, then Earth, then Fire."

I knew instantly that my plan had worked. I saw the flicker of light in Poseidon's eyes, and the coral reef around us pulsed with the faintest glimmer of energy.

Atlas' voice was hard when he spoke again. "Poseidon is taking on Ice, then Earth, then Fire, too."

Galatea gripped my arm. "That means you'll be in the Ice level with the giant, the Earth level with Kalypso, and the Fire level with Ceto. You need to be on your guard," she said, face tight with concern. She'd obviously been listening more carefully than I had.

"I will. And I'll be with Poseidon, thanks to you

shielding my thoughts and one tiny starfish." I grinned, holding her staff out.

She took it, a slightly puzzled frown on her face. "I'm glad I could help."

"I've had an idea!" Atlas' voice boomed across the room, loud enough that it made my pain lance through my skull. We turned to him, and I was alarmed to see that his placid, smug expression had been replaced with something bordering on manic.

"I think we should start now."

"What?" Kalypso's voice was crisp and clear in the stunned silence. "No, we need time to prepare."

"No, I don't think you do." Atlas' unhinged glare was trained on Poseidon. "Let's do this now. Off you go!"

The world flashed white, and the next thing I knew, I was underwater.

# ALMI

*M*y immediate instinct was to draw breath, and I barely stopped myself in time. Panic swamped me as I began to sink through the water, and I kicked my legs, trying to orientate myself.

I didn't have my belt. I had no water-root.

The overwhelming sense of being trapped pressed in on me, the weight of the water crushing me on every side. Something moved around me, freezing cold currents blasting my body, and then Poseidon's face was in front of me, his bright blue eyes beacons in the gloom. He gripped my face with his hands, then drew my lips to his.

*Air*, I realized dimly, as his mouth closed over mine.

He was giving me air.

He pulled away from me, eyes boring into mine. The burn in my lungs lessened and I tried to concentrate.

Where the fuck were those bubbles that had helped me last time?

The skirt of my dress tangled in my legs, and I stopped

kicking. Poseidon was holding me still in the water, and I needed to conserve my energy.

Bright red pulsed lower on Poseidon's body, and I realized it was Kryvo. Reaching out, I pulled him gently from Poseidon skin and placed him on my bare collarbone. The water was freezing, and he felt warm against my skin.

"Make those bubbles come back!" the little starfish squeaked as soon as his little stingers had latched on.

I shook my head, unable to answer him. I looked into Poseidon's eyes, wondering if he could speak to me.

His mouth moved, his words carrying to me through the water and sounding as though they were very far away. "We need to find a way of you breathing."

*No shit.*

I saw movement over his shoulder in the water, along with flashes of red. Fear made my skin feel icy cold as it got closer, and I realized what it was.

"Rotblood!" squeaked Kryvo. I gripped Poseidon's arm and pointed frantically over his shoulder.

He turned just in time, raising one of his fists. Water pulsed out from him, swirling in a glowing blue current as it powered toward the rotten, red shark. The current wrapped itself around the creature, and then the thing exploded.

Poseidon turned back to me, drawing me close and breathing air into my shaking body again. "We will not be able to keep this up for long," he said, the words slow and hard to decipher. A granite tendril worked its way across the side of his jaw.

Where were those damned bubbles? Who had sent

them last time? I hadn't even thought to ask Persephone or Galatea if they had helped, though I couldn't think of anyone else who would want to assist me.

*Whoever you are, please, please, please help me again now,* I prayed. If we didn't find the red shell, we would be trapped in here forever. Which in my case, wouldn't be very long, given that I was mortal and we were submerged in freezing, shark-infested water.

Something lifted my hair from my face. Something that wasn't Poseidon. A stream of tiny bubbles whizzed around me, faster and faster, until it settled around my face, just as it had done before.

Poseidon's eyebrows raised, and I took a tiny, experimental breath.

Air. Cool dry air.

"The bubbles are back!" I exclaimed aloud.

"You can breathe?"

"Yes."

"Tell me how later. Now, we need to find shells." Poseidon's gurgled voice was clipped and to the point, as though he was conserving words. "I can't afford to lose this Trial."

His face was as serious as I had ever seen it, the water lifting his white hair behind him, his tense body like a coiled spring. The importance of what he was saying settled over me.

When it had just been me, the aim of the game was just to survive. But now we were working together, the stakes had changed. We had to make sure Poseidon got his realm and his trident back. That meant actually doing well.

*Winning.*

I nodded, and he took my hand.

He moved through the water like a dart, pulling me along by his side. I didn't need to kick my legs or move my arms at all, so I just clung on tightly and kept my eyes open for anything that looked like a shell.

As we sped through the water, I assumed that we were under the sheet of ice that had been in the image in the flame dish, but all I could see was the dusky gloom of blue water, so filled with tiny particles that it was hard to see far. Below us was inky darkness, and no sound carried to my ears.

I hoped Poseidon had an idea where we were going, because I had none whatsoever.

"Look for shells," I told Kryvo, trying to distract myself from the cold by talking to the little starfish. The bubbles were still whizzing around my head, keeping a layer of air between my face and the water. My voice sounded completely normal to me, and Kryvo's little voice came back to me clearly.

"Not if they are anywhere near rotbloods," he shuddered.

"You did great, telling Poseidon what order to put the urns in," I told him, trying to cheer him up.

"I do not want to be stuck to him again," he said seriously.

"No?"

"No. He is… intense."

I inadvertently gripped the god's hand harder as we sped along through the water.

Intense was the word.

# ALMI

*A*fter a minute or two, when I was fairly sure I couldn't feel my feet—which were fortunately encased in sandals that laced halfway up my calf and therefore still on—I saw something. A solid wall of bright blue ice.

Almost the same color as Poseidon's eyes, the vertical expanse was like glass. My heart gave a little stutter when Poseidon pulled us closer.

There, encased in the ice wall but moving jerkily, as though trapped in mud, was the creature that had attacked him at the end of the last Trial. The beast that looked like it should have been in a nightmare version of Jurassic Park.

"What is that thing?"

It moved again inside the ice, easily twenty times my size, as we hovered the other side of the endless wall.

It was on its back, curved like a half-moon, arms and claws reaching up, scraping and twitching at its icy prison. One reptilian eye locked onto Poseidon and its massive mouth opened in obvious anger. A cracking noise sounded in the distance, and fear lurched through me.

"We should go. Now."

"It can't escape the ice," Poseidon's gurgled, slow reply came.

It moved again, its maw snapping closed, and one of its six brutally sharp arms jerking a few inches.

"All the same. Lots of shells, one hour to find them. We should leave him alone." My teeth were chattering as I spoke.

Poseidon glanced at me, then began to move, pulling me along with him.

I estimated it was another five minutes of swimming along the mammoth ice wall before a beam of light cut through the water like a laser before us.

Poseidon angled up toward it immediately, and relief rushed me as I saw a bright circle of light above us. As we swam higher, the water around us lightened, and I could see the layer of ice over our heads clearly. And the small, perfectly round hole in it.

Suspicion made me slow, pulling Poseidon's hand. "What if it's a trap? Surely shells should be under the water?"

He frowned at me. "Do you see any shells under here?"

He gestured at the empty expanse, the only thing catching my eye the moving silhouette of the monster trapped in the ice wall.

I shook my head. Slowly, he let go of my hand. My fingers were so numb with cold he had to uncurl them himself.

He swam to the hole, and anxiety gripped me as he

slowly moved his head up through it. His arms followed, and he heaved himself out of the water. I watched his legs disappear up and out, then looked for his shadow through the ice.

I could see nothing.

I kicked my legs and moved my arms in a wide arc, swimming closer to the hole, heart pounding.

Movement made me cry out in tense surprise, until I realized it was his arm plunging back into the water, his fingers extended.

Without hesitating, I reached out and grabbed his hand, letting him pull me out of the water.

The freezing air washed over my skin painfully as he yanked me up onto the ice. I stumbled, my numb feet not working properly, and wrapped my arms around my exposed chest. My sopping wet skirt clung to my legs as I looked around.

Well, it was marginally better than the emptiness under the ice, but not by much.

The ice wall we had been swimming along extended high above the water, forming the cliff that we had seen in the flame dish image. At its base, where the ice met the wall, was something that looked, from a distance, like it was made of metal. Something man- or god-made.

"D-d-d-d-o we n-n-n-eed t-t-to go over there?" I stuttered, pointing.

Poseidon scowled at me. "If we stayed in the water any longer you would have died from the cold."

"Th-th-that's hardly my fault," I protested. "I d-d-didn't ask to come out here in a fucking b-b-ballgown."

Baring his teeth, he undid the belt at his waist, sliding his ocean toga from his body.

I tried to keep my frozen face still, but I could feel my eyebrows raising.

When he'd completely removed the toga, I found myself staring at him in nothing but a small, relatively tight pair of black shorts, and one gold strap holding a dagger and some sort of flute across his shoulder that had been previously covered. A black leather thong was around his neck, a small blue gem on it hanging between his sculpted pecs.

I blinked at him. "You took your c-c-clothes off," I said thickly.

"I don't feel the cold." He held out his toga. "Take it," he barked, when I continued to stare at him.

I did, and his hand glowed around the fabric before he let go. "It will keep you warm. Put it on now, we have wasted enough time."

"I don't know how to wear a toga," I said, shaking out the huge piece of fabric. It looked like waves were rolling over it, shining with metallic threads as they crashed. It was beautiful.

"I don't give a shit how you wear it, just don't die of hypothermia!" He stamped his foot, jolting me into action.

"Right, got it, don't d-d-die," I said, wrapping the toga around myself like a blanket. Warmth enveloped me immediately, making me realize just how much my body was seizing up.

With one last glare, Poseidon turned and began striding across the ice toward the metal thing in the distance.

"Are you not worried about the ice breaking?" I called as I hurried after him.

He didn't reply, so I took that as a no.

I was, though, and took care to make sure that everywhere I put my feet looked solid before I stepped. It would be just my luck to fall through the ice straight into the waiting jaws of a frigging rotblood. And I knew there were more under there. Every now and then I saw a flash of something dark and red in the depths.

But then I caught a flash of something else in the ice, as I carefully avoided the area around another perfectly round hole.

Something shining like mother-of-pearl, catching the pale white light.

"Poseidon, wait!" I dropped to my knees, peering closely.

There, embedded in the ice, was a shell. Not a red shell that would get us out of here, but a shell nonetheless.

Poseidon appeared beside me, and I was momentarily distracted by the sheer amount of tanned flesh in my immediate vicinity, before he spoke.

"How do we get it out of the ice?"

"Your dagger?" I gestured at the little weapon on his strap. "Good thing one of us attended a ball armed."

"I am always armed," he said seriously.

I didn't doubt it.

He took the dagger in his right hand and pressed the tip to the ice. A loud cracking sounded, and I scooted backward on my knees.

"I'm going to wait just over here," I said.

"Good idea," he answered, without looking at me.

He began to dig the shell out of the ice, and thin cracks snaked out from where he worked. I kept moving toward the cliff and the metal structure as the cracks spread, but I was reluctant to get too far from him.

"The cracks are getting pretty big now," I called to him, at least ten feet away now.

I heard a small thudding noise, and Kyrvo squeaked in alarm as I looked down.

I was on ice thin enough to see through, straight down into the unblinking, onyx eyes of a rotblood. More rotten red shapes moved beneath the ice and as I looked out at Poseidon, I realized they were gathering under him too.

Making just one of the monsters explode had caused a reaction from the stone to show on his face. How many rotbloods would he be able to handle before he exerted too much power and turned into a statue again?

"Poseidon?" I started to shout, but he cut me off.

He didn't look up. He spoke one word, clearly and loudly. "Run."

# ALMI

*H*e stood up and cracking sounded so loudly I gasped. My legs moved instinctively, and before I knew it, I was sprinting full pelt toward the cliff, and what I desperately hoped was land.

Throwing a glance over my shoulder, I saw Poseidon running behind me, catching me up. Around him, the ice was breaking apart, the red-and-black, lava-like snouts of the demon sharks snapping at his feet as they tried to propel themselves up out of the water.

Why wasn't he flashing to safety? Surely gods didn't run!

"Faster!" he roared, and I turned back, urging more strength into my legs.

The ice under my feet heaved, and a small shriek escaped my lips as I dove to the side, leaping for another piece of ice as the one I had been racing across tilted into the water below. Red and black flashed in my peripheral vision, but I didn't stop to look.

Throwing myself at what I could now see was a metal platform, was the only thing in my mind. I caught the freezing cold railing of the platform and pulled myself onto it, the heavy material of my dress wrapping around my legs as I skidded, Poseidon's toga falling to the metal. Half a second later Poseidon's bare feet slammed onto the platform and he slowed to a stop, whirling back. The chunks of ice that had once been the perfect sheet covering the sea were sinking into the water, the rotbloods snapping at them.

"Christ on a cracker," I panted. "That was close."

Poseidon turned back to me, holding out the small white shell. "Do you have somewhere safe to store this?"

I glanced inadvertently down at his underwear, the only thing he was wearing, then nodded. He passed me the shell, and I tucked it into the tight bra I wore under the corset dress. He watched me, eyes flaring with light.

"Wear the toga," he growled, as I met his gaze. Nodding, I picked it up from where it had fallen, wrapping it around my shoulders. "We need to keep moving."

I turned away from the shark-infested water to inspect my surroundings. The ice cliff rose on our left, its surface like glass and the dark shape of the epic beast inside it no longer visible. The platform shuddered, and I peered over the edge to see the sharks biting at the metal posts it was standing on.

The other end of the platform, to my relief, was attached to land. Ice and snow-covered land, but land all the same.

I made my way across the metal, keen to get away from the sharks. "Don't they find it cold in there? They look like they're made of lava," I said. "Ice and lava don't seem to go together."

"They can survive in any environment. They are born of lava, but they are made of blood and rotten flesh."

I swallowed back my nausea.

"Hence the name," I mumbled. "What's the thing in the ice called?"

"A talontaur. And it's a she."

"Is it related to the one you killed before you turned to stone?"

Poseidon glanced at me, then shook his head. "It is the same one."

"How is that possible?"

"Demons and monsters of Olympus do not die. They regenerate. She will be trapped in there until she is at full power, and a god releases her."

"A god like you?"

"Or Ceto. But without my trident, I can't control her. Come."

Snow crunched under his feet as he began walking along the frozen ground.

"Your toes are going to fall off," I told him, walking after him and trying not to watch the way the muscles in his back moved as he strode along.

He ignored me.

"I am glad to be out of the water," Kryvo squeaked.

"You and me both," I told him. "But I don't know where we'll find shells out here."

We were on a shore of some description, but it was far

from the sandy beach on Sagittarius that had housed the treasure chest puzzle.

The smell in the air was of pine and frost, and the sound of the ocean was distinct in its absence, after being around it for so many days now.

I strained my ears, listening for anything at all, but only the odd cracking from the frozen sea behind us was audible, save for our footsteps.

We were hugging the ice wall, moving farther inland, toward a large copse of snow-covered trees. Nothing seemed to be on the ground, other than a few scrubby plants and boulders. I inspected everything we walked past carefully, just in case.

"Do you know where you're going?" I asked Poseidon, as he angled toward the trees.

"No."

"Then how do you know all the shells aren't under the water, and there's nothing up here?"

"Atlas wants me to lose. I am a water god. You are a sea nymph. He will make it hard for us by making the challenge one of dry land."

I frowned as I considered his words. "But Ceto and Kalypso are sea gods too."

"Neither are as powerful as me," he growled.

I opened my mouth to comment on the stone affliction, but remembered everything was being broadcast. Unsure whether to bring it up or not, I bit my lip.

"What-" I started, but Poseidon froze, holding up his hand.

"Listen," he whispered.

I did, catching the faint sound of a man shouting, then a screeching. "Polybotes?" I whispered.

"Maybe." He started up again, moving in the direction of the sound.

"How long do you think we have left?" I asked him.

"About half an hour," he replied quietly.

"Twenty-eight minutes," Kryvo squeaked. "I checked a palace clock when we started."

"Clever starfish," I told him, and he heated briefly on my skin.

We continued toward the copse of trees, and the light got darker as we moved away from the ice cliff. I guessed it was reflecting so much light that anything would feel dark in comparison.

The ground was still bare, just glistening frost-covered boulders and a smattering of snow. When we reached the first tree though, I paused.

They were conifers, the long thin branches covered in very dark green needles, which were, in turn, covered in snow. But something about them wasn't right.

Poseidon had moved farther into the copse, and I called his name softly.

"The trees," he answered. "There's something about them."

I turned to him as he took one branch at its base and shook. Powdery snow fell in a shower to the ground, and Poseidon shook the branch again. Slowly, the pine needles began to change color. In a few seconds, the whole branch, and then the whole tree, was yellow.

"What the…?"

"Try that one," Poseidon said, and I reached out and

did the same to the branch in front of me. The snow fell first, and then the tree turned blue.

I couldn't help the grin that sprang to my lips. "This is cool."

Light flared in Poseidon's eyes, then they narrowed. "Check all the trees. We need one shell-colored."

"White?"

"Or red."

Excitement buzzed through me as we began to move through the little copse of pines, shaking every branch we could reach. Eventually, all the snow fell from the one I was gripping and when the green pine-needles began to change color, it was to the exact same shade of white as the snow that had dropped to the ground.

"I have a white one!" I called.

"I have a red one," Poseidon's voice answered. He sounded alarmingly far away, but I didn't have time to worry about it, because the tree started to rumble.

The branches vibrated, and I took a step back, unsure what to do. "Any ideas, Kryvo?" I started to ask, when snow blasted up out of the ground in a circle around the trunk of the tree.

I took another stumbling step back, but I was too slow, and snow churned up around my feet, lifting my skirts and the toga away from me. I clung on, whirling, trying to move clear of the sudden snowstorm. Every time I tried to step out of the circle, I was blasted back. The only place I could see that was clear was underneath the low branches of the pine tree, so I ducked to my knees and began to crawl under.

The snow rose higher, whipping my wet hair around

my face and filling my nose and mouth as I crawled. I coughed, wiping uselessly at my face with one hand as I clung desperately to the toga with my other.

With a rush, a current of air flowed around me, warm and nothing like the stinging snow-filled air of the storm. Just like the bubbles, it swirled around my face, creating a barrier between me and the choking snow.

I took a gratefully deep breath, then forced my way under the tree. The needles scratched my bare shoulders as I tucked myself in, gripping the rough bark.

Concern for Poseidon rose in me, but I doubted snow would choke him. Snow was made of water, after all. I waited for what felt like an age, but was probably only a few minutes, until the snow died down and eventually stopped. Cautiously, I crawled out of the small space.

"Almi?" Poseidon's voice reached me, and then he was there, pulling me to my feet. The warm current of air had vanished, and I blinked up at him. His hair was wild and windswept.

"I hid from the snow under the tree," I said, and his eyes flickered to my hair. He reached out and pulled a white pine-needle from the strands.

"There are a few more," he said. His voice held a gentle quality that I had only heard him use when talking about his subjects before.

"I'll get them later. Did you get the red shell?"

He shook his head. "No. But the storm revealed a path. Did you get the white shell?"

I shook my head, turning back to the tree. As the only white one in what was now a sea of orange, blue, green, yellow and purple trees, it stood out.

"You know, you should make a forest like this in Aquarius, of multi-colored trees," I told him. "I would, if I was a god."

He looked at me a moment, shook his head, then looked back to the white tree. I scanned it too, looking for a shell, or a path.

"There." I followed Poseidon's pointing arm to the very tip of the tree. A shining mother-of-pearl nautilus shell perched up there like a frigging Christmas tree star.

Poseidon held out his hand, and it glowed a brief second before snow lifted from the ground in a flurry. It whipped quickly into a ribbon of water, melting fast, then flicked up to the top of the tree. When it whizzed back down again, it deposited the shell in Poseidon's waiting hand, then dripped lifeless back to the frozen ground.

I tried not to be impressed, but the simple act made me covet his powers more than watching him make rotten sharks explode.

It reminded me of the things Lily used to do with water, I realized with a pang of sadness.

For the first time since starting the Trial, her image flared to life in my mind.

*You're doing great,* she said.

I nodded, then held out my hand. Poseidon dropped the shell into it, then very deliberately turned away as I tucked it into my bra.

"Let's get this red shell," I said, to let him know I was done. He strode off through the vividly colored forest without turning back, and I rolled my eyes as I hurried after him.

# ALMI

"You know, you're not very polite," I said to his annoyingly pleasing bare shoulders.

"Nor are you."

I bristled at his response. "I'm very polite. Maybe not to you, but in general, I don't wander off when people are talking, and I look at them when they speak to me."

He glanced over his shoulder at me, a tiny sparkle of something that wasn't anger in his eyes.

I needed a frigging book to decipher his emotions. They were literally unrecognizable, he controlled them so well.

He pointed as we reached a tree with scarlet-colored pine-needles, and a very deliberate trail of the little red needles leading away from it, out of the copse.

"Looks suspicious," I said.

"We only have about fifteen minutes left. We need the red shell to leave this place, and I can't flash." Tension laced his words.

"How can Atlas remove your flashing and your talking-in-my-head thing?"

"When we agree to compete in Trials, we agree to the rules of the Trials," he ground out. "Now that he controls the Trials, he controls us."

I pulled a face, then looked up at the sky through the trees. "Atlas, if you're watching, you're a massive jerk," I yelled.

When I looked back down, Poseidon was shaking his head. "You are like a child," he said.

"Well, you're like an old man." *A really frigging hot old man.* "You should try acting like a child sometime. You might enjoy being a bit less serious."

"Whilst risking our lives in a deadly timed Trial, you're suggesting I goad the ancient Titan who put us here?" Anger was creeping into his words.

"Yes."

He stared at me a beat longer, then to my surprise tilted his head back and roared at the sky.

"Atlas, you are a weak-minded gràson."

"Feel better?" I asked him when he looked back down.

"Not really. We need to go."

He turned to follow the trail of red needles.

"What does gràson mean?"

"One who smells like a goat."

"Oh. Brutal. Have you ever considered using more… modern insults?"

"Often. I have been tempted to use many on you."

I poked my tongue out at his back, but I was sure that for the first time he was actually joking with me. This was an improvement in our relationship. If you could call the interactions between us over the last few days, or years, a relationship.

We followed the pine needles in silence, along a barren stretch of snowy ground toward the ice cliff.

The longer it took us to trek across the snow, the more I began to worry about the time. It had been easy to ignore it whilst we had been busy, running or shaking funny-colored trees around, but now I was becoming truly anxious. If we didn't find the red shell in time, surely the other Olympians would come and get Poseidon out of here?

"If we don't get the shell, can we find our own way home?"

"This is Apollo's realm, Capricorn, and if this area has been designated for the Trials, then it is entirely possible it is hidden from the view of the rest of Olympus."

Fear pulsed through me at his words. "Hidden from the other gods?"

"Probably, yes."

"But surely Apollo isn't going to give up a bit of his realm just to keep competitors stranded forever?"

Poseidon shrugged. "I would. Our realms are magic, and can accommodate much."

I shook my head, deciding not to comment on the moral questionability of keeping someone prisoner anywhere for eternity.

"Kryvo, how much time do we have?"

"Nine minutes and fifty seconds," he squeaked. Poseidon looked over his shoulder at me.

"The starfish knows the time?"

"Yes."

"How long?"

"Can't you hear him?"

"No. I could hear him when you stuck him to me." His expression darkened, and I understood why Kryvo didn't want to repeat the experience.

"Nine minutes," I said. The flash of concern in Poseidon's eyes was backed up by his quickening pace, and I felt my own feet moving faster.

When we reached the cliff a moment later, we saw that the ice had been carved into, a tall, thin section removed to create a path into the ice. The red needles led straight into it. I couldn't help pausing, despite the pressure of the time. The image of the two enormous, sky-high pieces of ice slipping back together and crushing us to death was impossible to avoid.

Poseidon stepped into the narrow passage though, and I swallowed, jutted out my chin, and followed. The ice reflected so much light that it was hard to see, and I found myself squinting. Not that there was anything to really look at. On our left was the chunk of ice that held the talontaur, and I could see it below us, below the sea-level, dark and slightly warped through the ice at this distance.

The ice on our right was empty, just a sheer lump of clear, cold glittering frozen water.

Or was it?

Something was moving in there. Something small and sparkling. Something red.

"Poseidon!" He turned to me, and I pointed.

"There's nothing there. We must not waste time." He started to turn back.

"I can see the shell! A small red shell, moving around in the ice."

He looked again. "There is nothing there. The trail of pine has not ended. We need to be faster." He turned and broke into a jog.

"But-" I started, but when I looked back at the shell, it was gone. "Shit," I swore, then jogged after the ocean god.

A roar rumbled through the passageway a few seconds later, and I tried not to let my fear still my motion. My first thought was that it was the ice, rumbling as the two colossal chunks moved back together. But I realized quickly that it wasn't. It was the noise of a man.

"Polybotes," hissed Poseidon, ahead of me. The passage was too narrow for two people to stand abreast. I was behind him so couldn't see a thing.

"Where?"

"Ahead."

"No shit," I snapped.

"There is a hole in the floor in a few feet. The shout came from down there."

Sure enough, in a couple of feet Poseidon slowed down, then stepped over a large hole in the ice. Movement caught my eye, and I turned to my right.

Polybotes was inside the ice. And whizzing around him like a damned snitch at a quidditch game was the red shell. He groped for it, but his body was in a space too small for him, and one arm was pinned at his side.

"It's a tunnel." Without another word, Poseidon dropped down into the hole in the ice. A second later, he appeared to my right, inside the ice. Even at his seven feet height, he was half the size of the giant. I watched as he ran toward Polybotes.

But then the red shell stopped flying around the giant's head and moved fast in the opposite direction. It zoomed along the tunnel, straight past Poseidon, and then me, into the left hunk of ice. I expected Poseidon to change direction, following it, but he just kept going toward the giant.

He hadn't seen it, I realized.

I looked down at the hole, knowing, but not willing to do what I needed to do.

"We could hide?" offered Kryvo.

"We're inside a massive transparent block of ice," I told him. "Literally the worst place to hide in the world."

"I'd argue, but you have four and a half minutes."

"Fuck." With a quick prayer, I dropped into the tunnel.

# ALMI

*I*t was no colder in the tunnel, but the surface beneath my sandals seemed slippier as I ran along the tube after the flying red shell. It was only seconds before I felt queasy. Claustrophobia crushed in on me as I realized that I didn't know how to get back if I got lost. I whirled, trying to see Poseidon, and spotted his dark form through the clear block behind me, engaged with the giant. Were they fighting? I was too far to see clearly.

"Poseidon!" I yelled. "The shell is this way!"

As if on cue, the shell zoomed past my face, tantalizingly close. I reached out for it, closing my fist around empty air just inches from it.

"Damn it!" I pelted after it as it zoomed off, so intent on following it that it was only when the light changed that I realized where I was headed.

The talontaur.

I was right above it, I realized as a dark shape filled the

ice below me. I slowed, looking down, and the blood in my veins felt as cold as the ice I was surrounded by.

Its head was turned up, and its eye was fixed on me. One of its crab-like legs was burrowing up through the ice, straight toward the tunnel I was standing in.

"Almi," I heard Poseidon's voice and whirled gratefully to see him running along the tunnel toward me.

"The shell is here somewhere," I panted.

"We need to get away from the talontaur. Now."

"We need to find the shell!" Poseidon reached me, and I could see stone snaking across the whole left side of his chest, creeping up his neck and along his jaw. Fear coursed through me. A cracking sounded, and we both looked down. The clawed leg had moved further through the ice.

"It's a trap," Poseidon growled.

"The whole frigging Trial is a trap, now help me get the red shell!"

It whizzed between us at my words, taunting us. I reached for it at the same time Poseidon did. He was quicker, but not quick enough. There was a bellow, and movement made me look behind Poseidon. Polybotes was lumbering down the tunnel toward us.

"Move!"

We ran, chasing after the red shell. It doubled back on itself, swooping down within grabbing distance repeatedly, but always quicker than we were.

"Try to catch it with your water," I yelled. Poseidon sent a ribbon of liquid over my head straight at the shell, but it was as though it had hit a waterproof barrier, the liquid dissipating as soon as it hit the shell. It splashed down onto the ground in front of me, and I was too slow to avoid the puddle. My foot slipped and my heart lurched as I lost my footing. I hit the ice hard, accidentally letting go of Poseidon's toga and my momentum causing me to slide on my skirts along the tunnel.

There was another crack as I scrabbled at the ice, trying to slow my movement. One long dark claw burst through the ice ahead of me.

The talontaur had broken through.

"Shit!" I squealed, spinning on my ass but still moving toward the claw.

A roar reverberated through the ice, this one definitely belonging to the monster, and cracks began to appear under my hands. I tried to jam my fingers into them, and the red shell zoomed past my face. Indecision crippled me a moment as I debated lunging for it, and then the world fell away from under me.

I was so shocked I couldn't even scream. The ice I had been sliding on had gone, breaking apart around me. I tumbled through the air, my body twisting so that I could see exactly where I was headed.

Sheer terror surged through me as I looked down into the open jaws of the monster. Poseidon couldn't defeat this thing again without turning to stone.

Something hit my middle, then my fall halted.

A stream of water was winding its way around my middle, lifting me up. The red shell whizzed past my face again, and the creature reared its head back, ready for an attempt to snap at my face.

"Sixty seconds," shrieked Kryvo, his voice barely audible over the sound of my pounding heart.

"Fuck!" I reached out for the shell, fury and desperation filling my whole body, adrenaline coursing through me.

The water holding me lost its tension and I looked up to see Polybotes throwing an almighty punch at Poseidon.

"Bastard shell! Come here! Please, please, please come here!"

I swiped at it as I started to fall again, and to my utter astonishment, something came out of my flailing hand.

I felt a pulse of energy, and a stream of shimmering air flowed from my palm, wrapping itself around the shell. The tiny red object immediately went limp, then came shooting back toward my hand.

"Poseidon!" I screamed as it landed in my palm. "I have the shell. Jump!"

The water tightened around me again, and without hesitation, the sea god jumped from the tunnel. He dropped through the air toward me, pulling on the water rope so that I zoomed up to meet him.

But Polybotes jumped too. Poseidon reached me in mid-air, grabbing my hand and jerking me toward him, just as Polybotes reached us. His weight was too much as he wrapped himself around Poseidon's legs, and together we fell fast.

"Get us out of here!" I shrieked at the shell, as we plummeted toward the open jaws of the talontaur.

# ALMI

*I* slammed into something solid, then felt the
weight of Poseidon on top of me. All the air
left my lungs, and I gasped for breath, but none would
come.

*You're just winded. Don't panic,* said Persephone's voice
in my head.

Hands pulled at my shoulders and then I could see as I
was dragged upright. We were in Poseidon's courtyard,
scores of people on the other side of the gates waving
flags and cheering and screaming. Persephone was
standing with Galatea and her guards in front of the iron
bars and she gave me an encouraging smile along with a
cheesy thumbs up as I met her eyes.

Atlas' voice boomed through the air. "The hour is up,
for all our competitors. The shells will be counted at a ball
graciously hosted by Apollo tonight. Use this time to rest,
competitors, for you will get little other chance."

I sucked in air that felt too thick as I clutched my
chest, mind reeling. The ground shuddered, and I turned

dazedly to see Polybotes stumbling his way to his feet. The giant's eyes met mine, then flicked to my closed fist.

"I nearly got left in there to die," he said, his rumbling voice strained.

I could barely breathe, let alone respond to him.

"Well caught," he said, and my eyebrows shot up in surprise. "If you hadn't got the red shell, we'd all be talon-taur food." With a small nod, he stomped off toward the palace.

"Well caught, indeed." When I turned to Poseidon there was a light in his face I hadn't seen before, and I felt weak for a whole bunch of new reasons. "We need to talk. Now."

I nodded mutely, and took his outstretched hand.

I wasn't at all surprised to find us on the lower level of the pegasi stables when the light from Poseidon's flash cleared.

Warm ocean wind blew across my face, and I finally felt like I could breathe properly. I closed my eyes, taking as long a breath as I could manage, before opening them again and focusing on Poseidon as I let it out. The ocean beyond the tower was calm, the sound of gentle waves and birdcalls soothing my reeling brain.

"I used magic."

Poseidon's eyes were dancing with blue light as he replied. "Yes."

"How?"

He looked down at my chest, and I did the same. The

turquoise in the center of my shell had spread, turning green as the ombre worked its way outward. "Your powers are awakening."

All the adrenaline that had been seeping away surged back through me as I pressed my fingers to my tattoo. "I'll be able to control water now?"

Poseidon shook his head. His bare shoulders were tense, but I didn't think it was with anger or overly severe control this time. "No. Not water. Almi. That was *air* magic."

I stared at him. "What?"

"I felt the power you used, and it wasn't water."

"But… I'm a sea nymph. Like Lily. She had water magic."

"Well, you don't. Those bubbles giving you air to breathe? I think you were doing that. The magical signature was the same."

My mouth fell open. "I was making the bubbles?"

"Yes. I think so."

"No, no this can't be right." Confusion warred with excitement. Magic of any type was a frigging gift. But I was a sea nymph, a creature of the ocean, a citizen of Aquarius. I belonged to the water, surely?

"Almi… Do you realize that you're the reason we're both here? Polybotes was right to thank you. You saved us all." His gaze bore into me, and I realized what the new emotion I was seeing in his face was.

Respect.

"I'm, erm, just better at spotting red stuff than you are, I think," I said awkwardly.

"You are fearless."

I snorted a laugh before I could stop myself. "The fuck am I. I was scared shitless the entire time."

"Yet you faced everything. And drew on a power you didn't even know you had."

He stepped toward me, waves beginning to roll across his irises. "The Oracle is never mistaken."

"What's the Oracle got to do with it?"

The intensity in his expression dropped, and he blinked. "Nothing. We need to test your magic." His words were matter of fact again, the quiet wonder in his tone gone, and he stepped backward.

A huge part of me had hoped he would come all the way, close the gap, and remind me of that torrent of passion and power he had inside him.

"Test it how?"

"Come."

I followed him up the steps to the pegasi pens.

"Blue?" I called the moment we emerged on the higher platform. I heard clopping hooves, then Blue nosed open the stable door of his pen. "Aren't you a sight for sore eyes," I said as he trotted over to me. His golden wings ruffled as he nuzzled at me, and I stroked my hand over his long snout, running my fingers through his blue mane.

"My hair is supposed to be this color," I murmured.

I felt a bit like I was in a dream. The full impact of what I'd done during the ice Trial hadn't really kicked in, though I knew what Poseidon had just said was true. I'd caught the red shell. Without me, we wouldn't have gotten out.

But it was the way I'd caught the shell that was causing the surreal haze buzzing through my mind.

*Magic*. At long, long, last, I had used magic.

But it was the wrong kind of magic.

"Your affinity with him, and the ship, could be explained by air magic," Poseidon said, nodding his head at Blue.

I turned to the god, raising my eyebrows in question, reluctant to let go of the pegasus. Kryvo gave me more comfort than I could ever have imagined a small slimy starfish could, but the solid bulk and heat of Blue at that moment was what I needed.

Well, what I *really* wanted was the bulk and heat of the moody sea god currently trying to turn my damned world upside-down. But since that didn't appear to be on offer, the flying horse would suffice. "How can I have air magic?"

"I don't know. But it would explain why living under-water all this time didn't awaken it."

I scowled at him, nearly a decade of resentment surfacing involuntarily. "Living underwater all this time?" I repeated angrily. "I lived in the fucking human realm all this time, thanks to you. How much magic do you think was going to surface there?"

He scowled back at me. "The point is that if you have magic now, we can use it."

"We? Huh." I turned back to the pegasus, burying my face in his neck.

*Get a grip, Almi,* I told myself. *This is not the time to pick a fight.*

*You're right. It's not,* said Lily, her face forcing its way into my head. *You were unbelievable out there, Almi. And now you have magic. Get whatever help you can from him, before the next Trial starts.*

I breathed in the horsey scent of Blue, and he whinnied softly.

"How do I use it?" I said, as evenly as I could, turning back to Poseidon. His eyes were hard, but he answered me.

"Feel the wind."

"I always feel the wind." Even as I said the words, I realized how true they were. I had always put it down to my slight claustrophobia, always needing to feel fresh air. But what if it was more than that?

"Good. Use it."

I gave him a look. "Use it? Just like that?"

"You did it in the ice."

"We were about to die in the ice. Same as when the bubbles came — I was about to drown. What if I can only use magic when I'm literally about to die?"

Poseidon shrugged. "Then you have less chance of dying."

I let out a long breath. "Not helpful. True, but not helpful."

"I beg to differ. When could access to magic be more helpful than when one is about to die?"

I glared at him. "You said something about testing my magic?"

He held his hand out. With a faint glow, a feather appeared in his palm. It was a plain feather, large and white. I expected the ocean breeze to blow it from his hand, but it stayed exactly where it was.

"Lift the feather. With magic."

I stepped away from Blue. "How?"

"Concentrate," he said.

"You're a terrible teacher," I muttered.

Kryvo's squeaky voice came to me. "He's right, Almi. I think you did make the bubbles yourself. That's air magic. You should try to use it now."

"Do you have better instructions than 'concentrate'?" I asked him quietly. Not quietly enough that Poseidon couldn't hear me, and I saw his face change from confusion to disbelief as he realized I was talking to the starfish stuck to my collarbone.

"Yes. I've been checking the paintings for air magic references since Poseidon mentioned it. You need to imagine that the element you are connected to is surrounding you, then call up enough emotion that it responds. Once it is there, you should be able to make it do as you wish."

I took a deep breath. "Right. I can do this."

I closed my eyes, and tried as hard as I could to feel the breeze moving across my skin. I opened my arms out wide, trying not to feel stupid, and mostly failing.

"Concentrate," I muttered.

The trouble was, I was so used to water, thinking about it, seeing it, pining for a connection to it, that I hadn't spent enough time thinking about air to know what to do.

I called up an image of a tornado in my head, the most air-based thing I could think of.

Almost within seconds of holding the idea, the tornado had taken on a life of its own. I could feel air whipping first around my arms, then my legs, then my whole body, lifting the skirt of my gown, and blasting at my cheeks. When I opened my eyes, I expected the imaginary feeling to drop away, but to my astonishment, my hair *was* snapping around my face, and when I looked down, my skirt was flying around my thighs. Nothing else in the stables was moving though, the flurry of wind contained purely around me.

I let out a bark of delight, and I saw a flash of emotion on Poseidon's face. He held out his palm. "Lift the feather."

I looked at the white feather. *Could you please lift the feather?* I asked the wind that was swirling around me. A slither of air sparked to life, shimmering greeny-blue, then shot toward the feather. Before I could command it to do anything else, it lifted the feather from Poseidon's palm and tossed it out of the stables, into the ocean below. My jaw fell open as the current of air did one little victory lap around Poseidon's head, lifting his loose silver hair from his shoulders, then bolted back to join the rest of the current whirling around me.

Ooh boy. It appeared my magic had a rebellious a streak that outdid mine.

# ALMI

"Oh!" My utterance fell away as the air turned in one last flurry around me, then vanished, melting away into the ocean breeze.

"Air magic," said Poseidon on an exhale.

"Air magic," I repeated. Thrills were rushing through me, a feeling like no other starting to work its way through all the internal chaos and fatigue. It was a feeling of rightness, a feeling of hope. And not one forced of desperation, like the hope that had kept me going my whole life, but one of true and sincere belief.

When I looked up at Poseidon, I realized I had felt a fleeting glimpse of this feeling before, just one day ago. Standing on the deck of the ship, staring at him.

Perhaps it hadn't been him that had felt so right. Perhaps it had been *me*, standing on the deck of a ship that flew through the air. A ship free from the binding of earth and ocean, designed to soar through the sky. I almost felt giddy when I thought about it.

Another long breath left Poseidon, and his eyes had

taken on that same wild intensity they had last time we were in the stables. But that time, I'd pissed him off.

"Want to go for a ride?" I asked, the question leaving my lips unbidden. Suddenly, all I wanted to do was feel the rush of wind over my face, the boundless freedom of soaring through the sky, just like I had on the ship, but with this new appreciation that was pounding through me.

I hadn't expected him to say yes. But he moved his hand to the little flute on his leather strap, pulled it free, then blew into it. A shrill, off-key whistle echoed through the air, and Blue stamped his feet.

Seconds later, the sound of hooves meeting wood made me spin around.

Another pegasus had landed, and my breath caught.

She was pure gold. Not just her wings, like Blue's, but her whole body; mane, tail — everything. But she looked weightless, her lithe movements so beautifully graceful.

"Oh my god, she's gorgeous."

"She is. She is called Chrysos." His tone was gentle, and I dragged my eyes from the golden pegasus to look at him.

The urge to go to him was almost unbearable.

How could a man be so hard, and yet have a tenderness toward these creatures that turned him into something else completely? Not soft, for sure. But... something else.

Before I could do anything about my inappropriate urges, he had moved to Chrysos, rubbing his hand down her neck, then leaping onto her back like a frigging pro. "You wanted to ride."

His eyes met mine in challenge, a spark in them that had nothing controlled about it at all.

Delicious excitement rose up in me. "How do I get on?" I asked, looking at Blue. Out of nowhere, a gust of wind blew behind me, and I knew what it wanted me to do. I reached up, gripped Blue's neck, and as soon as I jumped, the wind did the rest. It lifted me easily, sliding me onto the pegasus' back as though I had done all the work myself.

I looked at Poseidon gleefully, and the corner of his mouth quirked the tiniest bit.

"Reckon you can keep up?"

"Fuck yes."

Blue bounded for the edge of the stables, and a delighted scream burst from my chest as he launched himself into the air. My skirt flew out, catching like a sail, then pinning to my legs as the pegasus dove toward the waves.

Wind rushed over my face, stinging and strong and so much more energetic than it had ever seemed before.

Gold streaked by me, and I watched in awe as the golden pegasus plunged straight into the sea. She streaked under the surface, her gleaming gold coat and the silver hair of Poseidon visible under the waves as Blue galloped along with them, the salt in the air tangible as the ocean spray reached us.

Poseidon and Chrysos burst up from the water, a jet following them up and corkscrewing around them as they soared high.

"Go, Blue," I urged, and he beat his wings, racing up

after them. Pastel colored clouds filled the sky, coral pinks and soft yellow mingling with pale lavenders and peaches. The higher we got the more I saw little bursts of glittering air, whizzing around like shooting stars.

I was gripping Blue's mane hard, my thighs clamped around his haunches, but I had no fear of falling.

I urged Blue ahead of Poseidon, then called up the image of the tornado again. Wind rushed me, and I made my request of it.

*Carry us higher.*

There was a blast of warm current, then I heard a shout from Poseidon.

With a burst of speed that elicited a whinny from both pegasi, we were swept upward.

The wind whirled around us, whipping up the calm clouds, and pulling the flying horses to face each other.

My eyes locked onto Poseidon, and my pulse raced as heat swooped through me.

Unbridled joy was written across every inch of his face. Not a hint of control was left, his muscles bulging as he held onto Chrysos, his head thrown back as his hair whipped around his face, and his whole body radiating life.

*Take us down,* I asked the wind, and squeezed Blue tighter.

"Hold on!" I yelled, and then we were dropping through the sky like bullets.

As though getting in on the game, both Blue and Chrysos tucked their wings in, making our descent even faster. Fresh adrenaline surged through me as we plummeted toward the sea, the recent memory of dropping into the gaping jaws of certain death unavoidable.

As we got close to the water, I realized Blue wasn't pulling up. I took a breath, then called on the bubbles as we plunged into the sea.

They whooshed around my head as we powered through the water, Blue and Chrysos pulling up so that we stayed close to the surface. Chrysos was driving her legs hard, as though she were galloping on the ground, and I assumed Blue was doing the same. She pivoted, twisting so that she was tipping her rider upside down, and Poseidon pressed himself close to her neck.

Blue did the same, and laughter left my lips, until I saw the view. Being upside-down meant I was looking down now, and before us was Aquarius.

The hundreds of connected golden domes glowed beneath us, grand buildings and tall towers reaching the surface just visible. There were scores of animals; whales and dolphins and turtles and rays and eels and many other creatures too small to see, moving around the domes.

Blue righted himself as we soared past the palace stable tower, tipping me the right way again before bursting up through the waves, back into the sky.

I was breathless with excitement as he beat his wings, taking us higher, and I felt a stab of disappointment when he turned toward the stables.

He set us down, and Poseidon and Chrysos landed a beat after we did.

I slipped from his back, my legs leaden and my hands shaking. "Thanks, Blue. That was amazing."

I was wet again, my skirt heavy around my legs and my hair cool on my bare shoulders.

I felt a warm touch on my back, and I turned to Poseidon. He looked more alive than I'd ever seen him.

"You must rest," he said, seeing how unsteady I was.

"Probably. Could I have some more of those vials?"

He held out his other hand, two vials in it. "Could I have the shells?"

I nodded and fished them out of my bra. His gaze fixed on my chest, and his jaw tensed. I dropped the shells into his palm, picking up the vials in their place. "Fair trade," I smiled at him.

"Almi…" There was a strain to his voice that didn't match the restlessness in his eyes. "Why did you come back?"

My own elation dipped. "I told you. To save Lily."

"How were you planning to do that?"

I swallowed. Should I tell him? Was now the time? "I… I heard of a place that had healing powers. I wanted to try to find it."

"What place?"

I bit my lip. "Atlantis."

His eyes darkened instantly, his back stiffening. "The Font of Zoi," he murmured quietly.

"Yes."

He stared at me. "I have no idea how you found out about its existence, but if you know of it, I assume you also know I am its keeper?" I nodded. His jaw twitched. "That's why you came to the palace?"

"Yes."

"You thought to what, woo a trip to the deepest depths of the ocean from me?"

"No. I thought to steal your ship."

His mouth fell open. "You are unbelievable."

I resisted the urge to say something sarcastic. "Have you tried to use the font?"

"I don't know where you got your information from, but Atlantis is no longer accessible." His voice had turned hard, and for the first time since the end of the Trial, I saw tendrils of stone sneaking across his ribs.

"What?"

"It's not an option," he growled.

"But the book says it can heal anything. It could wake Lily up and cure the stone. We have to try!" I could feel fresh hope blossoming at the knowledge that he hadn't already tried to use the Font of Zoi. It could still be the answer.

"The Oracle said the heart of the ocean was the only way to cure the stone blight," he stated, folding his arms across his chest.

"We don't even know what the stupid heart of the ocean is! And besides, what about the sleeping sickness?"

"The Oracle said your sister would sleep until the gods weep. Not until you visited a long hidden, deadly realm," he snapped.

"Well, unless you want to tell me how the fuck I'm supposed to make a god weep, give me a better plan." I glared at him, and a gust of wind whipped around us. Blue and Chrysos both backed up.

"Your power is awakening. We may soon find out what the heart of the ocean is," he said. "That is the plan."

"It's a shit plan," I snapped.

Anger sparked in his eyes, and the sky around the tower darkened. "We have to win these cursed Trials, and then we will cure the blight. Do not presume to know better than an Olympian."

"Why the hell do you think you know more about Nereids and hearts of the damned ocean than I do? I am telling you, we do not have time to wait for this heart to show up!"

"This conversation is over," he snarled.

"Don't you fucking dare—"

But I was too late. Before I could begin to tell him what I would do to him if he flashed me away, I was standing in my bedroom, dripping wet and furious.

# POSEIDON

*S*he was getting too damn close.

Her face when she had brought the wind to life... Fuck, I'd almost thrown a decade of discipline away right then and there.

She was a damned force of nature, with no fucking concept of control.

I needed her like I needed water.

I wanted her like nothing I'd ever desired before.

Not just her touch, her kiss, her body. But that unbridled tenacity, her fierce courage. She was more than I had ever anticipated she would be, in every way. And I couldn't watch her come into her power any more than I could watch her die.


I had watched her every day for eight years. I'd seen her tears. Seen her grief. Seen her sorrow and loneliness.

I knew what she had thought of me. She believed me to be cold, hard, cruel. Hell, the world believed the same.

But she was starting to see the truth. Every time she looked at me, every time she touched my skin, every time she brought my soul to fucking life...

How could I be so damned stupid?

It had to stop.

It couldn't continue.

Or she would be the death of us both.

# ALMI

*I* smoothed down the skirt of my dress, trying not to grind my teeth as I did so.

"Are you alright?" Mov asked. "Do you not like the dress?"

"I love the dress," I told them, trying to smile. "I'd just rather be wearing pants and a shirt."

They scowled at me, before schooling their features again. "Why would you choose pants over this?" Mov gestured at the mirror.

My reflection showed a tight red dress, with a split high enough in the left leg that I could just about run in an emergency. It had puffed shoulder sleeves and a sweetheart neckline, just low enough to show my blossoming shell tattoo. My purple hair had a lot more blue running through it now and had been braided in a fishtail style, the plait placed strategically over my shoulder, hanging almost to my waist. Kryvo was, of course, on the side that wasn't obscured by my braid.

"It's lovely," I reassured Mov. "It's just that last time I

put on a dress, I didn't expect to immediately have to swim, run, fall and a ton of other shit, in it. Pants would have been easier."

"Do you think you are likely to have to compete in this dress?" they asked, frowning.

"I wouldn't rule anything out."

Mov lifted a finger to their lips thoughtfully. They disappeared into a closet, then came out a moment later, holding a black leather belt that was too small for any normal person's waist.

"We can strap a weapon to your thigh?"

Images of badass, sexy women in spy films flooded my brain and I nodded enthusiastically. "Yes. Let's definitely do that."

I had crashed hard when I'd gotten back to my room. Not until after I'd bellowed out some rage in the shower over Poseidon's dismissal of the font in Atlantis. But the anger, on top of everything else, had burned me out fast, and I'd slept long and soundly.

I'd awoken still pissed though. And not just at Poseidon.

The thing I was most pissed about was Atlas.

Atlas and these stupid fucking Trials.

I had magic now. Magic that I wasn't really sure how to control or what to do with, but I had it. It was helping me. Saving my damn life. I was finally ready, finally in with an actual shot at doing something useful for once, and I was stuck facing a load of deadly monsters for the entertainment of a lunatic god instead of saving Lily.

. . .

"I wonder what Poseidon did to Atlas' wife?" I mused aloud as the nymphs bustled about in the closet.

The more my confused feelings roiled around for the ocean god, the more I longed to know the answer to that question.

I had a connection to Poseidon, and I fundamentally struggled to believe he was cruel or unkind. Hard, sometimes misguided, and a tad merciless perhaps. But a lack of mercy was not the same as cruelty. Mercy could be learned. Or earned. Cruelty was inherent. In the blood. Unfixable.

Kryvo's voice reached me. "I found something in the palace about Atlas."

"About his wife?" My pulse quickened.

"Yes. Do you want to see?"

"Absolutely."

My vision clouded, and then I was looking at a domed ceiling, painted with an obscenely detailed image of what looked like a wedding.

Atlas' wedding, I realized, as I peered at the groom. Hera stood before them at the altar, her dark skin and peacock-colored headdress vibrant in the painting. I scanned the rows of attendees, and spotted Poseidon immediately. Zeus was by his side, and even in the painting, he looked bored. On the right side of the image were gods who weren't Olympians. Titans. So this must have been before the Titonamchy; the war that divided the great gods.

Jeez, that meant whatever had happened between the two of them had happened a long time ago.

I looked back to Poseidon, noticing his clenched fists and moody expression. That could mean nothing, though, I wouldn't have expected him to be the life and soul of a party.

The vision faded, and I bit back my disappointment. "Is that all there is?"

"I can keep looking." Kryvo sounded disappointed, and I hurried to console him.

"That was great," I enthused. "I just wish we knew what happened."

"Well, I don't know why Poseidon has a painting of Atlas' wedding in his palace at all," said the starfish.

"That's a really good point," I said with a frown. "Where is the painting?"

"The north-east wing. It's not used much by anyone except staff."


When the nymphs had finished working their magic, Galatea strode into the dressing room.

"Hey," I said, surprised by how happy I was to see her. "How's it going?"

"I am pleased you got out of the Trial alive," she said.

"Yeah. You and me both."

"I have been trying to find out how Atlas has so thoroughly infiltrated the palace."

"And? You find anything?"

"No." Galatea gestured for me to follow her, so I did. She marched along the corridors like she would know where she was headed even if she were blindfolded, and I wondered how long she had lived in the palace.

That thought made another spring to mind. "How old are you?"

She cast a look at me. "That is an impolite question."

"People keep telling me I'm impolite. I may as well live up to expectations," I shrugged.

She gave me a small scowl, then she shrugged, too. "Four hundred."

"Woah," I said. "And how many of those years have you spent here?"

"Almost all of them. Poseidon found me when I was very young."

"Found you?"

"Yes. We do not have time for my tales now, I am afraid. We are expected at Apollo's ball."

I screwed my face up. "What is it with you guys and balls?"

Galatea gave me a sympathetic look. "I do not care for them either, in truth." I took in her tight fighting garb and severe face and found myself unsurprised.

"Not a fan of twirling around on the dancefloor?"

"I would rather run rings around my enemies," she said.

I nodded. "Cool."

She frowned at me. "What does the temperature have to do with balls or enemies?"

"Nothing. Ignore me."

"So odd," she muttered, then resumed her strides toward a large, sweeping staircase carpeted in red. "The gods like balls and ceremonies because it gives them a chance to show off and size each other up," she said. "They love drama. Can't get by without it. There's nothing worse for an immortal than boredom."

"Where are Hera and Aphrodite? They haven't been at the last few gatherings."

"Hera has been missing for a while. Zeus fled Olympus, and it appears she has chosen him over the others." Her tone was clipped.

"Well, she is his wife."

"That matters not, when the moral choice is clear. Hera is a woman of integrity."

"And insane jealousy, if I remember correctly?" I muttered.

"On occasion, yes. But she is one of the better gods."

"From what Atlas said, she told him about my marriage to Poseidon so that he could seek revenge. I've got to be honest, she's not top of my list right now."

"Yes. That is troubling."

"Troubling. Yeah. I was going more for 'fucking inconvenient'. But troubling works too."

We reached the top of the staircase, where a massive archway led into a beautiful room I recognized immediately as Poseidon's throne room.

Poseidon stood from his throne, and I was surprised to see his ocean-toga.

"I thought I'd lost that," I said, staring.

"It is not a normal toga. It is enchanted," he said. "You are no longer angry with me?"

"Oh no, I'm still mad. I just got distracted for a second."

I was almost certain I saw a twitch of amusement in his face, which only made me more determined to remember I was annoyed with him.

"I have not seen you in red before."

I blinked. "You've spent like, six days with me. Most of which I was wearing brown and white."

"Yes."

I lifted my hands up. "That's it?"

"Yes."

"Jeez, and you say I'm the odd one."

"You've got to be odd to be number one," he said, his voice only just audible. I snapped my eyes to his, sparks surging through me. Why? Why would him quoting my own bullshit back at me cause such a physical reaction?

*Because he thinks you're funny.* Lily's voice in my head sounded amused. *And that makes you happy.*

*Funny? He doesn't think anything is funny! I've seen him smile once!*

*And what would you do to see him smile again?*

Anything.

The answer forced its way through any mental blocks I had with ease.

Fuck. Would I really do anything?

He stepped down from his throne toward me, oozing grandeur and power and cool stoicism. All things I had zero interest in. But his eyes… I was sure I could see raw, wild emotion deep in there, disguised as fierceness, carefully contained and locked away.

"When we are in Apollo's realm, you need to be wary of a number of things," he said.

"Apollo?" I suggested.

Poseidon shook his head. "No. He is cocky and somewhat overly jovial, but in your public position, you need not fear him. He is at war with the vampires right now, though. And they are certainly to be feared."

My jaw dropped. "Did you just say vampires?"

"Yes. Women who live by consuming warm blood."

"Well, shit. I didn't know Olympus had those."

He frowned. "All life began in Olympus. The ancient word for them is *lamia*. They have evolved much since the ancient times though."

"Why is Apollo at war with them?"

"He is the god of the sun," he answered, as though that made it obvious. Before I could ask him to elaborate, he was talking again. "Atlas will not be pleased that we were able to flout his attempts to separate us, or beat the ice Trial. It is of the utmost importance that you avoid him at all costs."

I nodded. "That's not a hard command to follow. He creeps me out."

"He has a lot of anger."

I couldn't help taking the opening. "Want to tell me why he hates you so much?"

"No. We only have a few minutes more until we will be flashed there. Do you have the vials I gave you?"

"Yes."

"Good. I strongly suspect that we will be sent to the earth Trial straight from the ball." His eyes roamed down my dress, and I was sure they lingered a little longer than was necessary on my exposed leg. I pointed my toe and bent my knee, like a burlesque dancer.

"That's why I got the split. So that I could run," I said in a mock sultry voice.

When he looked at me, his eyes were blazing with heat, and I gulped, tucking my leg back into my skirt immediately.

Galatea coughed behind me, and I felt my face flush.

"You're a leg man, huh?" I whispered awkwardly.

"Do not test me," he growled.

I hadn't realized what a test my leg was for him.

Or how much his reaction would please me.

*I told you,* said Lily. *You want him to want you.*

Before I could argue with my imaginary sister, the world flashed white.

# ALMI

The first thing I noticed was the glittering sheen of frost covering everything. We were in an outdoor courtyard, tall statues and Grecian fountains adorning the mosaic tiles, and creeping vines and purple wisteria winding around interspersed stone columns. The area was lit by hundreds of tiny floating lights, which shone just brightly enough to catch the sparkling frost that covered every single surface.

People milled around everywhere, many faces familiar now from the last few gatherings. I spotted Kalypso immediately, as she was only standing a few feet away, talking with an exceptionally handsome man with dark, dreadlocked hair, and a chest as broad as some of the gods.

"Where are we?" I asked Poseidon, but I got no answer. I turned and realized he'd already gone. Galatea gave me a vaguely sympathetic look. "I think you spooked him," she said.

"How?"

She pointed to my leg. "With that."

Before I could answer, Persephone came toward us, laying a hand on my shoulder and squeezing it. "You did so fucking well in that Trial!" Without even considering the action, I leaned forward and hugged her. The movement may have taken me by surprise, but she didn't seem fazed at all. She returned my embrace, then held me at arm's length, giving me a grinning once over.

"You don't look like you're in need of any healing. In fact, you look great."

I shook my head. "Thank you. Something amazing happened." Excitement fizzed through me as she leaned in, eyebrows raised in question. She was wearing a black gown with grassy-green trim across the low-cut front, and a tiara made from golden roses donned her white hair. She looked like someone from a movie or a video game, and normally, I would be intimidated by someone as beautiful as she was, but I trusted her instinctively.

Galatea moved closer so that she could hear me.

"I have some magic now," I whispered, and touched my fingers to my shell tattoo.

"That's great! Does that mean the heart of the ocean will show up?"

"That's what Poseidon is hoping. What it definitely means is that I can breathe underwater."

Galatea let out a sigh of relief. "Thank the gods for that," she said.

"For sure."

A nymph arrived with a tray of drinks, and we all took one. It was the same delicious fizzy wine as before, and I sipped gratefully.

"Where are we?" I asked.

Persephone held out her hand and gestured her head toward some railings at the edge of the courtyard. "Come see."

I took her hand and we walked across a neatly manicured lawn shining with frost. "Apollo is the god of the sun, so parts of his realm are intolerably hot. In order to balance that out, he has most of the rest of his realm made from ice."

We reached the stone railings and I peered over the edge.

We were on the top of a sheer cliff of ice. Water met the ice at the bottom, and was completely frozen over.

I looked at Persephone. "Is this where the Trial was?"

She nodded. "Yeah. We're on top of the ice cliff you guys were in."

"What about the talontaur?" Fear zipped through me, making my muscles tight.

"Hades said it's been moved. I don't know where, but look." She turned and pointed in turn to Hades, Artemis, Athena, Hephaestus and Dionysus. They were the only Olympians in our line of sight, all drinking and talking with creatures that looked like they had been invented by somebody on drugs. All except Hephaestus, who was staring glumly over the railings, nothing but an enormous leather apron covering his hulking torso. "With this many all-powerful beings here, you can relax."

"There are some all-powerful beings here that do the opposite of make me relax," Galatea growled, and I saw who her gaze was fixed on.

"Atlas." He was standing by a fountain with a very

pretty woman with neon blue skin and hair, and Ceto. Both Atlas and Ceto turned briefly our way, before resuming their conversation. Ceto's slimy octopus legs writhed on the tiles, her skin just like that of the rotbloods, lava-like ripples moving over her body.

Man, she creeped me out so much worse than the rest of them.

"There are some pretty powerful lamia here too," said Persephone, frowning. "They come from the Underworld originally - I had to fight an empousa once." She shuddered. "Fucking terrifying creatures. Anyway, Hades has been talking to Apollo a lot recently about the hostilities with the vampires. He can't control them once they leave the Underworld."

I was about to ask more, but a familiar face materialized in the crowd, and I gasped. "Silos!"

I rushed forward as he spotted me, a huge grin taking his face as he pushed past people to reach me. He wrapped his arms around me in a hug.

"Silos! How did you get here?"

"Dad." He beamed. "Almi, look at you!"

I did a twirl, and he laughed. "Ever think you'd see me in a dress?" I asked.

"Nope. But I'm glad I have. It suits you." His tone was soft, and I smiled at him.

"Thanks. And thanks for cheering me on. I saw you before."

"Are you serious? Of course I'm cheering you on! I can't believe you're Poseidon's *wife*. When the fuck were you going to mention that?"

I cocked my head, giving a small shrug. "You know I'd have told you if I could."

He nodded. "Yeah. Why did he make you live in the human world if you were married?"

"To keep me away from other people."

Silos frowned, then looked nervously over his shoulder, tensing. "Is he the jealous type? Do I need to keep my distance?"

I laughed. "Honestly, I'm just a business transaction to him. He needs me for something the Oracle at Delphi told him about. There's no jealousy in this marriage," I assured him.

His shoulders relaxed. "I can't believe you've almost been eaten by sea monsters twice."

I was happy he'd changed the subject. I didn't know what it meant that I'd much rather talk about nearly dying than Poseidon, but that appeared to be the case.

"I know. How's Lily?"

"The same." Compassion shone in his big brown eyes.

"I'm close now," I said. "I'm going to save her, Silos."

He nodded. "If anyone can, it's you."

I smiled at him, until a fizzing electric feeling rippled across my skin. I knew what it was, I'd felt it numerous times before now.

"Atlas," I murmured, turning and looking for the Titan. But I couldn't see him anywhere. Why had he sent that feeling? To let me know he was watching me? Just venting some anger at us for surviving today? Poseidon had said to be wary of him.

I looked back at Silos. "I have some pretty messed up

enemies here now," I told him. "It might be safer for you to keep your distance from me."

He opened his mouth, then closed it again, thinking.

"You know," he said eventually. "I'm going to guess you have a reason for saying that, and go with it. But Almi, if you need anything, or I can help you in any way…"

"Silos, you are helping me more than anyone in the world by keeping Lily safe. I owe you everything."

He smiled again, then hugged me.

"Keep kicking ass, Almi."

"You betcha."

# ALMI

"Who is he?" asked Galatea when I returned to the two women.

"My friend from when I was a kid. He's been taking care of my sister for me. Ever since Poseidon sent me away." Seeing Silos had forced out some of my new, softer feelings toward the ocean god, and reminded me of just what he had put me and Lily through.

"Do you still want me to visit your sister?" asked Persephone, voice gentle.

"Yes! Oh my god, yes, I would love you to," I told her. "The next time we get a long enough break from these Trials, I would be so grateful if we could go to her."

I didn't think Persephone could cure her, but I couldn't see how it could hurt. Any information would be useful, as would any slowing down of the process.

"Of course. Just use that rose I gave you to let me know you need me. Hephaestus made it for me. Well," she said, frowning. "Hades asked Hephaestus to make it for me. He's a little... shy around women."

"Isn't he married to like, the ultimate woman, Aphrodite?"

Anger sparked in Persephone's eyes. "Don't talk to me about that witch," she spat.

"Now, now," chided a male voice, deep and lyrical. "You mustn't speak ill of the Olympians." Apollo appeared beside us with a shimmer of gold. And gold was the only word I could think of as I took him in. His tousled golden hair flopped down over gleaming golden eyes. His toga too was gold, and fastened with a huge, golden, lyre brooch.

"Good evening, Apollo," Persephone said.

He threw a brief but devastating smile at her, then locked his eyes on me.

"You, Almi, are very, very interesting. Who knew the old water goat had a wife?"

I shifted uncomfortably. "Well, the whole world knows now."

"You are a sea nymph, yes?" I nodded. "Then…. Why do you have air magic?"

My stomach clenched, both with excitement and nerves. "You can feel my magic?"

"Sugar, I'm an elemental weather god. Of course I can."

I swallowed. "I'm only just learning how to use it," I admitted. Poseidon had said that Apollo wasn't a threat, and if he could feel my magic, there wasn't much point lying to him.

He grinned at me, and my chest tightened. He was frigging beautiful. Not in the same way as Poseidon — not at all. Poseidon was solid-mass-of-deep-and-mysterious-power kind of beautiful whereas Apollo was joyous-to-look-at kind of beautiful.

"Want a tip?"

"Sure."

"You can't control air. It is almost as wild as the ocean, and it may not be as strong or powerful, but everything relies on it. *Everything*. It has all the power."

I blinked at him. "I can't control it?"

"Nope. Don't even try. If you can win over the wind, you'll have an ally for life, but you can't bend air to any will."

I tried to process his words. "So, how do I—"

Before I could finish my question, he was gone, striding toward two women with tree bark for skin and green hair.

"Air magic?" Galatea was staring at me like I'd grown a second head.

"Yeah. Apparently."

"But… You're a Nereid."

"Yup." I wrung my hands and she continued to gape at me, confusion written across her face.

"If it keeps you alive, who gives a shit what kind of magic it is?" Persephone said.

I looked at her gratefully. "Yes. Exactly. Magic is magic, right?"

"Wrong." Galatea frowned. "Air magic is not of Aquarius."

Discomfort rolled through me. "Well, I am. I don't know how this has happened, but it has. And my shell is coloring. That happens to Nereids when they get their power, so... Even though I might still be broken, I *am* a Nereid."

I was speaking overly defensively, and I tried to relax. But Galatea's reaction was a mirror of my own worst thoughts.

What if I wasn't a Nereid? Which would mean... Lily wasn't really my sister.

Persephone threw a glare at Galatea as she laid her hand on my shoulder again. "Look, we all come into our own in different ways. Just because you're the first to do something one way, doesn't mean it's the wrong way. It's just... new."

"Or odd," I sighed, but her words forced their way through my paranoia. "Thanks," I told her, hoping my sincerity came across. "You're being really kind to me."

"People here are kinder than you think they are," she smiled. "And besides, it's true."

"I'll try to believe that."

"I am not trying to be unkind," said Galatea, her face still conflicted, but less accusatory. "I am sorry. I just find it confusing that the King of the Ocean would marry a being not of water."

"I don't think he knew at the time. In fact, I know he didn't. We both found out today."

"Air is a powerful element, like Apollo said," Galatea said, straightening. "I am sure you can command much respect with it."

"Command respect? Galatea, I'm not hankering after a general's job like yours. I want to survive this bullshit and cure my sister. Ideally, getting rid of this fucking stone thing altogether if we can. But I'm not after respect."

"You are a queen."

"You were the one who told me that would never happen! I specifically remember you telling me not to get my hopes up."

"That was before..." she gestured vaguely in the air, then pointed at my leg. "Before that."

"What?"

"Almi, I have never, ever seen him look at a woman like he did you. I have never seen his control so close to the edge. And I have been by his side for centuries."

My brain stuttered to an unhelpful halt. "What?"

Persephone gave a small, tinkling chuckle. "Do you fancy him?"

I turned to her, mouth open. "Look at him! How in the name of all things holy am I supposed to find him *unattractive*?"

She smirked at me.

"That doesn't mean I like him, though! He kept me from my only family for almost a decade! He's frigging miserable — which, I might point out, is the last quality I would look for in a guy, and on top of that, he's got me wrapped up in these bullshit Trials by doing something to another man's wife! I am not fucking interested."

I folded my arms over my chest and wished I hadn't spoken so loudly as the two women stared at me.

"Sure, you're not," said Persephone eventually, before taking a long sip of her drink, then holding up her empty glass. "Do you want another one?"

"Yes."

~

Neither woman brought up Poseidon again, which I was grateful for. Something I was also grateful for was the opportunity to ask about the other guests for the first time. Both Persephone and Galatea seemed happy to answer my questions about the different species and types of creatures.

The courtyard was beautiful, and though the sparkling frost covered the statues and the neat little trees, there was no chill in the air at all. The twinkling fairy-lights made it feel festive, and I found myself starting to relax. The absence of Atlas concerned me a little, but it definitely made things less tense, not having to watch for him. I had caught glimpses of Poseidon, here and there, talking to different folk. But he had avoided my eye, and I had done the same.

An area in the middle of the garden was made up of large square marble tiles, and people were dancing across them to music played by a woman plucking the golden strings of an enormous, gilded harp. She looked utterly lost in the tune, her fingers flying over the tight strings.

"She's a muse," Persephone said. "Fuck knows which one, there's like, nine, or something."

"And what is the grey thing that makes me want to drown myself?" I asked, pointing at the sea foam creature I'd seen the first night I'd arrived at the palace.

"That's an aphros," said Galatea. "I'm not a big fan of them myself. But they're an important part of Aquarius."

I was about to ask why, when someone started screaming. We all whirled, looking for the source of the noise. People began moving somewhere off behind the dancefloor, where the trees were thicker and there were fewer twinkling lights. I saw a glimmer of gold slither across the ground, disappearing into the undergrowth. A snake?

Persephone began to move quickly toward the commotion, and Galatea and I followed.

"What happened to him! Why is he like this?" a woman's voice was sobbing. My chest tightened, anxiety washing through me.

"No, this can't be… This is the man you arrived with tonight?"

"Yes, of course it is! He's my husband!" the woman half-shrieked back. Persephone pushed through the gathered guests, and when I squeezed through after her, I stumbled to a halt.

A merwoman, with matte white hair and green skin, was hanging from the arm of a statue. A statue of a merman. Tears streaked her face, and her chest was heaving as she sobbed.

"One minute, he was asking me to dance, and the next…" She broke down, sinking to her knees but not letting go of the statue's hand.

Sorrow welled up through me, edged with a colossal bout of fear.

*The stone blight.*

Poseidon had managed to keep it a secret so far. I scanned the faces of the crowd, looking for him, and not having to look for long. Folk parted instantly as he and Hades moved toward the woman and the stone edifice that used to be her husband.

Poseidons' face blanched as he took in the scene.

He turned to the assembled crowd. "Please, go back to the ball. This will be fixed, forthwith."

Nobody argued, and I knew why. A deep need to obey him thrummed through me, so against my own nature that I knew it was of a divine source.

I found myself taking a step back, before Persephone grabbed my forearm, holding me in place.

Everybody dissipated, and my new friend hurried to the grieving woman. She laid her hand on her arm as she ducked down to her, and the woman's sobs abated straight away.

"Sire," said Galatea, stepping to Poseidon.

"Take him to the palace, with the others." Poseidon's voice was hard, as hard as the man turned to stone before us.

For a split second, I considered objecting. I knew what came next. Poseidon would make her forget about him. But as I watched the woman being soothed by Persephone, abject grief in her face, I wondered how awful it would be for someone to take away her pain.

It would only be temporary.

*But would it?*

What if we failed to cure the blight? What if this merman existed as a statue for the rest of his life?

*What if Lily became a statue?*

"If we fail, you have to make them remember." I said the words out loud, and I wasn't even sure I was close enough for Poseidon to hear them, but his eyes snapped to mine.

"They will feel the pain all over again." His voice was as quiet as mine was, but I heard him clearly.

"Yes. But if their loss is permanent, it belongs to them. They need closure. They need their memories."

He gazed at me a long moment. "Granted." I raised my eyebrows, not fully sure what he meant by the word. "Your request is granted," he clarified gently.

A bubble of sadness coiled up through my center, rooting in my throat. "Thank you."

A thundering boom made everyone jump in surprise, and a few people cry out.

"What's that?" someone asked.

I already knew though. I could almost taste the unsettling electricity tang of Atlas' magic.

The crowd parted, revealing the Titan standing in the middle of the dancefloor, ten feet tall and wearing a white toga adorned with his interlocking ring sigil.

"Citizens of Olympus, esteemed gods," he boomed, bowing his head. "Are you enjoying yourself?"

Nobody answered him. I strongly suspected that nobody wanted him to win. The Olympians may be a little batshit crazy, but this guy? He was frigging nuts.

"Oh, I see you have experienced a little tragedy over there." He looked at the stone merman, and made a mock pout. "I don't believe he was anyone important, so best not to dwell on it."

Anger surged through me.

"Now, let me relieve you of your boredom! It's time to see how our contestants performed in the last Trial."

Ceto, Kalypso and Polybotes all melted out of the crowd, coming to stand in front of him. Poseidon and I stayed exactly where we were.

A flame dish shimmered into being before the Titan,

the flames leaping high, then showing five glass vases. There were little shells in the bottom of four of them.

"Polybotes, one shell." The giant grunted as a shell appeared in the bottom of one the vases.

"Kalypso, four shells." I raised my eyebrows as she smiled, and four shells appeared in a vase that already had three in it.

"Ceto, three shells." Her vase filled higher.

"Almi, three shells."

"Wait, what—?" I tried to interrupt, but he spoke louder.

"Poseidon, no shells." The empty vase in the image remained empty, whilst three shells appeared beside my existing one.

"No, they're his!" I shouted. Atlas turned to face me.

"The shells are counted at the moment the red shell is used. All three shells were on your person, my little queen."

The way he said the word queen somehow made me feel sick, and I glared at him. "You're a rotten fucking—"

Before I could finish, he roared again, turning back to the audience at large. "And now, let's really spice things up. Off we go, to the next Trial."

"Jackass!" I bellowed, as we were flashed away from the ball.

# ALMI

*I* was so furious when I opened my eyes under the water that I almost forgot to hold my breath.

I willed the bubbles to come to me, almost as desperate for the air so that I could fume about Atlas as to actually breathe.

The swirl of bubbles rushed toward me out of nowhere, whizzing around my face until I could see through it clearly.

*Thank you, clever new air magic,* I thought as I drew a breath and looked around myself, trying to find Poseidon.

My surroundings were significantly different to last time. The first thing I noticed was that the water was warm. The second thing I noticed was green. Green everywhere.

I was in some sort of underwater meadow. The entire ground below me—which I could see easily because the water was so crystal clear—was covered in a richly green, fluffy moss. Moss-covered boulders and huge plants lined the areas to either side of me, creating a channel.

My heart skipped a little when I used my arms to turn myself in a circle. I couldn't see Poseidon.

"Kryvo?"

"I'm here."

"Do you know anything about where we are?" I could recall what Atlas had said about tropical seagardens, but the little starfish might know more.

"Aphrodite's realm, Pisces, is made up of many small tropical islands, and I think we are in the channels running between them that are dedicated to her underwater plants."

"Okay. What's going to try to kill us here?"

"Pretty much all of the plants."

"Right."

"And Kalypso is in here with us somewhere. I would say she is pretty dangerous too."

"Agreed."

Feeling glad that I'd drunk all of Poseidon's vial before the ball and that his suspicion that we would be sent straight here from the party had been anticipated, I began to swim. I went with the faint current, rather than against it, hoping that was the right thing to do.

"Poseidon!" I called out. Making a noise would draw Kalypso's attention to me if she was nearby, but I figured it was worth the risk. I needed the ocean god with me.

I wasn't sure if that need was driven by fear of surviving without his help, or just wanting to be in his presence. I would have been lying if I didn't admit that he was starting to take up an extraordinarily large amount of space in my thoughts.

I rolled onto my back as I swam, so I could look up at the surface. I was only a few meters under the water, and for a moment, I was tempted to swim up and pop my head out, to see if that gave me any clues. But there was so much happening under the surface I decided I was more likely to find shells, and Poseidon, staying down.

The channel I was swimming along was curving gently, and I could see lots of brightly colored fish flitting about over the tops of the high boulders that made up the sides. When I rounded the corner, my eyes widened.

Opening before me was a landscape of mountains and valleys, all carpeted in thick, green seagrass. Tiny bubbles clung to the grasses before rippling to the surface, making the enormous bowl of water fizz before me. There were plants scattered amongst the green peaks as big as cars. Giant yellow plumed mushroom shaped things caught my gaze first, because they were so vivid in color. But there were patches where purple grasses, dotted with white flowers, lay like rugs over the green, and blue flowers in tall tubes like bluebells shot up between sturdier looking vines.

Between the vastness of the area, the fizzing in the water, and the gentle current, movement was everywhere. Instinct made me force out some of the calm beauty of the place and remember that this was a Trial designed to kill me. But my eyes flitted from one place to another, and I had no idea where to even start looking for shells.

I felt something behind me, my foot brushing something solid. I whipped the knife from my thigh-strap as I spun around, brandishing it in panic.

"It's me." Poseidon hovered in the clear water, his ocean toga looking too bold and blue in the green water world.

"Thank god. This place is immense," I said, on a small a sigh of relief.

"It will not be easy to find shells. Just about every one of these plants is lethal. This is Aphrodite's pet project." His voice sounded thick and gurgled, but it was easier to make out his words than it had been under the ice.

"Like a deadly underwater greenhouse."

He looked at me, then at the dagger in my hand. "You came armed this time."

"Yes."

"Good."

He swam past me, leaving the tributary and moving out over into what I was now terming 'the bowl' in my head.

I followed him, tucking the knife back into the band around my thigh and relishing the badass vibe it gave me.

It really did feel like I was swimming over mountains, the shapes of the green below me undulating and rolling exactly as the ranges had on Sagittarius. I wondered what the place would smell like, if we weren't underwater.

Poseidon swam low, dipping into one of the valleys, and I mimicked him. The air fizzing off the grasses intensified the deeper we went, and I got the distinct memory of being in a bath with a bath-bomb. Ahead, at the lowest point of the vividly bright valley, was a plant. It was as tall as Poseidon, standing alone and bold, and I recognized it immediately.

A Venus fly trap.

Except it was bright violet in color, and had a few... extras.

When we got closer, I could see the two halves of its leaf-shaped jaws were wide open, and the inside of them were baby pink. Instead of thin veined leaves, the plant looked thick and leathery, an almost hide-like texture covering its surface.

Lying in the middle of the lower leaf was a little white shell. Poseidon moved closer, and I grabbed his bare calf.

Tingles moved through my arm at the contact, and I let go quickly as he turned to me.

"It's a trap," I said.

"Clearly."

I pulled a face at him, and he ducked down, swimming to the grassy riverbed. He tugged up a handful of long grass, then swam back up.

Unlike the Venus fly traps I'd seen before, this plant didn't have the little spiny teeth-like protrusions around the edges of its leaves. In fact, there was very little that was threatening about it all, other than the jaw-like shape of the two thick leaves.

Poseidon swam over the top of it, then sprinkled the handful of grasses onto the lower leaf.

Teeth, actual ivory teeth, burst up from each leaf - not just around the edge but over the whole surface. The top leaf came slamming down onto the bottom one, mincing the grass into tiny shreds. Slowly, the leaf-jaws eased open again, the whole plant swaying slightly in the water.

"I don't like it," said Kryvo in a small voice.

"Me neither," I told him. "We're going to need something better than grass to get the shell."

I saw a ribbon of water come from Poseidon's palm, and shoot toward the shell. The second it brushed against the leaf though, the jaw slammed shut, squishing his water ribbon and making it dissipate.

*Air?* I projected my tentative thought. *Wanna have a go?*

Nothing happened.

I thought about how the wind had tossed the feather off the side of the stables and then ruffled Poseidon's hair earlier that day.

*Poseidon's water can't get the shell, but I bet you can.*

A corkscrew of tight bubbles whooshed through the water toward me, forming from the tiny fizzing bubbles coming off the grass.

A smile sprang to my lips, despite the seriousness of the situation.

"Well, hello!" I said aloud as the stream of air spiraled around me. "You have to touch only the shell, not the leaves," I told it.

Slowly at first, then more quickly, the air flowed over to the plant.

With a lightning fast dart of movement, the stream zoomed for the shell. The plant snapped shut and I held my breath as the stream whooshed back to me.

It had missed.

As the plant folded open again, I saw the shell still firmly on the leaf. Poseidon looked at me, then his ribbon of water snaked back to the trap.

Poseidon tried another three times, but to no avail. The plant was simply too quick.

"Come on, air," I told it. "One more go. We can do it."

I swam over the top of the massive plant, as close to it as I dared to get. It could easily trap my entire body between its leaf-jaws, piercing me a hundred times with all those lethal teeth.

The stream of air moved more slowly this time, almost creeping through the water toward the shell.

"Slowly," I whispered, as it got within an inch.

Both the stream and I froze as the leaf gave a tiny ripple, then stilled again.

"Super slowly," I breathed, and the stream moved again. Poseidon was watching, a few feet from me, but I tried to ignore him, focusing on the air. Millimeter by painful millimeter, it got closer to the shell. My pulse raced, and I would definitely have been sweating if we had been on dry land. My hands were clenched into fists, my nails digging into my palms as the air finally touched the shell.

The plant's jaw snapped closed, the teeth bursting out ready to impale the intruder.

But my stream of air zoomed back toward me with gusto, spinning me in circles with its strength in the water.

I squealed, and it slowed. I felt something pushing at my hand, cool and firm. When I looked down, the stream of air had turned narrow, trying to pry open my fist. I stretched out my fingers and the air dropped the little shell into my palm.

"Oh my god! You're amazing!"

The air stream started moving again, whizzing me around in another circle and almost making me drop the shell. "Woah!" I laughed. It stopped, instead forming a foot high whirlpool before me, bouncing in the water. "Thank you, very much," I beamed at it, before turning to Poseidon.

He eyed the little whirlpool warily, before swimming over to me. I held out the shell. "You'd better take this," I said.

Light sparked in his eyes, then he reached out, taking the shell and stowing it in a concealed pocket in his toga.

"Does your emotional support starfish have a time check?" he asked me, once the shell was safe.

"Kryvo?"

"Forty-six minutes," Kryvo squeaked.

Poseidon nodded and swam up the valley edge.

"You're welcome," I muttered, swimming after him.

## ALMI

When we emerged from the valley back out into the bowl, I was happy to let Poseidon take the lead. We swam for what felt like ages, almost everything I saw carpeting the ground below us bright green.

"I've been looking for any other starfish in the palace with views of deadly water plants," Kryvo said.

"Any luck?"

"Yes. A few. I'll let you know if they become relevant."

"What would I do without you, huh?"

"I doubt you would hide," he grumbled.

Eventually, the green under us started to change, as a vivid pink colored weed snaked its way through the grasses. After a few more meters it had smothered everything, turning the riverbed mountains completely pink.

I dipped closer to it, trying to look carefully for shells, or anything that could contain a shell. But if there were any there, they were too well hidden for me to spot.

Poseidon dipped suddenly ahead of me, and I assumed he had found something.

I swam toward him excitedly, then slowed.

He was down amongst the pink weeds, but not digging for a shell, like I thought he would be. The weeds were wrapped around his middle, trying to pull him down to the bottom. His hands were glowing as he swiped at them, but the weeds were too fast, turning him this way and that, and pinning his arms completely to his sides.

Why hadn't he blasted them off with magic already?

Worry filled me as I started to speed up again, but then I saw the dark-skinned figure of Kalypso, ten feet away. She wasn't being dragged down by the weeds — she was too high up. But she was holding her hand out, and I could just make out a rippling in the water coming from her palm, directed straight at Poseidon.

I pulled my knife from my leg band and sped toward him. As soon as I reached his thrashing form I began to hack at the weeds, but the dagger barely moved through them.

"In my toga," Poseidon snarled, and tried to turn toward me. A pink weed snaked its way around my wrist, and I snapped my hand back, trying to keep my body high above Poseidon's. Weight was crushing down on me though, a strong current of water pushing me. As the current moved over my face, the bubbles providing me air slowed, then vanished.

Shit.

I held my breath, reaching into the top of Poseidon's toga, where I knew he kept his dagger strapped to his chest.

Alarm at my lack of air and the pressure from Kalypso's magic distracted me from the spark I got when my fingers brushed his chest, and I tugged the dagger out.

It was significantly sharper than mine, and I sliced through the weeds in seconds.

Free, Poseidon burst up, soaring through the water straight at Kalypso.

She rose to meet him, and glowing currents crashed into each other between them as they both fired water magic at each other.

My bubbles whooshed back around me as Kalypso's magic was redirected, and I drew in a grateful breath.

Something brushed my ankle and I looked down, lifting my knees high in the water when I saw that it was a pink weed, reaching for me.

"Oh no you don't," I told it. I looked over at the fight between the two ocean gods. If Poseidon used too much power, he would turn to stone again. I had to help.

*Air? Fancy sending Kalypso somewhere far away from here?*

The tiny bubbles of air fizzing up through the water coalesced into a small spinning whirlpool again.

"I'd owe you one. Or two," I told it aloud.

With a bounce, the whirlpool zoomed toward Kalypso. It skirted close enough to Poseidon on its way to lift his toga, showing me the dark shorts I now knew he wore underneath, then smashed into Kalypso.

As it hit her, it expanded, lifting her high in the water and turning her over and over. Fortunately, she was wearing underwear too, as the skirt of her dark dress flipped up and I heard her give a roar of anger. The whirlpool grew again, then launched her bodily up through the surface of the water. A second later, far in the distance, I saw a disturbance in the water signaling her return to the water.

Poseidon turned slowly to me, and I snapped my hanging jaw closed.

I tried to look cool as Poseidon gazed at me, his eyes burning with blue light. Stone was creeping over his neck and up his jaw.

"That was impressive," he said carefully.

"Thanks." I looked at the whirlpool, still ten feet tall and churning near the surface. "And thank you!" I called to it. "You kicked that Titan's ass!"

With one last whizz, it dissipated.

"I suggest we swim in the opposite direction that she came back down in," Poseidon said.

"Lead the way, sire," I said, giving him a salute. A heady adrenaline was rushing through my body, a sense of surrealism taking over my rational thoughts.

I was in the goddess of love's lethal underwater garden, and I'd just used air magic to pitch a frigging Titan over a hundred feet.

How in the hell had I ended up here, all the way from the shitty little trailer in Oxford?

My sense of wonderment at my situation only increased as we continued to swim. The landscape beneath us changed again, the vicious pink weed petering out and replaced once more with bright green, bubbling grasses. But soon, there were also shoots. They started out quite small, maybe only a few feet. But the farther we got, the taller they grew, until they reached the surface of the water. We had moved away from the bowl, taking one of the tributaries that led off in the opposite direction as the now-probably-fuming Kalypso, and we had been swimming in a gentle bend, the bowl no longer visible behind us.

Soon, it was as though we were in an underwater forest, the colossal roots of the plants stretching up to the sun like tree-trunks around us.

They began to don canopies that looked like giant lily-pads above us, bright orange and purple, changing the color of the light seeping down through them and casting weird shadows over us as we moved.

I got the heightened sense of being in a dream, but I wasn't entirely sure it was a good one anymore. There was something both beautiful and eerie about the forest.

I slowed down as something alongside one of the tall roots caught my attention. It was a faceted column of some sort with a triangular top, sticking up out of the grassy riverbed. It was gray in color, and as I looked closer, I realized it was made from stone. As we neared it, an opening appeared in one side, small and dark.

Concern surged through me, the sense of danger arriving almost too late.

"Stop!"

Poseidon paused and turned to me just as something fired from the stone column, whizzing past his face by mere inches. If he hadn't turned, the thing would have hit him.

"What's wrong?"

"That thing just shot an arrow or something at you," I said, pointing to the column.

He turned, and I yelled again. "Move back!"

He did, but not before another arrow left the column, zooming toward him. He darted back out of its path. "I saw the arrow," he said slowly. "But not where it came from."

"That column."

"I do not see a column."

His gurgled voice was deadly serious, and I frowned.

"How can you not see it?"

"There is nothing there. Although I presume you speak the truth."

I snorted. "Why the hell would I lie?"

"My thoughts exactly. If there are sentinels, then we are likely on the right track to something worthwhile. Are there more?"

"Sentinels?" I asked, as I strained my eyes, trying to see further along the swaying tree-like roots. I caught a few glimpses of gray stone between the trunks.

"There are more. But if you can't see them, how are you going to carry on?"

He paused. "I can't. You will have to."

"Huh?"

"You can clearly handle yourself. You go. I will watch your back from here."

I swallowed hard, and Kryvo heated on my chest. "We can do this, right Kryvo?"

"No."

Lily's face filled my mind. *Of course you can. You just beat Kalypso.*

I screwed my face up. *Only because she was distracted by Poseidon and not expecting it.*

*Nonsense.*

"I'm not fast enough to get past the arrows," I said to Poseidon. "But you are. I think we have a better chance together."

It was true, I did think we had a better chance together. But I also really didn't want to carry on without him.

He regarded me a moment, silver hair floating behind him. "Agreed."

He held his hand out, and I took it. "Let's go low," I suggested, eyeing the height of the column.

As soon as Poseidon began to move lower, the stone column began to fire arrows. He was fast enough to duck under it, but when I looked left I realized we'd moved straight into the path of another, lower column.

"Go back up!"

He did.

I didn't dare to blink as we moved, swinging my head from left to right and shouting instructions as Poseidon kept us speeding through the gauntlet of arrows.

"Up!" I yelled, then, "Up again!" Arrows flew by, some a safe distance away and some so close I could feel the current they caused against my skin.

Poseidon kept zooming us forward until the thickening forest of roots and columns seemed to abruptly thin out, a large clearing coming into view.

"I think we're good," I gasped, as we burst into the clearing, scanning furiously for stone sentinels but seeing none.

"Thank fuck," Poseidon grunted, slowing us to a stop. His voice was strained.

"You okay?" I asked as I faced him.

He wasn't. I could see that immediately.

Blood streaked down his arm, and the stone was now covering more than half of the skin I could see.

"One hit me. I believe it is poisoned. I am weakening fast."

"Shit."

"We must find the red shell and leave here as soon as possible. I will need healing attention very soon."

"Shit, shit, shit."

Fear was working its way through me, and it wasn't just for losing him as an ally.

I was scared for him. The idea of him in pain, the tension in his voice, and the blood I could see — shining with silver as gods' blood did—was making me feel all kinds of wrong.

I needed him strong and healthy and... *happy*.

Why the hell did I need him happy?

*Not the time, Almi.* Lily's voice brought me out of my emotions.

"Not the time," I murmured.

Poseidon frowned at me. "The shell," he repeated, seriously. "I believe that may have something to do with it, given its color."

He pointed his uninjured arm at something enormous and red in the center of the clearing, and together, we swam toward it.

# ALMI

*T*he water seemed to heat as we got closer, and my brows rose as I took it in.

It was a flower of some sort, and it looked the tiniest bit familiar. It had a circular hole in the middle, the inside dark and foreboding, and was ringed with massive leaves that curled over the sides and were covered in bright orange dots.

"It's a corpse flower," said Kryvo.

"Corpse flower? Well, that doesn't sound good."

"If you take it out of the water, it smells like rotten flesh."

"Lovely."

"It's also toxic."

I could have guessed that from the brightness of its color. It was so red my eyes almost hurt to look at it.

"I'm going to go out on a limb and guess the shell is in that dangerous looking middle bit," I said.

Poseidon flicked a look at me. "Are you going to send your air magic in to check?"

ELIZA RAINE & ROSE WILSON

"Sure," I shrugged, as my heart rate quickened. Having magic was cool as fuck, but I was going to try to act as mature about it as I could.

*Air? Could you do me another favor?*

The bubbles immediately formed the little whirlpool again, and it bobbed through the water to me.

"Thank you. Poseidon here is in a bit of a hurry, 'cos he got hit by a poisoned arrow, so if you could just dart into that massive flower over there and grab the shell for me, I'd be super grateful."

"I'd be even more grateful if you didn't harass me whilst doing so," Poseidon added.

A small smile sprang to my lips, and warmth flowed through my chest as I looked at him.

He was in pain, and our lives were very much at risk, yet I was pretty sure the so-serious-he-might-hurt-himself god had just made a joke.

The whirlpool zoomed to Poseidon, lifted his hair over his head in the water, bounced for a second, then zoomed over to the big red flower.

"I'll take that as a no," Poseidon sighed.

"Don't look at me," I said, holding up my hands. "I'm told you can't control air, only ask it for favors." I grinned at him, and he shook his head.

A noise made us both turn to the flower, high-pitched and quiet at first, then lower and more melodic.

"Is the flower... singing?"

My little whirlpool was lowering itself into the hole in the middle. As I watched, all of the leaves contracted suddenly, the hole closing, then bursting open again and shooting something into the water. It was a fine, shining dust, gold and red sparkling glitter shooting out for tens of feet in every direction.

Including ours.

"Kryvo, how toxic is this thing?" I asked him quickly, already moving backward.

"Extremely. You'll go mad, then you'll die."

"And how does it distribute its toxin?" I tried to keep the panic from my voice, but I couldn't see the whirlpool anymore, and the glittery stuff was falling fast through the water toward us. We were trapped in the clearing, the stone columns lining every exit I could see back into the forest.

"From what I can tell from this mural it, erm…" He trailed off and I swallowed.

"Shoots it into clearings where its prey is trapped?"

"Yes."

The water all around us rippled, and my head swam as glitter descended over my vision. The music got louder, an enchanting melody that seemed to build with each second. A calmness came over me, and the forest seemed brighter somehow.

Movement over my head caught my eye, and I saw giant red lily pads extending from the forest edge, starting to cover the clearing. The light changed color, reds and oranges stark against the green riverbed.

"It's so beautiful," I breathed.

"You're beautiful."

I looked at Poseidon, my breath catching at the look on his face.

Hunger.

Raw, unbridled, hunger.

The waves crashed over his toga, and he was a vision of strength and ferocity in the calm, beautiful, eerie underwater gardens.

The music built, and the more I stared into his face, the more I couldn't give a shit about anything but him.

Even the stone, edging his face and covering his arms, looked beautiful.

"Why are you so unhappy?" The question left my lips, and the words were instantly lost to the melody filling the water.

"You."

"I make you unhappy?"

"Every day."

Pain lanced through me, confusion stabbing at my consciousness.

"I don't want you to be unhappy."

Within a heartbeat, he was in front of me, one arm around my waist, the other pushed into my hair, drawing my face to his.

We turned in the water, my skirt flowing out around me as we spun, the world falling away, soft light, warm water, and delicious music engulfing me.

His lips were inches from mine, and I had never seen the waves in his eyes so clearly.

"You...I'm supposed to hate you."

Anger and fear pulsed across his features, the waves

roaring in the endless depths of his irises. "You will be the death of us both," he said, then his mouth met mine.

Desire exploded through me, my legs lifting, wrapping around him of their own accord. His tongue played across mine, then he was crushing me closer, kissing me like he had on the ship, like a man who would give up anything in the world for this taste. The taste of something forbidden, something worth risking everything for.

I kissed him back, with everything I could to match him. I had no idea a kiss could say so much, mean so much. But in that moment, I would have given up everything for him.

*Everything?*

The word repeated in my mind, quietly at first, then loudly.

Loudly, and in a voice that wasn't my own.

I froze, and Poseidon tensed. Our lips came apart, and I was suddenly aware that something was wrong.

The light had changed, darkened. The only thing now clear in the gloom was the corpse flower, glowing a rich red in the middle of the clearing. The lily pads above us had turned dark and opaque, and claustrophobia closed in on me.

Poseidon was still gripping me, my legs still wrapped around him, when a scream tore through the water. I tightened my grip as both of us snapped our heads round, looking for the source of the sound.

It changed, turning into a long, awful wail that made me feel sick to my stomach.

"What—?"I started to say, then I saw Poseidon's face. Horror was etched into his expression, and he pushed me away, blasting me back through the water. I tried to right myself, then stopped still. There was something in the water behind him. Lots of somethings. Wraith-like figures were swimming out of the corpse flower, glowing red, barely visible, and they were converging on Poseidon.

Fear so strong it was crippling my muscles expanded through me, my throat tightening and breath hard to get. The shrieking wail got louder, and my terror increased with it.

"Kryvo!" I half sobbed the starfish's name as Poseidon continued to stare at me in horror, the wraiths swimming around him. Each time they brushed his skin I saw lumps of his flesh fall away, turning to stone before they drifted to the bottom of the river.

"They're all dead," the starfish choked. His voice was tiny, and I tried to move, but my limbs were immobile. I was sinking through the water, unable to kick my legs to keep myself afloat.

*Almi.*

Lily's voice was crystal clear in my mind, and I sucked in a breath.

*Almi, this is the flower's toxins. Swim to the flower, get the shell.*

"I can't. Poseidon…"

He was being torn apart by the wraiths before me, and I couldn't do a thing. I was going to watch him die.

I couldn't. I couldn't see him die.

I needed him.

*Almi, swim to the goddamn flower now!*

My sister never yelled.

She never swore.

The shock leaked through my stupefaction.

"It's not real," I gasped.

*It is not real. Kryvo said you would go mad, then die. Get to the damn shell.*

"It's not real!" I repeated, loudly this time, yelling the words at Poseidon. "It's not real!" The third time saying it seemed to finally unlock my legs, and I kicked them hard. The wraiths all turned to me.

My stomach knotted itself completely in fear, and I almost locked up again, but Lily was there in my head.

*Swim. You need to swim.*

Gritting my teeth, I turned away from them, and swam for the flower.

# ALMI

Tears streaked down my cheeks as I powered my way to the glowing flower. The closer I got, the louder the wailing scream got, so intense pain pounded through my head, and an overwhelming feeling of hopelessness seeped through me.

I forced myself on, through the barrier of awful sound around the corpse flower.

As I got over the top of it, my vision swam, everything wobbling and tipping from side to side.

Then the wraiths were *everywhere*.

They descended on me, smothering me with their translucent bodies, suffocating me.

"Swim down!" Kryvo's voice came to me, and I followed his instructions blindly, trying to angle my body down and kick my legs. I could feel my skirts getting stuck to my legs and anger began to replace my fear, frustration and terror bundling together, turning into something new.

"Keep going!"

My extended fingertips brushed against something, and a new vision filled my mind.

Lily.

On her pallet at Silos' home, the room burning around her. Flames licked at her bed, at her body, but they did her no damage. Because she was made completely of stone.

"No!"

"Almi, you're so close!" Kryvo's voice cut through the image, but when my own vision came back to me it was just the whirling bodies of the wraiths.

I kicked my legs hard and prayed.

*Air! Help me!*

With a blast of energy so strong I felt it to my core, the wraiths were thrown aside, leaving me a clear view straight down into the hole in the center of the plant. A solitary red shell was just within my grasp, and I lunged for it.

As I picked it up, another blast of the glittery stuff flew up around me, and a whirlpool as big as I was swept across me, picking me up and turning me face to face with Poseidon. Stone covered almost every inch of his skin, and I thrust the red shell toward him as black crept across the edges of my vision.

He wrapped his hand around mine, and everything vanished.

I found myself on a beach, white sand stretching in all directions. But I barely noticed it.

"Lily!" The image of the room burning around her stone body was seared into my skull, and the toxins still had me in their grip. Everything was spinning—the only thing keeping me upright was Poseidon.

We still had our hands gripped together around the shell, and when one of my legs gave out, he dropped to his knees with me.

"Almi," he murmured. "Almi."

I tried to focus on him, tried to see anything but the image of Lily.

His blue eyes bore through the flames in my head, and I clung to them.

"Poseidon."

He leaned forward, placing a kiss on my lips that was so tender it momentarily stilled my churning mind. "Almi," he murmured once more, then collapsed to the sand. I didn't have the strength to stop him pulling me down with him, and as I hit the ground, unconsciousness dragged me under.

When I awoke, all I could see was Lily. Flames were tearing down the room around her, and she lay lifeless, granite, in the center of the chaos.

"Lily!"

"It's okay, it's okay," a female voice soothed. "Lily's fine, it's a hallucination from the corpse flower's toxins."

I blinked up at Persephone's calm face. "What…" My words were cut off by a massive wave of nausea.

As if knowing, Persephone pressed a hand to my chest,

her golden vines flowing from her palm. The sickness vanished. "Good thing I'm good with plants," she smiled at me. "You should be dead."

"How's Poseidon?" I asked, taking a deep breath. "Where am I?"

"We're in your room."

"Kryvo!" Panicking, I pushed myself up.

I saw the starfish on the dresser, a paler red than he should have been. I struggled to get my legs out from under the covers, trying to get to him, but the sickness washed back over me, and I clamped my mouth shut and closed my eyes.

"Easy now." I felt myself pulled back to the bed, and my stomach settled again. "Is Kryvo your starfish?"

I nodded, unwilling to open my mouth in case I threw up.

"He's okay. Water creatures handle the toxins a bit differently. He'll need to sleep for quite a while, but he'll be fine."

Relief made me slump back into my pillows.

"As for your husband…" I sat up straight again, snapping my eyes open. "He's immortal, but the stone blight really has weakened him. He suffered from the poison in the arrow too, and it took a lot to get him conscious."

"But he's okay?"

"Yes." Her voice was uncertain, and I knew she wasn't telling me everything.

"What's wrong?"

"He is weak, Almi. So weak that I fear that overuse of his powers will render him a statue again."

"The blight is killing him," I whispered.

"Yes. I think so."

I bit down on my lip. "My power is finally showing up, I can communicate with air now. Does that mean the heart of the ocean will show up too?"

She shrugged. "Honestly, I don't know. Poseidon was the one who heard the prophecy from the Oracle, right?"

"Yes."

"Then you and he need to work this out. But I don't know you'll have much time before the next Trial. This is exactly what Atlas wants, each of you weaker every time."

I scowled. "Atlas is a cold, heartless asshole."

"Agreed. But he's not stupid. There is a ceremony in Aphrodite's palace tonight."

My stomach sank. "Shit. He's going to send us straight to the next Trial from there, isn't he."

"Probably. I should warn you, Aphrodite's palace is a little...tricky."

"Tricky?"

"I'll tell you when you've had some rest."

"Thank you. For saving us."

"You're welcome, Almi."

The next time I woke it was with the exact same image of Lily in the burning room filling my mind, swallowing me whole.

I heard myself scream as I thrashed out of the covers. "It was a dream," I panted aloud as the image faded and my room came into view.

"A bad dream."

My head jerked at the voice. "Poseidon!"

"Are you alright?" He looked concerned, his silver hair pushed back from his tanned face, his blue leather fighting clothes on. He was sitting in a chair that had been pulled up to my bedside and was leaning toward me.

"How long have you been here?"

"Not long. You were dreaming."

"Yes."

He gave me a long, intense look that never left my face. With sudden alarm, I looked down at myself. I was wearing a white shirt from the closet, I saw with relief.

Sending silent thanks to Persephone for dealing with my modesty while I'd been unconscious, I looked around the room. "Is there water anywhere? I'm thirsty."

He stood and moved to a tray on wheels that was covered in food and drink. "Persephone said not to eat too quickly, as it may make you sick," he said.

I nodded, eyeing him warily. "You are acting like my nurse." When his eyes met mine again, the memory of our kiss in the clearing crashed through my mind. I felt my cheeks heat.

"I felt the need to ensure your health," he said awkwardly.

"That, erm..." I took a quick breath. "That kiss. That was the flower toxins. Right?"

That didn't explain the kiss on the ship.

Or the way I felt every time my skin touched his.

Or my stupid burning desire for him to be happy.

"Right," he said. "Toxins."

"Toxins," I repeated, lifting a pastry covered in sugar from the tray, along with a glass of water.

He stepped back, putting some distance between us.

"Between toxins and marriage bonds, it's getting harder to hate you," I muttered around my pastry.

Emotion flashed in his eyes, and when he spoke his voice was soft. "You still hate me?"

I took a long swig of water from the glass, trying to work out how to answer him. My mind felt a little foggy still, but I was restless and painfully aware that I'd very nearly died. Deciding honesty couldn't hurt now, I replied as truthfully as I could.

"Yes. You took me from Lily. That was unforgivable."

"Unforgivable," he repeated quietly. "There is nothing that can not be forgiven." His eyes had turned hard, his jaw tight.

"I don't know if that is true."

"It must be," he said softly. "Forgiveness or revenge. They are all we have."

"What are you talking about?

"Nothing." His eyes locked on mine. "What were you dreaming about?"

"Jeez, you're hard to keep up with, you know that?" I chewed on my pastry and glared at him.

"What do you mean?" He looked genuinely bewildered, and a modicum of pity worked its way through my annoyance.

"You say stuff, and I don't know what you're talking about. It's all mysterious, cryptic nonsense. Or you lose your shit and just leave halfway through the conversation.

You're not easy to be around." Not that that was stopping me wanting to be around him.

"I... am not used to sharing thoughts of this nature with others," he said eventually. "I suppose I am not very good at it." He said the words like they tasted bad, and I thought that he probably didn't admit to not being good at things very often. Or at all.

"You and Galatea talk about everything," I said, still chewing.

"Not things like this."

"Like what?"

He glared back at me, the waves growing in his eyes and his hands twitching by his sides. "Emotions," he spat, eventually.

I raised my eyebrows. "This is you talking about your emotions?"

He let out an angry sigh. "*You* do not make it easy."

"You don't deserve it easy."

I couldn't help being hard with him, I was battling a decade of anger. But the cold, hard, controlled sea god was trying to talk to me about emotions?

"Look, the only person I share stuff like this with is my imaginary projection of my sister. So, it's not like I'm an expert," I admitted. "But, I think we have to be honest with each other if we're going to survive this."

"There are things you can't know."

I sighed. "What a surprise. Will you tell me what you know about the heart of the ocean?"

"I already have. I know no more than you do now."

"Great." I bit off another piece of pastry as I rolled my eyes.

"What were you dreaming about?" The urgency of his tone made me look at him.

"My sister. The flower made me see her completely turned to stone, and the building she was in was on fire." I felt tears fill my eyes as I spoke, and I cursed them inwardly. I didn't want to look weak. "It was very vivid. And upsetting."

"The image is still clear to you?"

"Yes."

"When we were in the clearing I... I saw the water wraiths tearing you apart." Strain edged his every word.

"I saw that too. They were pulling off chunks of your flesh." I shuddered at the memory.

"But it is your sister you see in your nightmares?" he asked.

I stared at him as I nodded, trying to make sense of what he was implying. That my nightmares should be about him? Or that he was having nightmares about me? His gaze bore into mine, and then light flickered in his eyes.

"Would it make you feel better to see her?"

"What?" I scrambled to the edge of the bed. "What do you mean?"

"I will take you to her. Now. To put your mind at ease."

"You would do that?"

"Yes. You saved my life. Again."

I paused. "So, you'll take me because you owe me?" An unexpected stab of disappointment that he was only taking me out of obligation pricked at my excitement.

He opened his mouth to say something, then closed it, simply nodding at me instead.

"Fine. Leave the room so I can get dressed," I told him, swallowing down anything else I might have wanted to say. If he was really going to take me to see Lily, this was the wrong time to risk pissing him off enough to do his vanishing-in-a-temper act.

# ALMI

*I* barely even noticed the clothes I pulled on from the closet. I couldn't think of anything I wanted more than to see Lily. To see that she wasn't turned to stone, and that the bakery wasn't burning around her. The image burst to life behind my eyelids every single time I closed them, even for a second.

My thoughts flashed to Poseidon as I hurriedly brushed my teeth. Was he seeing me torn apart by the wraiths every time he closed his eyes?

He was so damned hard to decipher. But I was growing certain that he cared about me.

I knew it must be the bond that was causing it, because I felt the same way. I was drawn to him, both physically, and in a deeper way - a way that meant his safety and happiness were not his problem alone any longer.

If that was how he felt about me, then I could deal with it. It was the marriage bond, and as annoying as it was, it was possibly the only thing keeping us both alive. Between his failing power and my growing magic, we had managed to survive three Trials now through combining our strengths.

Rushing from the bathroom, I moved to the dresser and peered closely at Kryvo. I couldn't see any movement, but when I hovered my fingers as close to him as I dared, I could feel a little bit of heat coming from his body. "Persephone said you were asleep, little buddy," I whispered to him. "I'm leaving for a short while, but I wanted you to know that you're safe here, and that you were frigging amazing. Sleep well, friend."

When I opened the door Poseidon was leaning against the frame, his stormy eyes conflicted and intense when they fell on me.

"Where are we going?" He held his hand out to me.

"Are you strong enough to flash us?" I wanted to get there as soon as possible, but I didn't want him to use power he couldn't afford to.

He scowled at me. "Flashing is child's play to a god," he growled.

"Fine. Fyka."

"That is your hometown."

"Yes," I nodded. "My friend has been taking care of Lily since you removed me from Aquarius." I glared at him, and he snatched my hand and flashed us out of the palace.

We were standing in the marketplace, and just about everybody within a hundred meters stopped what they were doing and stared. Poseidon wasn't known to be a hermit, but I didn't recall ever seeing the god in our little dome-town as a child.

I turned toward the bakery, and he followed me.

"Silos?" I called as I pushed the door open. It must have been around midday, because the place was packed with customers. A griffin spread his wings wide in surprise, hitting a merwoman in the face.

"He's out back," called a woman behind the counter, without looking up from wrapping a loaf of bread.

I pushed my way through the now silent group of people, to where I knew a section of the counter lifted to allow access to the back.

The matronly woman cast us a glance as we passed, and her mouth fell open as she did a double take. As one, most of the room dropped to one knee.

I shook my head as Poseidon inclined his at them.

"We know you're going to win the Trials, sire," a merman near the front said.

"Of course I am," Poseidon replied.

I rolled my eyes and kept moving.

"Silos?" I called again, once we were in the back part of the bakery, where both the ovens and the stairs were.

Just the fact that the building wasn't on fire was already making me feel better.

"Almi?"

A dark face emerged from a door, and Silos first grinned, then stared, as he saw Poseidon behind me.

He came out of the door fully and dropped to one knee. "You honor me and my bakery," he said.

"I'm here to see Lily," I said, and Silos lifted his head to look at me.

"Of course." I turned for the stairs, then paused when he spoke again. "I wasn't sure you'd made it," he said, his voice heavy with relief. I turned back to him, moving to give him a hug as he stood.

"I'm fine."

"Good."

When I turned back to the stairs, Poseidon was rigid. Ignoring him, I headed up the stairs.

I began to move quickly, the closer I got to her, and was practically running by the time I pushed open the door to her room. I rushed to her side, utter relief swamping me as I saw her flesh-colored skin. *Not stone.* Not the mother-of-pearl shine it should be either, but anything was better than stone. It had reached her shoulders, though, I saw as I pulled back the sheets.

I swallowed back the lump in my throat and sagged beside her. "Lily. Lily, I'm here," I muttered as I bent my head to hers.

A small noise reminded me that I wasn't alone, and I looked up to see Poseidon in the doorway. He was so large the room looked half the size, and all of a sudden, I didn't want him there. "You did this."

He shook his head gently. "I have made your life difficult," he said. "But I did not do this." He stepped further into the room, and I saw the stone spreading across his own flesh. "You can save her."

My heart almost stopped beating in my chest.

*You can save her.*

Nobody had ever said those words to me. Nobody other than me had ever believed them. A new hope coursed through me, as though the fact that somebody else believed the words might be true gave them actual possibility.

"I can save her?"

"You are the only person in Olympus who can save her. And me."

His words on the ship, when he had rescued me from the storm, rushed back to me.

*I will always save you.*

And now... Now it was up to me?

I gripped Lily's cool hand, dragging my eyes from him to her. "How?" Tears streaked down my cheeks as I stared at her lifeless face.

"First, we rid this realm of Atlas. Then," he took a long breath, and I moved my gaze back to his. "Then, we do whatever it takes. The Oracle, Persephone's powers, even Atlantis if we have to. We go wherever we need to, do whatever is required to heal the families this blight has cursed."

More tears spilled from my eyes.

I wasn't alone anymore.

The commitment in his statement was the most sincere thing I had ever heard. He would not stop until we found a cure. And I knew it wasn't just to save his own skin. I knew it as surely as I knew my own name. The King of the Sea loved his people, loved his subjects.

"And the magical sleep?" I breathed.

"The Oracle will tell us more. She will be our first visit, when these cursed Trials are over."

I nodded, squeezing Lily's hand. "This will be over soon," I told her. "And I'll get to talk to you. For real. See you smile for real."

A sob broke my words, and my eyelids forced themselves closed as emotion overwhelmed me.

Warm arms wrapped around my shoulders as they heaved, and rather than pull away from him I found myself leaning into the god.

I hadn't wanted him to see me cry. Ever. Nor would I ever have expected him to comfort me if I did.

But he tightened his grip around me, and just held me, and my sobs came harder.

"I love her," I said, through my tears, the words lost to his chest as I turned into him. I didn't let go of her, or wrap my arms around him, I just pressed my face to his solid warmth.

"I know. We will help her. I promise."

# POSEIDON

*I* thought I had felt my heart break a hundred times before, but watching her with her sister... Not from a distance, in secret, but close enough to see her hands shake, to hear every sob slice through me like a damned dagger to my heart — it was unbearable.

My control was becoming more tenuous every minute I spent in her presence. Watching the wraiths pull her body apart had almost broken me, and now the image was burned into my soul.

Never, ever would I let her be harmed.

*"You did this."*

That was what she had said.

She held me responsible for the pain and torment her loss caused her.

Every single part of me longed to be the opposite of that pain. To be the life, the healing joy, the freedom she so desperately craved.

But it was better this way.

I needed her to hate me.

# ALMI

"*I*'m really starting to like these dresses," I told Kryvo.

"They are not practical for warfare," he said.

"No."

"Or hiding," he added.

"This is true. How are you feeling?"

He was glued to my collarbone, and Persephone had assured me that the miniature version of the vials Poseidon had been giving me to boost my strength would ensure he would be fine.

"A little tired," he said. "I am struggling to reach the starfish further out in the palace."

"You don't have to do this."

"I'm your friend."

"I know, and I don't want you to get hurt."

"You might need my help."

"You are very helpful," I conceded. "But we should be okay without you."

He heated on my skin, and when he replied, his tone

was loaded with indignation. "If you don't want me there, I shall not come."

"Kryvo," I said softly. "That's not what I meant. You got poisoned by a deadly flower like eight hours ago."

"So did you."

"Yes, and I would definitely take more time to recover if it was on offer."

"Humph."

I shook my head. There was a knock on the dressing room door, and Galatea entered.

"Blue suits you," she said when she saw me.

I was wearing a dress that could have come straight out of a princess movie, layers of tulle in shades of blue puffing out from my hips. The top half was essentially two long pieces of draped fabric that went all the way over my shoulders, waistband to waistband. I'd had Roz pin it across my chest so that any vigorous movement wouldn't expose my chest to the world. Kryvo sat a little further out on my shoulder than usual, to avoid being covered by the fabric.

My tattoo was visible between the edges of the deep neckline. The turquoise green had spread into a forest green, then a much paler shade. Almost half of the shell was in color now.

"Thank you," I said. "How are you?"

"I have been better. But I have made some progress on the palace infiltration." Her face tightened, a slight snarl appearing. "Snakes."

"Snakes?"

"Yes. There have been multiple sightings of golden

snakes in the palace, and I think they have something to do with Atlas."

"I thought I saw a snake at Apollo's courtyard," I said.

Her focus sharpened. "Where?"

"Near the merman who turned to stone."

Galatea clenched her fists. "I will catch one of those slithery bastards," she growled. "And find out how they are getting in."

I inched away from her. "You're aware that you're terrifying, yes?"

She looked at me. "As terrifying as you are odd?"

"Yup."

"I can deal with that." She gave me a rare smile.

"How long until this stupid ceremony?"

"Half an hour. Are you armed?"

I lifted my skirt to show her my dagger in my leg strap.

It was weird to think that when I'd started all this, the gadgets and gizmos in my belt had been the best hope I had. Now, the magic of air was on my side. No more water-root or stink bombs.

"That dagger is pathetic," Galatea said. She moved her arm, fishing for something on one of the many leather straps crossing her lithe frame. "Here."

She passed me a knife, eight inches in length but weighing hardly a thing. It had a thin symmetrical blade and a handle made from a shiny shell-like substance, with turtles carved into it.

"It's gorgeous," I said.

"And sharp. Be careful."

"Thank you."

"It's a loan," she said sharply.

"Of course."

She nodded, satisfied, as I slipped it into the leg strap, in place of my blunt dagger. "I hope you will not have need of it, though that seems unlikely." A dark expression took her face. "You got just two shells last time," she muttered.

"Did you see how many the others got?"

"No, all the flame dishes in the palace would only show you two. But I heard a rumor Ceto did well."

I frowned. "Ceto scares me."

"They should all scare you," Galatea said.

"Hello?" Persephone's voice called just before she stepped through the door. "Hey, nice dressing room. Not going to lie - I'm a little jealous," she said, looking around at the pretty room.

I beamed at her. "Hi. Please can you tell Kryvo it's okay if he's too tired to come with me tonight?"

She looked at the little starfish, then at me. "Honey, you need all the help you can get. I'm not going to tell him any such thing."

"Oh."

"I told you," Kryvo squeaked.

"Look, Almi, I just wanted to stop by to warn you about Aphrodite's realm."

Galatea's frown deepened. "I hate Pisces," she muttered.

I raised my eyebrows in apprehension. "Aphrodite is... away right now. It's a long story involving Ares that I'll tell you about sometime over wine. But right now, her son Eros is running things in her place. And he's just as powerful in the, erm, intimacy department, as his mom."

I blinked. "Intimacy?"

Persephone sighed. "The magic of love gods can have a powerful effect on people. Particularly Eros, who is a god of desire. The magic can make you..." she paused, casting about for the right word. "A lot more open to things that might normally make you uncomfortable."

I looked at her in alarm. "Are you talking about sex?" I hissed.

"Well, yeah. And when I first heard about it, I freaked out, thinking that the magic would make me do things against my will, so I wanted to tell you that is absolutely not the case."

I felt my shoulders drop a little in relief. "Oh thank god."

"Yeah, thank Athena and Artemis in particular, they're the ones who put strict rules in place about that sort of thing," Galatea said, pride in her tone.

"Because Zeus is a colossal prick," Persephone said. "Anyway, being in Pisces will only heighten your existing desires. You don't need to worry about doing anything you'll regret."

I swallowed. "What if I'm not sure about my desires?"

Persephone gave me a knowing look. "Then you might get sure, real quick."

# ALMI

*M*y breath stalled in my chest when Persephone flashed us to Aphrodite's realm.

Just like Apollo's party, we were where the Trial had just taken place. We were in a long rectangular space reminiscent of a temple, with regular columns holding up the ceiling, but three of the walls were missing. The floor led straight onto the sand at each end, and the river at the front, and it was made of glass, the view beneath us of the sandy shoreline dropping away and the vivid green underwater landscape we had been trapped in spreading out into the distance. A flashing image of flames and stone leaped into my mind, and I dragged my eyes away.

The back wall was covered in doors, each one a different shape and style. Heat rushed my cheeks as I scanned the paintings around the doors. All of them depicted couples in various states of undress or arousal.

I turned instead to the ceiling, inky blue and covered

in twinkling stars, in contrast to the warm sunset colors swathing the sky outside.

The area was packed with people, more than I'd seen at Apollo's or Poseidon's. Beautiful men and women roamed the room with trays of drinks, wearing barely any clothing. My cheeks burned even hotter as a topless woman with purple skin and flame-red hair approached us.

"Cocktails?" she beamed.

Persephone took something bright blue with an umbrella in it. "Thanks."

I did the same. Galatea shook her head tersely, making a point of not looking at the woman's chest.

"Try to have a good time here," Persephone said to me, lifting her glass to mine. "I don't want to sound all doom-and-gloom, but..." I watched her try to say what she was thinking, knowing exactly what it was.

"It might be my last chance to have fun?"

She gave my arm a gentle squeeze. "You never know what's around the corner," she said.

I did, though. I knew what was coming. Since giving in to my emotions so physically in Lily's room, I had never been surer of my immediate future.

We were going to hand Atlas his ass, then we were going to cure the blight turning the citizens of Aquarius to stone. Including the two people dominating my thoughts.

I looked over the guests and spotted Poseidon easily. He was talking with Athena, his back to me. But the second my gaze landed on him, I saw him tense.

"Excuse me," I said to Persephone and Galatea, and made my way over.

Nerves flitted through my stomach as I approached, both because I'd let Poseidon see so much of my emotion earlier, but also because he was with a freaking Olympian. One I admired.

"Athena," I said, bowing my head respectfully as I reached them.

She locked her eyes on me, and so did the huge owl on her shoulder. "Almi," she said. "You are doing well, for one so untrained." Her voice was deep and lyrical, and commanded instant respect.

"Thank you."

She nodded, looked at Poseidon pointedly, then turned away to talk to someone else.

"Why are you polite to her, and rude to me?" Poseidon said as soon as she was gone.

"Because she doesn't radiate go-fuck-yourself vibes all the time."

He frowned. "I beg to differ."

I laughed. "Fine, she does, but she doesn't do it in an arrogant way. She does it in a way that suggests she's earned it."

He stared at me a beat, then cast his eyes down my body so fast I might have missed it. "Your tattoo has more color."

"Yes. I hope that means I'm getting stronger."

"It is—" He clamped his mouth shut, as though he had been about to say something he shouldn't.

"It's what? What do you know about it?" I asked, stepping forward excitedly.

His eyes were bright with blue light. "It is beautiful."

"O-oh." Warmth flooded my chest, and the happiness those few words caused shocked me. "You think so?"

"Yes." The muscles in his neck were straining, and his chest was rising and falling too slowly, like he was breathing overly deeply.

"Thank you."

"I find many things of the ocean beautiful," he said, a forced flippancy to his tone. I might have been stung, except that the sincerity of his words didn't match the first sentence. He was covering up, pretending he hadn't meant what he'd said.

"So, you think we'll go straight to the next Trial from here?" I asked, changing the subject.

"It seems likely. Though Atlas is not here yet."

"Where is our host?" I asked, looking around the room. I had never seen Eros, also known in human myth as Cupid, before. He was rumored to be worth looking at.

Poseidon's face darkened. "Fortunately, not here. You should be warned that Aphrodite's bloodline, and her realm itself, can heighten some urges."

"Persephone has already briefed me," I said. "Do you know if my friend is here?"

Silos would bust something to be in a forbidden realm, especially with a bunch of topless women and sex paintings on the walls.

Shadows flashed across the light in Poseidon's eyes. "The baker?"

"Yes. Silos."

"Who is he to you?"

I jerked my head back, in both surprise and indigna-

403

tion at his forceful tone. "My friend. As previously stated, a number of times," I said, not trying to keep the defensiveness out of my tone.

"Is he aware that you are friends?"

"He's taken care of Lily for almost a decade; I don't think he would have done that if he wasn't my friend," I said, frowning.

"I meant, is he aware that you are no more than friends," he growled.

Anger coursed through me, replacing the warm feeling from before. "What the hell is that to you?"

He stepped closer to me. "We are wed."

I gaped at him. "Are you shitting me? You do not get to marry me, dump me in a different damn world for eight years, then claim me as your wife when it suits you!"

"Do you love him?"

The question was so abrupt, my tirade sputtered out completely. "Love him?" Poseidon just glared at me, his jaw so tight he may as well have been made from frigging stone again. "He's my friend! My best friend! What the hell is wrong with you?"

"You," he hissed.

"*I'm* what's wrong with you?" I said incredulously. "You need to take a look in the mirror buddy, because you are frigging nuts."

"So you do not love him?"

I shook my head, then downed most of my drink before I could lose my shit and throw it over him. "No, your watery lordship," I said, waving my hand at him angrily. "I love him as my friend and for what he has done for my family. Nothing more. Happy now?"

"No."

"What a fucking surprise." I finished the rest of the drink, barely noticing that it tasted like fresh strawberries.

"Have you lain with him?"

"Oh, for fucks sake." I turned, trying to flag down a server.

"Answer me."

"No." I swiped up a drink from a man wearing nothing but a piece of string masquerading as underwear.

"No, you will not answer me, or no you have not lain with him?"

"Jeez, I haven't *lain* with anyone, if you must know!"

Waves rushed his eyes, and he seemed to swell with power.

I gulped at my new drink, something watermelon flavored and particularly lovely. It did nothing to calm my burning face.

"I must leave."

"The party?"

"No. Your vicinity." With that he whirled away, leaving me staring at his back in disbelief.

"That man…" I fumed.

"God," Kryvo corrected me.

"God or not, he's a frigging nutcase."

"I think he finds you hard to be around."

"The feeling is mutual."

I heard a voice behind me, deep and powerful. "Whenever I see you, you are talking to yourself." I ground my teeth and closed my eyes. I *really* did not want to speak with the owner of that voice. I considered moving away, but my legs turned my body without me telling them to. I glared as I found myself face to face with Atlas.

# ALMI

"What do you want?"

"I want you to know what kind of god your husband is."

"I don't care."

Atlas raised his eyebrows. "Am I supposed to believe you are in it for the power? The status? The world didn't even know who you were just a week ago. If you don't care about him, and you don't want to be a queen, what is it you want, little Almi?"

"What I want is none of your damn business, Atlas. Fuck off."

Anger darkened his face, flames roaring around him for a split second. The image of Lily burning flashed into my mind, and I must have reacted, because Atlas's gaze sharpened. "You are afraid of fire?"

"No."

"I could *make* you afraid of fire." His voice had dropped to a seductive, infinitely unsettling tone. Actual flames began to lick up around his toga-clad body.

"Leave me alone."

"No, I don't think I will. So far, you and Poseidon have felt little of the torment you both deserve. I need to up my game."

"You're insane. You know that?"

He laughed, the hint of mania I'd seen a few times in his eyes evident in the sound. "I am a Titan, Almi. Do you know what that means?"

"You're old."

"I'm more than old. I was here at the start. I am a part of the source of the very world you live in. Do you know what happens when a being this primordial, this *colossal*, experiences pain?"

I shook my head, unwilling to speak. He was advancing on me, the smell of electricity and fire rolling from him, the air thick.

"Love and loss. There's nothing more powerful. I will have my revenge, and there is nothing a pathetic little sea nymph and a broken, redundant Olympian can do to stop it."

I glared back at him, refusing to flinch, but desperate for him to leave.

"She told you to fuck off."

Poseidon's voice was loaded with power, and although I still couldn't turn around, I felt his presence behind me, and smelled the fresh scent of the ocean.

Atlas' unhinged gaze settled over my shoulder. "Are you enjoying the irony of your predicament?" he hissed.

I felt another wave of power wash over me, and the flames flickering over the Titan dulled. "You are responsible?"

"You must have guessed by now? Although, I suppose you are quite stupid."

"How long has it been since you were awoken?" Poseidon growled.

Atlas laughed. "I'm not wasting my time on you two, when there are so many more pleasant ways to pass moments in Aphrodite's realm. I think Kalypso is waiting for me, with a drink."

With one last craze-filled look, he strode away. My limbs loosened as he left, and I turned to Poseidon. He looked furious, and stone was spreading across his exposed skin.

"What was he talking about?"

"He is causing the stone blight."

"What?" I gaped at the sea god.

"I suspected he was, and it is important that it is confirmed. I must inform Galatea."

"So, that's why only Aquarius is suffering from the ailment? It's an attack on you."

"Yes. But my people are paying." Soft rage laced his bitter words.

"What did you do? Why did he say it was ironic?"

I didn't expect him to tell me, but when he looked into my eyes I didn't see the tight refusal that I had on previously asking about his feud with Atlas. Instead, more sadness filled the depths of his fierce blue eyes. "I do not want to tell you."

"Why not?"

"Many reasons."

"Are you... ashamed of what you did?" I barely whispered the words, somehow feeling like I was treading on thinner ice talking to him like this than when I yelled or swore at him.

"Yes. I do not regret my actions. But I do not wish to relive them. Or speak of them." He straightened as he spoke, his commanding presence growing, leaving no room to ask more.

I nodded. It was more than he had given me before, and he had been honest. That was enough. For today, at least.

"Do you, erm, want to dance?" The question left my lips of its own volition. A harp was playing, but there was a deep beat behind it, and it was penetrating my consciousness somehow, pulling me to it.

Poseidon looked at me, eyes sparking with light. "Music in the realm of love is a dangerous thing," he said, his voice husky. "It has a power of its own."

"I like it," I said.

"You're supposed to like it." He looked at me a second longer, before speaking again. "I need to talk to Galatea about the blight. I will return."

I watched him leave, wondering why the hell I'd asked him to dance.

I'd been mad at him getting all jealous about Silos literally less than ten minutes earlier.

*You weren't really mad.* Lily's voice popped into my head, her image floating swiftly into my mind. *You want him to be jealous.*

I sucked on my cocktail, refusing to answer. Mainly because she was right. Embarrassing as it was to admit to him that I was a virgin, there was a part of me that couldn't believe a god like Poseidon would give a shit about my relationship status. It was the same part of me that couldn't stomach the idea of him with someone else.

*It's the marriage bond,* I told Lily. *It must be.*

*Yeah, sure. Nothing to do with the fact that he's seven solid feet of muscle, wrapped in the raw power of the ocean, and he looks at you like you're the only thing that could tip him over the edge.*

I leaped on her words, ignoring the ones I didn't want to respond to. *Why is that? Why does he always act like he's about to lose control when he's around me? Maybe it's the stone illness, making him edgy.*

Lily laughed. *Dance with him. I think you'll work it out for yourself.*

I gulped more watermelon drink. *Work what out?*

*The tension between you two. And don't worry, I will be making myself scarce, I promise.*

*Lily! As if anything like that would—*

"Do you still want to dance?" Poseidon melted out of the crowd, hand held out toward me.

"I, erm, I'm—" All my confidence vanished.

"Technically, you are my queen. And I think it would be good to show Atlas some solidarity. It will anger him."

"Well. In the name of angering that jerk, let's dance," I said, steeling myself and taking his hand.

# ALMI

*W*e weren't the only ones on the dance floor. Couples were everywhere, many with their eyes closed, and a rhythmic sway to their movements as they pressed against one another.

"How can dancing to a harp be sexy?"

A few faces turned my way as I mumbled the words, drawn by Poseidon's presence. "This is the realm of love. Eros is here now." He pointed, and I saw a man standing at the edge of the room, framed by the water beyond.

Not just any man. He was ridiculously attractive, and not in a way that was dignified or regal, but in a way that made me think all sorts of things I usually only thought about when I was alone. He was broad and muscular, and wearing human clothes, tight pants and a shirt. His hair was dirty blond and I could see his bright blue eyes clearly as they fell on us.

"We must converse with him, as is polite." Poseidon's voice was sharp, and I wondered if there was something between the two gods as we made our way to the water's edge.

"Poseidon," Eros nodded as we reached him. "And Almi," he said, turning to me.

"Hello," I answered. I felt no waves of power like I did from the other Olympians, just a pleasant, relaxing sort of feeling.

"I'm sorry about my mom's sea garden trying to kill you," he smiled at me.

"I doubt that," Poseidon answered, before I could speak.

Eros looked slowly at him. "How is my mother?"

"Ask Hades."

"Sadly, he is engaged with Apollo, elsewhere, this evening." Eros' smile was still present, but there was a palpable tension between the two of them.

"Well, Aphrodite is in his care now."

A tense second or two passed, then Eros' full-lipped smile broadened, reaching his eyes. "You know, she can get a little crazy at times. Going after Ares like that..." He shrugged. "I'm sure a short spell in the Underworld won't do her any harm. And it's given me a chance to redecorate." He grinned as he nodded at the back wall.

"Very classy," Poseidon said, rolling his eyes.

Eros ignored him, looking to me instead. "Don't let this one fool you," he said. "This grumpy, stoic, boring vibe he puts out? It's all bullshit. I'm a god of desire, and let me tell you, this guy is fucking full to the brim with that shit. It's near killing him keeping it under control all the time."

I swallowed, my cheeks heating, as Eros' sparkling eyes bore into mine.

"Enough, Eros," Poseidon growled.

The god looked at Poseidon. "I'm just saying it how it is. If you don't let some of that shit out, it'll kill you. You'll explode."

"You are immature, and utterly unpracticed in self-control. I need no advice from you."

"Wrong. On a number of accounts. And anyway, who said I was talking about sex? Which, incidentally, there is nothing immature about."

The way he said the word sex made heat wash over me, leaving me even more flustered.

Poseidon growled his name in warning. "I said, enough."

"Desire is a broad word, Mr. Sea King. Deny yourself everything you want, and it won't just be your own life you ruin."

"I have had enough of your advice for one evening," Poseidon snapped suddenly.

Eros shrugged again, his smile still firmly in place. "Your funeral. Have a nice time, Almi. Make the most of the place."

He winked at me before he turned away, and I could have sworn the volume of the music increased, a new note on the harp setting my nerves tingling as the sensual beat pounded enticingly behind the melodic tune.

"He's got a point, you know."

"He's an idiot."

I turned to Poseidon, trying to tamper down the swirling heat wrapping around me, and my heightening senses. "I'm not talking about, you know, *sex*, either." I coughed awkwardly. "When we were in the stables, I could see how much you miss flying. You should let yourself do more things you want to."

The memory of that smile, only seen twice and seared into my damn brain, leaped to my mind. "You should smile more."

His hard gaze softened at my words, and emotion filled his eyes. "You speak of things you do not understand."

"Then make me understand."

I could see his indecision as he stared at me. "The prophecy," he said eventually.

"What about it?"

"You did not hear it all." Poseidon's chest lifted as he took a long breath. "The part you do not know is important. To both of us. I want to take you to the Oracle. I want you to hear the rest."

A fluttering in my stomach accompanied his words. I had spent years wondering about the prophecy, hating the Oracle for ruining mine and my sister's lives. The words of the prophecy came to me clearly.

*'He who possesses the heart of a Nereid shall possess the Heart of the Ocean. True love is not a necessity, pure possession will seal the deal.'*

But... there had been more. A part I had ignored, because it had no relevance to our situation at all, and because Poseidon had cut it off, mid-sentence. I struggled to remember it.

Something about true love not going unnoticed?

I needed to get to the sketchbook, check what had been said.

"Why can't you just tell me?" I asked Poseidon.

"Firstly, I am hopeful that it may have changed. Secondly, you will have a hundred more questions that I can't answer, but the Oracle might be able to."

"Do prophecies change?"

"Rarely. But sometimes."

"If it involves me, then I have a right to know. Just tell me."

"We can only win these Trials as a team, and I am not willing to jeopardize our lives, and the safety of my realm, with personal matters right now. We must wait until the Trials are over, and I have dealt with Atlas."

"Personal matters?" I muttered, glaring at him. "That's what you're calling this? Lily's life might depend on these *personal matters*. Hell, everyone affected by the blight could depend on them."

"If I don't win these Trials, they will no longer be my subjects to rescue."

The gravity of his words slowly sunk in. I remembered what Athena had said about how dangerous Atlas taking one of the twelve realms could be to Olympus, and how important it was that Poseidon win.

He was right. Atlas was the far more immediate danger.

"I am sorry."

I blinked in shock at his words. I had been about to agree with him, commit to winning the Trials. I had not expected an apology.

"For not telling me about the prophecy?"

He stepped close, startling me as he lifted my hand in his and pressed it to his hard chest. "Yes. For that. But I am also sorry for what I have done to you and your sister. I am sorry for the pain I have caused you. I am sorry for the time you have been alone."

"You are?"

"I am."

He bent his head, and brushed his lips against mine, the lightness clearly a request for permission.

"I thought you wanted to dance?" I whispered.

"I do not dance," he said. "I want to watch you dance."

"You do?" I asked, surprised.

"I do. Dance for me."

He pulled me into his arms, slipping one arm around my waist.

I didn't argue with him. I closed my eyes, and allowed myself to enter the music, the feel of his hands against my body, the scent of him around me, the electricity in the air all surrounding me, pulling me in and sweeping me away.

I let go, for the first time in what felt like forever, nothing hammering at my mind, compelling me to action. I was completely at peace, lost to the deep, sensual beat of the music. I was warm within the circle of his arms, and if he had ever been my enemy, I knew I now had nothing to fear.

I felt the light brush of his lips against my neck, the gentle brush of his breath against my ear. When my eyes flickered open, he was watching me, his eyes vibrant, powerful, and sparkling with blue fire.

Feeling bold, I placed both my hands on his chest, letting them run down his torso, over his impressive six-pack and back up to his shoulders. I arched my neck and kissed him, my tongue reaching out to taste his firm lips. He responded with a groan, his arms tightening around me and pulling me closer. His kiss deepened. I felt his hands slide over the bare skin of my back, down to my bottom, pulling me up against him. An ache rose within me, and I embraced it.

"Do you know where all those doors at the back of the room lead?" he growled against my mouth.

"No," I breathed back.

"They are magic. Private rooms for guests of Aphrodite who want to be alone. They give the occupant exactly what they want, when they want it." He moved his head back to gaze down into my face. Another request for permission, I realized, and nerves fired through me as I dazedly worked out what he was suggesting.

"I... I didn't know that," I said, trying to slow my racing heart, and building desire. "Like the Room of Requirement but for sex?" I made an awkward attempt at a joke, panic trickling through me along with pounding need.

"I have no idea what you are talking about, but I know what you require. Have you really, truly never been touched?" His voice was tense.

"Never."

"I will take my time. I will make your long wait worth every second."

# ALMI

*H*is mouth closed over mine again, and I clung to him, lost in the feel of his lips, his tongue, the way his body moved with mine. I heard the music change, but I didn't care. I wanted, needed, to be with him.

He took my hand in his and led me through the crowd of dancers gyrating to the new tune. Nobody so much as cast a glance at us.

"Choose a door."

Almost breathless with anticipation, I didn't even look at the decorations on them, just pushed the nearest one open.

I stepped into something that looked like it had been dreamed up in a Disney movie. A dirty Disney movie.

A huge, four-poster bed, with a canopy of soft drapes stood in the center of the room. The bedding was a rich navy blue, and the walls were adorned with more soft hanging fabric, in teals and turquoises. All of them were

419

adorned with exquisite illustrations of couples pleasuring each other.

I turned back to Poseidon, and before I could say a thing, his huge hands gripped my hips and he lifted me from my feet, kicking the door closed behind him.

He set me down on the massive bed, kneeling between my parted legs, the skirt of my dress tangling between us.

A tiny voice pushed through my hazy desire. "Almi?"

Kryvo!

"Can you send my starfish back to my room please?" I whispered.

A smile pulled at the corner of Poseidon's mouth, and there was a tiny flash by my collar.

He leaned forward, kissing along my jaw, down my neck. "Do you know what I wanted to do when I saw you tonight?" he whispered, his voice husky with desire.

I shook my head.

"I wanted to lay you on a bed and do this," he growled, and then he pulled me to him, and kissed me once more. It was a possessive, demanding kiss, and my body responded to every move. I was lost in a sea of anticipation. I moaned as he pulled away again.

He moved back and undid the clasp on his toga. I watched as he did, mesmerized by his smooth skin, the play of muscles under his tanned flesh. He reached for me again, this time running his hands up my shins, slowly lifting the fabric of my skirts.

A tiny worm of fear worked through me at the foreign touch, and he paused. He lifted his hand to my jaw, stroking a thumb along my lip.

"I will just give you a taste of the pleasure you deserve. And only if you want it."

"We're not going to..." I fumbled for the right word, trying not to sound immature or stupid. "Go all the way?" I mumbled eventually.

He tensed, his bare chest heaving as he sucked in a breath. "I would do anything to claim you right here, right now, Almi," he growled. "But no. I just want to show you how good you can feel."

I tried to force out my desperation for him long enough to think rationally.

I wanted him. I knew that. And I trusted him. He wouldn't push me any further than I wanted to go.

I nodded. "Show me."


He pulled me even tighter against him, his fingers brushing against my skin as he kissed me deeply. I could feel his arousal hard against my stomach, and knowing he wanted me as much as I wanted him made even more desire fire through my body.

I moaned, wrapping my arms around him, but he pulled back, eyes burning blue.

Slowly, he lifted my skirts higher, exposing my panties. He didn't move any faster as he hooked his fingers into the waistband of my underwear. I lifted my hips to let him remove them.

A tidal wave of self-consciousness slammed into me as he stared at my nakedness - the only man who ever had. I instinctively brought my knees back together as far as I could with him kneeling between them.

His eyes locked on mine, wilder than I'd ever seen them.

"You are perfect. So perfect."

Some of the discomfort leaked away at his words. He touched my jaw once more, drawing my face to his, and I opened my legs again to let him lean into me, to plant soft kisses along my neck.

"So perfect."

The rest of my awkward fear vanished with each kiss, each careful caress of his hands.

He slipped his hand back to my knee, rubbing his thumb in slow circles but not moving any further up my leg. I whimpered and arched my back, needing more. His eyes cut to mine.

I reached forward, tentatively running my fingers down his chest, across his stomach and lower. He groaned as my fingers brushed against him, and a massive bolt of need stunned me as I realized how big he was.

*How in the hell would that work?*

Slowly, he lifted my hand away from him, and I reluctantly let him. "Let me concentrate on you," he growled.

There was something in his eyes that I didn't understand. Something reverent, almost.

I watched, breathless, as his hands slid up my thighs, then lifted my hips as he slid his fingers between my legs, kissing me again at the same time. His tongue probed, seeking entry. I opened my mouth, allowing him in and his tongue slid against mine at the same time he ran one finger along my wetness.

He spoke against my lips, his tone coarse, heavy with need that my entire body was mirroring. "I want you to feel good." His finger stroked along me again, and I gasped. "I want to touch you until you can barely breathe."

He began to rub small circles over me, concentrated on my clitoris, and it felt nothing like it had when I had tried on my own,

"Oh my god." My words were lost to his mouth, and I bucked against his hand, wanting more pressure.

But instead, he stopped, dipping his fingers to my entrance. I felt myself tense, and he paused.

"Do you trust me?" His finger flicked against me, gentle and exquisite.

I nodded. "Yes."

He pressed one finger into me, and my head tipped back, my eyes closing. I could feel the intensity of his stare, but all I could focus on was the unexpected, unfamiliar pleasure of his touch.

My stomach muscles contracted as he moved his finger inside me, stroking, exploring, and a long moan escaped my mouth as he pulled it out slowly, only to slide back in again with a second.

A slight bite of pain emanated from my core, but it faded in an instant, replaced by a pressure that I could barely tolerate, yet never wanted to end.

His thumb moved, and the gentle pressure on my clitoris returned. Another, louder moan sounded from my throat, and I heard him growl.

"Look at me."

I opened my eyes, lifting my head and staring into his burning eyes. I was trembling, my body tensing against the incredible feeling of his touch. He leaned closer, scratching his teeth along my throat, his fingers moving faster inside me. The pressure built as he watched my face, and he spoke again, the strain in his voice palpable.

"I want your first orgasm to be something you'll never forget."

A thousand butterflies took flight in my stomach, and I forgot to breathe as the pressure built into something I could no longer contain. Before I knew what was happening, a sense of falling and a flash of heat had me crying out. My hands gripped his shoulders as my head fell back, and my entire body convulsed with pleasure, every nerve ending on fire.

I lurched forward, pressing my face against his neck, whimpering as my orgasm poured through me, obliterating every other emotion.

"That's it," he growled, his lips moving along my jaw. "Let go."

And I did. My vision came in and out of focus as I came down from the eruption of pleasure, and I realized with a jolt of embarrassment that I was mumbling his name. He kissed along my throat, across my collar and my chest, back up to my lips, fingers stroking gently across me, playing, teasing me back to reality.

Then his kisses moved, and I sat up sharply, my eyes flying open as I felt his lips on my inner thigh.

"What are--"

"Lie back. This time, when you come, I want to hear my name. Loudly."

I moaned, my chest tight, and dropped my head back onto the pillow as his tongue and lips moved to my other thigh.

The pressure was building again already, and I could

feel him watching me as his lips and tongue moved along my skin, closer, closer to my aching center. Just when I thought I couldn't take any more of the need, his tongue flicked over me and my nerves were so raw that a bolt of sensation shot straight up my spine. I jerked under him, and his hands clamped over my hips, holding me still.

"Fuck, you taste divine."

I answered him with a moan. His tongue moved, swirling, gently at first, then harder as I pressed myself against him. I felt his finger, stroking along me, then slowly sliding inside me.

"Oh fuck," I gasped, as raw pleasure exploded through me. But before it could take me over completely, he withdrew his fingers, and the pressure of his tongue lessened to a tickle.

"Not yet, my queen."

My senses all fuzzed together.

"Please," I gasped, scrambling to my elbows so that I could look into his face.

He was beautiful. Hard and powerful and fierce and wild. I would be his if he asked me. At that moment, I would do any single thing he asked of me.

My emotions must have been clear on my face, because dark, wild desire flashed in his eyes, and then his mouth closed over me, his fingers working their blissful magic once more. I dropped back onto the pillows and allowed his hands and his mouth and his tongue and the fire in his eyes to take charge of my body.

He took me to the edge three more times, and each time, he pulled back and kept me from letting go completely. His breath was hot against my core, his fingers moving with agonizing slowness as I writhed, begging. I felt like I was burning up, every single cell crying out for his touch.

I didn't know how much more I could take, but I never wanted it to end.

"Now."

He growled one word against me, and it was enough.

My back arched and I came, but instead of the freefall it had been the last time, I was thrown into a maelstrom of pleasure. My core pulsed, my skin prickling and my toes curling as I cried out his name, wave after wave of release crashing over me.

"Yes," he growled, his fingers inside me, his tongue on my clit. "That's it."

He kept going until I was shaking, my body near collapse, my entire mind consumed by the pleasure his hands and his mouth were delivering. Only when the last tremors had faded did he ease back, planting soft kisses along my thighs.

I sucked in air, trembling. When my eyes cleared and I could focus again, he was standing, watching me. His erection was obvious under his toga, and it sent fresh waves of need pounding through me. What would it feel like, for him to slide that inside me instead of his fingers?

My core pulsed at the thought, and I sat up, pushing my hair from my face. "I want you," I said, my own voice hoarse.

His hands clenched at his sides, power bright in his eyes. "No."

"But—"

He cut me off, his voice louder than it needed to be.

"Almi, I am begging you. Do you have any idea how much I want you? To feel you around my cock, to fuck you until you scream my name over and over?" He ground his teeth as my eyes widened. "No, you must stop." Waves rolled in his eyes, his jaw tense.

I stared at him a moment longer, trying to wrestle my feelings under control.

I wanted him so badly it hurt. And I could see and hear how much he wanted it too.

If he didn't want to do this today, here, then he must have his reasons. And honestly, I could understand. When I forced myself to think rationally through my heady desires, this wasn't the place I wanted to lose my virginity either.

I had no doubt in my mind that it was with him that I would do so though. I was connected to him far more deeply than I could ever have guessed. His expertise went farther than clever fingers or tongue. It was as though he'd known me, known my body, known my limits.

"Then kiss me," I said.

Some of the tension relaxed in his shoulders, his eyes softening. He moved back to the bed, and I arranged my skirt across my legs, trying to prove to him that I wasn't going to try to mount him. Though it took more willpower than I knew I had when he did sit beside me, cock clear through the fabric of his toga, not to climb into his lap.

I bit my lip as my eyes snagged on it, then dragged them to his face. "That was… amazing."

"I didn't hurt you?"

I shook my head. "Not a bit."

"I will never hurt you. I meant what I said before. I will always save you. Always."

I wanted to ask him why. I wanted to understand how he could feel so intensely for a woman he had ignored his whole life. But instead, I found myself leaning forward and touching my lips to his, pushing my hand into his hair, and pulling him close to me.

"And I you," I said, the words coming instinctively.

A gong sounded, and pain pierced my skull, sharp and startling and so unlike the explosion of pleasure I had just experienced.

"It is time to count the shells!" There was a harsh flash of red light, and suddenly I was standing in the main room again. My skin burned as I felt about myself, making sure my skirts were straight and trying not to look like we'd been up to exactly what we *had* been up to — although I was probably of the least interest in the room. Some unfortunate folk had clearly been enjoying the palace's atmosphere a little more... *unclothed* than I had been. I tried not to look, as humans and creatures alike scrabbled to arrange themselves more modestly.

Poseidon was beside me, and he gripped my hand, glaring at Atlas. The Titan was leaning against a column, smiling unsettlingly at everyone. Kalypso was a few feet from him, Polybotes towered over everybody in the room on my left, and Ceto was at the front of the group, everyone giving her a wide berth.

"Hey, the pleasure rooms in this realm are completely private, you can't just summon people out of them!" Eros came stamping through the crowd, his gorgeous smile conspicuously absent.

"I think you'll find I can," Atlas said. "Your pathetic Olympian magic is no match for my Titan power, as I just demonstrated."

Anger and a teeny hint of fear worked its way through me. Atlas *was* strong. He had infiltrated Poseidon's palace, and so far, little seemed beyond his capability.

"You will not be welcome here again." Eros folded his arms across his toga-clad chest.

"I weep for my loss," Atlas said sarcastically. "I'm sure your mother will beg to have me in her palace when the Poseidon Trials are over. In fact, I'm sure your mother will beg to have me, period."

Atlas' manic smile was back, and power burst from Eros as massive white wings erupted from his back.

Athena and Poseidon stepped forward together, along with the Hawaiian-shirt-wearing Dionysus and a man with short red hair, who I was sure was Hermes.

"Atlas, we agreed to these Trials and nothing more. Please conduct them presently." Athena's lyrical, deep voice was so formal she reminded me of a schoolteacher. "Eros, we will be leaving your realm imminently, please step back." She oozed command, and I wasn't surprised when Eros did as she asked him. He kept his furious glare trained on Atlas though.

"As you wish, mighty Athena," Atlas said with a mock bow. He waved his hand as he straightened, and the flame dish appeared, showing the vases full of shells. "Kalypso found two shells, bringing her score to nine." The beautiful water goddess scowled. "Now, after finding three shells, Ceto is at ten." The mother of sea monsters squelched on the glass floor as her vase filled higher. "Polybotes got two shells, making his total five." Atlas fixed his eyes on me. "Which means that with her two shells, Almi is just ahead of him, at six."

"No." I shook my head hard. "I got no shells in the last Trial, they were Poseidon's."

"No, I was watching. I saw you get both of them."

"Last time you said it was who was holding them when the Trial ended!"

He shrugged. "I changed my mind."

Fury coursed through me, but when Poseidon squeezed my hand and I looked at him, I didn't see my anger reflected in his face.

"We will talk alone," he said, so quietly I was pretty sure only I heard him.

"So, that means Poseidon still has zero shells!" Atlas announced, holding his arms up. "The mighty King of the Sea, and he can't win one solitary shell." He tutted, shaking his head. "Time for another go, I think."

With a flash, the room vanished.

# ALMI

*I* wasn't surprised when I found myself in water, but I was surprised by how dark it was. I thrashed around in a panic, trying to get my bearings, and sending a silent plea for the breathing bubbles.

I felt them before I saw them, rushing around my face, cool compared to the water. Tentatively I parted my lips. Air, not water flowed between them.

"Thanks, air," I said gratefully, slowing my movements and trying to see what was around me.

The only light was not coming from above me, but below me, which had caused my disorientation. It was coming from a river of glowing lava, hot jets of water shooting up from the cracks in the black rock of the ground. As my eyes adjusted to the gloom, I started to pick out details, though I was unable to see Poseidon.

The landscape was like something from a nightmare, where hell met the bottom of the ocean.

A faint glow caught my eye and I tensed, until I realized it wasn't red, like the lava or the rotbloods. It was blue.

Poseidon, I saw with relief. He moved through the water with no resistance at all, reaching me fast.

"Are you okay?" his gurgled voice asked.

"Yes. But— I don't have Kryvo."

The realization smacked into me.

"He's safe," Poseidon said, taking my hand. "We must hurry. We have to find as many shells as we can."

"What's the point? He just gives them to me anyway."

"Which is a good thing. If they were split between us, neither of us would have a chance of beating Ceto or Kalypso by now."

He was right, I realized, as my brain caught up. "Ha!"

A tiny smile pulled at Poseidon's lips in the darkness. "He has shot himself in the foot, trying to humiliate me. Come."

We swam through the water, the river of lava beneath us widening, the speed of the sludgy orange liquid picking up as we moved along it. Something flickered with light, and I tugged on Poseidon's hand as I twisted to look. He stopped instantly, and I let go of him and turned to what had caught my attention.

It was a giant clam shell by the side of the river of lava, closed but pulsing with a very faint blue light.

Poseidon zoomed down toward it, and I followed him, swimming fast but not so fast I would tire myself out. By the time I reached him he was trying to prize open the huge shell with his hands. It was as wide as I was tall, the back half of it fused to the rocky ground. The water was hot so close to the lava.

Poseidon lifted his arm over his shoulder and slid his dagger out of the back of his ocean-toga. With an obvious effort, he wedged the tip of the blade into the clam. Slowly, the shell began to creak open.

I barely kept back a scream as the clam sprang open suddenly, spewing forth hundreds of tiny snakes. All of them were burning red or orange, looking as though they were made from the lava itself. They wiggled through the water at speed in every direction, and before I could do a thing, a handful of the foot-long snakes had reached me. They whipped me with their tails as they surrounded me, leaving searing hot pain where they touched my skin. I yanked the blade Galatea had loaned me from my leg strap and swiped at a snake that had just whipped its tail across the top of my arm. It hissed as I made contact.

I heard a distant growling sound and looked back at the clam. Poseidon was hacking away at a mass of the little snakes in the very middle of the now open shell, trying to get them away from whatever it was they were protecting in the middle.

"Air, if you could help out right now, I'd sure be grateful!"

Pain shot through my wrist, and I beat at the snake that was trying to wind itself around my arm. Blisters were popping up on my skin where they'd touched me, and I gritted my teeth and brandished my blade at the bright, burning serpents.

Another roar reached me through the water, and an explosion of the lava snakes blasted away from Poseidon, revealing a black chest the size of a jewelry box. He tipped forward in the water, snapping the lid open fast and swiping up a tiny, gleaming, white shell. He whizzed through the water toward me, grabbed my wrist and pulled me away from the snakes. I winced as his hands touched the blistered skin on my arm, and his head snapped round to mine.

Anger flashed in his bright eyes as he saw the evidence of the little lava serpents.

"One shell down," I said, as cheerfully as I could.

He slowed a little, having put some distance between us and the snakes, then passed me the shell. I took it, inserting it carefully into my bra, and he gestured for us to keep moving.

It was so dark it would have been easy to get lost, and I was glad when Poseidon began following the glowing river again.

An eerie orange glow fell over the black rock as more and more of the ground was covered in the surging molten red liquid. Just a moment later, the ground beneath us fell away, and the river of lava turned into a frigging *waterfall* of lava.

It was as beautiful as it was terrifying, streams of bright red and orange crashing over the edge of the rocky cliff into a massive pool far below us. Poseidon tilted his body in the water and headed down, keeping us a fair distance from the lavafall.

I could see movement in the lava as it fell, as though life churned inside it. I was just thinking how unnatural the whole thing felt, when a rotblood materialized from the falling lava. The inky red, blood-like liquid that the creature was made from swirled in tendrils out of the lava and solidified into the shark-shaped monster, and its huge mouth opened, rows and rows of sharp teeth visible as it sped through the water.

# ALMI

*F*ear gripped me, but as I began to react I realized it wasn't swimming toward us. Poseidon slowed, jerked us back and stopped, then pointed.

Ceto.

The goddess was deeper than us, down by the huge pool, and she was trying to fish something out of the lava with a long, jagged bit of rock. The rotblood was heading straight for her.

At the last moment, she looked up and saw the demon shark creature. I expected her to swim away, but all she did was flick one of her tentacles, her expression barely even changing. Bright red liquid oozed from the tentacle, clouding around the rotblood. It jerked in the water, coming to a complete stop just a few feet over her head. With one final convulsion, it floated down the rocks beside her, unmoving.

"I do not want to be poisoned again."

Poseidon looked at me. "We will go back the way we came."

But no sooner had we started to turn, when a cackling sound reached me, followed by a blast of warm water.

We both whirled back to see Ceto rising in the water, red eyes fixed on us.

"Air!" Poseidon gave my hand a hard squeeze, before letting go of it. I was both touched and alarmed he appeared to think I could handle myself.

Three of Ceto's tentacles wriggled before us, her skin rippling just like the rotbloods. Liquid poured from the three tentacles, red, green, and black in color. Poseidon held up his hand, and a ribbon of water shot from his palm, expanding into a wall as it moved toward her.

A small change in the movement of the water around me suddenly turned into a large change, and a ribbon of air appeared in front of me, tightening into the little whirlpool.

"Hey!" I said, delightedly. "Help get rid of the poison!"

The little whirlpool whizzed off, spinning around Poseidon enough to lift his toga, before charging toward his wall of water. The second the two met, a blast of energy rolled through me, starting at the top of my head, and flowing deliciously through my whole body. My skin tingled, and all I could think about was him. When I locked my eyes on his face, he turned, and I knew without question that he could feel it too. A new light shone in his eyes, not the usual, piercing blue, but a blue so pale it was almost silver.

A loud hiss made us both look back, where our hybrid whirlpool had smashed into Ceto. It was ten feet high, glowing blue water spinning with the air magic, which also had a faint silver glow. Was that what I had seen in Poseidon's eyes just then? A reflection of my air magic when the two had met?

Colored inks flew from Ceto's tentacles as she struggled. She was getting free.

"I know you've got your hands full and all, but if you get a chance, see if she has any shells on her," I told the air.

My mouth fell open as the whirlpool abruptly tipped, turning Ceto completely upside-down. The goddess made an awful grating, growling sound that set my teeth on edge, then a huge swell of dark water began to form around her.

A sense of danger seeped through me, feeling her magic build. Poseidon grabbed for my hand. "Time to go."

"Wait! We can beat her."

Poseidon raised an eyebrow, and I saw the stone edging his jaw.

But he nodded. "On the count of three, we send her flying, just like Kalypso."

"Might have to be a count of one," I said, as I turned back to her. She was surrounded by a swirling black mass of red-veined lava, our whirlpool significantly slower around her, as though it were struggling to contain her.

"Now!"

I threw as much mental command as I could into my plea as Poseidon held up both his hands. "Send her as far from here as you can!"

The whirlpool glowed silver and blue, so bright I had to shield my eyes. Ceto hissed again, and then the whole thing rose through the water, taking her with it as it got high above the lavafall crater. The spinning got faster, and then Ceto burst out of the side of the whirlpool, her slimy body flying through the water, quickly lost to the gloom.

"Fuck! Did you see that?" I turned to Poseidon, unable to keep my excitement hidden. His eyes were still alive with glowing energy when they met mine. Surprising me, he moved forward, planting a brief but fierce kiss on my lips.

When he pulled away I moved with him, wanting more, but my little whirlpool forced its way between us, dancing through the gloomy water. There, in the middle of the swirling air and illuminated by its faint silver glow, was a shell.

"You little thief!" I exclaimed. "You actually managed to steal one of her shells? You're so clever!"

The whirlpool soared up and around us, lifting Poseidon's toga once again as it went, and I laughed as he scowled at it.

"We must move on. Without your emotional support starfish, we do not know how much time we have left." He reached for my hand as I felt a pang of unease at not having Kryvo with me.

"Yes. More shells."

We moved back into the lavafall crater, where there was a series of small, interconnected pools of lava, the ooze dripping from one into the other over the gentle slope. Poseidon headed straight for where Ceto had been, and I saw a small wooden chest sitting on a little island in one of the pools. My little whirlpool had accompanied us, flitting around us like it was on a serious caffeine rush, never staying still for a second. Not that I minded. I was quite happy to have air with me.

"Can you get the chest?" I asked it.

It zoomed toward the middle of the lava pool, and as it spun around the box, the lid flipped open. Poseidon swam higher so that we could see into it, but there was no shell. There was a small piece of paper.

My whirlpool shrunk, so that it was only six inches tall, and dipped into the chest. When it rose, the paper was in its center, and it whizzed back to me.

I unfolded the paper, and Poseidon moved closer to see. There was a crude drawing of a curved shape, and a dotted line crossing it, with an X at the end.

"I think it means under the lavafall."

"What? As in, go through the frigging lava?"

"Yes. It would be challenging enough for a deadly trial."

I looked nervously at the torrent of lava plunging over the drop-off and into the pool below. "The same lavafall that burps out demon sharks?"

"Yes. The very same."

"We need to do what we did before. Combine the water with your air," Poseidon said.

I nodded. "To make a clearing through the lava?"

"Exactly."

"You up for that?" I asked my whirlpool. It bounced in

the water, then expanded suddenly, making itself the same size as me.

Poseidon lifted his hand, ribbons of water flowing from his palm. Almost majestically, they threaded themselves into the whirlpool, beams of shining light spinning before us. I felt the same bolt of energy take over my body, the heady, intoxicating feeling filling me from head to toe.

The whirlpool moved, tipping and narrowing so that it became a horizontal tube. With a flourish, it powered toward the lava fall, stopping in the center. The lava flowed over each side of it, a perfect tunnel created through the sheet of molten liquid. I started to celebrate, turning to Poseidon, but a dull pain entered my head, seeping through me. The top of the tunnel dipped, and Poseidon squeezed my hand.

"Focus. We must go now. Do not lose concentration."

I did as he said, pouring all my thoughts into the whirlpool.

*Keep the tunnel open and steady. You can do it,* I thought, as I got closer. Heat overwhelmed me, and the tunnel side vanished, allowing lava to pour down exactly where we would be if we were inside.

"Focus!"

*The heat won't kill you,* Lily's voice said in my mind. *Concentrate on the air. Feel it. Imagine standing on the deck of that Crosswind, the wind whipping around you, taking you anywhere you want to go. Feel the wind.*

I did as she said, not risking closing my eyes, but trying to transport all my other senses just as she had described.

"We'll go one at a time. You first."

Poseidon let go of my hand, and with a deep breath and a sick feeling in my stomach, I swam through the air tunnel.

I was through in less than a second, but it felt like an age. I didn't stop to take in my new surroundings, just whirled around to see Poseidon coming through safely. As soon as he was by my side the whirlpool squished to nothing, the pain leeching through me vanishing.

"Air? Are you okay?"

There was movement on the now complete curtain of lava right in front of us, and I held my breath, terrified of a rotblood bursting forth.

But it was my little whirlpool that emerged. It spun fast, tiny droplets of lava soaring from it, almost like a dog shaking itself.

"You did good," I told it. To my surprise, it moved to Poseidon, nudging at his palms.

"I think it likes your water," I said.

"They are a good team." His eyes fixed on mine, and I knew he wasn't just talking about the magic.

A cracking sound forced us to look away from each other.

The cliff behind us was lit clearly by the lavafall that we were now behind, and the rock was shifting, creaking and cracking as we watched. It didn't look like it was in imminent danger of collapsing, more that it had its own life.

Poseidon took my hand, and we headed deeper, sticking close to the wall. It wasn't long before we came across a very wide, shallow cave.

. . .

Keeping my eyes wide open in preparation for rotbloods, I scanned the cave. It was lit by an orange glow coming from the cracks in the black rock at the back. We swam cautiously along the length of the cave, and I wished Kryvo was there to tell us how much time we had. And to distract me from my growing unease.

"There," I said, pointing.

There was a stone statue, standing in the cave a little further along. We swam toward it, and I couldn't help my curiosity as its details became clear.

It was clearly very old, the stone chipped and worn. It was of a woman, very beautiful, wearing a toga and an extravagant crown. But rather than sit on hair, the crown was wrapped around a nest of snakes. There must have been a dozen making up her hair, and the detail in their faces was exquisite.

Poseidon jerked to a stop as we got within a few feet.

"She's beautiful," I said.

"We need to find the shell." His clipped tone made me remember the time pressure we were under, and I nodded.

I became aware of movement in my peripheral vision, and turned my head, hoping it was my whirlpool.

It wasn't. The glowing red swirls of a rotblood were growing clearer as it moved through the cave toward us.

Poseidon pulled my hand, making me look the other way. Another rotblood.

"Quickly."

I swam to the statue, looking carefully at the snakes first, as they drew the most attention.

When I reached forward to touch it though, Poseidon

slapped my hands away, pressing his own fingertips to the stone before I could object. I frowned at first the tension on his face, then the relief when nothing happened.

"It may have been a trap. Come on, help me search."

I nodded. "Air, can you hold off the rotbloods for a few minutes?" When I turned to locate the whirlpool, my stomach clenched. There were at least five more demon sharks closing in.

The whirlpool expanded, zooming protectively around us and the statue. "Thank you," I whispered, then turned back to the statue. Poseidon was running his hands over the snakes, so I dipped in the water, inspecting the rest of the carving.

She was wearing a belt, I saw, and in the center was an emblem so worn I couldn't make it out. It was orb-like in shape, and I ran my fingers around it, trying to see if it would reveal anything not immediately obvious.

I tugged a little too hard, and the orb came off in my hand. "Shit," I muttered, turning it over. There was a tiny hole in the back. "Poseidon!"

He turned to me and I held it up. A ribbon of water left his fingertip, and narrowed into a tiny point, slipping into the pinprick hole.

Red light flashed to my side, and I glanced sideways to see my whirlpool ram into a rotblood, sending it powering backward, before zooming to my other side to deal with another one.

I felt a pop, and looked back at the stone orb in my hand. It had opened a crack. I tried to open it the rest of the way, but it wouldn't budge. I could just make out something written in the ancient language on the inside lip of the opening though. I held it up to Poseidon, trying to ignore the barrage of gnashing teeth trying to get past my whirlpool to get to us.

"What does it say?"

I could have sworn I saw a flicker of fear in his eyes, before he spoke one word. "Ekdíkisi."

The orb snapped open all the way, revealing a tiny red shell in its center. I reached for it, and everything went dark.

# ALMI

The palace courtyard materialized around me, and I blinked around in stunned triumph. We had done it. My *magic* had done it. It had helped us beat Ceto, survive the tests and traps, and even better – get shells.

"Three shells!" I turned, clutching at Poseidon's arm, and stilled at the wildness in his eyes as I made contact with him.

*Freedom.*

The feeling powered through me, so strong, so over-whelming, that everything else faded away but the promise in his eyes.

*A life spent soaring through the sky, blasting through the waves, sea, wind and endless, boundless time and space—*

"Almi." My name on Poseidon's lips cut off the stream of vivid thoughts, and without hesitation I lifted myself onto my tiptoes and crushed my lips to his.

I gave no thought to the folk around us, or the fact that we might be being broadcast. And nor did he.

He returned my passion with an unrivaled intensity of his own, wrapping his powerful arm around me and pulling me tight against him. Tight enough that I could feel how much he wanted me.

His tongue found mine, and desire coursed through my whole body, hot and almost painful in its urgency.

"Sire!" Galatea's shrill voice forced us apart, and I panted slightly as I turned to his first-in-command, trying not to hate her for interrupting our celebration.

When I saw the expression on her face though...something was wrong.

"It's the man you had us watch," she breathed. Poseidon tensed, eyes flicking uneasily to me. "You must come. Now."

I didn't even have time to open my mouth and ask what was happening before we flashed away.

"The bakery?" A sick feeling rolled through my gut as I blinked up at Silos' bakery. "You were watching Silos?" My words were a hoarse whisper. Poseidon didn't answer, just turned and followed Galatea toward the door. I hurried after them, fear spreading through me, as I glanced at the upper floor. *To the room where Lily was.*

The second I entered the bakery, my fear solidified into something much worse.

"Silos!" I ran forward, pushing past both Poseidon and Galatea, to where my friend was standing. "No!"

Stone. He was made from stone.

I was vaguely aware that there were more statues in the bakery, as though every one of his customers had also been turned to stone while he had been serving them.

My mind spinning, I raced for the door at the back, to the staircase.

I took the steps two at a time, bursting into Lily's room with a crash.

"Almi!" Poseidon's voice roared my name as the door slammed open.

Her bed was empty.

For a second, I couldn't breathe, my mind blanking completely.

I had been terrified of finding her as a statue, but not there at all?

"She's gone! Poseidon, she's gone!" I burst back into the bakery and froze.

Atlas was standing next to Silos' stone form, leaning against him like he was some sort of furniture.

"Where is she?" My words came out a scream, and Atlas laughed.

I looked at Poseidon, my eyes filling with angry, terrified tears. Unbridled fury filled his.

"The heart of a Nereid, huh?" Atlas said.

I'd thought I was already scared for my sister, but now I knew I was.

"You dare fucking touch her—"

He stepped forward, swiping his hand, and my threats fell away. I was moving my mouth, but no sound was coming out. Frustration made my entire body heat, and more furious tears streamed down my face.

"The thing is, Almi, Poseidon, and whoever the fuck you are,"—he said, waving a hand at Galatea—"you don't seem to understand the gravity of your situation. Almi, you especially, are under-informed." He turned his maniacal grin on me. "I've been on a little trip to see the Oracle."

"Atlas! We are mid-Trials, you can't interfere! What have you done with her sister?"

"I am not interfering. I am simply ensuring that I am in a fit state to rule your realm, when one of my minions win. By taking possession of the heart of the ocean. I assume, Almi, that he has told you the entire prophecy?"

I glared at him, and when that didn't feel like it expressed my feelings well enough, I spat at him.

His eyes darkened, and flames leapt up across his skin. "You're a vile little thing," he hissed. "I can see why he hid you away for so long."

"Why are you doing this now? Wait until the Trials are over, and I will face you one-on-one," Poseidon said.

"He knows you two will win," said Galatea, her voice loud and clear. I could have kissed her for the furious look her sentence brought to Atlas' face.

*She was right.* He was doing this because we'd just got so many shells.

Power erupted from him, a stream of fire slamming into Galatea. A wall of water burst up in front of her the same second it hit, dousing most, but not all, of the flames.

"Stop!" I screamed, visions of the bakery in flames rushing me. But no sound came out.

I ran at the Titan. He turned to me, his flames powering at me instead. But almost as though he was realizing an error, his face changed, and the fire vanished.

449

He began to laugh again. "No, no, no! I mustn't kill you! Death would be far, far too good for the wife of this monster." He turned to Poseidon, who hadn't moved. It finally occurred to me that that wasn't right, and I saw the strain in his body as he fought against some invisible force. Stone crept over his skin.

He was pinned by Atlas' power, just as I had been before.

"Where is Lily?" he ground out. Fresh tears started down my cheeks at hearing him say my sister's name.

"You want to find out? Forfeit your place in the Trials."

"I can't do that."

"Then her sister stays with me. I'm sure I can wed an unconscious sea nymph."

"I can't just hand over my realm to you."

Emotion was coursing through me. I knew Poseidon couldn't give up his realm. But how could he leave Lily in the hands of this monster?

There had to be another way.

Desperate words flowed from my lips, pleas and curses alike, but no sound came out. Hopeless frustration was causing a rage to build inside me like I had never felt.

"Then I keep the girl." Atlas shrugged his shoulders. "If your wife is of no further use to me, then perhaps it is time to repay the favor you did mine." Fire roared around him, and he turned to me.

"Atlas!" Poseidon roared, and I saw true fear in the sea god's face. Power exploded from him. I sent a desperate plea to the air to come and help me, to defend me from the maniac who had my sister.

And the air answered.

A fucking tornado burst to life before me, whipping around the gods flames and flinging them back at him. Atlas snarled as a tidal wave of water crashed over him. I screamed in dismay as the statue of Silos was knocked to the ground, along with all the other stone citizens in the bakery, and then the side wall of the building. Everyone froze for a split second as the building creaked, and I looked desperately at Poseidon.

Galatea ran to the middle of the room, her staff held high and glowing. A shield of water spewed from it as the building began to collapse around us, every statue safe inside it.

"You are pathetic!" Atlas cackled over the sound of crashing destruction. There was a flash of red, and then he was before me, his hand shooting out and gripping me by my neck. "Do you want to meet my wife, Almi? She's keen to meet you, I know." His breath seared my skin—it was so hot, and he was so close.

*Air! Help!*

The tornado slammed into us, knocking him sideways and dislodging his grip on my throat, and then Poseidon launched himself at the god. The two men rolled to the ground, water and flame crashing over them both as they fought.

"She's on her way!" Atlas yelled gleefully as he sprang to his feet. Poseidon landed his fist square in Atlas' face as he leapt up after him, and Atlas stumbled back, silver liquid running from his nose. His eyes turned completely black and when he spoke his voice was no longer his, but something out of a freaking horror film, so loud it sounded like it was coming from the earth itself.

"She's here. And she has your sister." He turned to me, his demonic eyes making my head spin and my stomach churn.

*Lily was here?*

"Do you want your sister back?"

Hope soared. "Yes!" My word actually sounded out loud, my voice returned. "Lily!"

"You'll need to convince my wife to give her to you."

I spun, looking for her. Golden snakes slithered toward us, through Galatea's shield of water. A hand pushed through the shield, green and long-fingered.

I heard Poseidon speak. "Almi, you have to go."

"What? No, not without Lily!"

"It's too dangerous."

I whirled to face him. "No! No, don't you dare take me from her again!"

"I'll get her back." His eyes were hard, filled with tortured emotion. "I promise."

I opened my mouth, but the world flashed white before I could say another word.


THE STORY CONTINUES IN SACRIFICE OF THE BRAVE KING

# SACRIFICE OF THE
# BRAVE KING

# ALMI

*I* tugged at the bedroom door. It was still locked.

I was alone and shaking, tears streaming down my face.

I had never felt so helpless.

"Why?" I yelled at the locked door. "Why are you doing this?"

I didn't know if I was raging at Poseidon or Atlas.

At that point, I fucking hated them both.

Things had finally been going well. *Better* than well. We had gotten ahead in the Trials, my magic getting stronger, our foes easier to beat. We had a very real chance of winning.

My magic growing was increasing our chances of finding the Heart of the Ocean — which meant I was getting closer to saving Lily.

And then... Then Atlas took her.

I picked up the nearest thing to me — a glass of water on the stand inside the door — and hurled it at the wall with another bellow of rage. "Fucking asshole," I screamed.

I had done nothing to him. Lily had done nothing to him.

And Poseidon... I had been starting to believe he was far more to me than an ally. But then he had sent me away. Again.

How could he? I had as much power as he did, who the fuck did he think he was to decide it was too dangerous for me?

I might have been able to talk Atlas around, or my air magic might have smashed them to pieces — there might have been a hundred ways I could have gotten Lily back. But Poseidon didn't trust me. He didn't respect me.

He just fucking sent me away.

My eyes burned as furious tears kept coming, and I looked around for something to hurl.

He had betrayed me.

Atlas may have taken my sister—and fury filled me at the thought—but Poseidon had brought me as close to him as I had ever been to anyone and then betrayed my trust. He had treated me like a child, a weakling; useless. I was used to feeling fury. But betrayal was new.

"Asshole!" I launched the entire wooden stand at the wall. A leg snapped off as it made contact, before clattering to the ground.

A small squeak reached my ears over the rush of pounding blood.

"Kryvo?"

"Almi." He sounded terrified, and a tiny bit of my rage melted away. Enough for me to hurry over to the dresser. "Please don't throw anything in my direction," he whispered.

"I'm sorry." My voice broke on the word, and my angry tears were replaced by a heaving sob that took me by surprise.

"What happened?" he asked, his voice still tiny.

I slumped onto the stool at the dresser, lifting him carefully from his cushion. I suddenly craved his warmth and the feeling of not being alone so hard I could have kissed the little starfish. I set him on my palm, and his suckers hooked in.

"Atlas killed Silos and took my sister," I choked.

"What? Why? How?"

"Poseidon was having Silos watched, and he and everyone in the bakery had been turned to stone by the time we got there, and Lily was gone." Never-ending tears rolled down my face and I swiped at them. "And then Atlas showed up, and said he had taken Lily. He tried to get Poseidon to forfeit the Trials in return for giving her back, and when Poseidon said no, Atlas said he had no need for me anymore. He said his wife was coming, and I think he meant to kill me. He said his wife had my sister with her. But before she got there Poseidon flashed me here."

Kryvo said nothing a moment, then spoke. "I need more details. Tell me again. Slowly."

"I can't! I need to get back there, to get Lily!"

"Why did Poseidon flash you away?"

"He said it was too dangerous for me to be there, but

he can barely use his magic! Persephone said the poison weakened him, and—" I banged my fist on the dresser as emotion overwhelmed me.

I was scared for Poseidon, I realized angrily.

I didn't want to be scared for him! I wanted to hate him. But the truth was, Atlas could kill him. Easily. And the thought of that was so intolerable that fresh emotion surged up inside me.

"He has Galatea with him," I said, trying to take a calming breath. "She is strong. He's not alone."

"Almi... There may be a good reason he sent you away."

My memory flashed on the green hand pushing through Galatea's shield, and I shuddered.

"I have to get back there. Now. I have to help. I have to get my sister back."

A voice suddenly boomed through my room, reverberating through the walls. "Your sister is safe. I will return to the palace as soon as I can."

"Poseidon?" I stared up at the walls, momentarily stunned. "Poseidon!" I yelled again. "Tell me what the fuck is happening!"

Nothing but silence answered me. My tears had stopped, though.

*He was safe. And Lily was safe.*

Nothing was more important than that.

"Where is he? Why the hell isn't he back here right now? I need to know what's happening!" I stood up, restless energy and adrenaline coursing through me. I kicked at the foot of the bed as I tried to swallow down my anger and failed.

"For once I wish he'd just fucking answer my questions, instead of being so cryptic and mysterious and pigheaded and—"

Kryvo cut my tirade off. "We could get answers ourselves."

"What?"

"This is probably a bad idea, but... He told you there was more of the prophecy."

"Yes."

"After you, erm, sent me away," he said, awkwardly, "did he tell you any more?"

"No."

"I have been searching the palace for anything about the Heart of the Ocean, and I can find nothing. I think..." He took a small pause. "I think we should go and see the Oracle."

I blinked. "Poseidon said he would take me to the Oracle, once the Trials were over. And... And Atlas said something about her." I sifted through my blurry memories of what had just happened. "He said he had been to see her, and that I was under-informed."

"I think we should take advantage of Poseidon not being here. I think you need to know everything you can about yourself, and how you are connected to the blight. Look at your shell."

I turned to the mirror and sucked in a breath. The green color was seeping into yellow, tinged with orange at the edges. The shell was three-quarters filled with color.

I bit down on my lip as I wiped the drying tears from my cheeks.

I had so many questions that Poseidon wouldn't

answer. He had just shown me how little he trusted me, how little respect he had for me. Why should I trust him to decide what I should and shouldn't know about my own destiny?

The green hand pushing through the water flashed into my head again, the image becoming hard to shift. Had that been Atlas' wife?

"Will the Oracle tell me what Poseidon did to Atlas' wife?"

"She might, if it is relevant. We need to go before Poseidon comes back."

"We're locked in. I don't know how to get out."

"We know a goddess who might help us," he said.

I lifted him to my face. "Kryvo, you're a fucking genius."

He flushed hot on my hand, before I set him back down on his cushion and ran to where my belt was slung on an armchair.

I rummaged through the pouches until I produced Persephone's gold rose. I clutched it tight, closed my eyes, and spoke aloud.

"Persephone, I hope you can hear me. I need your help."

The smell of the forest washed over me, and when my eyelids fluttered open, Persephone stood before me.

"Thank you, thank you, thank you for coming," I said in a rush.

"What's happening? Are you okay?"

"No. I'm not. Poseidon has locked me in here, *'for my own safety'*, and I'm done putting up with his bullshit."

Persephone cocked her head at me. Her slight build was clad in black jeans and a yellow blouse, her white hair tied up in a big messy bun on top of head. "You looked like you were getting on pretty well, last time I saw you."

"Well, that was before."

"Before what?"

I took a breath, then told her everything, as compactly as I could. "I just need you to get me to the stables. From there, I can get Blue and manage on my own."

She snorted at me, folding her arms. "I don't doubt for minute that you can manage on your own, but I don't think you *should*."

I stared at her. "You won't help me?"

"Of course I will, but I'm coming with you."

"What?"

"Do you know where to find Delphi and the Oracle?"

"No, but I think my starfish does."

She shook her head. "What kind of friend would I be, if I let you go roaming around Apollo's realm, or pissing off Oracles, by yourself? Get that dress off, get some pants on, and let's go, before Poseidon gets here."

# ALMI

*I* hurriedly changed my clothes in the bathroom, nerves thrilling through me.

*The Oracle.*

I was actually going to see the Oracle. The woman I had been blaming, alongside Poseidon, for my sister's condition for years. She was the only person who might have answers. And boy, did I have a lot of questions. So many questions.

Persephone coming with me gave me more comfort than I would ever admit. She had magic, connections, and knowledge. She would make this trip a hundred times easier and give me a real chance of getting there before Poseidon could interfere.

I half jogged out of the bathroom, wearing black woolen pants from the closet, and a shirt over my vest, my tattoo on show. Kryvo was stuck to my shoulder, and I'd braided my increasingly bright blue hair over the other shoulder with little care, just wanting it out of the way. Persephone regarded me briefly.

"You sort of look like a sexy pirate, except those pants are… not so sexy."

"I want answers from the Oracle, not a night of passion with her."

"All the same," Persephone said with a shrug. "Let me see if I can try out a new trick Hecate taught me." She waved her hand at me, a green vine shooting out. As soon as it made contact with my pants, they changed, the woolen material smoothing out and fitting snugly against my thighs.

"You've given me leather pants," I said, staring.

"Yup. You ready to go?"

I nodded, and we flashed.

❧

"Wow."

My mouth fell open as I took in what I was seeing. The temple of Delphi, I assumed. It was white marble, with a triangular roof and Greek style columns, and looked fairly unremarkable, aside from two tall iron dishes at the top of the steps to the entrance, flickering with blue light.

What was remarkable was where the temple was positioned.

The top of a mountain. The *very* top of a mountain.

We were standing on a small marble platform jutting out of the front of the temple, and there were no railings, the smooth stone surface offering nothing in the way of grip. It felt like we were balanced precariously on the tip of the peak, the platform at risk of tipping either way at any point.

The view was dizzying. I didn't know how high up we were, but I could see an entire range of mountains stretching out below and beyond us, all snow-capped and surrounded by pastel-colored Olympus clouds.

"It's beautiful," I breathed, turning in a slow and careful circle.

"No, it's not." Persephone's voice was unsteady, and her face was white when I turned to her.

"You okay?"

"I freaking hate heights," she said, taking a slow backward step toward the temple. I moved to her, taking her shaking arm.

"You can flash to safety if you need to, any time," I said reassuringly.

She nodded. "I know, or my knees would already have given out. This is good for me. Facing my fears and all that."

"You're doing great." Together, we moved carefully to the steps leading inside the temple. As we reached the top of them, a lyrical voice sang out of nowhere.

"Only one may enter."

Persephone looked at me. "Have you got my rose on you?"

"Yes," I nodded.

Relief washed over her face. "Good. I'm leaving. Call me when you want me to come get you."

"I really, really appreciate your help." She had been willing to stay on the top of the mountain and deal with her fear, just for me.

"Be careful," she smiled at me, then disappeared in a

flash. I took one last look at the incredible vista, then headed into the gloom of the temple.

The inside looked nothing like I thought it would. In fact, it looked nothing like I thought anything would.

The walls and ceiling were gold, and in the shining surfaces were scratched hundreds and hundreds of words in languages I couldn't read. Light radiated from the walls, reflecting off the enormous pool that dominated the central area of the temple.

I stared as I came to a stop at the top of a set of stairs leading down to the water. There was a stone platform in the middle of the pool, covered in a bed of cushions and a bowl of fruit. The scent of lavender permeated the air.

The water in front of the platform rippled, drawing my eye. The water looked as golden as the walls, and slowly a figure rose from the liquid. A woman, head shrouded in hessian, dark skin glowing and youthful, and her amber eyes bright.

The Oracle of Delphi.

"Almi." Her voice sounded clear and deep. The water around her rippled, light shimmering in golden rings.

"Hello." I was more nervous than I had expected to be, sweat pricking at my skin.

"I have been expecting you for some time."

"Well, you can see into the future, so..." I shrugged awkwardly.

"Incorrect. I do not see into the future. I am aware of certainties, and I can see links and bonds."

"You told Poseidon he had to marry me."

"Also incorrect. I told the King of the Sea that if he possessed the heart of a nereid, he would also possess the Heart of the Ocean."

"Which meant marrying me."

She raised her shoulders in the slightest of shrugs. "That is how Poseidon chose to interpret the prophecy. Is that what you wish to talk to me about?"

I almost said yes, but shook my head. "No. I have two questions," I said, holding my hand up. The smell of lavender was becoming overpowering. "One, what is the Heart of the Ocean?"

She lifted her arms from the water painfully slowly. Her skin was veined with gold, and more water rippled out around her. "The Heart of the ocean is not a heart at all."

I stared at her. "Right. Want to be any more vague?"

A tiny smile played at her lips. "You do not see what is before you, Queen Almi."

"I'm not a Queen."

"You are."

"Whatever. What is the Heart of the Ocean if it's not a heart?"

"You will find out, soon enough."

I glared at her and she stared back. "Fine," I hissed eventually. I clearly wasn't getting any more from her. "Question two, is there any way to cure the stone blight without the Heart of the Ocean?"

"No."

I growled in frustration. "Are you sure?"

"Yes. You are the only one who may find it."

"How?"

"You are not of the ocean."

"Yeah, I just found that out. I have air magic. But that doesn't answer my question."

"Everything needs air. Fire, water, earth. None exist without each other, and air is at the heart of everything."

"Are you saying my air magic will help get the Heart of the Ocean?"

"Your full power will lead you to it."

Relief washed over me. It was as we had suspected. When my shell tattoo was filled with color and my power fully present, we would be able to find the stupid heart.

"I have answered your two questions. Is there anything else?"

I bit my lip as I considered.

I knew what I wanted to ask her something else, but a tiny bit of me felt I was betraying Poseidon by doing so.

*He sent me away, and he doesn't trust me,* I told myself.

I would regret not asking when I had the chance.

"What was the whole prophecy you gave Poseidon about marrying a Nereid?"

"What do you mean, the whole prophecy?" She tilted her head slowly, the fabric swathing her not moving at all.

"I heard the first bit, about marrying a Nereid. Then something about true love, but it was cut off."

She moved her arms around slowly, expression darkening. "Poseidon has not told you?"

"No. He told me there was more to it than I was aware of, but he wouldn't tell me what it was."

She brought her arms back down, palms flat on the water, and flames fired to life across the back of her hands, spreading across the surface of the pool like oil.

Her eyes turned milky, and the flames leaped high around her, the whole pool on fire. I stepped forward, unsure what to do and my nerves edging on panic, but then she spoke.

"He who possesses the heart of a Nereid shall possess the Heart of the Ocean. True love is not a necessity, pure possession will seal the deal. But be warned. True love will never go unnoticed. Should a Nereid fall in love, she will die, her mortal body cast aside, and her soul made extinct."

I stared at the woman in the flames, her words ringing in my ears. My whole body felt like it had been doused in ice.

*If I fell in love, I'd die?*

"Poseidon knew this?" My words were a mumble, my mouth not working properly.

"He has known a long time."

"He didn't tell me. He didn't tell me I couldn't fall in love."

"You *can* fall in love. But the moment true love is reciprocal, you will die. If you fall for someone who does not love you back, then your body and soul will be safe. Be warned though, unrequited love wreaks havoc on the mind. Not a much better fate than death, I suspect."

I had given up on love years ago. The revelation that falling in love might kill me shouldn't have mattered. But... There was something between Poseidon and I. Something beyond our physical attraction, something that hit me on a level I had never felt before. All I could see in my mind as the Oracle spoke was his face, hard and severe, and those beautiful eyes filled with raw, boundless power.

Did I really believe I might fall in love with him? The god who'd wrecked my life?

I replayed her words again, trying to work them out in my head, trying to understand why thoughts of Poseidon were dominating my reaction to the revelation.

*Should a Nereid fall in love, she will die, her mortal body cast aside, and her soul made extinct.*

Did that mean all Nereids? Or just me?

"Is this the same for all Nereids?" I asked the Oracle aloud.

"You are the only one left."

"No, my sister is alive."

"Lily is neither alive, nor dead, while she sleeps."

"Why is she asleep?" My words came out abrupt and angry, my emotion beginning to creep free of my control. "And what does gods weeping have to do with her?"

"She sleeps to awaken you."

My heart skipped a beat. "What?"

"The closer she moves to death, the farther you move toward power."

"No." I felt the hard stone hit my knees as I dropped to the tiles, my head swimming. "No, that can't be true."

"Everything I say to you is true."

"I'm getting my magic because Lily is dying?"

"Yes."

"No. No, this can't be right." The repercussions of what she was saying hammered through me, and I felt sick. "The only way to cure the stone blight is with the Heart of the Ocean," I whispered.

"Yes."

"And the only way to get that is for me to get my full power."

"Yes."

"Which means…" I trailed off, unable to finish the sentence, my throat closing.

The Oracle finished it for me. "Lily must die to cure the rest of Aquarius — including its King."

# ALMI

For a moment, I couldn't breathe. My throat was closing completely, and I couldn't get any air into my darkening mind.

The implications of what the woman in the pool before me had just said were too much for me to process, too huge for me to make sense of.

To save Poseidon and all those people, my sister had to die. And it would be me who killed her. My magic.

As if on cue, my throat opened as though it were being forced, air rushing into my body.

I gasped as I realized it was my air magic, trying to help me. I looked down at the shell on my chest, two-thirds filled with color.

Anger bordering on rage gushed trough my body. "No!"

"I am sorry."

I snapped my eyes from my tattoo to the Oracle. "Bullshit! Nobody is fucking sorry! Nobody! You, Poseidon,

Atlas — you're all just playing some fucked-up game, and the person who loses is my sister!"

The rage had broken free, and I was vaguely aware of my hair whipping around my face, my shirt blowing against my skin, and my legs straightening, lifting me from my knees.

"Why? Why does she have to pay?" *And why did I have to be the one who would kill her?*

A sob tore from my throat. The flames around the Oracle rose higher. "Fate. You are bound to the life you are living."

"No! I am free! I make my own decisions!" I knew even as I yelled the words they were futile. I hadn't been in control of my life for even a moment of it. Control was an illusion.

"You do not."

"What if I refuse? What if I don't want this stupid fucking magic?" The air whipping around me fell away in an instant. An uncomfortable feeling of danger swirled through my anger.

"If you refuse your magic, in order to keep your sister alive, then you will never find the Heart of the Ocean."

"And Poseidon will die?"

The Oracle nodded. "Along with the citizens of Aquarius affected by the stone blight."

A wave of hopelessness crashed over me, and I pressed my hands to my face, as though I could force some clarity into my overloaded head.

I already knew what Lily would do, what she would say to me if she were there.

There was no way in Olympus that she would put her own life over others. But it wasn't her choice. It was mine.

"There must be another way," I said, removing my hands, desperation in my voice as I stared at the Oracle. "There has to be. What about Atlantis?"

The Oracle tilted her head slowly. "What do you know of Atlantis?"

"It has a font that can heal anything. Can it heal Lily?"

"The Font of Zoi is the reason you are in this position now."

"What?"

"Almi." The deep male voice saying my name didn't belong to the Oracle. I focused my gaze over her shoulder, my eyes landing on Poseidon.

My breath caught again, more black dots invading my vision as emotion threatened to overwhelm me. He was covered in stone. Hardly any patches of his warm, tanned skin showed at all as he stepped to the side of the pool, moving stiffly toward me.

"You should have told me." I couldn't help the words leaving my mouth. He glanced at the Oracle, then back to me.

"Told you what?"

"All of it."

"All of the prophecy?" He was speaking gently, as though I were a bomb he was scared of setting off.

"Yes. All of the prophecy. And about Lily."

His expression darkened, and he frowned. "What of Lily?" he asked carefully.

"She is dying because of me."

He was close enough now that I could see the emotion

in his face when he reacted. Surprise. And sadness. *He hadn't known.*

"She is safe now," he said.

He hadn't known that my power was killing her. And he had saved her from Atlas.

Tears spilled down my cheeks as my anger with him leaked away. "Where is she?"

"You need to rest."

"Where is she?"

"In the palace. With the others."

"My magic is killing her. When I get it all, she'll die."

He reached out an arm, and his touch was rough and cool. The touch of stone. "I'm sorry."

"You need help," I said, looking down dazedly at his arm.

"Yes. Let me take you home, then I must see the dragon."

I looked from him to the Oracle. "Tell me about Atlantis first," I said.

She gave me a sad smile. "Poseidon can tell you about Atlantis. Once he is healed." She moved her sightless eyes to him, and there was no doubting her words were a command aimed directly at the ocean god.

He nodded slowly. "I will."

When the light from Poseidon's flash cleared, I found myself back in my room and Poseidon gone.

I didn't even check to see if the door was locked. No anger welled up in me this time. Just bone-deep sadness.

I moved to the dresser, lifted Kryvo from my shoulder and onto his cushion. "You okay?" he asked quietly.

"Not really." I made my way to the bed, climbed onto the huge mattress, then fell, face-first onto the pillows. Blessed darkness engulfed my vision, and I let the hot, silent tears come.

I knew what I had to do now.

I had to talk to my sister.

Whether or not the Lily who lived in my head was my own projection or really her made no difference. I needed her. And I needed to tell her how sorry I was.

"Lily?" The fabric around my face muffled my voice, and I was glad. I didn't want to see or hear anything, except her.

*Almi.*

Her hair was as bright blue as I'd ever seen it, her skin glittering and shining with pearly pastels, as she materialized in my head. I let her image fill every part of my mind.

"I'm sorry. I'm so, so sorry."

*I'm not.*

"What?"

*I've always known you were destined for something big, little sister. And I was right. You're going to save the whole damn realm.* Her smile was big and warm. *I'm thrilled.*

"But... I'm killing you."

*Almi, I've not lived any kind of life for nearly a decade. I only wanted to come back for you. Because you wanted me. My purpose was always to help.* Her big blue eyes were filled with sincerity. *How better can I help than to give you what you need to save Aquarius?*

"It's not fair."

*No, it's not.*

"I need you. I need you to come back."

*No, you don't.*

"Yes, I do! I've been trying to get you back forever. I can't give up now!" I punched at the pillows either side of my head.

*You wouldn't be giving up. You would be embracing what you and I were born to do. Between us, we'll save Aquarius. And save the man who loves you.*

I stilled. "Loves me?"

Lily smiled again, this time playfully. *You know, you're very naive, for a woman of your age.*

"Poseidon doesn't love me."

*That is a conversation for you two to have, not one for me to be involved in.*

I lay in the pillows, silent for a moment, tears still streaming into the bedding. "Lily, I can't be the cause of your death. I just… can't."

*You mean you won't.*

"Fine. I won't. I can refuse the magic. I know I can."

*And watch Poseidon die? Watch the families of Aquarius fall to the blight, one by one? Watch what's left of the realm fall to Atlas and his cronies?*

I didn't answer, fear and anger swirling about in my head and mixing into frustration. I could do that no more than I could cause Lily's death, and she knew it.

*Almi, if you don't cure Poseidon of the stone blight soon, then you two will lose the Poseidon Trials. That affects the whole of Olympus. It is no exaggeration to say that the fate of this world lies with you.*

I pushed myself out of the pillows, rolling onto my

back and staring angrily at the ceiling. "I am not equipped to save the fucking world. You just said it yourself, I'm naive. Everyone thinks I'm odd. And I'm on my own."

*You're odd, for sure, but you are most definitely not on your own. You have Kryvo, Galatea, Persephone, and Poseidon. You are surrounded by people who care for you.*

As I thought about it, I started to believe she was right. She wasn't just trying to comfort me. Persephone was my friend. If I hadn't known that before today, I was given proof when she clung to a mountain top for me, despite being terrified. Kryvo constantly faced his own fears to help me. Galatea had started looking at me with respect instead of suspicion, and I was pretty sure she would describe herself as caring for me in her own way. And Poseidon... Poseidon was something else to me. Not a friend. But I was sure he cared for me.

Did he love me?

*Could* he love me?

He'd sent me away to be on my own, unable to help my sister. He couldn't have done that if he loved me.

Shaking my head, I forced the thoughts away. "If I have all these powerful gods and friends around me, then surely there's another way. Poseidon is going to tell me something about Atlantis."

*The Oracle was clear. There's only one way. Please don't get your hopes up.*

"That's a hard habit to break, Lily. I've been getting my hopes up for as long as I can remember."

She chuckled. *And thank the gods for that. You're tenacious. You're a survivor.*

"I'll never be as strong as you are."

*You'll be stronger,* Lily whispered. *I just had boring old water magic. You have something incredible. Air that can merge with water, with fire, with earth. Did you see how your power blended with Poseidon's?*

My mind flicked through memories of the last Trial, and the elation I had felt afterward. And the deepening of the bond with Poseidon, the unspoken connection that had become impossible to suppress.

"Does all magic merge like that?"

*It depends. At the Academy, they told us that certain types of magic could work together, but not usually from two different people. And only under the control of powerful gods.*

"I'm not a god."

*No, but you are married to one. One of the most powerful in Olympus. Brother of Zeus and Hades, King of the Sea.* She grinned. *Ideal husband material.*

I let out a long breath, shaking my head slowly. "I can't lose you, Lily."

*You'll always have your memories.*

"I need more than that. I need to wake you up."

*You need to save the world.*

# POSEIDON

"What did you tell her?"

Fear rolled through me, my limbs, my face, my skin, all starting to feel numb as the stone crawled across my body.

The Oracle stared at me with sightless eyes. "You should have told her yourself."

"You told her the rest of the prophecy. About falling in love being the cause of her death." I felt sick, emotion making me angry.

"She was less concerned with that than learning that she will be the cause of her sister's death."

"Explain."

"Her magic comes at a cost. For her to reach her full potential, her sister must die."

"Then she will refuse the power. She loves her sister more than anything in Olympus." There was no way Almi would be a part of killing her own sister.

The Oracle shook her head. "Then she will not be able

to obtain the Heart of the Ocean. And then you will die. You and all the inhabitants of Aquarius. Atlas will get the revenge he so desperately desires."

Horror coiled in my gut at her words.

This couldn't be. How could Almi have been put in such an impossible position?

"Are you speaking the words of a prophecy, or is this your opinion?" I ground out.

"Lily must die, for Almi to save your life. That is prophecy."

Rage exploded through me, and I felt the stone tighten over my skin, blocking my power form erupting.

"I have vowed to save her sister."

"Then you have vowed to mark your own end. And that of your kingdom."

"Who did this? Why is this happening to her and Lily?"

"Almi has the potential to carry phenomenal power. That must be tempered. Tested. Proven."

"By killing her own sister?"

"By being forced to make a decision for the greater good."

"This is cruelty beyond measure."

"It is life in Olympus. Life wielding enormous power."

"It is hatred and bitterness and resentment."

"Emotions you know much about. Emotions you have caused in abundance in others."

"You are referring to Atlas?"

"You have brought this upon yourself, Sea King. And the unrequited love you feel for your bride? You have done her no favors. Saved her from nothing."

I didn't hear another word from the deity's mouth. My head was spinning, my rage barely under control, and my body succumbing to the stone.

*Hades!* I sent the plea for help to my brother, just as my legs gave out, and blackness swamped me.

## ALMI

*A* gentle knock at my door snapped me from my reverie.

I didn't know how long I'd been sitting on the bed, trying to work out what the hell I was supposed to do next.

I leapt up, hoping it was Poseidon come to tell me about Atlantis, but already knowing from the knock that it wasn't him. It had been too soft.

I pulled the door open and saw Persephone. "Hi." She looked me up and down and frowned. "You look terrible."

"I feel terrible."

She nodded, as though making up her mind. "We'll go to my place. I've got some stuff that will make you feel better."

I looked at her, and my concern must have been evident, because she reached her hands up, gently clasping my shoulders. "Medicine. Maybe some wine. Nothing weird."

"Is it a bit early for wine?" I realized I didn't even know what time of day it was.

"It's never too early for wine. Also, no. It's the middle of the night."

I nodded, dazedly, then stopped. "I can't. I have to wait for Poseidon. The Oracle said he had to tell me something important."

Persephone's expression tightened, and alarm shot through me. "That's sort of why I came. Hades had to take him to the dragon again. She's a miserable dragon in the first place, and now she's being really grumpy."

"What happened?" Fear for Poseidon, unwanted but fierce, slammed through me.

"He's not in a good way. She's only been able to get rid of some of the stone this time, and she told Hades she won't help him again, because it's too draining for her."

"Oh gods." I rubbed my hand across my face. "Is he okay?"

"The longer he gets to rest between now and the next Trial, the better. I, erm…" She looked at me guiltily. "I sedated him."

"You sedated him?"

"It was the only way I could get him to rest. He has to let his body regenerate, or the stone will take over," she said apologetically. "If we can keep him unconscious for a full day, and he barely uses any power when he wakes, then he stands a chance of surviving another Trial." She squeezed my shoulders as she spoke, trying to reassure me. She was only partially successful.

I needed to know about Atlantis. I needed to know if

the Font of Zoi was an alternative to an even more awful decision.

*Poseidon, or Lily.*

If it were just those two, then the choice would be my sister. But it wasn't that simple.

Tears filled my eyes, unbidden.

Persephone pulled me into to her, wrapping her arms around me. "Hey, it's okay, we'll save him," she said. "You'll save him."

That only made the tears fall faster. "But saving him… Saving him means…" I tried to get the words out, but my throat closed again, the numbness that had fallen over me in my solitude abandoning me.

Persephone held me at arm's length, looking into my face and frowning with concern. "Saving him means what?" Realization washed over her features. "The Oracle didn't give you good news, did she?"

I shook my head, and she moved past me, into my room to pick up Kryvo's cushion. "Take your clever little friend, and we'll go to my place. You need fixing up, and if you tell me whatever that mountain-top dwelling weirdo said to you, we'll work it out together."

"Wow," squeaked Kryvo, as we materialized in what I assumed was Persephone's place.

It was as though a greenhouse had had a baby with a gothic castle. The whole structure was made from intricate wrought iron, and almost every wall between the iron frame was made from glass. Gold and red roses were intertwined around the iron, a stark contrast to the mass of green beyond the glass walls. It looked like a luscious jungle out there, with hundreds of types of trees and plants growing beside each other. Even someone as lacking in plant knowledge as I could see that a lot of the species shouldn't be found growing side by side.

"Wow," I repeated the starfish's word. I refocused on the room we were in, seeing that it was a large living and dining room in one. The floor was a rich dark wood, and the dining area was raised a few steps to separate it. An iron chandelier hung low over an organic-shaped tabletop made from one beautiful slab of polished wood. In front of the glass walls, surrounding a fire dish flickering with a warm glow, were a series of huge chintzy pink armchairs. Green potted ferns dotted the room, and there were brightly colored orchids on many of the surfaces.

I tipped my head back to look up, seeing the lofty ceiling far above us, glittering with lights that looked like stars.

"You like it?" Persephone smiled at me.

"It's stunning."

"We can only live here six months of the year. On the surface of the underworld, I mean. The rest of the time we have to live underground, in Hades' palace. I had a lot of windows to make up for when I designed this place."

"I'd love to hear how you two got together," I said, as she led me to the armchairs.

"And I'd love to tell you, but not now. We've got some more important matters to attend to. Sit."

I did, and she moved to a long counter along the back of the dining area. She clattered around a few moments, and I let the comfy couch take my weight, closing my eyes and trying to clear and organize my thoughts so that I could make some sort of sense to my new friend.

"So. Tell me what happened with the Oracle."

I opened my eyes, and she was pulling leaves off a couple of plants and putting them into a small mortar. She ground them up, and vines snaked from her palms, wrapping around the stone bowl.

I watched with fascination. "What are you doing?"

"Making something that will restore your strength faster than those vials Poseidon has been giving you."

"Thank you."

"You're welcome. Now, tell me."


As calmly as I could, I told Persephone what the Oracle had said. I tried to keep my emotion at bay, delivering the information as concisely as possible. By the time I had told her everything though, silent tears were streaming down my cheeks again.

She walked over to me, handing me a steaming mug of something that smelled like blackcurrants. I took it, and sipped cautiously. Warmth spread through my whole body.

"I'm so sorry, Almi. This is a seriously shitty situation to be in." Persephone's face was filled with sympathy as she sat down on the armchair next to mine.

"Lily says we are destined to save the world together. She says she's not mad or upset about it."

Persephone's face creased into a frown, concern

replacing the sympathy. "Lily says?" she repeated. "I thought she's been unconscious for years?"

I let out a long breath as I realized what I'd said. I hadn't meant to tell her that I spoke to Lily. The words had slipped out, my control over myself and my emotions was so tenuous. "I talk to her in my head," I admitted quietly. "I get a really vivid image of her, and she talks back."

Persephone looked surprised, then thoughtful. "Do you think it's actually her?"

I shrugged. "At first, I thought it was my grief and loneliness, when I was in the human world with nobody to turn to. But...she's so much like her, not me. She thinks of things I don't, and she knows things I don't. Which makes me wonder if I even could be making her up myself."

"You would be amazed what our subconscious knows about us that we don't," said Persephone gently.

"So you think I'm making her up?"

"I don't know. You said she had powerful magic when she was awake?"

"Yes."

"Any telepathic magic?"

"Erm, no. Just water."

"Hmm. Well, either way, she told you she is not upset about you embracing your power to find the Heart of the Ocean?"

I swallowed hard. "She was always selfless. But I've spent my whole adult life trying to save her. I can't give up now. I can't." Desperation perforated my every word.

I expected Persephone to tell me that the right thing to

do was let Lily die in order to save everyone else. I knew that was what any sane person would tell me to do. But she didn't.

"What about Atlantis?" she asked.

"The Oracle told Poseidon he had to tell me something about it."

"Something that would help cure the blight?"

I bit my lip as I remembered what the deity had said. "She said there was no way to cure the blight without the Heart of the Ocean. And the only way to get it was for me to get my full power." My shoulders sagged.

"There has to be a way around this."

I looked at her determined expression. "You think?"

"Yes. Prophecies are almost as tricky as gods. There's always another way."

A surge of hope flooded my system as I gripped the mug. All I'd needed was to hear someone else say there might be another way. "Do you have any ideas?"

"No. You have to survive the Trials and keep Poseidon alive. And I don't see how you can do that without your magic."

I sat back guiltily. "I think I may have pissed my air magic off. In the temple."

Persephone looked alarmed. "How?"

"I kind of said I didn't want it."

"Right. Well. Hopefully, there was no harm done and you can just apologize?"

"Apollo said air was fickle, and hard to control."

"Hmm. We'll work on that next. In the meantime, what are you going to do about the love thing?"

"Love thing?"

She looked at me like I'd just suffered a head injury. "Almi, if you fall in love with your husband, you're going to die. Does that not strike you as something we need to address?"

I held my hand up. "Whoa, now. There is a whole load of reasons why that does not cause me concern right now." I drained the contents of my mug, already feeling stronger. "Number one, he's a massive grumpy idiot who represents everything I can't stand in life. Number two, I wouldn't even know how to fall in love. I love my sister, and that's it. I have no capacity or desire to love anyone else. Number three, I'll only die if the love is reciprocated." I looked pointedly at Persephone. "So, nothing to worry about."

She just stared at me, eyes wide and brows raised.

"What?" I said, unable to take the long silence.

"I'm trying to work out where to even begin," she said.

"You mentioned wine?"

Persephone nodded. "Wine is a very good place to begin."

# ALMI

When we both had glasses of something amber-colored and fizzy, Persephone cleared her throat. "I think you're in more danger than you think, Almi."

"In what way?"

"I'm not going to risk moving you closer to that danger, but you need to be more prepared than you currently are."

"I'm not following you."

"I am not going to say anything to make you like Poseidon any more than you do now."

"In case you accidentally make me fall in love with him?" I scoffed.

She didn't laugh. In fact, she looked as serious as I'd ever seen her. "Almi, I'd bet my entire life and everything I own on one thing. He loves you."

I scowled. "Lily thinks so too. But you guys don't know what the marriage bond is like." I paused. "Well, maybe you do, since you're married to his brother. This constant pull toward each other, this weird electricity thing we get whenever we touch - it could so easily be misinterpreted as something more."

Persephone's green eyes filled with something that could have been sorrow. "Almi, if it turns into something more, you'll die. You get that, right?"

"Yes, but I don't love him. And I don't think he loves me. He might be drawn to me, and fancy me, but that's not love."

"What happened at Aphrodite's palace?"

My cheeks heated. "We, erm, you know…"

"You had sex?" She looked almost relieved.

"No. But we were, erm, close." I swallowed, and decided to bare heart and soul. After all, there wasn't much she didn't know about me anymore. "I haven't been with anyone before, and he stopped it before it went any further because of that."

"Oh gods." Persephone rubbed her hand over her pale face. "Almi, no guy, god, or anything with a damn dick, is going to turn down sex unless love is involved!"

"Oh," I said, my cheeks burning now. I took a long glug of wine. "Oh," I said again, at a loss for any other words to say.

Could the fierce sea god really love me?

How? He barely even knew me. Surely he couldn't fall in love with someone within a week?

"Poseidon has been sullen and angry since I've known him. But that wild look in his eyes when he looks at you? I have never seen that before. And the anger is different now. Not humming under the surface, but clawing to get free. He is different around you, for sure."

"Oh." In an attempt to use another word than *oh*, I looked down at Kryvo, who was stuck to my collarbone. "What do you think, Kryvo?" I prayed the starfish would say the sea god thought I was odd and wanted nothing to with me.

No sooner than I had the thought was it followed by a prickle of alarm.

*I didn't want Poseidon to want nothing to do with me.*

Shit. Flashes of the way he had made me feel in Aphrodite's palace came to me, and I buried them quickly.

"You keep kissing him when I'm stuck to you," the starfish said, matter-of-factly.

"That's not an opinion."

"You two are connected. There is an energy between you, and the magic you both have binds."

I thought about our ride on Blue and Chrysos, and the way our power had merged in the last Trial. More unease washed through me.

"We are connected," I repeated. "Not in love. There's a difference."

"You need to be careful. Try not to spend too much time alone with him," said Persephone.

"How? We have to finish the Trials. Or at least, *try* to finish the Trials." I drank more wine. "This is a fucking mess," I muttered.

Persephone gave me a sympathetic look that turned quickly to resolute. "Concentrate on surviving the Trials, hold on to the things about Poseidon that piss you off, and then we'll work out the Heart of the Ocean. That's the plan."

"Yes." It wasn't a new plan, but it was the only one we had. And I wasn't doing it alone. I knew the woman beside me would help me, no matter what. I reached out and squeezed her hand, a movement uncharacteristic for me, but it felt right. "Thank you. Lily has been my only friend for a long time. I'm so grateful for your help."

She squeezed my hand back. "I could do with a friend here, too, and I think you're great."

Warmth flowed through me again, along with hope.

We would find another way.

We talked for another hour or so, and Persephone seemed to make a point of picking subjects that had nothing to do with the Trials or Lily or Poseidon. We talked about the human world, about where she grew up in New York and the life I'd lived in my trailer. We talked about music and movies and the sorts of things normal people got to talk about.

When Hades flashed into the room, I nearly dropped my drink in surprise.

"Oh, I didn't know you had company," he said, moving to Persephone and bending down to kiss her. "How is Poseidon?"

"He needs to sleep. And Almi had an unsettling visit with the Oracle." Hades looked at me, understanding swirling in his silver eyes. "That woman could be described as a lot worse than unsettling." He eyed the wine in my hand. "Be careful," he told me. "Persephone has a volatile history with Dionysus' wine."

I raised an eyebrow, and she giggled. "When I was human, I couldn't handle it. You're not human, you'll be fine," she reassured me.

A flash drew all our attentions to the flame dish. Flames roared up high, bright white, then fell away to reveal an image of Atlas' face. A long silver scratch ran down the side of his face, and I gasped in surprise. Had that happened during the fight I was spirited away from?

"Good evening, Olympus." His voice was hard and dry, all his charm gone. "The next Trial will be the last of the Poseidon Trials."

Relief hammered through me. I glanced at Persephone and saw the same feeling mirrored on her face. "Thank the gods for that."

"It is time the world knew what the King of the Ocean is capable of. What kind of a god he truly is." My skin tightened, and I leaned forward. "I was the ruler of a great city in Olympus once. My wife and I ruled happily, until Poseidon interfered." Red flames burst to life in his irises and then began to lick over his skin.

"Fuck," Hades swore.

"The god you all revere sank my city to the bottom of the ocean. He was responsible for the deaths of hundreds of innocent people."

The sound of blood pounding in my ears got louder. "No," I whispered.

"And I only wish that the fate that befell my beloved wife was as simple as death," the Titan snarled. "For the final

Trial, our competitors will navigate my sunken city, and find as many shells as they can. But be warned; the monsters there are worse than anything in the shallows. Time in the depths has turned my once great city into a lethal maze, and rotbloods will be the least of your worries. You begin at dawn. Find my city, find the shells. End the Trials."

The flames flashed up again, swallowing the image. When they died down, Atlas was gone.

"Shit," Hades swore again. The temperature in the room increased. I stared numbly at the fire.

"Did he really kill hundreds of people and sink an entire city?" My words were a mumble.

"You must ask him," Hades' said. "It is not my place to speak of it."

"War can be brutal," said Persephone gently.

"This was before the war," Hades muttered. "These two have had a rivalry going back centuries, but my brother would never tell me what happened."

"He said he was ashamed," I said quietly.

Hades looked at me. "He told you of it?"

"No. He told me he didn't want to speak of it because he was ashamed."

Hades let out a long sigh. "We have all done things of which we are ashamed. None more so than the gods."

"You've killed hundreds of innocent people?" I snapped, then regretted it when I saw his grave face.

"I am the God of Death," he said, power ringing out around him. "I have done things you can't even begin to imagine."

Persephone got up slowly from her chair, the movement diffusing the power rolling from Hades. "I will have to wake him earlier than I'd hoped," she said gently.

Hades looked at her, then nodded. "He needs to tell his wife what he has done. They need to make a plan to get through this."

# ALMI

*P*ersephone flashed us back to the palace, directly to Poseidon's throne room. I looked at the giant wave throne, the surly god distinctly absent.

"I'll bring him here when I've woken him," Persephone said, then flashed away.

I let out a long breath, then heard a cough behind me. Whirling, I saw Galatea. She had a huge bruise under her left eye, and her staff was scratched.

"Galatea, what happened?"

"I was going to ask you the same." She looked tired, but her blue eyes were alert as always. She leaned against a statue of an orca and glanced at the huge throne. "He flashed me out of there."

"Me too." He had removed both of his allies. Two women who had power and could have helped him. "Fucking idiot." I shook my head.

Galatea flinched, but she didn't reprimand me for blaspheming. "My sentiments also," she said. "I understand the dragon and Persephone have healed him."

497

"Yes. Persephone says he won't be able to use much power when he comes round."

Galatea nodded. "You saw Atlas' announcement about the last Trial?" Her words were tentative, and I nodded. "And the part about him sinking a city?" I nodded again. She took a long breath. "I do not know the full story, but trust me when I tell you that Poseidon is not a cruel god. He never has been."

"Is he... a murderer?"

"There are no gods in Olympus not responsible for death," she said resignedly. "But Poseidon has a good heart."

She would say that, though, she was unwaveringly loyal to the sea god.

"Well, I hope he will tell me about both Atlas, and Atlantis, when he is roused," I said. Even as the words left my mouth, something in my mind clicked.

Galatea looked intently at me. "They are one and the same, Almi."

My mind whirred as I stared back at her.

*Atlas.*

*Atlantis.*

"Atlantis is Atlas' city?"

Galatea nodded. "Yes. It was named for him. It was a magnificent city, with enough power to rival a realm."

"And a font that could create life," I murmured.

Galatea frowned. "How do you know of that?"

"She knows more than she thinks she does." Poseidon's voice rang out behind us, and we both turned.

He was standing tall, wearing the tight blue pants and no shirt, straps holding weapons criss-crossing his chest.

But half his chest was the color of granite. It snaked up his neck, just creeping over the left side of his jaw.

My heart seemed to slow in my chest as I looked at him, his wild eyes boring into mine.

"What happened between you and Atlas?" demanded Galatea before I could say a word. I couldn't help admiring the authority in her tone as she addressed her king. This woman was not taking no for an answer, no matter who she was speaking to.

"We had a conversation." Poseidon's voice was laced with barely restrained anger, but I didn't think it was directed at her. Galatea banged her staff on the ground, not bothering to try to restrain her own anger.

"Sire, you could have been killed! What were you thinking, sending both me and Almi away? We do not need protecting, you do!"

"Yeah!" Galatea's outburst had summed up my feelings exactly.

Poseidon turned his angry eyes to his general. "Do you really believe, for even a moment, that I think you incapable or weak?" Galatea said nothing, but doubt flickered through her eyes. "I removed both of you because I knew what was coming, and it was not something either of you could help with."

"We're back to this cryptic bullshit again?" I fisted my hands on my hips, my patience at its end. Persephone had fixed my body with her tea, but emotionally I was spent. "I'm done only getting half the story, Poseidon. You hear me? Done." I folded my arms over my chest and glared at him.

He looked between me and Galatea, then let out a long

breath. "Atlas' wife is not a foe either of you can face."

"Why not? I threw a water Titan half a damned mile through the ocean, and Galatea is as hard as nails!"

"I will tell you what happened, but you must let me start at the start."

I dropped my arms. "Fine."

"We shall go the east wing."

"Why?"

"There is a painting. It will help me to make you understand."

Make me understand? That did not sound good. Trepidation coursed through me as I turned to follow him out of the throne room.

Galatea coughed again, and he turned. "Sire... I apologize for my outburst. If this is a conversation you wish to have with your wife alone, then I trust you to keep me informed later."

Poseidon gave her a tiny, grateful smile. Not the full-on smile that had seared itself into my brain, but a rare expression, nonetheless. "I will appraise you of what we are facing as soon as we are back from the east wing. Thank you, Galatea."


We didn't exchange a single word as we walked through the halls of the palace. The further we got, the more nervous I became. How the hell had I not made the connection between Atlas and Atlantis before? The Titan had named the city after himself, and I'd totally failed to notice the names were connected.

Would it have made any difference if I had realized?

Probably not. But it explained why Poseidon had been so reluctant to talk about the sunken city. I tried to recall what the book had said about it. Clearly the author had been lacking some vital information.

I wrung my hands as we made our way down a long winding staircase, natural light diminishing, and the glass walls replaced by white marble.

I felt like a leaf bobbing along a river, or a feather floating on the breeze—all my grounding gone, and nowhere to cling to for comfort.

My time with Persephone had helped re-instate my hope for Lily. Rather, it had made me believe that there could be — *had to be* — another way to save everyone without losing her.

But when it came to Poseidon…I didn't know how to feel. I didn't understand anything about being a god. Not only a god, one of the three most powerful, ruling gods of Olympus. The power and responsibility he wielded, the friendships and threats he would have faced in his life…. His life was worlds away from mine. Galatea had just referred to me as his wife, but that wasn't how it felt, despite the undeniable bond between us.

As if hearing my thoughts, he glanced over his shoulder at me. His white hair was swept back with a simple gold circlet, and I had a clear view of his stormy eyes.

Could I trust him? Had he been the cause of hundreds of innocents' deaths, as Atlas had said? What if he was about to show me how horrific he really was?

What if the reason he was so damn miserable was because he was truly bad at his core.

*What if I was bound to a monster?*

# ALMI

e entered a room at the bottom of a dark staircase. It was gloomy, and the air was musty, a slightly damp scent to it. Drapes hung along the walls, and they were covered in thick dust. The only light came from the ceiling, which glowed, just like the one in my room but more faintly. Poseidon clapped his hands quietly, and the light increased enough that I could see properly.

The room was much longer than I originally thought, and lining both sides were statues. Some marble, some stone, and many broken. A dark blue carpet ran down the middle, and when I stepped onto it a cloud of dust rose around my feet.

"There are no starfish in here," Kryvo squeaked, so only I could hear him.

So Kryvo hadn't seen anything in this room before. I peered at the first statue as we started down the carpet. It was of a satyr, holding up a set of panpipes and looking devilishly cheerful. A flash of concern filled me that these were people who been afflicted by the stone blight, but that thought fled when I reached out and touched it. It looked nothing like the stone that had been creeping over Lily's limbs or crawling across Poseidon's face. That stone was dark grey and mottled. This was ash-veined white marble. And the satyr looked happy, not like a being about to be turned to stone.

We kept walking, and I noticed that very few of the statues were of sea creatures — unlike the rest of the palace. Maybe that's why Kryvo's starfish friends were absent.

When we were halfway down the hall, Poseidon stopped. Reaching out, he gripped the edge of a set of dusty red drapes, and tugged hard. The fabric fell to the floor, the metal pole coming with it and clattering on the tiles as a huge cloud of dust puffed up around us.

When it cleared, I saw the mural painted on the wall behind the drapes.

I took a step back before I'd realized my legs had moved. Kryvo heated on my collarbone, as goosebumps rose across my skin.

The green hand.

I was looking at what that green hand had been attached to.

And I'd seen the creature before, but not like this… It was the same as statue in the last trial that we had found hidden behind the lavafall. A beautiful woman with snakes for hair.

But here… Here she was portrayed very differently.

Her figure was lunging out of the painting, so lifelike it had startled me. The snakes covering her head were all standing on end, teeth bared, evil in their eyes and their scales gleaming gold. Her whole body was green and scaled, her long taloned hands scratching at the viewer of the image. And her eyes... They were reptilian—bright yellow and slitted vertically.

The haunting beauty of the woman was still there, under the ferocious anger. Humanity resided in those snake-like eyes, I was sure. Her high, dignified cheekbones, and beautiful, full red lips spoke of what she had once been.

I knew with utter certainty who I was looking at.

"Atlas' wife."

"Yes. She was not in this form when he married her."

I turned to Poseidon, my breath a little short. "What happened to her?" I dropped my voice, almost not wanting to know the answer. "Did you do this to her?"

Poseidon's eyes burned bright blue a moment, and I expected him to drop my gaze. But he held it. "No."

Relief flooded me.

"But I am responsible."

My stomach tightened again. "How?"

"Her name is Medusa. Atlas and I were close once, and I was very fond of Medusa, until I unwittingly discovered that she had a human lover. That is not uncommon amongst the gods, and I agreed to say nothing when she told me there was no seriousness to the affair. But the man she was betraying her husband with died. She came to me, knowing that I was powerful and had the ear of Zeus and Hades. She begged me to bring her lover back. I refused. Bringing life back from the dead is a power only all twelve Olympians can achieve, and they must all agree. Doing so would have been akin to me taking a stand against Atlas. Using the Olympians to save the lover of my friend's wife was not something I was willing to do." He let out a long sigh and looked back at the painting. "I underestimated her grief and determination. Atlas is a primordial Titan, and his city housed one of the most powerful artifacts ever created. Not even the gods know how it was created."

"The Font of Zoi," I breathed.

"Yes. While Atlas was visiting with Zeus, Medusa stole into the palace and tried to use the Font to bring back her lover. The Font turned on her. It created life, but in the form of a monster. And it used her body as a vessel."

I shuddered as I looked from his face back to the painting. "I read the font only backfired if used will ill-intent," I whispered.

"She was grief-stricken, and angry. With me. The massive surge of power from the font reached me first, because Atlantis was so close to my realm. I got to the palace before anyone else did. She was turning before my eyes, and I could do nothing to stop it happening. Through her pain, she told me that me and my realm would pay. I believe she had tried to use the font not just to bring back her lover, but to inflict harm on me or Aquarius. When Atlas and Zeus arrived moments later, she rose as you see her here. She told Atlas I had tried to seduce her, then used the Font to turn her into a monster when she had refused. If my brother, Zeus, hadn't been there, Atlas would have killed me on the spot. Hades arrived, and we fought, only defeating Atlas as more Olympians arrived to help. We combined our powers to banish Atlas. It is not possible to kill a Titan, but we were able to send him into an indefinite sleep."

He looked back at me, his eyes bright and intense. "Medusa escaped though. And she has the power to turn people to stone."

"Stone," I repeated. A sick feeling rolled through my gut as the pieces snapped into place.

"Stone. Before I could catch her, she had turned the entire population of Atlantis to stone. If you look into her eyes, you become a statue."

"Did you look into her eyes?"

"Yes, but I am a god. I was not affected. At the time."

"What did you do with her?"

He took a breath. "I didn't know if there was any chance of saving the people in Atlantis. But the Font was too dangerous to be used again, and I knew Medusa was too dangerous to be allowed to live."

"So you sank Atlantis."

He nodded. "Yes. And I bound her to the city."

"She sank with it?"

"Yes."

"She's spent centuries trapped alone in a city full of statues she created at the bottom of the ocean?" The horror of it made me feel even more sick.

"It was that or kill her."

I honestly wasn't sure which was worse. "And when Zeus woke up Atlas, he went down to Atlantis, found her and freed her?"

"Yes. I believe the golden snakes Galatea has been

tracking are spreading the blight, and I think Atlas created them in Medusa's honor. And to make it clear to me that I deserve this. This is Atlas' revenge. He wants to turn my realm to stone, as he believes I made his own wife do to his."

"And that means... As your wife, he wants to turn me into a monster?"

Light flared in Poseidon's eyes, waves crashing over his irises. "The last Trial is in Atlantis. The Font is in Atlantis." He nodded gravely. "I do believe that is what he will try to do."

# ALMI

*J* stared at Poseidon, my mind reeling.

Part of me was relieved. Relieved that the god before me wasn't the brute I had feared he was. Relieved that my gut was right, that the connection I had with him had read his soul, and his heart, correctly.

And at least so much of what was happening to Aquarius and its king made sense to me now. I had no idea how Lily and her sleeping sickness fit into anything, and I still knew nothing about the Heart of the Ocean, but Atlas and the stone blight... "It's a perfect revenge," I said softly, looking back at the image of Medusa.

"Yes. I do not know if I was infected by Medusa's stare centuries ago, and it only flared up when he freed her, or if I have been infected like everyone else has. Galatea believes the snakes are passing the blight to the citizens."

"And you think Atlas created the snakes? They are not a part of Medusa's magic?"

"No, I think he created them so that I would know what they meant."

I looked back at him. "Did you not suspect Atlas when people started turning to stone?"

"Nobody has seen the Titans for centuries. The ones we managed to send to sleep vanished from their prisons as one, many years ago and we still do not know who was responsible. Until Oceanus was found and awoken last year, the original, primordial Titans were presumed lost to the world."

I blinked at him, reminded once more of how different his life must have been from mine. "Do you think he could use the font to turn me into..." I pointed at the painting. "That?"

Distant thunder rolled, and a tendril of stone wound across his cheek. "I will not allow him to."

"You mustn't use any power," I said, instinctively reaching out and touching his arm. A protective surge made me want to close the gap and embrace him, but something stopped me.

Sensing my hesitation, he spoke again. "I did not want to remove you and Galatea from the bakery. But I do not know a way of defending against the stone stare of the snakes, other than by being a god. I had no choice." His words were earnest and soft, and any residual anger I had melted away.

"Honestly, looking at her, I'm sort of glad you did," I whispered back. "Why do you even have this painting in here?"

"It is impossible for most to look at her directly, so I kept a painting, in case I ever needed to show a mortal."

"Why, if you thought you'd sent her to the bottom of the ocean for eternity?" I suppressed another shudder.

Emotion filled his eyes and they moved to her reptilian ones in the picture. "I could have asked the Olympians to bring him back. Her lover. And I didn't. She went mad with grief."

"Are you sure she wasn't nuts to begin with?"

"She was vibrant, and clever, and perhaps a little cruel." He tilted his head, lost in his memory. "But the pain of grief is real."

I nodded. "Yes." The thought of losing my sister was unbearable. And now, the thought of losing Poseidon, Kryvo, or Persephone sent stabs of fear and denial through me too.

"I didn't know how deeply she loved him."

"Would it have changed your decision to help her if you had?"

He didn't answer for a while. Then he turned his head, fixing his eyes on me. "Many things have changed since then," he said quietly.

"Is that a yes?"

His hair fell forward across his face as he shook his head. "No." He lifted an arm, gesturing at the image. "I suppose I painted this to remind me that she had once been human. And that decisions have consequences. Even the decisions of a god and a king."

The magnitude of his words sunk in slowly, and for the first time, I had a clear picture of the man standing in front of me.

He understood love and grief. He felt regret, remorse, and responsibility. He didn't take his position as a god and a king lightly, even a fraction. His rigid control and his seriousness all suddenly made sense.

He feared making the wrong decision.

He feared losing control, because he understood, and feared, the consequences of his actions so keenly.

There could be no impulse decisions, no spontaneous actions — because he wouldn't know or be able to control the outcome.

Everything had to be measured, weighed, and evaluated, lest the consequences be as dire as Medusa.

I stared up at him, trying to work out what to say. I felt like I'd been given a window into the man's soul, a glimpse of the god that I shouldn't have. And it unsettled me a little. Not because I feared him, but the opposite. My respect for him was growing by the second. And for someone like me, respect was everything.

I pulled at the least serious thing I could, unwilling to go any deeper into his mind.

"You painted this? You're pretty good."

"I paint better seascapes," he said, and I could hear a quirk of dry amusement in his low voice.

I stepped into him, winding my arms around his waist, and pressing my face to his solid chest. He tensed a moment, then his hand traced its way down my spine, before flattening on the small of my back and pulling me harder into his body.

I wanted to kiss him, so badly. I wanted him to know I understood, and that he had done nothing wrong. That Medusa would probably have flipped out and fucked everything up on her own. But I dared not say a thing that would risk deepening our bond. *Risk making my heart ache for him any more than it was starting to.*

"We must work out a way to survive, and win, the

Atlantis Trial," said Poseidon, and I was relieved that he was changing the subject to something more practical.

And he was right. I needed to find a way to get air to work with me enough to survive the damn Trial and keep Poseidon alive, but not enough to fully embrace my power and kill my sister.

"I think I pissed off my air magic," I said into his chest.

"Then you'd better apologize."

## ALMI

*A* weirdly comfortable silence fell between us as he led me out of the dusty hall and back up the winding staircases of the palace.

"You know, we could get to the pegasus stables a lot quicker if you let me flash us there," Poseidon said, giving me a sideways glance. I'd told him not to flash us anywhere, as despite his protests that it didn't use much magic, I figured the fact that only gods could do it suggested otherwise.

"I want to see how to get there without flashing," I said. Which was partially true. I was nervous about trying to talk to air again. The platform at the top of the stables was the perfect place to try though, given that it was the place I'd first connected consciously with my magic. Plus, I would get to see Blue.

"You can't," Poseidon said.

"What?"

"You can't reach my personal stables without flashing."

"Then how are we going to get there?"

He threw me another glance, and I swore I could see a hint of excitement in the look. "The palace has secrets."

"Tell me about it," I said.

He quirked an eyebrow. "You have seen some of them?"

I looked briefly down at the starfish attached to my skin. "Yep."

He followed my look, and his brows drew together. I thought he would ask more, but he said nothing.

I followed him all the way to his throne room, where he moved to a towering statue of a merman. It was at the back of the round room, and the figure had his head tilted back and a trident pointed at the ceiling. The marble merman was as tall as Poseidon, which he demonstrated by reaching up and gripping the middle prong of the trident, which few would have been able to reach.

Blue light rippled across the room, and a loud click sounded. I gasped as the ceiling above us began to change, bright light flooding through the intricate images painted there.

Within moments, the domed ceiling had vanished completely, and clear sky showed above us, the pastel-colored clouds of Olympus rolling over us.

"But... but... we're underwater?"

Poseidon's lips quirked, then he put his fingers to his lips and whistled. Nothing happened for a moment, then two tiny dots appeared in the bright sky above us. Blue and Chrysos came into focus as they flew down toward us, and my heart filled with happiness to see the pegasus.

"Blue!" He landed gracefully in front of me, looking

massive and regal in the throne room. I reached out, running my hand along his snout. He snorted happily.

"Ready?" Poseidon had moved next to me, and he gripped my waist when I nodded, lifting me easily onto the pegasus. Blue stamped his feet, and we took off.

As soon as the fresh ocean air hit me, I felt a trickle of calm penetrate the emotional churn of the last few hours. I closed my eyes, gripping Blue's mane and letting the breeze engulf me.

"I'm sorry if I gave you the impression that I didn't want you," I said out loud. My words were a whisper, the wind snatching them from my lips as I spoke them. "The thing is, I love my sister. And embracing you might kill her." I took a deep breath as I felt Blue swoop and a big gust of air blew over me, making my hair whip around my face. "And that would... Well, it would break me. Into a million pieces. That could never be put back together again." I thought I felt the wind still for a fraction of a second, before it gusted around me even harder. "Do you think we can do what we were doing before? You help me out, just until I work all of this out?"

I opened one eye hopefully, then the other.

A little whirlwind whipped around me, lifting Blue's mane and bouncing off my arms.

"Hello!" I said gleefully. The sight of my little air friend filled me with as much joy as seeing Blue did, and not because I needed the magic. Because I *wanted* it.

The whirlwind zoomed away, and I twisted to watch it make for Poseidon and Chrysos. With a flourish, it spun around the sea god, lifting his hair, then Chrysos' tail. The gold pegasus whinnied and kicked out in annoyance, and I laughed aloud.

Chrysos sped up so that Poseidon was right alongside me. "It looks like you've been forgiven," the god said drily, eyeing the mischievous little tornado as it whooshed after him.

I beamed at him. "It looks that way."

My smile seemed to soften him, and a faint shadow of my grin tugged at his lips. "We must go to my ship. I would like to show you around before we set out on this last Trial." There was a grave finality to his words that I didn't like at all.

"Can I get my stuff first?"

"Yes. I need to appraise Galatea of what we are facing in Medusa. I should have told her before now."

"Probably."

"Take Blue back to the throne room and pack your things. I will meet you on the ship in an hour."

# ALMI

*I* stared down at the belt on my bed, everything I owned rammed into the bewitched pockets.

"I think that's everything," I said.

"Why are you speaking like you're not coming back?" Kryvo's nerves were evident in his squeaky voice.

"I'm not sure," I lied.

There had been an undeniable finality in Poseidon's tone when he'd told me to come and pack, and I knew he felt the same way I did.

This was it. The last Trial.

If any of Atlas' cronies won, it was game over. If I accidentally embraced my full power and killed my sister, I didn't know what I would do, but I was pretty sure it wouldn't involve coming back to the palace. And if I felt any more strongly about the complicated, tortured god who held the title of my husband... Well, that might be game over, too. That was, if Persephone was right, and he loved me.

Shaking off the thought, I picked up the belt and

strapped it on. For the first time, I felt appropriately dressed for a Trial. I felt strong and alert, probably thanks to Persephone's healing magic. The shell tattoo was three-quarters filled with color, but my desire to admire it had vanished.

"Are you sure you want to come with me?" I asked Kryvo.

"I'm not going to dignify that with an answer," he said huffily.

I smiled. "Just checking. I knew you wouldn't abandon me at the last hurdle," I told him. He heated on my skin.

"Can we take my cushion please? I think it may be a long trip to the bottom of the ocean."

I picked up his cushion and stowed it in the belt.

It probably would be a long trip. And if the author of the book had got anything right, it was a dangerous one, too. Poseidon no longer had any control over the creatures that inhabited the sea's depths.

I sucked in a breath. "So. My goals are," I raised my hand and ticked them off on my fingers. "Reach Atlantis without being eaten, find the most shells and win the Trial, use my power without fully embracing it, don't fall in love, and don't get turned into a monster by a primordial, all powerful god."

"You forgot cure the stone blight and save Aquarius."

"Shit."

"Shit," repeated the little starfish.

~

When I got back to the throne room, I was surprised to see not only Poseidon there, but Hades, Persephone, and Galatea.

"I made you these," said Persephone, stepping forward and handing me four vials of brown liquid. "It's the tea from my place, but I've added a little extra. It will heal most mild-to-serious wounds, but only with rest."

"Thank you," I said gratefully, tucking them into a pouch on my belt.

"I hope you don't need them. And I'm sorry we can't help you more," she said, before wrapping me in a warm hug. "Know that we would if we could."

"I know," I told her. She stepped back, and Hades' stare caught my eye.

*Look after my brother,* he said, but his voice sounded in my mind. I nodded. Galatea stepped forward, holding her hand out formally.

"I want you to know that I believe you to be the best chance our king has. And that I am confident that you will save our realm from destruction." I took her proffered hand, trying to suppress an awkward grin as she shook it.

"I'll do my best," I said.

"I know you will. By the way, I still think you're odd." She gave me a true smile, her face lighting up with wry amusement.

Impulsively, I tugged on her arm, pulling her into a brief hug. She stiffened and looked a little alarmed when I pushed her away again.

"I've decided to own being odd."

"Probably for the best," she nodded. "Look, I want you to have something." She pulled her dagger from its sheath and handed it to me. It was the one she had lent me for the last Trial.

"But..." She had given me the strong impression that the dagger was important to her before, and the intricate carving on the handle suggested it was valuable. I looked up from the dagger to her. "This is yours."

"And now it is yours. If I can't be involved in taking down that scumbag Atlas, then at least you can take my weapon into battle with you."

"Are you sure?"

"I am. You have earned it, Almi."

"Thank you. I am honored."

"Prove it, by winning."

I nodded and tucked the knife into the strap on my leg —now on the outside of my tight leather pants.

"Are you ready?" Poseidon asked.

I looked around the throne room. All the people here had become my friends, including Kryvo and Blue. I felt a surge of reluctance to leave, the idea of there not being a bunch of life-threatening shit going on around us and being able to just enjoy time with these people, suddenly filling my mind.

I'd never wanted anything other than Lily before. And now...? Now I wanted a life. In this place, with these people.

I still wanted Lily. Jeez, did I still want Lily. But I wanted Lily to meet my new friends, enjoy their company, play with my air magic, explore the Palace, feel what it was like to ride Blue — and a hundred other things this life could offer us.

"Almi?" Poseidon's voice was soft and broke me from my unexpected reverie.

"Yes. I'm sorry. I'm ready." I looked at Persephone. "Thanks for everything. If we don't see each other again, you saved my life, and, as soppy as it sounds, proved to me that I can have friends." I looked at Galatea. "You too. Thank you both."

Persephone gave me an encouraging smile, and Galatea looked even more awkward. "We'll see you just as soon as you're back," Persephone said firmly.

"Preferably victorious and with his trident returned," added Hades, nodding at his brother.

Poseidon gave him a look, then lifted me onto Blue's back. I closed my eyes quickly, allowing just a second for the emotion to wash over me. Then, gathering my resolve, I squeezed the pegasus with my thighs. "Let's go, Blue," I whispered, and the pegasus launched himself into the air.

As soon as we reached the empty sky above Aquarius, my little whirlwind appeared, dancing around us as we soared higher.

I couldn't see Poseidon's ship anywhere, but Blue seemed to know where he was going, so I clung on and enjoyed the ride.

After a few moments, we burst through a large, coral-colored cloud, and as if a veil was lifted, Poseidon's gleaming ship was revealed in all its magnificence. Blue touched down on the bridge and Poseidon landed a few feet away. His hair was windswept, and his emotionally charged gaze fell on me as he leaped down from Chrysos.

"You care for them." It was a statement, not a question.

He strode toward me with an almost alarming sense of purpose. I eased myself down from Blue's back.

"Yes."

"You earned the respect of my general and my brother."

"More by luck than by judgement, I think," I shrugged awkwardly. Poseidon came to a stop a foot away from me.

"You are more than you think you are, Almi." Storm clouds swept across his eyes.

"Perhaps." A few days ago, I would have argued. But with my unfolding power, and the responsibility of so many lives weighing on me, I *had* to be more than I thought I was. I didn't have a choice.

"I wish I could show you."

I frowned at his words. "Show me what?"

He shook his head. Tight control gradually retook his features, the storm in his eyes dying away. "The ship. I need to show you the ship."

Normally, I would have pushed him to find out what he had really been about to say. But in my gut I knew it would be too dangerous to hear it. I could see the undercurrent of desire in his face, feel his need rolling from him.

"Yes. Show me the ship."

We stared at each other a beat longer, then he whirled around. I waited long enough for my pulse to slow and followed him.

# ALMI

We made our way down a short set of steps to the main deck of the ship. The glorious solar sails stood huge and proud over us, glittering like liquid metal. Poseidon moved to the railings, and I followed.

"There are crossbows mounted at regular intervals along the ship's rails," he told me, his tone all business. "They refill with bolts made from a similar material as the solar sails. That means the deeper we go, the less light there is and the less ammo we have."

"Like a battery that runs out in the dark."

He threw a small frown over his shoulder at me. "I do not know what a battery is."

"Like a store of power, that runs out when you use it all."

"Then yes."

"How does the ship keep going without light to power the sails?"

This time, when he looked over his shoulder at me, he

wore an expression laced with pride. "This ship is special. She is the only vessel in all Olympus that can switch out her sails to pagos sails."

"Pagos sails?"

"They are powered by the cold."

"And it's cold under the sea?"

"Yes. The lava breaking through the surface in the last Trial was due to us being on the border of the black-smith god's volcanic realm, but most of the ocean floor is cool. And the depths we will need to go to are extremely cold."

I frowned. I'd had enough of cold water in the Trial on Apollo's realm. "I may need to borrow your toga again," I said.

"With any luck, we will not get wet. I have barely any water magic left, and your magic is air," he said wryly.

"If you have the only ship that can move through water, how will the others get down to Atlantis?"

Poseidon shrugged. "Ceto is a sea monster, so she will have no problems. And Kalypso is a water Titan. She will be able to devise something, I am sure. Polybotes though, I do not know. Giants have strong ties to Hephaestus' forges—he may be able to seek help there." He turned back to the large crossbow mounted on the railing. "To fire, you send your will into the weapon, just as you did to steer the crosswind in the first Trial."

I followed him around the deck of the ship, making a mental note of everything he told me about how it worked. We went through what to do if the sails were damaged, how the enormous harpoon gun on the peaked front of the ship worked, and where all the emergency hatches to get below deck if the haulers weren't working were.

The irony of Poseidon himself teaching me how to control the ship I had originally planned to steal from him was not lost on me as we made our way back up the steps to the bridge.

He spoke as though I would need to know these things in his absence, and such a large part of me wanted to stop him, unwilling to entertain the idea of losing him for any reason. But there was no point. He would feel better if he thought I could operate the ship without him, and the knowledge sure as hell couldn't hurt.

He told me how to brace myself properly when holding the huge ship's wheel, so that it didn't wipe me off my feet if it spun, and he showed me yet another weapon in the back of the bridge, this one more like a freaking cannon.

"The other thing you need to be aware of on the bridge is the pegasus pen."

"The what now?"

He pointed to a gleaming gold metal sigil on the planks, on the left side of the ship. The gold was shaped like a winged horse. He dropped into a crouch, the movement making his shoulders muscles bulge and a shimmy of appreciation work its way through me.

He pressed his fingertips to the metal symbol. "Think of Blue when you touch it," he said. A whirring sounded, and then I saw movement beyond the railings. When I reached them to look over the edge, a whole section of the ship was sliding out, and a small, roofless stable was contained within the section.

"That's amazing!"

"They will sleep and rest there. There are very few instances where they would want to be inside the stable when it is stowed inside the ship, as they are incredibly claustrophobic creatures."

I nodded in understanding. "I can empathize."

"You are claustrophobic?" he asked me.

"I don't like the thought of being trapped."

"Does anyone?"

I gave him a pointed look. "You choose your own walls, mighty one," I said, giving him a mock bow to emphasize my point. "You can go anywhere, do anything. The decision not to lies with you."

Light burned bright in his eyes a moment, then he turned back to the railings. "The last thing above deck is the underwater shield." He moved back to the ship's wheel and pointed at the trident carved into the very center. "Touch that and will for protection from the water. A magical shield will encompass the ship."

"Including the side-stable?"

"Yes."

"Cool."

"You are cold?"

"No, it's a human word for something good."

His frown lifted. "Humans both intrigue and bore me."

"Then you've met the wrong humans. They are far from boring, trust me."

He cocked his head. "If we survive this, will you show me the human world?"

Both his demeanor and the question itself were so un-godlike that I was momentarily stuck for words. He sounded like a normal guy, asking someone out on a date.

He straightened when I failed to answer. "If you still resent me for forcing you to spend so much time there, then I understand."

"No, I just didn't expect you to ask me that."

He paused. "Does that mean you do not resent me?"

I scowled. "Oh, I still resent you. But I guess there were some pretty awesome places in the human world. California was particularly fun." I wondered how much more fun it would be to visit with an almighty water god. The thought of Poseidon in Hawaiian shorts on a surfboard, performing mind-blowing tricks on the waves, made me smile.

"That's the one—." Poseidon started to say, then closed his mouth abruptly.

"The one what?"

A muscle in his jaw ticked as he kept his lips clamped together. When I realized he wasn't going to answer me, I shook my head. "And you say I'm the odd one. Anyway, yes. If we survive this, I'll show you the places I enjoyed in the human world."

"I would like that." The words sounded like they were being dragged from his lips. "I must show you below deck, now."

# ALMI

*O*nce again, I decided not to push the ocean god. If he thought it best to keep what he'd been about to say to himself, there was probably a good reason.

I followed him into the hauler at the back of the bridge. Unlike the one that hung on the outside of the boat, this one moved down the middle, sinking into the planks just like a wooden elevator.

When it reached the bottom, Poseidon broke the slightly awkward silence. "There are two levels down here. The lowest is all weapons and cargo, and the other is cabins and the galley."

"Is the galley the kitchen?"

"Yes." There was no door on the hauler, and he gestured out at the space before us without stepping out of it. "This is the cargo hold."

There were many large wooden crates and peculiar shaped objects covered in sheets. Round porthole windows let in rays of light, but it was still gloomy. Under each porthole window was a cannon, poking through the hull of the ship.

"Do these cannons reload magically too?"

"Yes. And unlike the ones up top, they can fire light and cold powered ammunition."

"So they'll work when we're really deep?"

"They will. And they are controlled by the ship herself. She will defend herself from threat, but you will need to steer her, as she can only fire the weapons, not aim or move herself."

"Okay."

The hauler began to move upward again, taking us to the next level up.

This time, I found myself looking down a long, nicely decorated corridor. Double doors at the end were carved in the shape of a seashell and glimmered with the same mother-of-pearl shine as my sister's skin.

Poseidon stepped out of the hauler and began to stride down the corridor. "These are guest cabins." He gestured at the wooden doors we passed, stopping when he reached one with a large cresting wave painted on it. "This one is the galley."

He pushed the door open, and I peered in.

All the surfaces were a rich, dark wood, and the walls were painted pale blue. There were sinks and counter-tops, knife racks, and cupboards. "Kitchen," I said with a nod. "Got it."

"Can you cook?"

The question was another unexpected one. "Today is an Almi-pop-quiz," I said, looking at him.

"What is a pop quiz?"

I chuckled. "It doesn't matter. Yes. I can cook. My trailer used to be parked near an Italian restaurant and they used to give away all the food they hadn't sold that was going bad. I make mean pasta."

"Then you are cooking on this voyage."

I raised an eyebrow. "We're calling it a voyage now, are we?"

"Any large undertaking on my ship should be called a voyage," he said, his shoulders squaring.

"I prefer voyage to Trial," I said. "Can you cook?"

"Of course."

"Then why am I cooking on this voyage?"

"I am a king." There was a playfulness to his tone, not an arrogance, and I decided to play along.

"Oh, I see." I bent low. "I shall make my king the finest Italian food that has ever passed his lips."

"I do not know what an Italian is, but I look forward to it."

I grinned at him. He stared at me a beat, then turned away. My smile slipped.

"This is the mess room, or dining room." He pushed open another door to reveal a room that looked fit for a king to eat in. Cherrywood paneling lined a space housing a long table, and the portholes along the hull side of the room were lined with gleaming gold rings. Sea creatures were painted across the ceiling in the same style as his throne room, and I instantly wanted to spend time in there.

"It's lovely."

"Yes." He closed the door. "My chambers are there." He pointed to the double doors at the end. "You may stay in this room." He pointed to a different door at the left end of the corridor, which presumably shared a wall with his.

I moved past him and pushed open the door.

It was nice; a small neat single bed against one wall, two small porthole windows letting in light, and a chest filled with sheets and what looked like shirts. The walls were the same pale blue as the galley. There was a door that I assumed led to a bathroom.

"You know, a gentleman would give the lady the bigger room," I said, stepping back into the corridor and eyeing the huge doors to his room.

He said nothing, but the muscle in his jaw ticked again.

"Since we're having a tour, I'd better see your room too."

Before he could stop me, I pushed the doors to his room open.

"Whoa."

The room was at the front of the ship, so it was a V-shape, and it took up the *whole* of the front of the ship. Instead of porthole windows, enormous full height picture windows lined the back walls. A bed in the shape of a clamshell stood grandly in the center of the room, and somehow managed to look classy, rather than tacky. I stepped into the room, turning in a slow circle. The ceiling, unsurprisingly now, was painted with a beautiful coral scene, turtles, merfolk, dolphins, whales, seahorses, and hippocampi flitting about amongst the underwater garden.

Along the back wall of the room, on either side of the door, were tall bookcases covered with ornaments, small statues and books. A door led to what must have been the room opposite mine in the corridor. A bathroom? I walked to it and pushed it open.

Bathroom didn't come close. It was an indoor beach. Soft white sand covered the floor that wasn't taken up by what had to be described as a pool, rather than a bathtub. The far wall was a waterfall, water running from a split in the wall into the sparkling green pool. Shining mirrors alternated with large windows, reflecting the bright light around the room. It didn't smell of soap, like a normal bathroom, but of the sea, fresh and inviting.

I gaped at Poseidon. "Can I at least have a bath in here?"

His eyes darkened, his jaw working as he dropped his head. "If you remove your clothing in this room, I will not be held responsible for my actions," he growled.

Color leapt to my cheeks and I swallowed. My hands itched to pull my shirt straight off. But that was a bad idea, and we both knew it.

"This is a nice room," I said dumbly instead.

"Would you like it?" he ground out.

I blinked at him. "Who the hell is answering no to that?"

"I have not offered my quarters to anyone my entire, long, life. So I do not know who is saying no to that."

I tried to find some amusement in his tone, but he was a seven-foot tower of tightly coiled energy, and I was getting the distinct feeling that if I pushed him much further, he might explode. "Why are you offering it to me then?"

"You are my wife."

My heart skipped a beat. *Wife*. I'd been his wife my whole adult life, but I'd never actually been treated as such. I looked back at the bed, then at him.

"I don't know if you'll fit in the single bed in the other room."

His eyes flashed. "You misunderstand me. I did not offer to swap rooms with you."

Heat swirled through me on a low, long swoop. "You mean… share?"

I looked back at the enormous bed covered in rich navy silk sheets. Vivid images filled my head, us in the pool together, his whole glorious body on show, me lying back on the bed, his magnificent form towering over me.

"Yes. I mean share."

"Is that a good idea?" My voice was a hoarse whisper.

"No."

"Right."

My face heated so much it was uncomfortable. I turned and walked deliberately past him, to the open doors to his rooms. "I need some air."

"That *is* a good idea."


I headed for the hauler at the other end of the corridor, and only noticed when I reached it that Poseidon hadn't followed me. I saw him disappear into the galley and was relieved.

When I got to the top deck, the cool ocean air calmed

the heat that had been taking over my body. Sharing a room with him wasn't just a bad idea, it was freaking dangerous. My mind skipped gleefully back to how he had made me feel in Aphrodite's palace, causing some of the heat to return instantly to my face. And south of my belly

I could be in serious danger of falling in love with him, I thought ruefully.

If I was being honest with myself though, the gentle questions he'd been asking me that suggested he genuinely wanted to get to know me were just as dangerous.

Distance.

We may have been stuck on the ship together, our goals intricately intertwined and our destinies hand in hand, but I had to keep as much distance as I could between myself and the ticking timebomb that was my husband.

# ALMI

ootsteps made me turn from where I was leaning on the railing. Poseidon came toward me, holding two steaming mugs, and held one out to me.

"Thank you." He just nodded. "How long is the voyage down to Atlantis?" I asked him, trying to stay focused on the practical.

"Two days."

"I read something about sea monsters guarding the route."

He looked grave as he leaned against the railing next to me. "Yes. Two of the most dangerous creatures to inhabit the seas." My stomach squished in apprehension.

"The most dangerous? Worse than the talontaur?" I'd heard stories growing up of the most monstrous sea creatures in Poseidon's seas, and some of them had kept me and my vivid imagination awake at night.

"Worse than the talontaur," Poseidon said. I looked at him, dread forming now in my gut as images from my childhood nightmares flashed before me. *Please don't say-*

"Scylla and Charybdis."

"Fuck," I said on a breath. "And you can't control them?"

"Not without my trident."

The heat that had been engulfing me vanished, replaced by icy fear. I gripped the warm mug, and took a sip. Cinnamon filled my mouth and chased away some of the cold.

"You know these monsters though, right? That must give us some sort of advantage?"

"I designed them, with Ceto and her brother."

"Good. So, you must know their weaknesses?"

He gave a dry snort. "They do not have weaknesses." He straightened suddenly, frowning. "That's not actually true." His words were slow and thoughtful, and I could practically see the cogs turning. "They hate each other."

"Why?"

"What do you know about them?"

"Only what I was told by my sister when I was little."

"Which was?"

"They are so terrifying that people go mad when they encounter them. Scylla is a six-headed sea dragon, and Charybdis is a giant whirlpool with a meat grinder at the bottom."

Poseidon quirked a brow. "Meat grinder is not a bad analogy. Charybdis is more like a giant worm, with a circular mouth and hundreds of layers of teeth. The pull of his whirlpool is enormous, and once you are in his grasp it is near impossible to get out."

"And Scylla? Is he really a six-headed dragon?"

"Yes. *She* has six heads, all on long necks, a mane of lethal spiked horns and a jaw full of teeth on each."

"Obviously," I muttered, and took another sip of cinnamon tea. "When I was a kid, Scylla and Charybdis were used to make a point of learning about having to make hard decisions."

"Yes. The two creatures are rarely separated and were designed to guard passageways. The person wishing to get through must travel close to one of the monsters, and the passageway will be too narrow to avoid them both. They must choose what they believe to be the lesser of two evils."

Another stab of irony clouted me. *Learning to choose between the lesser of two evils. Killing my sister or killing a whole realm.* I looked away from Poseidon, staring over the edge of the ship to the water below. "Meat grinder or multi-headed dragon. Which is worse?"

"In our situation, I do not know. But, Scylla's body is fused to a mountain, far below sea level. Charybdis, though tethered to Scylla, can be moved. With an effort."

"You think we can separate them enough to get through the middle?"

Poseidon shook his head, and a dangerous gleam filled his eyes. "I think we try to do the opposite. I think we try to move Charybdis toward Scylla."

"Let them fight while we scoot past?"

"It would be the fight of centuries," he murmured, and he sounded regretful.

"You're worried they will hurt each other?"

"No, I'm sorry I will not be able to see it if we pull this

off. They are some of the most magnificent killing machines in Olympus."

Poseidon really had led a different life than the one I had. Glee at watching two lethal monsters kill each other was really more of an all-powerful, ancient-god thing than it was an Almi thing.

He glanced at me when I said nothing. "They'll be reborn if they are killed in battle," he said, clearly trying to reassure me.

"Oh. Erm, good."

Once again, Poseidon had been thinking about the repercussions of his actions. I wondered if forcing the monsters to fight would have been a viable strategy for him if they didn't come back to life if they died. I had a feeling the answer was no.

"It will take a great deal of your power to move a monster like Charybdis." Poseidon looked into my eyes, serious and stern. "Do you think you can do it? I am not sure how much I will be able to assist."

I swallowed, trying to decide how truthful to be with him. After a moment's thought, I opted for full honesty. There wasn't any point in lying. If he felt even half as connected to me as I did to him, he would know. "I won't fully embrace my power."

His face didn't change. I didn't even see the telltale flicker of bright blue in his eyes that often gave away his emotions. "How much power do you think you can call on without embracing it fully?"

"I have no idea," I shrugged. His lack of anger or disappointment at my confession was unnerving me. "I expected you to give me a lecture."

"Would you like one?"

"No."

"I can't control your decisions, Almi. Only my own." He looked away from me. "I will not be the one to tell you to cause your sister's death."

Gratitude swamped me, along with a healthy dose of relief. He wasn't going to try to talk me into taking my power. Not even to save his own life, or his realm.

Fresh guilt began to invade the relief. "I'm not refusing to find the Heart of the Ocean or anything," I said quickly. "I'm not giving up. I just think there must be another way, and I won't risk Lily's life until I know there isn't."

He met my eyes again. "One step at a time. We will win these Trials. And then we will cure this blight."

I held my mug out. "To winning the Poseidon Trials."

After a beat, he held his own out and chinked it against mine in a toast. "To winning the Poseidon Trials," he repeated, and we both drank.

When Atlas' voice rang out around us an hour later, my nerves were a jangle of restless knots. "To the starting line, competitors!" There was a flash of light, and the whole ship was transported.

We were hovering over an expanse of clear ocean, and in front of us, lounging on a throne on a marble platform floating high enough for us to see him clearly, was Atlas. He was massive, almost the same size as Polybotes the giant. He was wearing gleaming gold armor from neck to toe, and flames licked over the metal at irregular intervals.

His eyes were bright red, and his dark hair was topped with an elaborate gold headdress made up of interlocking rings.

"Let us recap the scores! Kalypso got one shell in the last Trial and now has ten." High above us a vessel flashed into existence. It was a ship very similar in shape and size to Poseidon's, but it was made of alternating sections of black metal and water. I could see straight through large parts of the hull, and actual fish were swimming around in the watery walls.

"That's frigging awesome," I breathed.

Poseidon frowned at me. "You are not supposed to be impressed by the enemy."

"She has a ship made out of water," I said, looking at him. "There's no scenario in which that's not cool."

He rolled his eyes, but he didn't actually look annoyed.

Kalypso's ship vanished, and Ceto took its place, enlarged so much she was as big as a frigging house. Her tentacles whipped at the air, her soulless black eyes looking over our ship as the red liquid ran like rivers over her leathery flesh. "Ceto is our current leader with eleven shells."

I pulled a face as she vanished, and Polybotes appeared instead. He was standing in a round metal sphere, not a great deal larger than he was. Strips of the sphere were made of glass, like the segments of an orange, and the ball appeared to be equipped with coiled chains and at least two crossbow-style weapons. "The giants in the forges have indeed assisted him," Poseidon muttered.

"They made him that?" I gaped at Poseidon and he nodded.

"It looks like their work. He'd better hope it can withstand the depths." The sea god didn't sound all that convinced that it would.

"Polybotes managed an impressive three shells in the last Trial and has eight overall."

The next flash took me utterly by surprise. The ship and Poseidon vanished around me, reappearing where the other contestants had, high above the ocean surface.

I, on the other hand, stayed exactly where I was. It took less than a second for me to plummet into the freezing waves. I had time to gulp in a breath, and then I was kicking my legs, trying to ignore the shock of the cold and my blistering rage, as I swam back up to the surface. I heard Atlas' voice as my head broke the waves.

"Poseidon has yet to score a single shell."

I looked up and saw Blue's distinct wings as he dove off the edge of the ship, making straight for me. He didn't get far, though, before there was another flash, and the ship and I swapped places.

"Lastly, we have Almi, who appears not to have a vessel to travel to the sunken city of Atlantis in!" Atlas' voice was mocking as I found myself suspended high over the ocean, and Poseidon's ship.

A tingle of panic ran through me, both at the sheer height I was dangling at, but also at the thought that I wouldn't be able to share Poseidon's ship. After all, we were technically competing with one another.

Blue charged through the sky toward me, ducking under me as Atlas' voice rang out again. "Almi is second to last, with nine shells. And it now seems she is traveling to the bottom of the sea on a pegasus." He actually laughed this time, and Blue let out an angry whinny as whatever was holding me in place in mid-air vanished, and I slipped awkwardly as I tried to right myself on his back.

"Thank you, Blue," I said as I gripped his mane. I knew the pegasus' anger was directed at the asshole Titan and not me.

"Let the final Trial commence!"

# ALMI

*B*lue tucked in his wings and dove. I expected him to make for Poseidon's ship, but instead, he angled straight at the surface of the sea. I sent out a silent plea to air for the breathing bubbles and held my breath for the second time.

I was more prepared for the cold as we plunged under the water. Bubbles zoomed toward me, wrapping around my head and filling my mouth with air as Blue spread out his wings and gave them a hard beat. I could feel his legs kicking hard under us, and we kept moving deeper.

As the air before my eyes settled, I twisted my head and watched as the other competitors sank in their various vessels around me. Kalypso's distinctive black panels were the most obvious, and she was still closest to the surface. Polybotes' sphere was sinking steadily, and Ceto's inky form was already far below me. Poseidon's ship was at the same level as Blue.

The front was tipped forward slightly, the gleaming gold sails slicing through the water. Poseidon was standing at the helm, gripping the wheel, and the sight of him made my breath catch.

He was magnificent. His white hair billowed behind him in the water, and the light rippling through the water and reflecting off the sails played across his solid chest.

As I watched, the color of the light changed, the gleaming liquid gold sails darkening. As though navy ink had been poured down them, the gold melted away, and they reminded me of a breathtaking night sky, covered in glittering stars. They still looked as though the material was made of liquid metal, but now deep and rich and dark.

A bubble started to grow from the middle mast as I stared, expanding into a dome just like the ones that covered the cities in Aquarius, a slight golden shimmer to it. Poseidon moved his head, locking his eyes on me. Without a word from me, Blue shifted, and we powered toward the ship.

Blue slipped through the shield with no resistance at all, and I let out a heavy breath of relief. He landed on the main deck, and my bubbles pulled away from my face to form the little whirlwind.

"Thank the gods for that," I muttered, as I slid from Blue's back. "And thank the gods for you." I patted Blue's haunches, and he stamped his feet before spreading his wings and shaking them. I squealed as water covered me from head to foot. My whirlwind rushed me, spinning around me in a flash, lifting my hair and pulling my shirt from my belt. I squealed again as it spun me around, spluttering a laugh as I realized it had almost dried me completely.

"And thank you too!" It zoomed around my head, just half a foot high again. Tucking my shirt back in, I set off for the bridge at a jog.

"You know, I worried Atlas was going to find a way to keep us separated," I said to Poseidon as I stepped off the last step and onto the bridge.

He didn't look at me, and I frowned and sped up. "Everything okay?"

"The ship," he ground out.

"Your face," I murmured, coming to a stop next to him. *Stone.* So much stone. "What's wrong with the ship?"

"When you and Blue landed, it all but stopped responding to me. It's taking everything I have to keep her on course."

"Atlas," I said in a hiss. "He *has* found a way to try to keep us apart."

Poseidon gave me a very brief sideways glance. "He could not interfere with my ship."

"Are you sure?"

"Yes. It would be like interfering with Chrysos or Blue."

"Then maybe the ship just doesn't like me." I laid my hand on the wheel next to his, and felt the vessel judder underneath me.

Poseidon's eyes snapped to mine. "You are right. She does not trust you." His own eyes darkened briefly, as though he wondered if that meant he shouldn't trust me either.

I released the wheel and put my hand over the top of Poseidon's instead.

*Can you hear me?* I asked the ship.

We jerked again.

*I'm going to take that as a yes. We're going to need you to put on the performance of your life today. Poseidon's life, trident and realm are dependent on it.*

An image flashed into my head, unbidden. It was dark and disconnected, but I saw myself, I saw golden snakes, and I saw Poseidon on his knees, stone covering his body.

I was so shocked I pulled my hand from Poseidon's. "Did you see that?"

"See what?"

"I think the ship just showed me something."

Poseidon's face creased thoughtfully. "She is powerful, and the ships have mental connections. I suppose it is possible. What did you see?"

"Something that hasn't happened."

"No. That is not possible."

I heard Kryvo's voice, small and I was fairly sure only for me. "Put me on the wheel. I can feel the ship, a bit like the statues in the palace."

I lifted him from my collar and laid him on the wood. His little tentacles wrapped around a spoke.

"What are you doing?" Poseidon looked at me and I waved a hand at him.

"Starfish stuff."

"We are losing speed. We need to do something."

"I'm trying to."

Kryvo spoke again. "She does not like you. She believes that you will be the cause of Poseidon's death."

"What? How? Why?" The questions came out one after another, and Poseidon looked at Kryvo, then me.

"She doesn't know any of those things, only that you are a bad omen for her king."

I ground my teeth. "He's supposed to be the cause of my damned death!" I protested. "Not the other way around!"

Poseidon fell so still next to me that, for a second, I worried he may have turned to stone again. I looked at his face and saw he had closed his eyes.

"Is he talking to the ship?" I whispered to Kryvo.

"I think so," the starfish whispered back.

After a minute that felt like a freaking hour, I felt the ship start to speed up. When Poseidon opened his eyes, we were moving at almost twice the speed we had been. He reached for my hand, and I let him take it. Studiously ignoring the zing of electricity that shot between us, he wrapped my fingers around the spoke of the wheel. "Almi, meet *Mossy*."

I felt a flash of heat under my fingertips. *Hi. I'm not trying to kill your king. I promise.*

The heat cooled instantly, and the same image I'd seen before popped into my head. I tried to hold onto it, to make out more detail than I'd seen last time, but it was just as fragmented as it was before. Just as it slipped away though, I thought I saw myself lying on the ground at Poseidon's feet, pale, unmoving, and lifeless.

I let go of the wheel.

"What happened" Poseidon looked at me, concern in his bright eyes.

"I just saw the image again. I thought I saw..." I trailed

off, unwilling to say what I'd seen. "It was weird," I finished lamely. "The ship's moving faster, what did you say to her?"

"How important it was that we win this Trial."

"Good."

I picked up Kryvo and put him back on my collarbone. I didn't know if it was normal that I now craved his reassuring presence, or if that made me even odder than everyone already thought I was.

At this point, I wasn't really sure I cared.

"How long will it take us to get to Scylla and Charybdis?" I asked.

"About a day."

"What?" I stared at him. "A whole day?"

"We are going deeper than most minds can comprehend."

"Oh. So… We *are* going to have to choose a bedroom at some point."

He looked at me. "There are many creatures guarding the deep. I suggest one of us stays on watch at all times."

"Good idea. Maybe we can build a blanket-fort up here."

He blinked. "A blanket-fort? Is this a human thing?"

"No, Lily and I built blanket-forts all the time."

"Explain this fort-building to me."

His grip on the ship's wheel had relaxed, and I was confident *Mossy* was doing most of the work now. "You get a load of sheets, a couple chairs, cushions, some snacks and a drink, and you build a fort," I said.

He cocked his head, thinking. "A furniture fortress?"

I laughed. "That sounds like an upgrade. But yes. Exactly that. If you have fairy lights, then you're acing it."

He considered me a moment. "You would rather sleep in a structure made of soft furnishings on the bridge, than in a bedroom?"

"I'd rather sleep anywhere that keeps us close," I said, then felt color rush my cheeks. "For safety, I mean," I added in a rush. "It's all very well for you to keep watch, but without your magic you might need me quickly."

"I concur."

"Really?"

"Yes. You keep watch, and I will gather the necessary equipment."

# ALMI

*W*atching the god of the sea, one of the three ruling Kings of Olympus, and the most serious man I'd ever met, build a fortress out of cushions was a frigging delight.

And it was an excellent blanket-fort. Or more accurately, a fortress. He'd brought up four of the overly grand dining chairs, a whole load of sheets, and armfuls of cushions over three feet wide.

"Are those from your bed?" I asked him as he arranged a series of smaller black velvet cushions across the back of the makeshift mattress.

"Everything is from my bed," he grunted from inside the fort.

Lily shimmered into being in my head. *Almi, I know I said I wouldn't get involved with you two, but you do realize sleeping with him up here is the same as sleeping with him in his bed, right? I only mention it because if you fall in love with him, you'll die. And then so will he and all of Aquarius.*

*Jeez, not much pressure then,* I replied. *We're taking turns.*

*Don't worry. I'm not falling in love with him. And I'm still not convinced he loves me.*

Her face did that thing where she was clearly about to say something and thought better of it it. *Fine. Keep it that way.*

*I will.*

*Good. Know that if you don't, and you two get too close, you're going to get me popping up in your head. I'll do whatever takes to keep my baby sister safe.*

I groaned out loud and Poseidon turned from where he was kneeling in the den. "Am I doing it wrong?"

"No. No, you're doing great."

*Lily, I'm not going to get too close to him. I swear.*

*Good.*

I turned to face the darkening water around us as my sister's face vanished from my mind. As we got deeper, less light penetrated the ocean, and there was something unsettling about the endless inky gloom. We'd lost sight of the other ships a long time ago, though we had seemed to be ahead of Polybotes and Kalypso, and behind Ceto.

"What happens if we get to the sea monsters after everyone else?" I asked.

Poseidon appeared beside me, startling me. "The fortress is ready."

"Oh. Right." I turned and dropped to my knees at the entrance to the makeshift tent, dutifully admiring his handiwork. "It's lovely," I told him. He frowned.

"It is adequate?"

"Yes."

"As good as you made as a child?"

I paused as I looked at the beautiful wood of the chairs, and the rich velvet cushions. "It's fancier," I said.

"Is that good?"

I sat down on the mattress he'd made, swivelling on my butt to look at him. He was bent over and looking at me anxiously. My heart swelled a little at the sight.

"Why are you so keen to do a good job?"

He paused, then said, "A king takes pride in all his tasks."

"Right."

"And you are a queen."

My heart skipped a beat. "It's as good as when I was a kid," I confirmed.

He looked satisfied as he dropped down to the planks, drawing his knees up and resting his muscular arms across them.

"If the others reach the monsters before us, we may be lucky. They may remove them from our path."

"Are any of them strong enough to do that?"

"Ceto and Kalypso might be."

"If we lose, who would be the best and worst to win in our place?"

He gave me a dark look. "We will not lose."

"Uh-huh. But if we do."

I thought he wouldn't answer me, but then he spoke. "Kalypso would be my preference to win."

"Really?"

"She is the only one who might challenge Atlas. I don't believe that she would hand my realm over to him."

I thought about the hunger in her eyes when she'd

cornered me in the dining hall. "I agree. Why do you think they are all competing for him?"

"He'll have bargained with them or blackmailed them. Polybotes might just be competing for his own revenge."

"Dare I ask what you did to him?"

"I am the creator of all giants. He has not agreed with all of my decisions."

I decided to ask him to elaborate later, not that I figured he would actually tell me anymore about his history with the giant.

"What do you think he's got on Ceto?"

"She will have been the easiest to bring around." I could hear the anger in his voice immediately. "If he offered her freedom in exchange for the realm if she wins, then she will not have hesitated."

"She scares the living shit out of me," I said.

He glanced at me. "She is designed to do just that. Her brother is worse, though he is incredibly stupid." He let out a long sigh. "We combined our magic to create incredible creatures - Scylla and Charybdis included. I am disappointed, though not surprised, that she has broken our tenuous bond."

For some unfathomable reason, hearing him talk about a bond to someone else, even a woman who was half rotten sea monster, made me irritable. "And Kalypso?" I asked. "What do you think he has on her?"

"I wish I knew. She has power and a place of privilege in Aphrodite's realm."

"Why is she not a part of your realm if she is a water goddess?"

"When the Titans lost the war, she asked me for a

place in Aquarius. Her father is Oceanus, the most powerful water god to have ever existed. He fought against his own kind in the war, helping the Olympians. Zeus spent a long time trying to make Titan descendants unwelcome in Olympian society, and he wouldn't allow me to accept someone as strong as Kalypso in my palace."

More irritation flowed through me at the idea of Kalypso living in Poseidon's palace, but I shoved it down. "Did that piss her dad off?"

"Yes. Oceanus removed himself from Olympus. It is my belief that he caused all the other primordial Titans to disappear."

"And Kalypso went to Aphrodite?"

"Aphrodite went to her," he corrected me. "Kalypso is beautiful, fierce and powerful. Just the sort of friend Aphrodite likes at court."

"Why didn't Zeus stop Aphrodite like he did you?"

Poseidon snorted. "Stop the goddess of love from doing what she wanted? You are aware of my almighty brother's reputation with women?"

I nodded. "I heard it wasn't just women."

"You heard right. Zeus will put his dick in anything that moves."

"Huh. So Aphrodite seduced him?"

"She seduced him every few months, whenever she wanted something."

Fresh irritation rolled through me, and I cursed this new jealous streak that had risen up out of nowhere as my mouth opened without my permission. "Did she ever seduce you?"

His eyes snapped to mine. "No."

"Oh."

A tense silence descended, and I pretended to inspect my nails for dirt.

"Do you want to sleep now, or take the first watch?" Poseidon asked eventually.

"As I'm already in the fortress, I guess I'll sleep now, if that's okay with you?"

"Good. I will wake you in three hours or so." He stood up and disappeared from my view.

I flopped back onto the cushions with a heavy breath. Just spending time around him was starting to feel dangerous. Every minute, every sentence, every flash of emotion made me warm to him more. And worse, made me doubt my insistence that he didn't have feelings for me.

# ALMI

*I* slept fitfully, but my grogginess when Poseidon woke me vanished fast. When I crawled out of the tent, clutching Kryvo on his little cushion, the sea god was waiting with a plate covered in hot bacon and toast. I stretched, then took the plate from him.

"Thank you. I thought I was cooking pasta?"

"I heard this meat was popular with humans."

"You found bacon just for me?"

"*Mossy* did."

"The ship?"

"Yes."

"How? Has she decided she doesn't hate me yet?"

Poseidon turned to the railings. It was really dark around us now, the only light coming from the gentle glow of the shield over us. "She can conjure whatever food is required. She is no normal ship."

I decided not to point out that he had ignored my second question. "I read about her, in my book. She sounds very special."

He rubbed his hand along the wood fondly. "She is."

"Anything happen while you were on watch?" I moved to the wheel, reluctant to touch the wood myself, lest I be bombarded with more weird images.

"No. I think we are about six hours away now."

"Good. You need more rest than me, according to Persephone. You should sleep as long as you can."

I expected him to argue, or try to be all proud and testosterone-y, but he surprised me by nodding. "Agreed. The more I sleep now, the more I may be of use in battle."

Sensible guy. Of course.

"Enjoy the fortress," I said as he dropped to his knees and crawled inside.

"Wake me if anything happens." I heard his deep voice from under the sheet.

"I will."


I sat down on the deck, leaning my back against the railings and plopping Kryvo's cushion down in front of me so that I could tuck into my bacon and toast. "Did you get any sleep, Kryvo?" I asked around a mouthful of salty deliciousness.

"Yes. A little."

"Good."

"Almi?"

"Uh-huh?" I swallowed my too-large mouthful.

"I am worried."

"You and me both, little friend."

"I'm serious."

"So am I." I set down my empty plate, then gently lifted the starfish onto my palm. "What's wrong?"

"I do not see how you can face Medusa and survive."

"I don't plan to face her," I told him. "I plan to do exactly what you would tell me to do and hide from her."

"You do?" he said hopefully.

"Yes. If Poseidon knows of no way for me to survive her stare, then I'd be an idiot to do anything else."

"Do you think she will be in Atlantis?"

"Yes. But I'm more worried about getting to Atlantis right now." I stood up as I spoke, turning to look out into the dark beyond. The ship was still tilted slightly downward at the front, but for the most part we were just sinking into the depths. I didn't even want to know how much distance there was between us and the surface. The thought made my chest tight.

"Scylla and Charybdis?" asked Kryvo.

"Yeah. Hopefully, the others will get there first and deal with them." I was only half joking.

"They will not harm Ceto. She is their mother."

"Hmmm. She's supposed to have given up all familial advantage," I said doubtfully.

"Would you like to see them? There are a few paintings in the palace I could show you."

I considered his offer as I stared out into the dark. Part of me thought I should be prepared. The other part thought that if I knew what we were about to face I'd want to turn and run. Only, there was nowhere to run.

"Tell me about them, instead," I said. "Anything you think might be helpful."

"Okay." The little starfish sounded less frightened, now

he had something to do. "Scylla's body is fused to a mountain, and she can't move. She has six long necks that look like they can bend in any direction, and each head has a long thin jaw with lots of teeth. In both images of her I can see, she is picking prey off the deck of ships with her multiple heads."

"Okay," I said, beginning to regret asking him. A flash of light in the dark blue beyond made me pause. "Hold on a moment, Kryvo," I whispered. "What was that?"

The light flashed again, then again. I stared as a creature drifted into view. It was huge, about half the size of our ship, but I knew instantly that it meant us no harm.

"It's a hippocampus," said Kryvo. "But not like the ones you get in Aquarius."

He was right. The hippocampi in Aquarius were like seahorses crossed with actual horses, their tails curled up and round, but with the heads and front legs of a stallion. They were usually blue or green.

This creature, though… It too had the curled tail of a seahorse and the head and top-torso of a horse, but it was almost white. Lights, intensely bright blue, flashed all along it in quick pulses. The mane flowing from its massive head was rippling with silver light, and its eyes were the same color, bright and filled with intelligence.

"It's beautiful."

"And deadly."

I was starting to believe that most beautiful things were deadly. "Tell me about Charybdis," I said as it drifted out of view.

"There are more pictures of Charybdis, including an image of when he nearly ate Persephone."

"What?"

"Persephone faced the Hades Trials, and she had to collect a gemstone whilst riding a hippocampus and avoiding being sucked into Charybdis' mouth."

"Well," I said, a little stunned. "If we survive this, I'll be wanting to hear that story."

"It proves that what Poseidon said was true — Charybdis is the one that can be moved."

"Does he just look like a whirlpool?"

"If the whirlpool had a massive worm mouth with many rings of teeth at the bottom, then yes."

"Right."

An hour passed by, and I became increasingly more restless, sitting on the deck with nothing but my anxiety and many unanswered questions to concentrate on. "Do you know any stories, Kryvo?"

"There are many in the palace."

"Could you tell me one? Preferably one with happy ending."

"I shall look for something appropriate," he said.

When five and a half hours had passed, and I'd raided the galley twice for more helpings of bacon, I crouched in front of the blanket-fort.

"Poseidon?"

He sat up immediately, hand moving to the knife at his side. He relaxed as he saw me.

"Did you sleep in all that stuff?" All his leather strapping was still across his chest. I blushed as I realized I was openly staring at his pecs.

"Yes."

"Right. Did you sleep okay?"

"Yes."

"Would you like some bacon?"

He paused. "Yes."

Poseidon ate, and I told him about the hippocampus we'd seen. His eyes turned wistful as I spoke.

"They are truly magnificent creatures. You are fortunate to have seen one."

"I felt fortunate," I told him. "How will we know when we are close?"

Before he could answer me, the ship jerked beneath us. Poseidon moved fast, laying his hand on the ship's wheel when he reached it.

"We are close," he said drily.

I peered out over the railings and saw that there was light coming from beneath us. It was blue, nothing like the warm glow of the shield, and it flashed and moved. We continued our descent until I could see solid rock. "Is that the ocean floor?"

"Yes."

The pale blue light was beaming up from cracks in the rock, which widened out into a river of icy light, flowing faster than the ocean water it was submerged in. It formed an illuminated path that lit the side of a massive, dark mountain on our left.

"Is that the mountain Scylla is attached to?" I whispered.

"It's a dormant volcano, but yes." The ship leveled out, and began to follow the river of light.

As soon as we rounded the mountain, I got my first glimpse of the two legendary sea monsters.

Scylla was indeed fused to the mountainside, as Poseidon had said. Snaking out from the rock were six long necks, covered in gleaming barbs. A tail protruded from the rock too, swinging back and forth, its reach as long as the neck's. The heads on the end of each neck made my legs feel weak. The jaws were abnormally long, clearly designed to stab between sails on ships, picking off prey exactly as Kryvo had described. The teeth lining each jaw were so huge the mouths didn't close properly. Worse, each head was easily the size of a car.

Charybdis was lower than the other monster, the whirlpool part of him set into the ground on the opposite side of the river. But poking up out of the middle of the whirlpool was the ugliest, most grotesque-looking worm I'd ever seen. The whole thing's head was a mouth, circular and lined with layer after layer of needle-sharp teeth.

The monsters were lit by the eery, pale blue, flickering light of the river, and the ocean around us was impenetrably black. The gap between the two colossal creatures was barely bigger than the ship, but on the other side, rippling with silver light, was a round portal.

"Air, I'm gonna need some serious help, here," I muttered.

# ALMI

My little whirlwind zoomed about excitedly. "It's alright for you, you're not about to get eaten by sea monsters," I muttered. It stilled, as though trying to show me it could be serious. "Are you ready to kick some sea monster butt?"

It bounced up and down.

"I'm going to need you to be about ten times bigger, and seriously strong. Think you can do that?"

It bounced again.

"And I'm also going to need you to not kill my sister. You got it?"

It hesitated, then bounced again, not quite as vigorously as before. I got the distinct impression the hesitation was due to doubt, rather than an actual desire to harm Lily.

"Look." Poseidon's deep voice caught my attention, and I followed his pointing arm.

Kalypso.

Her black and water ship was hovering right near the

river, and it looked as though she was either unable or unwilling to move between the two creatures. *Mossy* dropped lower, moving closer to the Titan's ship, and I saw a huge tear in the black metal part of the hull, as though a tooth had dragged clean through the metal.

"Poseidon!" Her voice boomed through the water, echoing with a gurgling sound. "Almi!"

"What do we do?" I asked Poseidon. Our ship slowed to a stop beside hers. She was standing on the bridge. There was no shield keeping the water out of her way, and it made me wonder briefly why Poseidon had one. After all, he could breathe underwater as easily as he could breathe on land.

"You will not be able to pass," Kalypso called before Poseidon could answer my question.

"You don't know that," I called back.

"We stand a better chance working together."

I raised my eyebrows in surprise. "She wants to work together?" I hissed at Poseidon.

He turned to me, his voice low. "She can't get past alone."

"Then we should take advantage and leave her here, surely?"

Doubt flickered over his face. "Almi... I have no question that your magic is strong. But you will not embrace it all." I frowned, wanting to protest but not sure I could. "And besides, if we manage to pull off our plan and force the two monsters to fight each other, she will be just as able to sail past them as we will."

I screwed up my face. He was right. Our plan would remove the monsters from *everyone's* path. If we couldn't use Poseidon's power, then the addition of a water Titan's magic might be more helpful than I wanted to admit. I thought about what Poseidon had said earlier, about Kalypso being the only one of the competitors who might not give up the realm of Aquarius to Atlas if she were to win. "Fine," I said.

We both turned to Kalypso. "I want to move Charybdis," called Poseidon.

Kalypso leaped off the bridge of her ship and darted through the water toward us, so fast it took me by surprise. Clearly Poseidon had the same thought because his knife was in his hand in a flash.

"I am not here to fight you," Kalypso said as she reached the edge of our shield, just a few feet away from us. Her watery hair caught the icy light, her dark skin almost giving off its own glow. She was truly magnificent under the water; it was where she belonged. "Did you just say you wish to *move* Charybdis?"

"Yes. Pit the two creatures against each other. I believe it is the only way to distract them."

Kalypso nodded slowly. "Yes. I like this plan." She looked at me. "Having been on the receiving end of your blustery friend, I know your strength." She glared at my little whirlwind, and it zoomed around my head, taunting her.

"Between us, we should be able to do this," I said, keeping my shoulders squared and my voice confident.

"Agreed." She looked back to Poseidon. "And you? Will you be adding your now-less-than-considerable abilities to this quest?"

"I shall steer my ship," he ground out. I couldn't

imagine he was enjoying admitting he could do nothing to help.

A strange wail rippled through the water, and we all turned our heads to look at the source. Scylla's heads all ducked and turned to us, the blue light of the river lighting them from beneath. As one, the six jaws opened, and I shuddered as the wail sounded again. Forked tongues flicked out between the too-big teeth, and as they moved the barbs covering each neck flashed, showing themselves to be black and slick with something that caught the light.

In response to the wail was a slicing, gnashing sound that was so high-pitched it made my head hurt. The hideous-looking worm thing that was Charybdis was rising out of the spinning whirlpool, its round mouth vibrating in the water.

"Are they communicating with each other?" asked Kalypso.

"I don't know. But let's not waste any more time."

"I concur. Are you ready, land-lover?" She looked at me and I scowled.

"Land-lover?"

"You have no affinity with water. I can tell that even from spending very little time with you."

"Air-lover might be more accurate, then," I said, trying not to let her words get to me. They were true, and I'd known it my whole life, but that didn't change the years of wishing they weren't. I was a sea nymph, for god's sake, I was supposed to have a connection to the water.

Kalypso rolled her eyes. "I am bored with this. It is

time to show the world what I am made of." She held up her hands, and the water around them began to churn.

"Come on, air, let's show this jumped-up Titan we're just as good as she is," I said to my whirlwind. It bounced, then flew through the shield.

For a moment, I thought it might try to combine itself with Kalypso's magic, as it had with Poseidon's to get us under the lavafall. But even the thought of combining my magic with hers made an uneasy sensation roll in my gut, and the whirlwind flew straight past the Titan, toward Charybdis.

I swallowed, nerves and fear twisting inside me. I had no idea how what I was doing.

"Lift the worm out of its hole," said Poseidon. "Then throw it at Scylla."

I looked at the grotesque flailing worm that could have swallowed my trailer whole.

"Easy," I muttered.

I projected my thoughts at my air friend. *We need to lift the worm out of the hole and throw it at the dragon heads.*

The whirlwind was growing as it approached Charybdis, and Kalypso's churning water was racing along beside it.


The worm roared when the two magics hit it.

I cried out in both surprise and pain at the sound, clapping my hands over my ears. I felt my connection to the whirlwind slip as my concentration was ruptured, and I forced myself to focus through the discomfort.

*Dig it out of the hole!*

The whirlwind tightened into a spinning rod and dipped between the worm's huge, wavering body and the whirlpool it was housed in. Kalypso's water was wrapping around it like a lasso, and it thrashed even harder.

With a whoosh, my air zoomed back into sight, it too wrapping itself around the worm's body but starting from the bottom of the whirlpool.

"On the count of three," called Kalypso. "One..." My cord of air glistened in the light of the river as it kept tightening itself around the worm. "Two..." Kalypso's shimmering jet of water was now firmly wound around the thing's head too, underneath the gnashing ring of teeth. "Three!"

I sent a blast of mental power at my air, and Charybdis shrieked again as he was jerked a meter out of the whirlpool. I felt a pull myself, my chest tightening and my mind going fuzzy.

"Hold on!" Poseidon's voice was laced with excitement, and that spurred me on. I kept channelling my thoughts, trying to fight back the exhaustion that was overcoming my body.

The worm jerked again, and again, and then he began to move slowly at first, then faster. The pull on my body lessened, and then the creature was free, pulled completely from the spinning water. It thrashed and flailed in the water, and Kalypso shouted again.

"Now!"

*Now*! I repeated the command to the air, and the worm went pelting through the water toward Scylla's waiting jaws.

The second the teeth closed over the worm's body, the

ship moved beneath my feet. Kalypso threw an unreadable glance at me, then she was zooming back to her own ship. My air magic rushed toward us as we raced along the river.

I had no idea how long the two creatures would be distracted by each other, but clearly Poseidon was taking no chances.

I moved from the railings, once my whirlwind was safely back through the shield, and jogged to Poseidon.

"You did well," he said when I reached him at the wheel.

"Air did well," I said.

We had reached the monsters now, and my gaze was drawn to the epic battle. Poseidon had kept the ship low to the river, aiming straight for the center of the portal at the end of it, which meant the monsters towered over the sails of our ship as we sped along. Five of Scylla's heads had the worm in their mouths, and the sixth was snapping at its face. The worm's body dripped with red slime, and the sheer size of the two creatures made my knees weak.

We were almost past them when the sixth head froze. I watched, almost in slow motion as Charybdis' worm head moved in unison with it, snapping to us.

"Poseidon, I think they've seen us." I felt my legs moving me backward, even though backing up would achieve nothing.

"Shit," he swore, and the ship sped up a fraction more.

It wasn't enough though.

Scylla's sixth head dove at us, lightning fast. For a moment, I thought she'd taken a wild and inaccurate stab as the huge jaw slammed into the lower part of the deck, nowhere near where Poseidon and I were standing. Then I heard a loud whinny.

"Blue!" I shrieked. Without hesitation, I sent my whirlwind toward the snapping jaws. This close, I could see Scylla's leathery hide was deep red in color, and the barbs were indeed dripping with something that looked like oil, flecks of it falling onto the planks and sizzling.

My whirlwind was ten feet tall when it reached the head, and it smashed into it with such force that both the head and the ship jolted. It beat against the snapping jaws, and Blue galloped across the deck toward us, away from the head, followed by Chrysos.

There was another shriek, and the ship jerked to a stop. "Poseidon?" I looked at him, panic rising. He looked back at me, then ran to the railings.

Scylla was still holding the worm part of Charybdis in her mouths, but now the giant round worm-mouth was spinning, sucking everything in its path into it. Including us.

There was movement on our right, and Kalypso's ship soared past us. She'd let us go first, which meant the monsters had two chances of being distracted from her, first by each other, then by us.

"Asshole!" I roared at her. She locked eyes with mine, then blasted beyond us.

*Mossy* heaved, but rather than move forward, she was sucked sideways, toward the meat-grinder mouth.

"Air!"

But my whirlwind was still beating against the snapping sixth head of Scylla, and I could see that if it let up for even a moment, we would be dragon food.

"Shit, shit, shit." I whirled on the spot, looking for anything that might help us, as the ship began kept lurching inexorably toward Charybdis' mouth. Debris and rock were flying past us, anything not anchored down sucked into its maw. The ship cannons were firing, but they were either missing their target, or the ammunition was ineffective.

All we'd done was made sure we had to beat both monsters, instead of one, I realized in horror, as the blanket-fort flew past my head.

Poseidon ran back to the wheel, closed his eyes, and yelled for me to hold on to something. I raced to the wheel, too, wrapping my arms around it.

"What about the pegasi?"

"They made it to the stable. I'm closing them inside the ship!" *Mossy* spun abruptly so that the front was facing the churning maw, instead of the bridge. There was a roar that I was sure was Scylla, and I turned my head in time to see it snap at the main mast of the ship. The whirlwind could only do so much without my constant energy and focus driving it, and I felt a stab of terror as the dragon's teeth sank into the wood of the mast. The whole thing creaked loudly, then began to tip.

The mast crashed to the deck, the beautiful sail tangling around it as it fell. The view ahead of us now was clear, and my heart skipped a beat. The front of the ship was just meters from Charybdis' churning teeth and endless black gullet.

# ALMI

"My children." A melodic voice rang through the sounds of our ship being torn apart, and abruptly, everything stilled. The ship stopped moving, Scylla's heads stopped snapping, and the writhing body of Charybdis froze.

Poseidon was the only thing that moved, and he turned, gazing over his shoulder.

I followed his look, and gasped.

Ceto was behind us, and she was easily as big as the two sea monsters. Her octopus half was low to the ocean floor, her tentacles on either side of the river, holding her colossal body above the glowing water.

Her human half somehow looked completely different than it did on dry land.

The blue light played over her red and black skin, and her black eyes were massive as she surveyed the scene. She looked fearsome and regal, rather than grotesque. I found myself wanting to bow to her.

"My children, you are being used."

I held my breath, not daring to even whisper in the silence that had descended, lest our trip into Charybdis' gullet be resumed.

"Consuming the King is not on your list of tasks today. Pray, let us pass, and I will return you to your rightful positions." Her black eyes moved briefly to Poseidon, then back to the monsters.

Slowly, ever so slowly, the other five heads of Scylla let go of Charybdis' body. The ship shuddered beneath us, then stuttered forward, like a car struggling to start.

Poseidon turned to face the sea goddess as the water flashed red around us, and Charybdis vanished. I moved cautiously to the railings. He was back inside the whirlpool, which was whirling to life around his body.

"Why have you saved our lives?" Poseidon called to Ceto, still towering over us all.

A slow smile spread across her face. "A favor here and there can save one's own life," she said. Her voice, so scratchy on land, was beautiful underwater.

Poseidon paused, then bowed his head. "Consider us in your debt," he said.

She gave a low chuckle. "Oh, I do, Sea King."

There was another flash of red, and then she was a third of the size, and hovering right beside our ship. Her voice rang out, but this time it was in my head. *There is more at stake than you know, Sea King and his Queen. When I need the favor returning, I expect you to deliver.*

Then she was gone, zooming toward the portal and vanishing into it.

A low, pained wail came from Scylla at the departure of his mistress.

"We should go, like, now," I said, casting a glance at the six-headed beast.

Poseidon gripped the wheel. "Come on, *Mossy*. I know you've been injured, but it's not far." The ship inched forward, but it was more of a limp than a sprint. Another wail came from Scylla.

"Air? Fancy giving us a jumpstart?" My whirlwind sprang to life beside me, then whooshed outside the shield. It vanished from view, and a second later, the ship began moving.

"Thanks, air!" I hollered, as we began to power toward the portal.

Questions were whirring through my adrenaline-fuelled brain as we reached the swirling mass of silver water that made up the portal, but apprehension, along with sheer exhaustion, stopped me from voicing any of them. I just clung to the railings as the prow of the ship pushed through the portal, and then the rest of us followed.

For a brief moment, there was just swirling water crashing over our shield, but then we broke through the other side. My eyes widened as I took in the scene before us.

About five miles away, gleaming in the dark and resting on the ocean floor, was a city. The dome encompassing it wasn't the soft gold of the domes in Aquarius but a cold white silver, which illuminated the ruins inside. Large temples and a massive palace in the center were crumbled remains of what they must once have been. We were too far away for me to make out anything other than the larger buildings inside.

But it was clearly once a grand place. I looked at Poseidon.

"Is that it? Atlantis?"

"Yes. Save your energy and your magic. *Mossy* will get us there in about half an hour, I think, and we need time to eat and recover."

I nodded, and projected my thoughts to air. *The ship is going to take it from here, have a rest.*

Poseidon turned away from the wheel, and his bright eyes locked on mine.

"Why did Ceto just help us?" I asked him, moving closer.

"She is still loyal to me."

"She's competing against you to win your realm and trident! That hardly seems like loyalty."

"She just saved our lives, Almi. She broke the rules, commanded her brethren, and saved us."

"What was she talking about when she said-"

Poseidon held his hand up, halting me. "She told us in private for a reason," he said, voice low enough that I struggled to hear him from just a few feet away.

"Okay. Well, what did it mean?"

"It means, if we can't win, we help Ceto win. At all costs."

I would have expected to feel uncomfortable at the idea of willing Ceto to win over Kalypso, but the last few minutes had made me think otherwise. "She's pretty fucking impressive underwater," I muttered.

"You should see me at full power."

I looked up at him in surprise, and realized I wasn't the only one feeling the adrenaline rush from our life-and-death battle. He looked alive, that same wildness in his face I'd seen in a few of the Trials.

"I'd like that," I said, before I could stop myself. His eyes darkened with what I was sure was desire, and I gulped. "We just almost died," I said, trying to backpedal.

"Yes. But here we are." His intense, burning gaze kept boring into me.

I grasped for something to say that would douse the intensifying emotion blazing between us. "It's a good thing we don't need *Mossy* for much longer." I gestured at the fallen mast and saw pain cross his face, breaking the spell.

"She can be repaired. But not any time soon." His stare moved and rested on Atlantis. "Almi, if we come across Medusa on our hunt for shells, you must-"

"Run and hide," I cut him off. "I know. I may be odd, but I'm not stupid."

Slowly, he reached his arm out for me. Equally slowly, I stepped forward and took his outstretched hand. He tugged me into him, and I let out a hard breath as an overwhelming feeling of *rightness* engulfed me. His scent, his presence... his everything.

I needed him.

The feeling whacked into me, and when my arm brushed against the stone covering the side of his ribs, a hard lump formed in my throat.

How the hell could I choose between him and my sister? Between him and fucking anything?

## POSEIDON

*I*t had been more decades than I could recall since the war with the Titans, and the only time I had ever believed my immortal life to be in danger.

Until now. The stone blight was not just slowly killing me; it was making me vulnerable to every threat I faced during the Trials.

But when staring down death at the jaws of a monster of my own creation, I found myself caring nothing for my own life, only for that of the woman now in my arms.

I wanted to tell her so many things. To explain my actions, to ease her frustration.

I nearly had, a dozen times.

The need to tell her how I truly felt, to say those three words to her aloud, was burning a damned hole into my heart.

I didn't know if she could ever love me. The desire to make her understand was tortuous. Watching her pain was worse. I would take her burdens in a heartbeat, would that I could.

My jaw clenched so hard it hurt as her fingers brushed the stone covering my ribs.

The world needed us to win the Poseidon Trials. Aquarius and Olympus needed us to defeat Atlas. They needed us to find the Heart of the Ocean and rid the world of the stone blight.

But once Atlas and the blight were dealt with?

Then I would make things right.

I would tell Almi all the things I couldn't now. I could apologize and rid myself of the searing guilt that plagued me daily.

Almi would be happy.

My deal with Atlas had ensured that. She would live the life she had always wanted to live.

And it did not matter that she could not love me, because I would not be there to live it with her.

# ALMI

When we got close to the city I could see a pier jutting out of the dome, and Kalypso's ship was moored against it. Every building in sight either had sections missing, was crumbling to pieces, or was completely destroyed. It was a city of ruins, something I could imagine a human archaeologist would go nuts for.

*Mossy* pulled up alongside the pier, and I took a deep breath.

I had eaten as much as I could manage and put bread and dried meat in my magicked belt in case we needed more later. We had also drunk a vial each of Poseidon's energy stuff. Blue and Chrysos were on the bridge with us, stamping their feet and looking more ready to go than I felt.

This was the end. I knew it was, as surely as I knew I loved Lily.

We would either leave this place as victors, or we wouldn't leave at all.

The thought of spending eternity in the sunken, ruined city, as still and stone as everything else in it, made me want to keep my feet firmly on the planks of the deck.

But then Blue nudged me, and Kryvo spoke. "We will find all the shells." His quavering voice didn't hold a note of confidence, but the fact that he was trying to buoy me forced me into action.

"Of course we will, little friend. Of course we will."

I tried to lift myself onto Blue, and felt Poseidon's hands on my waist. Heat swooped through me as he lifted me easily onto the pegasus' back.

"Thanks."

He pulled himself onto Chrysos, and I caught his wince at the inflexibility of his side that was mostly covered in stone. "Are you ready?"

"As I'll ever be." Which was code for *I'll never be*.


The pegasi took off, the two of them bursting through the shield around the ship and swooping through the water to the dome. The distance was short enough that I didn't need the breathing bubbles, but my little whirlwind shot after us, whizzing around at my side.

I expected that we would need to find a point where water met the dome in order to get in, just like the domes in Aquarius, but Poseidon was ahead of me and he guided Chrysos straight at the silver barrier.

He and pegasus slipped straight through the dome, so I shrugged and followed him. Silence met us as we broke through the dome covering Atlantis.

As Blue descended, I got a better look at the buildings

around me. I could see that they would once have been grand, even the smaller ones. All pale, polished stone or marble, many of the surfaces were decorated with gilded patterns — or at least they had been once. The sound of the pegasi's hooves touching down on the flagstone ground echoed around us, and it wasn't until I twisted my body and slid off Blue's back that I saw the first statue.

I froze, my breath catching. It was a woman, her arm halfway up to shield her face, which wore an expression of true fear. Her other arm was extended by her side, holding back a boy of about ten. He was gazing in the same direction as the woman I assumed was his mother, but his expression was one of awe.

I stepped toward the stone figures. Guilt and pressure weighed down on me as a new thought occurred to me. What if the Heart of the Ocean could bring these people back from the stone? What if it wasn't just Aquarius who could be healed, but the ancient people of Atlantis too?

I felt something on my shoulder and whirled. "Don't dwell on them," Poseidon said, his voice heavy with sadness.

"Poseidon, do you think the Heart of the Ocean can cure these people too?"

"Cure? Almi..." He looked at me as though he wasn't sure what to say, his jaw tight. "Almi, the people who have been turned fully to stone... I do not know if they are alive inside there."

"You mean, if they're already stone they can't be cured?" Fear lanced through me, and a fresh wave of grief built inside me. "But Silos!"

"I do not know for certain," he said quickly. "But I do not think you should risk raising your hopes."

"You kept them all, though, in your palace, all the people turned to stone! You talked about saving them." I could hear the desperation in my voice.

"Of course I did. I couldn't give up any chance of hope. But I do not want you to think it is your fault if they cannot be saved."

I turned back to the stone woman. Could she be saved?

My eyes moved to her child. Would the lives of these strangers be worth the cost? Could I pay with my sister's life?

What if I did, and they stayed as they were now, cold and lifeless?

Before the overwhelming doubt could burrow its way in any further, Poseidon gripped my shoulder, spinning me back to face him.

"Focus on the task at hand. Find shells. Beat Atlas. You are under no pressure to decide anything now. Do you understand me?"

I stared into his face, feeling the weight lift slightly at his words.

Respite. I was finding respite in the form of deadly Trials and avoiding being turned into a monster, or stone. But honestly? *Anything* was preferable to deciding whether or not to end my sister's life.

We walked through the fallen city in silence, Blue and Chrysos staying close. There were stone people everywhere, some clearly aware of their impending fate, and some caught oblivious. My overactive imagination couldn't help but picture what it must have been like, Medusa stalking through the streets, turning everyone who looked at her to stone.

As we walked, I tried to make myself look at anything other than the people. The architecture was exactly what the human world thought of as ancient Greece. Temples with triangular roofs and tall columns, simple square buildings decorated with intricate carvings and paintings of landscapes, animals, and people. I didn't see a single building still standing as it would have been in its full glory, though it was easy to see how magnificent the city would once have been. Dark green moss grew across the pale ruins, and there was a dampness to the air that smelled of slightly sweet decay. When I looked up, rather than see the vivid blue ocean above me like in Aquarius, I just saw navy-hued darkness.

"Was Atlantis always underwater?" I asked Poseidon. I kept my voice hushed, as seemed to befit our environment.

"No. It was an island."

"Oh."

"I covered it with a silver dome when I sank it because I couldn't use a gold one. Gold is for Aquarius."

"Why create a dome at all?"

He glanced at me. "Medusa. She is not a being of the ocean."

The reminder that he had sent her to live alone down here for centuries made my skin crawl. "Did you ever consider that death might be kinder?"

There was a long silence before he answered. "Yes. Many times."

"Then…" I trailed off, unwilling to finish the question.

"Why didn't I kill her?" He finished for me. "I tried to. Twice."

My mind flashed on the passage I'd read I the book, about Poseidon making two trips to Atlantis with sick people, and returning with them healed.

"I read about you visiting Atlantis twice," I said slowly. "The author of the book believed you were taking sick people to the Font of Zoi."

"A ruse."

"What?"

"That was a ruse. Back then, the citizens of Olympus still had distant memories of the font so it was easy to play on their beliefs. I had no sick person with me, either time, though I let the world believe I had."

"You just came down here to kill Medusa?"

"Yes."

"And?"

"And I failed."

I looked around, uneasiness crawling all over me. Poseidon had failed to defeat her twice at full strength. And now we were in her territory, on her and Atlas' terms, and Poseidon was practically powerless.

I shuddered as I imagined her stepping out from behind every splintered column and shattered wall we passed.

"How did the city end up all destroyed?" I feared I already knew the answer.

"Most of the damage was done when it sank to the

bottom of the ocean. The damage in the west," he waved his hand to our left, "was done the last time I came here."

I swallowed. "Fighting Medusa?"

"Yes."

"Where is the Font of Zoi?" I asked, changing the subject. "In fact, what is a font?"

"It's just a fancy word for a fountain. There used to be a palace in the center of the city that housed it, but it was destroyed when Medusa was turned."

"Was the font not damaged?"

Poseidon glanced at me as we walked. "The Font of Zoi is more ancient than anything else in Olympus. It cannot be damaged."

"Oh. Good." I tried to ignore a family of stone statues on my right, standing crowed in a lopsided doorway. "Should we go there? To the old palace?"

Before Poseidon could answer me, Blue whinnied loudly ahead of us. He was in sight, and he was poking his large head into a crumbling doorway, stamping his feet.

We both broke into a jog to reach him. "What's up, Blue?"

The building he was interested in was remarkably intact, compared with a lot of the others around it. Walls stood only half crumbled between chipped columns, and when I looked up, I could see that a large part of the peaked roof was still there. It looked like it might once have been a temple. I peered through the precarious archway and saw that Blue was looking down at the marble tiles on the floor. Carved into the first one was the image of a shell.

"Look."

Poseidon moved behind me to look where I was pointing, his proximity making my skin tingle and my pulse quicken.

"I guess we've found our first test," he said grimly.

# ALMI

The inside of the temple was gloomy, light only entering through cracks in the ceiling and illuminating a narrow corridor that served as the entrance. Trepidation filled me, knowing that anything could be lurking in the dark, waiting for us.

"Air?" My whirlwind sprang to life beside me, and I felt a little better.

"I shall enter first."

I opened my mouth to protest, but he had already stepped past me. I shook my head, and silently urged my whirlwind to move to his side.

Cautiously, we made our way into the ruins of the temple. As we walked down the dark hallway, I saw more shells carved on the large tiles beneath our feet. The marble would once have been shining and polished, but now dust covered everything. Poseidon paused in front of me, and I almost bumped into his back, I was concentrating so hard on the floor.

"What's wrong?"

"There is a new carving on the tiles." I stepped to his side and saw a carving of a snake on the central tile. The corridor was three tiles wide, and on the next row there was a carving of a tree on the left tile, nothing on the middle one, and a shark on the third. It was too dark to see what was carved into the tiles further on, but I could see faintly that there were images.

"Do you think it is some sort of puzzle?"

"I don't know." He twisted slightly and pulled a small throwing star from one of his leather straps. He tossed it onto the tiles before us. With a small clatter it landed on the shark. Nothing happened for a beat, then the tile flared with fire before disintegrating completely. Warm, flickering light came from the hole now in the corridor floor, and I gaped as I leaned forward, trying to see what was under there.

"Lava." Poseidon was taller than me and could see further.

"Shit. How do we know which tiles to step on?"

"I don't know."

"How many of those throwing stars do you have?"

"One more."

"Huh." I squinted down the corridor, totally unable to see where it ended. "I'm not sure that's going to get us very far."

"I think we should step on the tiles with no carvings." He sounded decisive.

I frowned at him. "Why?"

"Because I don't understand trees or snakes."

I blinked. "Do you understand sharks?"

"Yes."

"And the shark tile would have sent us to a fiery death."

He paused. "I see your point. But I still think we should jump over the first row, and land on the blank central tile."

I let out a sigh. I had no better ideas. "Throw your other star, to check it's safe."

He pulled the sharp little weapon from his strap, and carefully threw it onto the blank middle tile on the second row. The marble flared with fire, then melted away into dust, making the hole in the corridor floor twice as wide.

I put my hands on my hips. "That went well."

"At least we know which tile is safe in that row now," he said. "The tree tile."

I pointed down the indeterminably long corridor. "I have no idea how many of these we have to deal with, but I'm guessing quite a few."

"Then we had better get moving."

I sighed. The first row would be easy for Poseidon to get over, his legs were that much longer than mine. But I would have to jump. "'I'm going first," I said, keen to make sure my landing area was clear.

"Fine."

I held my breath and resisted the urge to close my eyes as I jumped over the first row, onto the tree tile. I saw a flare of light around my legs as I landed, felt heat, then the ground beneath me suddenly felt wrong. A scream gasped from my lips as the tile began to fall away from under me.

"Almi!" As Poseidon yelled my name I felt wind whipping around me, and then I was moving up instead of down. My whirlwind had expanded and wrapped around me, lifting me completely clear of the tile floor.

"Can you take me to the end of the corridor?" Adrenaline rushed through me as I whispered the question. The whirlwind whizzed a little faster, and then we were flying over the ground, zooming along the corridor.

I tried to take deep breaths as we raced along, a small opening letting in light coming into view at what I assumed was the end of the corridor. As we got closer, the opening got larger, until it became an arched doorway. Gently, my whirlwind set me down on my feet, right in the middle of the doorway. I gripped the stone frame of the arch as I stared into the room beyond.

"Almi! Almi, are you alright?" Poseidon's voice bellowed from the other end of the hallway.

"Yes!" I yelled back, unable to take my eyes from what I was seeing. "Can you bring Poseidon across the tiles?" I asked my whirlwind. With a little flurry that I took as a *yes*, it set off back up the corridor.

I heard a masculine cry, then a minute later the whirling current of air set the sea king down beside me. "Almi, I thought-" His words tailed off as he noticed what was in the room before us.

Treasure.

The room glowed gold, and not because of some magic ceiling or lighting device, but because it was filled from floor to ceiling with gold.

The whole space was set six feet below us, stone steps leading down to the room, which explained how it was so intact compared to the outside of the building. It looked like something a dragon should have been guarding, piles and piles of golden coins stacked everywhere, huge wooden chests standing open and brimming over with gems of every size and color imaginable.

"We have to find one tiny shell in all this," I breathed. "Where has it all come from?"

"Medusa must have been hoarding it. She's had many years to amass it all."

"You mean she's spent all these years combing through a dead city stealing everyone's valuables?" I stared at him.

He shrugged. "She had little else to do. And she is greedy and aroused by wealth and power."

I shook my head as I turned back to the room. Poseidon stepped onto the first stair, and I instinctively reached out and grabbed his shoulder. "Wait! What if it's like the Cave of Wonders, and if you touch anything but the shell, everything tries to kill you?"

He looked at me as though I'd hit my head. "What?"

"Don't touch anything except the shell," I said.

"How are we supposed to find the shell without touching anything?" He swung his arm out, gesturing at the ten-foot-high piles of treasure.

"I don't know," I scowled. "Just… be careful."

Together, we made our way down the stone steps, into the trove. The parts of the walls that I could see showed the Olympian gods on their thrones, regal and formal. Athena's owl perched on her shoulder, and part of Zeus was obscured by a colossal, gilded statue of what looked like an orchid. There was barely any floor space available to walk on, and I let out a low whistle as we passed a carved ship almost as big as I was, exquisite in its detail.

"We could be here for days."

"We do not have days."

"No shit." I looked at my whirlwind, now in little form and bouncing along beside me. "Do you know where the shell is?"

It zoomed around me head a couple times, then settled by my shoulder. "I'm taking that as a no. Kryvo? Any ideas?"

"No. Sorry. But I think you're right not to touch anything you don't need to."

"Kryvo says I'm right—"

Poseidon held up his hand. "Shh. Do you hear that?"

I fell silent, listening. After a second, I heard the slight clinking of metal. "Is that coins moving?" I whispered.

"I think so," he whispered back. As he turned in a slow circle, he pulled his blade from his one of his chest straps.

I mimicked him, drawing Galatea's dagger from my thigh. Fear trickled through me as my eyes darted between the piles of coins. My gaze froze as I spotted movement. A single coin, tumbling quietly down the side of one of the larger heaps of treasure.

"There!" I breathed, pointing. As Poseidon turned to the pile, it exploded. Coins, gems, goblets, and trinkets flew everywhere, showering the room as a massive snake erupted from where it had been hidden in the mountain of treasure. I barely had time to react as the reptile's enormous mouth snapped at Poseidon. He leapt backward, slashing his knife at the creature, as my whirlwind flew between them. It buffeted the snake's face, keeping it at bay long enough for me to take it in. It was as gold as the room we were in, gleaming with metallic scales, and it was so long I couldn't even see the end of its tail. It slithered away from the whirlwind, trying to move around behind us. I heard a loud crash, and when I looked in that direction, a slab of marble had descended over the doorway we had entered through. We were trapped.

Panic surged inside me, and I felt my connection to the whirlwind strengthen in response. "We need a way out!" I didn't know if I was telling Poseidon or my whirlwind, but both reacted. Poseidon jumped over the snake's body as it rounded him, moving in to snap its jaws at him again. Fangs glistened with saliva, and its head was as large as Poseidon's chest. He slashed fast with the knife, making contact just behind the snake's head. The creature hissed, retreating a little.

My whirlwind had abandoned the snake and was zooming up and down the walls, as though it was looking for something. I risked closing my eyes, so that I could try to concentrate on my magic.

It was looking for gusts of air or draughts, I realized as I let my senses merge with the air. It was looking for a way out, just as I had asked it to.

Something slammed into my legs, and my eyes flew open. Pain flared up from my shin, and I stumbled to the ground, the golden tail of the snake whipping past my face.

I tried to scrabble back to my feet, but I was too slow. The tail wound around my waist, yanking me up off the ground. Poseidon was still hacking at the snake's face as it lunged repeatedly for him, and I belatedly remembered Galatea's dagger in my hand. With a shout, I brought it stabbing down into the golden scales. When the blade first met them I thought it wouldn't pierce the shiny armor plating, but then the resistance vanished, and the steel sank into the snake's tail. It let out a hiss, then flicked me hurling from its grasp.

I couldn't help my shout of pain as I slammed into the solid stone wall. The air left my chest as I hit, then I crashed the few feet to the ground, landing awkwardly. Something cracked in my ankle, and pain so fierce it made me briefly dizzy washed through me. Fighting nausea, I tried to stand, failing on my first attempt. The pain in my leg was too much, and I sank back onto my butt.

"Almi!" Poseidon roared my name, but the snake wasn't letting up. The tail came powering back toward me.

I sent a silent plea to air, and my whirlwind charged into the fray, forcing the tail away from me before it got close.

A loud crack sounded behind me, and I leaned back, looking up at where the sound had come from.

There was a three-foot crack in the stone where I had hit the wall. As I watched, the crack grew. Slowly at first, then almost too fast to comprehend, it snaked its way up the wall, moving across the ceiling. The sound of stone breaking apart grew, and the snake paused. Casting its slitted reptilian eyes toward the ceiling, the snake gave a small quiver, then spun away from Poseidon, retreating into the mountain of coins and gold it had come from.

I tipped myself forward, onto my hands and knees. If I couldn't stand, then I would crawl. "Poseidon, I think we need to get out of here!" He was at my side in seconds, trying to pull me to my feet. My whirlwind was at my other side, trying to keep me upright. The cracking sounds had turned to crashing sounds. I threw a glance behind me just in time to see that the wall I'd hit was coming down. A mass of slabs and broken chunks of stone were tumbling toward us.

My whirlwind grew, spinning around us so fast that when the first few hunks of rock fell over our heads, they were blasted away. But the slabs were getting bigger, and there were too many of them for it to keep out. Especially with me weakening by the moment. My head was spinning, the pain in my leg drawing too much of my attention.

"The ceiling has come away on that side. We may be able to get out," Poseidon called, pointing up.

"How? If the whirlwind stops, we'll be crushed!" The stone debris built up around us in a ring, and if the whirlwind stopped shielding us for even a second, we'd be crushed by the collapsing building.

"Chrysos!" roared Poseidon. Gold wings flashed into view above us immediately. The pegasus swooped down, heedless of the falling rock, diving into the clearing the whirlwind created. There was nowhere near enough room for the horse to touch down, but Poseidon wound one arm tightly around my waist, and then jumped high as Chrysos reached us. To both my horror and astonishment, he caught onto the pegasus' neck, and the winged horse immediately began to beat her wings, lifting us out of the falling structure.

# ALMI

"*D*on't let go!" I shrieked, dangling from Poseidon's arm, and trying not to look at him dangling from Chrysos' neck. "He's super strong, he's super strong," I chanted, squeezing my eyes closed.

"I *am* super strong," Poseidon said, and I opened my eyes as Chrysos cleared the top of the building and soared the short distance back to the road. Poseidon landed lightly, tilting me gently to my feet. Chrysos' hooves clacked on the ground as she landed next to where Blue was anxiously chattering his teeth.

"Thanks, Chrysos," I panted. "I think my ankle is broken," I said, as I tried to put the tiniest bit of weight on it and searing pain met the movement. I stumbled, and Poseidon tightened his grip around me.

"We must rest."

"But we didn't get any shells." Guilt crashed through me, along with a surge of anger. We'd risked our frigging

597

lives in that temple, and didn't even have a shell to show for it.

"Winning is not as important as living," he said seriously, looking at me. "Persephone's potion will heal your ankle quickly, but only with rest."

Another wave of dizziness and pain rocked me. "What if someone else finds the red shell and ends the Trial?"

"Then we leave this place without facing Medusa. That in itself will be a win."

"But your trident! Your realm." I stared at him.

"I'll win them back. Once I am healed."

I knew he didn't believe that. I could hear it in his voice, see it in his face. "Bullshit."

"Almi, I'm not arguing with you. If you want to force the truth from me, then fine. There is no way Atlas will allow this to end before we face his wife. This whole fucking sabotage of the Poseidon Trials is about his revenge with me."

I blinked, and let the words sink in.

He was right. Atlas was in charge. He was playing us, and everyone else.

"Fine. We'll rest."


Leaning on Poseidon's arm, I tried to hobble alongside him in search of a reasonably stable-looking place to rest. But I only got a few steps before being forced to take weight off my injured leg completely. I tried to hop, but Poseidon stopped moving, frowning down at me.

"You could give me a piggyback?" I said, trying to

make light of the fact that not being able to walk in a place as dangerous as this was a pretty big problem.

Poseidon narrowed his eyes, then in one swift movement bent down and scooped me up in his arms.

I suppressed a squeak, throwing my own arms around his neck in surprise. Tingles ran along me everywhere my skin pressed against his, and my breath came a little shorter. Avoiding my eyes, the sea god began to stride toward the building.

"Am I not heavy?" I asked awkwardly.

"My magic is weakened, not my body," he growled.

"Oh." He was seven feet tall and pure muscle. I probably weighed nothing to him. "Good to know."

He raised an eyebrow, finally flicking his eyes to mine. "That my body is in fine working condition?"

I gulped. "Yes."

"Have no doubt."

I didn't.


Half a mile later, he ducked cautiously under the crumbling doorway of the pale stone building, alert and tense as he looked around. Dusty light filtered in through cracks on the walls and ceiling, and as I looked around I saw that the place had once been someone's home. Mercifully, there were no statues inside. The room we had entered was one large living space, with a kitchen counter at the back, a long dining table in the middle and tall, expensive looking couches at the front. The soft furnishings had disintegrated to nothing, and I doubted the table-legs would hold if we put any weight on the tabletop. There was only one floor to the building, and three closed doors that I could see. Poseidon set me back on my feet gently.

"I'll check the other rooms," he said quietly. I nodded and steadied myself by gripping the arm of the couch behind me. To my surprise, it felt sturdy, if a little grimy.

Poseidon announced the building as clear a few minutes later. Some of my tension relaxing, I sank down onto my butt. Dust puffed up in a cloud around me, and Kryvo made an unhappy sound.

I coughed and Poseidon came over, waving the dust away with his hands. "I fear it will not be a comfortable rest. But I will secure the door, and at least it will be a safe one. Eat."

I did as I was told, undoing my belt and pulling things from the pouches. First, I drank the potion that Persephone had given us, and then I ate the meat-filled pastries we'd loaded up with from *Mossy's* galley.

When Poseidon returned from barricading the door with the top of the dining table, I passed him the remaining pastries. He lowered himself to sit beside me and ate.

"I have sent the pegasi back to the ship. I am not accustomed to nearly dying."

I wasn't immediately sure what to say. "I guess being immortal hasn't prepared you for that, huh?"

He had an intense look in his eyes as he stared at me. "No. It has not."

"How long have you been sick with the stone blight?"

"A while. But it has never felt like the encounters of the last few hours."

"You know, we nearly died quite a few times over the last week. You forgotten the corpse flower?" I shuddered just thinking about the toxic underwater plant.

"I was unconscious by the time I was almost dead," he said. "I was not staring down the jaws of death."

"What about when we nearly fell in the talontaur's mouth?" His mouth quirked at the corners, and I scowled. "How the hell is anything about that creature funny?"

"You do not like to be wrong."

"No. Does anyone?"

"Certainly not. But it is a particular trait of gods and royalty." His smile was spreading slowly, and my stomach squished. "You are more suited to the position of queen than you are, Almi."

I snorted, unable to hold his gaze. "Nonsense. I'm inexperienced, impulsive, and I usually have no idea what I'm doing."

"Yet you always find a way. You never give up. That is courageous."

"It's pigheaded stubbornness. Driven by my need to save Lily."

"You are good of heart. You help others when it has nothing to do with your sister. Like that boy in that town-"

He cut off sharply.

"Poseidon," I said slowly. "What boy in what town are you referring to?" My stomach was flipping as I spoke. I knew what boy he meant. But there was no possible way he could know about that.

The wild look filled his eyes, stormy and bright. "The boy you stole food for. The homeless boy."

When I had been in Germany, looking for the book, a boy of about eight, homeless and hungry, had begun hanging around my trailer. I had a pretty good routine of stealing bread and juice off the back of a delivery trolley that made its way around the neighborhood early, and I started taking a little bit extra to give to the boy. We spoke no words of shared language, but I had formed a bond with the kid. When I'd moved on, I'd worried about him a long time.

"How can you know about that?" I could feel energy rolling off the god, and I felt a little breathless.

"You were never alone, Almi," he said eventually.

"How do you know about the homeless kid?" I repeated.

"I watched you."

My mind blanked a moment, a million emotions rushing me. "You *watched* me?"

Poseidon held his hands up, speaking quickly. "Not permanently, or in a way that would take liberties. On my honor." He pressed a hand to his chest. "I would use my power to check in on you from time to time, nothing more."

I stared, still utterly confused. "Why? Why would you spy on me?"

"I was not spying on you. Although I appreciate it might feel like that. I was ensuring that you were safe."

"Protecting your asset?" I tried to struggle to my feet, needing space, needing to be further away from him. But my leg wouldn't allow it, and I fell hard onto my ass again.

Poseidon moved to help me, but I threw him a look that suggested if he came anywhere near me I'd kill him, and he stilled.

"Protecting my wife." His voice dropped low.

"Do you have any idea what it feels like to be told that a god has been secretly watching you your whole life?"

His jaw tightened. "I have been periodically making sure you were safe. That is all."

The implications of what he was saying sent thoughts barreling through my head. "You must have known I had the metafora compass. You must have known I was coming back to steal your ship."

He shook his head. "No. I stopped checking in on you over a year ago."

"Why?"

He took a long breath, his eyes loaded with unidentifiable emotion when he brought them back to my livid gaze. "It was too painful. I was falling in love with you."

My tumbling anger stumbled to a halt. I swallowed, staring. "How?" My word was a hoarse bark. "How can you fall in love with someone you don't know? Someone whose life you've ruined?"

"You fought back. You were always positive. You were everything I didn't have in my life. I found myself wanting you more and more." He held his hand up again. "I mean you, not your body. I never, ever watched you inappropriately. I wouldn't do that to anybody, least of all a woman I respect as much as you."

"I don't understand," I said on a breath, rubbing my hands over my face. Emotion overwhelmed me, disparate pieces of information ringing in my ears.

If I accepted that he was telling the truth and hadn't been perving on me in the shower for nearly a decade, then I found myself less angry with him. He had been looking out for me, which fit in with the man I was learning he was — one who did feel the consequences of his actions and wouldn't marry a girl and then dump her in a different world without another thought.

"I knew. The first day I met you and your sister."

"Knew what?" I was almost too scared to meet his eyes again.

"That it was you I was destined to fall in love with. Even then, with no power, you glowed like a fucking beacon to me. But I knew the rest of the prophecy. I knew that if we fell in love, you would die. But I also knew I needed the Heart of the Ocean. I had no choice. To save your life, I had to marry your sister.

When that went wrong, it was too dangerous to keep you anywhere near me, so I sent you to the human world. I naively thought you might feel less inadequate there than somewhere you were surrounded by people with power. I couldn't stay away, though. I watched you. And the more I saw of your spirit, I knew I had been right. I saw what I had done to you, separating you from Lily. I began to hate myself for it, but the more you hated me, the less likely I was to be the cause of your death. So I embraced it. I resigned myself to a life where my wife, the woman I desired more than life itself, had to hate me. I had to be the cause of your misery."

# ALMI

*M*y head was spinning by the time he stopped speaking. "I need you to leave." My voice was surprisingly calm.

His tight face darkened. "It is dangerous here. I can't leave you."

"Just go over there, to another room or something," I said, waving my hand a touch desperately, belying my level tone. "I need some space. Now."

Slowly, he stood up. With one last piercing look at me, he strode away.

When I heard the soft closing of a door, I tipped my head forward and let out a shuddering breath, silent tears flooding from my eyes.

My whole damned life had been a lie. I had spent years feeling so alone it hurt, and someone had been in love with me that whole time. Not just someone, my own fucking husband. The man I had been learning to hate more and more every minute I was away from my home and my sister.

But he'd done it all to try to save me. He had sacrificed his desire, made himself miserable, learned to hate himself as much as I had, to do what he thought he had to in order to keep me safe.

The pain in his face when he had spoken had been unbearable to watch. Was that why I had just sent him away?

I closed my eyes. *Lily?*

My mental voice was tiny when I said my sister's name.

There was no answer.

*Lily? Lily, I need you.*

Nothing.

"Poseidon!" I called his name, and the god ran back into the room, knife out and his body tense. He looked around for the threat, before his eyes landed on me. "She's not responding. Lily isn't responding."

He dropped to his knees before me, tucking his knife away. "Atlantis is probably blocking the mental communication," he said gently. Slowly, he reached his hand out, wiping a tear from my cheek with his rough thumb. A new one replaced it instantly.

"You think she's really talking to me? It's not me making her up?"

He nodded. "Yes."

"What if I can't talk to her because she's dead?" The words barely sounded as I said them, my voice breaking on the last one.

"She is not." His hand moved so that he was cupping the side of my face reassuringly.

"You don't know that! What if I used too much power,

and—"

His other hand moved, so that he was holding my jaw on both sides, forcing me to look directly at him. "Lily is safe. Atlantis is through a portal, and I am sure that is what is blocking her." He spoke slowly and firmly, and I found myself calming.

"Can you talk to you brother?"

"I do not want to risk using my power. But you are strong enough to try."

I blinked at him, then screwed my eyes shut. *Persephone? Can you hear me?*

There was no response. My heart rate slowed a little more.

"I don't think it's working," I told Poseidon. His grip on my face relaxed, and without thinking, my own hand shot up to stop his moving away.

He froze, staring at me. Waves crashed in his beautiful eyes. "I'm sorry," he said. "For everything I have done. And for telling you today. I should not have."

"You could have done it differently. You could have sent Lily with me."

"I wish I could. But she was sick, and I couldn't risk anyone else trying to get to her for the Heart of the Ocean. In my realm, I knew she was safe."

"You could have let me know I wasn't alone. You could have told me why I was sent away."

He nodded. "I believed you would just start again in the human realm, your memory of me angry and distant. I had no idea of the love between you and your sister. I am sorry. I got it so wrong."

For a second, he looked so human, so pained and

regretful. "You really did get it wrong." He cast his eyes down, unable to hold my tear-filled gaze. "But for the right reasons." His eyes darted back to mine, flaring with light.

"You will forgive me?"

"No. But I think I understand you."

He said nothing for a long moment, and being so close to him was becoming unbearable. The urge to move my lips to his was warring hard with the urge to slap him across the face. He had controlled my entire life, made every decision about my future for me without my knowledge, and then secretly watched me. And he had done everything he possibly could to put my life above his happiness.

"I will take understanding over forgiveness," he said eventually. Slowly, he stood up, running his fingers along my jaw as he did so, his reluctance to remove them from my skin almost tangible.

My hand flew up to stop his moving, but as I got within in an inch of touching him, I forced it back down.

This was dangerous territory. I could feel the charged emotion between us like I could feel my magic when I used it. It was real and powerful. And potentially lethal.

I hadn't known how I could love a man who had torn my family apart. But the god I'd learned to hate had been a lie.

Poseidon had been forced into so many situations he couldn't win, and he was painfully aware of the consequences of his actions.

He did not do anything lightly. He did not perform his tasks with his own satisfaction as his motivation. And what he had done to me and Lily was just the same. Self-ishness had not driven his choices. There hadn't been a right course of action that he'd willfully ignored.

I didn't love him. But I no longer believed that I couldn't.

And as I stared into his eyes, I knew Lily and Persephone had been right.

He loved me.

# ALMI

"I think I will give you that space," he said, his voice husky.

I nodded. "Yes. But Poseidon?"

His unearthly blue eyes bore into mine. "Yes?"

"Come back. I don't want to sleep alone."

"Anything, for my Queen."

He turned, striding away from me, toward one of the doors. I slumped, leaning my back against the couch and rubbing my hands over my face. What a mess. What a disastrous fucking mess.

"He is an extraordinarily complicated man." Kryvo's squeaky voice was thoughtful.

"That's an understatement," I muttered, instantly feeling a little less alone for hearing the starfish.

"But I suppose that you are fairly complicated too."

"Really? I'm simple."

"Your goals are simple. But your situation is not."

I rubbed my thumbs across my temples. "It's simpler than it seems. Poseidon and all of Aquarius, or Lily."

"That's if you survive long enough to need to make that decision."

"Thanks for the reminder."

"Almi, you need some sort of blindfold for when you are back out there. Looking into Medusa's eyes will end all of this instantly."

I nodded, the practical advice what I needed to help drag me from my emotional rollercoaster.

Poseidon was in love with me. I needed to accept that, appreciate the danger that carried, and move on. The more I dwelled on what he had done for me, or at least, what he had tried to do for me, the more I risked my own feelings deepening. And if I died I wouldn't be able to save him or Lily.

"Yes. Very good idea, Kryvo." I gathered as much control over my thoughts as I could, trying to focus on anything that wasn't the sea god or my sister. "Can you tell me another story from your murals?"

"Of course. What kind of story would you like?"

"Nothing romantic. Got anything heroic? A come-back-from-unlikely-odds tale?"

"I have just the thing."

As Kryvo told me stories from the paintings in the palace, I collected stale-smelling cushions from the couches and made an uncomfortable bed on the floor. The throbbing in my ankle had lessened considerably, and I let the little starfish lull me to sleep, focusing enough on his words and the escapism of his stories to block out my own tumbling thoughts. I woke briefly when Poseidon joined me, his massive presence a comfort. He stayed a foot away from me, and I suppressed my groggy desire to tuck myself against his body. I had firsthand experience of how he could make me feel, so I knew for sure that intimacy could literally kill me.

That didn't stop me dreaming about him the second I slipped back into sleep though.

It was a good thing that Poseidon was no longer next to me when I woke the next day. Desire pounded through me, the tingling memories of my dream impossible to shift.

"Snap out of it, Almi," I muttered as I sat up, looking around for the god. "He spied on you for almost a decade. He's an asshole."

Except he wasn't. And I knew it. I'd known it since he'd saved me from the rotblood when I'd tried to reach his palace. That day seemed like a lifetime ago.

"How is your ankle?" His voice startled me, and I swiveled on my butt to see him coming in through the no-longer barricaded door.

Carefully, I stood, testing my leg.

I couldn't believe that I had been completely unable to put weight on the same foot just the day before. The injury was healed. I lifted my uninjured leg, putting all of my weight on the bad ankle. It was fine. No trace of any damage, no pain or discomfort. Not even a twinge.

"If you're watching, Persephone, you're my hero," I said, speaking to the gloomy room in general.

I packed up the things I'd taken out of my belt, munching on a hunk of dried meat as I did.

"Kryvo suggested I make some sort of blindfold," I told Poseidon when he asked me if I was ready to leave. He was being overly formal, and I knew he was as concerned about our precarious emotional connection as I was.

"Excellent idea." He gripped on of the leather straps across his chest and it glowed briefly blue.

"You shouldn't be using any magic!"

He shook his head at my protest. "It's not my magic. It's the toga's magic." Slowly, he drew his fingers away from the light, the watery material of his toga appearing between his fingertips, expanding fast.

"That's awesome."

He raised an eyebrow, then fished his knife from another strap. Carefully, he cut a slice of fabric from the bottom of the toga. I watched with a twinge of regret.

"I'm not surprised your ship doesn't like me. I bet your toga isn't much of a fan either."

"Both can be repaired," he said, straightening and handing me the strip of aqua-green fabric. Tiny white-tipped waves rolled across it, and I felt inexplicably attached to it. "You, on the other hand, cannot be repaired, if you are turned to stone. Be careful, Almi."

I broke his intense gaze and nodded. "Always. Let's go."

Blue and Chrysos were outside in the street when we left our temporary shelter, and Blue trotted to me as soon as he saw me.

"Morning, gorgeous," I said to the pegasus as he nudged my hands hard with his snout. "You sleep okay?" He whinnied at me, flicking his tail uneasily. I couldn't blame him for his anxiety. There was something unnerving about the streets of the silent, sunken city of Atlantis, even without the constant worry of Medusa lurking about. The light in the whole place was wrong, the only illumination coming from the icy silver dome over our heads. Beyond that the darkness was suffocating, and if I looked up too long panic started to build inside me.

"We must go to the palace." I looked at Poseidon in surprise. "I thought you said that's where they will expect you to go?"

"It is. I am tired of these games. I want this done." What he wasn't saying aloud was that he was weakening with every passing day. I could feel the energy coming from him depleting, his powerful aura less each day.

"I'm right there with you," I said with a nod. "Let's get this over with."

# ALMI

*W*e walked for what I thought was about an hour, Poseidon confident in the direction. Eventually we rounded a corner and the monotony of grey stone was finally interrupted. And not by anything I would have expected.

Green moss had grown all over all the fallen stone, and ivy crawled up the columns that still stood, along with some of the statues.

Thirty feet away, blocking the road we were walking, was a ten-foot-tall hedge. Perfectly trimmed into a large rectangle, and vivid green against the cool grey and pale blue of the rest of our surroundings, it looked anything but innocent. There was a small gap carved into the middle of it. An entrance.

"I think we're about to enter a maze."

Poseidon looked at me. "You mean a labyrinth?"

I nodded. "What is the difference?"

"A labyrinth is filled with things ready to kill you."

"Then yeah, I guess we're about to enter a labyrinth." I

thought about what I knew about mazes, or labyrinths. You had to get to the middle. Mild claustrophobia simmered when I thought about being trapped or lost in an endless deadly maze. "Can't we just ride Blue and Chrysos to the middle?" I suggested hopefully.

Poseidon looked at the pegasi, stopped still next to us. Chrysos flexed her stunning golden wings , as if to say she was up for it.

As Poseidon opened his mouth to answer, though, a loud buzzing started.

"What's that?" My whirlwind sprang to life beside me, and Poseidon had his blade drawn. The sound was coming from above us though.

A swarm of something dropped through the air above us, separating as they got closer. They were small and gleaming gold, and they looked a lot like bees. No, hornets. Huge stingers on their butts angled toward us as Poseidon and I slashed with our daggers, trying to keep them back. My whirlwind zoomed about, blasting them away. One of the pegasi made an awful shrieking whinny.

"Blue!" The pegasus had launched himself into the air in a frenzy, his wings beating at the swarm of creatures around him, his mouth frothing as he snapped his jaws at them. But they were relentless. The swarm had abandoned me and Poseidon, instead splitting themselves between the two winged horses. Chrysos was stamping and jumping, trying to keep her wings tucked in, but I could see the creatures landing on her broad flanks, their stingers piercing the hide.

Blue made another awful sound, and fear and anger had me surging toward them. My whirlwind was trying to bat them back, but there were so many, and it could only help one pegasus at a time.

"Go back to the ship!" shouted Poseidon. Blue's eyes found mine, as though he wanted my permission to leave.

"Go!"

Chrysos launched into the air, and with one last frantic look, Blue soared off through the sky, leaving most of the swarm unable to keep up.

My whirlwind shot back to my side, ready to defend me from the remaining golden insects, but with another loud buzz, they flew off, melting into the hedge before us.

I stood panting slightly, furious that Blue had been attacked. "Do you think they were sent just to stop us flying?"

"Yes." Poseidon looked as furious as I felt.

"Fuckers."

He nodded. "They will pay."

"Fucking right, they will." The angry adrenaline had been just what I needed to shift my trepidation. "They'll pay now. Let's go." Without giving myself time to panic, I strode into the labyrinth, Poseidon right by my side.

The hedges rose high on either side of us, dense enough I couldn't see through them, and tall enough that we wouldn't be able to climb over them. The air had cooled, and the pine scent held a tinge of sweet rot. Silence swallowed us as we walked, so complete it was as unnerving as the solid walls of green surrounding us.

The path was straight, and it was a few moments before we reached a fork. "Left or right?" I whispered.

"If we always turn the same way, we should find the center."

"Okay. Let's go left."

Poseidon turned, and we carried on, daggers drawn. There was the distinct feeling of being watched, and it made my skin crawl. The more corners we turned, the more I became convinced there would be something waiting for us round each one. Someone waiting for us. Medusa.

Poseidon paused before me, and my heart skipped a beat, pumped up as I was. "What's wrong?"

"There's something ahead." I squinted. I could make out something grey along the long straight path in front of us.

"Shall we go back? Or try to find a turning?" There were no gaps in the hedge on our left, but I could see one further down on the right. But that would ruin our plan of always turning left.

"Let's see what it is," he murmured.

I nodded, my whirlwind expanding slightly beside me in response to my building fear.

It was a statue. We didn't need to go much further before the stone structure became clear. It was in the middle of the path, about as large as Poseidon, and it was of a cyclops. Even from a distance I could see how detailed its features were, and I wondered if it had once lived, or if it was a product of the imagination of a talented sculptor.

"The hedges," whispered Poseidon. I looked left and

right, and started in surprise. Stone faces filled the gaps between the thick foliage.

"That's why I feel like I'm being watched," I hissed. "Jeez. They're creepy as hell."

"I think we should go past the cyclops."

"I agree." We had stuck to the left-turning plan so far, and I had no intention of undoing our progress and getting lost.

Slowly, we inched our way toward the imposing statue. I knew it was made of stone, but that didn't stop my nerves as we reached it. The monster's face was a mask of anger, his fists the size of my head.

A tiny cracking sound reached my ear as Poseidon squeezed past the statue, trying not to touch the hedge.

"What was that?"

"Just keep moving," he said, voice tight.

I did as he said, slipping more easily past the cyclops on the other side. Another cracking sound pierced the eerie silence. I looked back at the statue. It looked solid, and I could see no movement.

I looked ahead again, seeing a turning on out left in a few feet. "There," I pointed, and we picked up our pace.

The path that came into view when we turned was peppered with statues and I faltered. A flash of gold caught my eye at ground level.

"Snake."

Tiny golden snakes were slithering across the path between the statues. I watched as one wound its way around the closest one, a small satyr with evil looking eyes.

"I don't like this."

"If it is getting more dangerous, then we are on the right path," Poseidon replied grimly.

"Small comfort."

We moved forward, my every sense on high alert. Tiny hissing sounds perforated the heavy silence, making me even more on edge.

The satyr blinked.

A yelp of shock left me, and it was as though the sound brought everything around us to life. About half the statues moved, the satyr springing forward. For a thing made of stone, he moved effortlessly. A roar behind him drew my attention, and I saw a stone griffin swiping at another statue that appeared to be inanimate.

My whirlwind danced forward, catching the satyrs heavy arm as it started to swing. Poseidon ran beyond it, launching his dagger at the griffin.

In the water, my air had removed my enemies by blasting them away, and I compelled my whirlwind to do exactly that. But these were no ordinary stone beasts. The resistance I felt when the whirlwind tried to heave the satyr off the ground was massive.

"You lifted Charybdis, you can do this!" But I felt myself exhausting fast, and knew this stone was magicked with something strong. Titan magic.

"Run! Our best bet is to run past them!" Poseidon called from ahead of me. Taking a deep breath, I did as he said, and sprinted past the satyr.

My whirlwind followed me immediately, and as I caught up with Poseidon, who was sparring with the mean-looking griffin, he tucked in his knife arm and began to run with me. We ducked and dived the swiping, lumbering statues as we sprinted, leaping over golden snakes that I was sure were increasing in size.

We almost missed a left turn, but I skidded to a stop. "Here!"

We barreled around the corner and saw a mercifully empty path ahead. "Are they following?" We both turned, my whirlwind bouncing, ready. But there was nothing behind us, and silence had settled once more.

I leaned over, gripping my knees as I tried to get my breath back. I was not much fitter than I'd been when I'd last sprinted that fast, away from a stacked librarian when I'd stolen the book. I shook my head as I straightened. So much had changed since then.

"Are you alright?"

"Yes. Running isn't my thing."

"We should keep moving." A snake slithered across the path before us, making me jerk up straight. It was three or four times the size of the first one I had seen, thick and long and shining with gold scales as it moved between the hedges.

"Agreed."

We resumed walking, and I tried to ignore the continued stone faces in the hedges. Most were humanoid, and all had detailed eyes that followed us as we kept turning left. A steady stream of snakes crossed our path, and with each one I knew we were getting closer to an attack of some sort. It made no sense that they were ignoring us.

After what felt like another hour, but was probably less, I heard a low loud slithering sound. Poseidon slowed at the same time I did. The noise of twigs snapping and foliage scraping increased.

"Are you thinking what I'm thinking?" I whispered, pulse racing.

"Our golden friend from yesterday," Poseidon growled.

I tensed, my whirlwind growing again. "I owe him one. He fucked my leg up." My bravado was only partially real. The giant snake scared the shit out of me. Not as much as the idea of wandering the cursed maze for the rest of time, but plenty enough to make my knees feel funny.

Sure enough, seconds later, a massive golden snake head appeared around the corner ahead of us. Its huge, forked tongue flicked out at us, hovering and tasting the air as we froze. Its powerful body, filling the entire pathway and scraping on the hedges as it moved, slithered into view behind the head.

"What's our plan?" I hissed, trying not to sound frantic and failing.

"Snakes have a weak point at the back of their skulls. You distract it, I'll stab it."

Before I could say a word in reply, Poseidon roared, and ran at the snake.

"Go!" I threw my arm forward, and my whirlwind rushed after him.

The snake had little time to react before Poseidon reached it. He threw himself low to the ground, skidding under its raised head, then grabbing onto its neck. His arms could barely close around it, it was so large, but he swung himself up and onto the thing's back.

The snake thrashed and hissed, its tail flicking up behind him and powering down, toward Poseidon. My whirlwind got there first, though, slamming into the oncoming tail that had made such easy work of me the day before. As if getting revenge for me, the whirlwind hammered angrily at the snake's tail, hindering any chance it had at all of reaching Poseidon.

The creature thrashed its head so hard Poseidon could barely keep any kind of purchase on it. Its jaws were wide open, fangs bared. It could probably have swallowed me whole. Poseidon wasn't going to be able to defeat it on its own.

Gathering my courage, I ran forward. Throwing my arms in the air, I yelled at the snake. "You broke my ankle, you big ugly brute!"

The snake paused for the briefest second. A second was all Poseidon needed. He raised his blade with both hands and expertly brought it plunging down, right behind the monster's head. IThe thing's eyes flashed with surprise, then flared red before it collapsed to the ground.

Poseidon's gaze locked on mine, and he tugged his dagger free, leaping off the snake's back.

An hissing wail echoed through the air, angry and chilling.

"I think we just killed Medusa's guard dog," said Poseidon.

I swallowed, looking at the dead snake. "That was impressive," I murmured.

"It's one more reason for her to hate me. We are close."

"To the center of the maze?"

"To the Font of Zoi. I can feel it. You should be able to too."

I concentrated on the air, trying to feel for magic. A thrumming was coming from our left. A lively, dangerous sort of thrumming.

Together, we left the golden snake on the ground, and headed for the font.

# ALMI

*P*oseidon hadn't been kidding when he'd said a font was just a fancy name for a fountain. And it wasn't even a fancy-looking fountain. I could see a simple stone pedestal in the center of the maze, the stone the same gray color as the stone that covered Poseidon's skin. There was a bowl on top of the pedestal, smooth, and a shade paler, and water gently bubbled up in the middle of it, only rising a few inches off the surface before splashing back down.

For all its simple appearance, nobody would have believed the font to be harmless. It oozed power, the air around us thick with thrumming energy. It only added to my tension as I looked around cautiously.

The space seemed to be clear of anything living, only the foreboding green of the hedges surrounding us.

Something flashed red above the font, and my focus honed in on it. A red shell, flitting a few feet above the bubbling water.

"Look!" I moved to step closer, but Poseidon gripped my arm.

"It is too easy. Something is wrong." His voice was a hiss, and fresh trepidation took me.

A golden snake slithered into the clearing on the other side. It sped toward the font, then began to twine its way around the base. A second later, another snake followed, then another.

A low, booming laugh began to sound, almost too low to make out at first, then gaining in volume.

"I can't tell you how much I wished that you had gotten here first, Poseidon." Atlas voice echoed around us. "My wife has been expecting you, but she found poor old Polybotes instead."

The air behind the font shimmered, and a ten-foot-tall statue appeared.

Polybotes.

His face was a mask of anger, his hands half raised to cover his eyes.

My stomach was knotting itself in fear, anticipation making me feel sick.

"You are not supposed to interfere with the Trial! You gave Athena your word," shouted Poseidon, anger hard on his face as he stared at the stone giant.

"You were not supposed to do a great many things, sea king," Atlas snarled. With a flash of red light he appeared in the clearing, in front of the font. "I destroyed the palace that used to house this font after my wife told me what you tried to make her do in there." Every word dripped with hateful venom, and flames licked over his armor. "And now its new home is where you shall watch your own wife meet the same fate."

"Your wife lied to you." I said the words loudly, and both men turned to look at me.

"Is that what he told you?" Atlas spat.

"Yes. And I believe him."

"Of course you do. It does not make it true."

"Have you asked her?"

"I will not insult her honor by doing any such thing!" he roared, and his manic rage instantly made me understand why Poseidon had not bothered to try to defend himself with the truth. Atlas would clearly have it no other way, there would be no convincing him that his wife had been in the wrong or lied to him.

Kryvo's tiny, urgent voice came to me. "Almi, she is coming. I can feel her magic, you need to shield your eyes, now."

I pulled out the strip of fabric from Poseidon's toga that he had cut me, and quickly tied it around my head, flush over eyes.

The darkness swallowed me, and I felt desperately helpless as Atlas began to laugh.

"That will not save you, silly little Queen."

Panic that had started as a creeping feeling washed over me in waves as I heard slithering noises around me, followed by the movement of my whirlwind.

"Poseidon?" I tried to keep my voice quiet and free of alarm, but I knew I had failed.

"I am here," he answered just as quietly.

"This isn't going to work. I can't see. I can't fight or control my air if I can't see."

Atlas' laughter was getting louder, and so was the slithering sound.

My little starfish spoke, his voice barely audible over both sounds. "I have found a starfish! I can show you what is happening through their eyes!"

"What? How have you found—" I started to say, but words failed me as a vision descended over the blackness.

I was looking at the scene from the center of the courtyard, and I realized dimly that the starfish Kryvo had found and was using to show me the view was on the font itself. I could see myself standing next to Poseidon, my whirlwind high and fast next to me, and Poseidon's blade drawn. I could hardly see Atlas as he was standing next to the font, only his side making into my fixed view.

None of that seemed important though, compared with what was moving into the clearing with us.

There were so many golden snakes slithering across the ground and around the bottom of the font now that almost the whole ground was covered, and they parted like water for the bare green feet gliding through them.

Medusa.

She was exactly as Poseidon's painting had depicted. Beautiful and terrifying. An ivory white toga covered most of her scaled green skin, and the snakes making up her hair were as bright as Atlas' golden armor. Her piercing eyes were fixed on me, and I shuddered. I knew for certain that if it weren't for the blindfold, I'd be stone already.

"Poseidon. Long time no see."

Her voice was a hiss that made my skin crawl, and I sucked in a breath as fear made my heart beat even faster.

"This is your last chance to tell your husband the truth," Poseidon said.

She laughed, soft and even more hiss-like. "My last chance? We have faced each other before, and you have never offered such ultimatums." She paused, tilting her head. All the golden snakes rose together. "Ah, but you are as good as dead already, you poor immortal." She tipped her head back and laughed again, loudly this time. The sound made me feel sick.

"Husband dear, I told you I infected him last time."

"You were right, my darling. And now these little friends have infected his whole realm, and soon all of Olympus."

"No. This ends today."

"Wrong," said Atlas. "The only thing that can cure the stone blight is the Heart of the Ocean. And I shall soon be in possession of that."

"How?" The single word escaped my lips.

Medusa's hiss answered me. "Why are you wearing that ugly blindfold, little queen? Show me your beauty and take it off," she said, sickly sweet. My whirlwind sped up, whipping a path in front of me, then back again, like a guard dog might to warn off a threat. The disorientation of watching myself from the font made me feel off balance as I pulled Galatea's dagger from my thigh.

"The heart of a Nereid," Atlas said, stepping closer to me and Poseidon and putting his back into my line of sight. I watched his shoulders shrug. "Poseidon interpreted the Oracle's prophecy differently than I did. He took the term possession to mean ownership by marriage. But I took the liberty of checking in at Delphi myself, and can confirm that cutting the heart from the chest, locking it in a box and declaring it as my own will work just as efficiently."

Poseidon's face turned so dark with anger, if he'd had his full power I would have run away from him myself. "You will not touch her."

"I have two to choose from," Atlas said, and snapped his fingers.

Lily appeared in the middle of the clearing.

My heart skipped a beat as everything around me stilled, shock taking over my senses.

She was asleep, barely any skin on her exposed face and arms not covered in stone. The golden snakes slithered over her body, and impulse took over.

"Get off her!" I began to move forward, kicking at the snakes. Medusa opened her mouth, a hideous hiss issuing from it, and Poseidon's hand shot out, yanking me back by the shoulder.

"You cannot harm her!" Poseidon shouted.

"Yes, yes, yes, I remember our deal." Atlas waved his hand dismissively. "This sleeping sister is only my back up, in case my wife accidentally kills yours. I am very keen that little Almi here is the one whose heart I cut out and keep. I am hopeful that whatever creature the font turns her into doesn't need her heart to keep her alive." I couldn't see Atlas' face, but his voice sounded as crazy as I had ever heard it.

I tried to work his words out, tried to think of anything I could do. "What deal is he talking about?" I said, turning my blind head to Poseidon. "Why is Lily here? I thought you said she was safe in the palace!"

"Enough!" Atlas clapped his hands again, before Poseidon could say anything. "Say goodbye to your husband, Almi. I was never afforded the opportunity to do so with my wife, before Poseidon turned her into what you see now."

"I have come to terms with this body, husband dear," Medusa hissed. "I have not however, come to terms with being sent to live for centuries alone at the bottom of the godforsaken ocean."

For an instant, I saw regret on Poseidon's face. Then Medusa attacked.

## ALMI

*M*y whirlwind sprang to my defense, and gratitude for the fact that I could see through the starfish statue flooded me as I directed it toward the shrieking snake-woman.

The need to defend not just myself but my unconscious sister and the powerless Poseidon was booming in my mind, and the whirlwind smashed into Medusa before she could get close to me, her clawed hands raised and ready.

Atlas roared and hurled fire toward me. Before I could react, a wall of water erupted from Poseidon, shielding us both from the fire and instantly dousing it. Medusa barreled forward again, trying to force her way through my whirlwind, which was buffeting her this way and that.

Atlas hurled more fire at us, and fear for Poseidon flooded me. He couldn't keep using his power without turning to stone. But I couldn't fight Atlas *and* Medusa with my air, I needed his help. I didn't know how to split the whirlwind, didn't have the strength or power to control two separate forces. Frustration and fear were building up in my gut, adrenaline only fueling them.

"You can't kill me, and you know it!" shouted Poseidon.

Atlas' response was loud, madness lacing his words. "I don't want to kill you, sea king. I want to maim you. I want to hurt you. I want to immobilize you, so that you can do nothing but bleed and weep, while the woman you loves is turned into a monster."

An explosion of hatred poured through me, the idea of Poseidon hurt intolerable. My sister's unconscious form on the ground before me, her body being used as bait in this fucked-up bid for revenge against a man I had come to realize would do no harm to an innocent, was suddenly too much.

The roiling emotions hardened inside me, forming a giant ball of pure rage. The whirlwind split in two.

I stared, shocked for a second, then pressure crushed in on my head as the power of the two separate columns of wind churned around in me. I directed one to keep Medusa away from Poseidon, and as I tried to compel the other one toward Atlas, I saw the dark form of Kalypso running into the clearing. I watched her eyes flick over the scene, and her shudder as she saw Medusa. When her gaze fell on the font, her dark eyes sparkled.

"Yes, my daughter!" roared Atlas. "Take the red shell! You and Ceto are even, if you take it now, you will win!"

Daughter? Well that fucking explained a lot.

Throwing her arm up across her eyes, Kalypso ran toward the font.

I compelled one of the whirlwinds toward her, trying to stop her reaching the font. But her outstretched arm was too close, and the implications of what she was about to do roared through my head.

She would win. She would win the Trident, Aquarius, and control of Poseidon's life. And she would let Atlas tear it apart. The snakes would fill Aquarius, turning everyone to stone, completing the Titan's revenge. And then? Atlas' maniacal cackle echoed through the clearing as she got close.

And then he would challenge the whole of Olympus. I was certain.

I knew what I had to do. Crushing sadness weighed down on me, so hard it made my vision blur.

But the decision had been made.

It had been made for me.

It was simply impossible to trade the lives of hundreds for one.

A sob tore from my throat, and a sharp feeling hit me in the chest. For a split second, I thought some sort of dart had been thrown at me, then I felt the rage no longer pouring through me, but *from* me.

My whirlwinds shuddered a second, then grew, pulsing with bright silver light. In my chest, the feeling was turning from painful to downright explosive.

My head swam as power coursed from my body, out into the mass of air before me. Golden snakes were picked up from where they were trying to escape and hurled through the air.

My head swam with the rush of power, and somewhere deep inside, fear crawled up through me.

Power.

*So much power.*

I hurled both whirlwinds at Kalypso, just as her hand was inches from the red shell.

She screamed as she flew thirty feet in the air. Atlas gaped, and with a sickening satisfaction, I launched the goddess as far away from the font as I could manage.

I reached up, desperate to tear the blindfold from my eyes. I needed to see my tattoo.

I needed to know for sure if I really had just embraced my power.

*If I had killed my sister.*

"Almi, no!" Poseidon's voice wasn't just insistent, it held actual power, and my hand halted where it was.

With one tiny thought, I threw his magic from me, lifting my hand the rest of the way.

"Almi, she'll kill you! She'll kill you instantly!" Kryvo's voice was shrill, but my fingers tugged the blindfold away, regardless.

I had my head angled down, and the vision from the font faded, my own eyes stinging and blurry in the light as my chest came into view.

My tattoo.

It was beautiful. As bright and as vivid as Lily's had ever been.

I'd have given anything in the world at that moment to rid every speck of color from my skin.

"I'm sorry!" My words were a sob, and I screwed my eyes closed and dropped to my knees.

When I was sure I was looking at the floor, I opened them again, crawling through the mass of snakes toward my sister. They hissed and bit at me, hundreds of lacerations covering my skin as I powered through them. I didn't care.

"Keep her away!" I screamed at air. Anger and resentment laced my words, but so did unbridled power. I was a ticking fucking time-bomb, so loaded with power it was making my head swim and everything blur. The fact that I hadn't been yanked off my knees by Medusa suggested that air was doing as I had commanded.

I reached Lily, pulling her head onto my lap. Tears were streaming down my face so thick and fast I couldn't see properly. For a second, I thought her eyes moved.

I shouted again, the noise animal and strangled and pure grief.

Lily's eyes flickered open.

"Lily?" I was crying so hard the word barely sounded.

"Almi," my sister croaked.

"Lily!" I pulled her too me, trying to hug her mostly stone body, my heart smashing so hard against my ribs. "Lily, you're awake! You're alive!"

I moved so that her head was in my lap again, and I could look into her face. She beamed at me. "I'm so proud of you."

"What's happening?"

"A few things, I think," she smiled. "First, I am awake because your grief caused Poseidon enough pain that he wept a tear for you. Gods don't cry, Almi."

I started at her, the words of the prophecy ringing in

my ears. She will sleep until the gods weep. All this time, making Poseidon cry would have woken her?

"What about my power?"

Her smile softened. "Don't blame yourself, Almi. It was always going to happen like this. You made the right decision. I'm just so pleased I got to say goodbye."

"No, no, you're awake now! It's going to be okay!"

"Listen to me, Almi. There's not much time. Poseidon made a deal after he flashed you out of the bakery. My life, for his."

"What?"

"The only way he could stop Atlas from cutting out my heart was to offer up his own life. Poseidon agreed that if I was still alive and safe at the end of the Trials then Atlas could have his life, to do with as he wished. But if I died, then Atlas had to remove his trident as a prize in the Trials, and give it back to Poseidon."

"But..."

"I know it wasn't the plan, but by embracing your power, you've broken that deal."

My mouth opened and closed as I tried to make sense of what she was saying. Only one thing was repeating. "You're dying."

"Yes. I've been dying for a decade, Almi. It's time. And like I said before, how lucky am I to have helped my little sister save the world?" Her smile was sad and soft, and fresh grief crashed through me.

"Please. Please stay with me."

"I've stayed as long as I can. You have someone else to love now."

"No." I shook my head, eyes blurred with tears.

"I love you, Almi."

"I love you," I sobbed back.

I knew when it happened, just a second later. I felt the life leave her. And with it went all rational thought.

The time-bomb exploded.

## ALMI

*W*hen I looked up, it wasn't with the thought of avoiding Medusa's stare. It was with the thought of annihilating her completely.

A sense of utter invincibility had taken me, and somehow, somewhere, I knew I had changed. Poseidon said he was immune to her gaze because he was a god. Well, the power roaring through my veins now had to equal that of a fucking god, and I was going to use it.

I didn't speak a word of command as I rose to my feet, but air whooshed to me instantly. It whirled around me, creating a barrier like the one it did when I was underwater. With no fear inside me at all, I took in the scene before me.

While I had been with Lily, Ceto had reached the clearing. And to my relief, she was fighting alongside us. Snakes poured from Medusa's outstretched claws, and they covered the sea monster's body. Inky red liquid burst from the spots all over her tentacles as Ceto blasted the snakes back at Medusa.

Poseidon was facing Atlas, my silver-glowing whirlwind beating against the fire god every time a flame even tried to leave his fingertips.

As I started to move toward them, gold light beamed from Poseidon's hands, and I heard him cry out in surprise. Both he and Atlas froze as the light flared too bright to look at, then died away. There, gleaming in Poseidon's open hands, was his golden trident.

Atlas turned to look at me, then down at Lily, his face an angry snarl. Poseidon looked at me too and his expression made my shattered heart skip a beat. There was no triumph in the return of his precious trident. Only pure sorrow. Lily's words spoke loudly in my mind.

I'd been so overwhelmed with grief, so astonished to hear her actual voice, the impact of what he'd done had been lost.

But now, staring at him, seeing my own pain echoed in his fierce eyes, it hit me.

He had traded his life for hers.

He was willing to die, to save my sister. For me.


Searing pain lanced through my gut, and I gasped as it reached my chest, a crushing agony gripping me, forcing me to my knees once more.

Atlas' snarl turned into a delighted grin as Poseidon shouted my name. He began to run toward me, but there was a shriek from Ceto, and then Poseidon's legs were suddenly stone. He beat at his limbs with the golden trident, roaring in helpless fury, but it was no good. I tried to suck in air as my chest continued to tighten, dropping to my hands and starting to crawl toward Poseidon.

Atlas cackled loudly, and fire roared to life on the ground, rushing me. My whirlwind swept into my vision, blowing the flames out instantly. Fresh fire sprang up to replace it though.

I kept crawling, only one thought in my mind, my eyes locked on Poseidon's.

I knew what was happening to me.

This was the day all the prophecies would come true, it would seem.

Poseidon loved me.

And I loved him.


"Almi, please, no." Poseidon's voice reached me as I got closer, choking for air. My whirlwind was beating back Atlas and his fire, and a barrier of air was spinning around me, so fast it was clear.

The stone was spreading up Poseidon's waist now.

"I won't let you die." It was hard to get the words out, the invisible band squeezing my chest not allowing enough air into my body.

"Almi, run. Call Blue and run."

I drew on the immense power still coursing through me and dragged myself to my feet. "It's too late." I tried to smile, but the fear on his face was too much. "You offered your own life for hers."

"I would do anything for you."

"And I you. I love you."

Something snapped in his eyes, all the barely contained control leaving him completely. "This can not happen!" His voice was an anguished roar. "Take me! Take me and leave the nereids to live!"

I didn't know who he was yelling the plea at, but I couldn't stand the grief in his voice. I moved the last step toward him, pressing myself against the little flesh he had left, clasping my hands to his face.

"It wasn't supposed to happen like this. You and your sister were supposed to get the life I deprived you of." Regret and fear and bone-deep sorrow laced his tone as his wild eyes bore into mine. "It wasn't supposed to happen like this."

I gasped in a breath, before pressing my lips to his. "It's not your fault," I breathed, drawing back. "You did every-thing you could. The prophecy was clear. I'm going to die." I knew the pain in my chest was my oncoming death. But the sight of the man I had only just accepted that I loved turning into a godammned statue had filled me with an eerily calm, resolute rage. "If I'm going down, I'm taking them with me." If there was any chance at all that killing Medusa and Atlas would save Poseidon from the stone, then I was going to do everything I could to make it happen.

He shook his head, but I kissed him again. "I love you," I gasped against his lips. The words were like a balm, and I drew strength from them.

When he spoke them back, actual strength flowed through me, my spine straightening and my chest easing just a little. "I love you Almi. I always have."

I stepped back, and saw that the stone had almost reached his shoulders.

It was now or never.

# ALMI

*J*ust as I turned to Atlas, Kryvo's voice reached me. "Almi! Almi, the starfish on the font!"

Atlas fixed his hate-filled eyes on mine. Behind him, Ceto and Medusa were still locked in battle.

"It's too late, Kryvo. I'm so sorry."

"No! You must take me to the font! You must!"

He would be safer on the font, I realized, as Atlas began to advance toward me. I had no plan, as such. Just that I was going out with as big a bang as I could manage, and I was taking these fucking assholes with me. And I didn't want to do that with my friend attached to me.

Mustering my strength, I ran the few short steps to the font. I pulled Kryvo from my shoulder as I went, ready to set him onto the stone before Atlas could attack, but I faltered when I saw the fountain.

There were *hundreds* of starfish carved into the stone of the font.

I held my hand out to touch one, air magic swirling

around me and my shield expanding. As the air moved over the font, the starfish began to burst to life, just as Kryvo had. One by one, they peeled away from the stone and flew into the pool of water. The sounds of fighting fell away as I stared, my heart hammering.

Kryvo quivered in my hand. "You brought me to life," he squeaked. "I can feel your magic now, you brought me to life!"

He was right. I remembered how the air had blown in from the open bedroom window before he had come to life on my mirror.

A weird crashing realization filled me, knowledge that was coming from somewhere filled with magic drawing me to the truth.

"Kryvo, it's you," I whispered. My vision was swimming, and I could feel more and more magic building inside me. My chest burned with the pressure.

Somehow, I knew what I had to do. Magic compelled me, and I lifted the little starfish to my face as heat seared up my back. My air buffeted me, my magic warring with the Titan on my behalf behind me.

"Kryvo, you're going to save them all, you brave little starfish. You're the Heart of the Ocean."

Gently, I dropped him into the font with all the other starfish. The water pulsed, and I heard his voice in my head.

"Almi!"

"You're going to save Poseidon and all the people of Aquarius!" I told him again, watching as the water got brighter and brighter. I knew he would be safe. More than safe. He would become something new, something brilliant. "You're a hero, little Kryvo," I whispered.

Tears that I thought I had run out of sprang to my eyes again, and as the water got so bright it hurt, I turned back to Atlas.

I took as deep a breath as I could manage. I refused to look at Poseidon. I couldn't stand to see if the stone had taken him. Couldn't stand to tell him goodbye.

The Titan's furious eyes bore into mine, mania within them.

"Medusa!" I shouted as loud as my breathless body would allow. Atlas faltered at my summons, but behind me, I saw the two goddesses pause.

Ceto's voice rang in my mind. *You wish me to stop fighting her?*

*Yes.*

In a second, the woman was in front of me, standing beside her husband. I looked straight at her. The barrier of air between us would filter her deadly stare.

"You underestimated her, husband," she hissed to Atlas.

He snarled, and flames roared up around him. I felt the heat of the magic from the font behind me first, though, and then it began to flow around me, a thick tension building to a crescendo.

"What is happening? Why is the font—" Medusa's panicked words were cut off by a boom so deep it made the ground shake. Energy flowed from the font, and I held my arms out as it washed over me.

Healing energy.

It would do no good for me. The Heart of the Ocean

was never destined to save my life. But I turned my head, eyes misty with tears, and watched as the stone melted from Poseidon's body, rolling off his form like liquid.

A scream snapped my attention back ahead. The stone had left Lily's body too, pooling beneath her where she lay, then flowing across the ground. *Toward Medusa.* The stone that had left Poseidon was doing the same, and as it reached Medusa's feet it began to wind its way up her body.

"What's happening?" she shrieked, trying to move. Atlas scratched at the stone covering his wife's body, fury and fear on his face.

"You are being punished." Poseidon's voice rang out, and then he was beside me, pulling me tight against his body. Overpowering relief crashed over me, making me sag against him. I had failed to save Lily. But I had saved Poseidon. My air barrier expanded, encompassing him, too, and his trident gleamed gold. Water flowed from its tip into my air magic, making it gleam brighter silver.

"Make it stop!" Medusa screamed. Atlas turned to us, advancing a few steps then faltering, as though he didn't want to leave his wife.

"Make it stop, now!" he repeated, launching fire from his hands toward us.

The flames hit the water-wind wall of magic between us and petered out instantly.

"The font takes ill-will lethally," said Poseidon. "And your wife holds centuries of ill-will. Tell him the truth, Medusa. Clear your conscience, and the Underworld may treat you differently."

"I hate you!" she shrieked.

A new energy built around us, and as I looked at Atlas' terrified, maniacal face, I realized it was coming from him. All the warnings about the ancient Titan's strength washed over me, and fresh fear rose in me.

"Poseidon, you have to get out of here. Grab the red shell, and go," I said, turning into him.

He gripped my jaw, pressing a crushing kiss to my mouth before answering. "No. I will not leave you."

"I am dying, anyway. Please, live for both of us. And live the way you want, free and joyous."

He stared down at me, but the fear and sadness had gone. "I will fix this."

"Leave."

Medusa's frantic screams were increasing, so loud I only just heard Ceto in my head.

*My King, Queen, Atlas' power is becoming unstable. We need to leave.*

Medusa's screams cut off abruptly, and Atlas roared. I knew before I turned that she would be a statue.

"You will pay for this, ocean god!" Power hammered against our barrier, coming from every angle. I staggered, unable to take the attack, and the pressure in my chest magnified.

"Leave, Poseidon!" Ceto shouted. I was vaguely aware of her by the font, her hand hovering by the red shell. Kryvo floated above the fountain, only now he was covered in shining crystals and pearls.

Poseidon shouted as he launched power back at the Titan, and for the first time, I felt him as he should be.

The raw, colossal power of the ocean, unhindered by the stone blight. He was glorious.

Black swam in front of my eyes, and my throat closed tighter.

I slipped, and Poseidon pulled me upright.

"Let me go. Leave."

Heat swamped me, and I realized through my dizziness that we were surrounded by fire. My air magic was dying.

Poseidon bellowed, then water washed over me, making my already breathless chest work even harder.

"I love you." My legs crumpled as I gasped the words. More black crowded my vision; fire and water and the tang of power fading away as the pain flashed into agony. The excruciating feeling faded as quickly as it came, and a delicious serenity took me.

Then everything was gone.

# POSEIDON

"*H*ow does it feel, Poseidon? To watch your wife die?"

Atlas had not a drop of sanity left in him as he roared the words. I knew my own was teetering on the edge. I couldn't look at Almi's body on the ground beside me, or the little control that remained would flee me.

I knew what I needed to do. And I couldn't do it alone, not from the most inaccessible place in all of Olympus.

*Ceto, take the shell. End this.*

I couldn't win the Trials, nor could Almi. But he'd said Ceto and Kalypso were even on shells. And I needed the Trial over. I would have to take my chances with the sea goddess.

Power coursed through me, the feeling so welcome after such a long absence. I raised my trident high above my head.

"Creatures of the ocean, sea gods and goddesses of Olympus, hear my plea! This Titan wishes you ill! The Trials are over, and he must be dealt with!"

With an almighty push of power, I sent all my strength into the ocean beyond the dome around me. Atlas roared again, and Ceto launched inky black water at him as fire burst from his palms.

I cast my gaze up, feeling the response of the deep around me, answering my call. As I stared, creatures of all manner appeared beyond the glowing silver dome. Whales that had never seen daylight, twenty-feet long sea snakes and eels, fish of every size and shape, seals, dolphins, hippocampi, all swam alongside creatures many believed only existed in myth. Creatures as huge and terrifying as the talontaur, monsters that could only be seen by those who were guilty of horrific crimes, and deadly ocean wraiths arrived to aid me. When I saw the merfolk of the deep reach the dome, I knew that meant Ceto's brother, Phorkus, had answered my call. He was the god of the deep, and these creatures were his kin. Sure enough, I saw his inky, rotten form beyond the dome, shaped like his tentacled sister.

My trident grew hot in my hands as the hundreds of sea creatures kept flocking to the dome, to answer the call of their King. Light spewed from the tip of the trident, and as it hit the dome, everything shone gold.

"Rise!" I shouted the command, pouring my gloriously returned strength into the words. The creatures beyond the dome moved in a frenzy, and then the ground beneath my feet began to shake as the mass of creatures lent their strength in lifting Atlantis from the ocean floor.

We rose, slowly at first, then faster as more and more of my brethren answered my call. Kalypso appeared behind Atlas, and I prepared to call back some of my power to fight her, but she cast her eyes down to my feet where Almi's body lay, then back to mine. She nodded once, then shot jets of water from her palm at the scrabbling Atlas.

When daylight appeared above us, the sea animals began to dive away, the creatures of the deep unable to tolerate the light.

"Thank you. Your loyalty shall be honored," I boomed, then used my own power to raise Atlantis the rest of the way.

We burst through the surface, and I didn't need to send my next plea.

There was a series of flashing lights all around us, and as they cleared, I found myself surrounded by my kin.

Hades was beside me, Persephone to his left. Athena was to my right, and beyond her I saw the rest of the Olympians lined up opposite the insane Titan, with the exceptions of Zeus, Hera and Aphrodite.

"You broke the rules, Atlas," Athena said.

The Titan screamed, throwing his arm up and indicating the terrifying statue that used to be his wife. "He broke the rules! Centuries ago, he tried to defile my wife!"

"No. The Font of Zoi is older than all of us. Its magic is beyond question. *It* deemed her unworthy. The monster Medusa became was a representation of her true nature. She did that, not Poseidon." Athena's voice rang with melodic wisdom.

"Lies!" With a searing burst of heat, Kalypso's water and Ceto's inky ribbons disintegrated.

No words needed to be exchanged between me and

my brother. In unison, Hades and I launched power at the Titan. Athena, Ares, Apollo, and Artemis added streams of glowing magic to ours, and Atlas screamed in pain. Hephaestus, then Dionysus, then Hermes added their own power, and Atlas rose from the ground.

"To Tartarus?" growled Hades. He was in his smoke form, huge and oozing terror that would have sent a mortal mad.

"To Tartarus," I agreed. As one, we focused out power. I pictured the horrific fiery pit of hell that was the underworld prison, Tartarus. Hades rose from the ground too, his bright blue power swirling with light. Bodies formed from the light, an army of corpses, ready to take their prisoner. Athena called out a battle cry, and I poured every drop of power I had into the stream wrapping around Atlas. He shrieked as Hades' army swamped him. There was a flash of blue light, and the god of the dead vanished, along with Atlas.

"Poseidon, she's… she's…." Persephone was on her knees, her golden vines wrapped around Almi's form. Her eyes were filled with tears, and her voice shook. "She's dead."

"Not for long," I growled. I bent, scooping my wife up in my arms. Persephone's vines vanished immediately, and I swallowed down bile at the feeling of Almi's cold, lifeless skin.

"Brethren. Will you bring her back?"

Athena looked at me sadly. "Without Zeus, we can not.

All the Olympian gods are needed for this feat. I am sorry, Poseidon."

I turned away from the goddess.

"Zoi! Behold the last of the Nereids! You save species from extinction, and the Nereids are worth saving. I beseech you!" My voice broke on the last sentence, and I lay Almi down in front of the font. Her starfish, encrusted in jewels and hovering over the font, pulsed with light.

"Poseidon, if the font doesn't deem her worthy, she may return a monster."

I ignored Athena.

"Kryvo. Tell me what to do."

I heard the starfish's tiny voice in my head. *Give her water.*

I leaned forward, scooping water up from the font in my hands. I knelt carefully and looked at her face for the first time since the life at left her.

I couldn't bear it. Anguish beyond anything I had ever known made my chest feel like it was shattering.

*Give her the water.* Kryvo's voice seeped through the pain. I bent over her and tipped the water from the font over her colorless lips.

Nothing happened. Silence dominated. Absolutely nothing happened.

Then the ocean breeze gusted over us, a tiny whirlwind appearing beside me. It danced toward Almi's face and as it reached the droplets of water running uselessly down her face, it gathered them up, and made a miniature whirlpool of air and water.

Carefully, delicately, it moved to her tattoo. I watched, my breath held, as it appeared to melt into her skin. The center of the shell tattoo flared with life and color, vivid green. I didn't dare release my breath as the color swirled out, filling the shell, and then rippled over the rest of her skin. The pallid tone faded, lively pink replacing it. Then her chest moved, her lungs filling. She gasped, and her eyes flickered open.

# ALMI

*L*ight pricked at the darkness.

"What…" I tried to say, but my throat didn't work. I wasn't breathing, I realized abruptly. Panic swamped me as I tried to orient myself, tried to open my eyes or make my chest work. With a rush, I felt air flow down my throat and fill my lungs. My eyelids cracked open, and through the haze, I saw Poseidon.

Memories crashed through me as I stared up at his face.

*His smile.*

That devastating smile was stretched across his face, and then his hand was on my cheek, brushing my hair back.

"Almi," he breathed.

My head pounded, and my vision was blurry.

"What…" I tried again, but air whooshed over my face, and a little whirlwind came into focus.

Something stirred in my gut, alien and raw and not

unpleasant. The whirlwind expanded, whizzing around me, and Poseidon's smile slipped.

"What are you doing?" he barked, his fingers tightening around my shoulders. I was vaguely aware that I was lying on the ground, but then the whirlwind tightened around me and pulled me from Poseidon's grasp. He cried out and Persephone appeared beside him as I was lifted higher into the air. She said something to him, and a jet of water burst from his palm toward the whirlwind. The pain and disorientation was leaving me, the feeling in my gut spreading through me instead.

*I was supposed to be dead.*

The realization hammered into me as I stared down into Poseidon's confused face.

*I had died.*

How was I back?

I felt something warm and slightly sharp against my hand and looked down.

"Kryvo." He was beautiful.

"He saved you," the little starfish said gleefully, as an image of Poseidon calling all of the creatures of the sea burst to life behind my eyelids. I watched as Atlantis rose from the ocean, and the Olympians arrived and cast Atlas into Tartarus.

Numbness still suffocated my mind, even as I felt the power building inside me. I watched as Poseidon lifted my body, and carried me to the font.

"He brought me back," I murmured.

"The font brought you back. It deemed you worthy."

I opened my eyes, dispelling the vision. "What's happening now?"

"You are being reborn with the Heart of the Ocean."

"That's you?"

"Yes."

"I don't understand."

"I belong to you. You have my power now, as well as your own."

"Your power?"

"Yes. Immortality. You're a goddess now, Almi." I could hear the glee in his voice.

The whirlwind around us spun even faster, and I tried to get my brain to catch up as I hovered within it. "A goddess?"

"Yes. Embrace it."

As he said the words, the air stopped spinning. For a second I thought I would plummet to the floor, but a torrent of magic exploded inside me, and the whole world froze.

That same weird, expanding knowledge I'd had in front of the font filled me. I could be anywhere I wanted, instantly. And I knew exactly where that was.

I flashed, right into Poseidon's arms.


"You're back." He gripped my face, kissing me everywhere. I laughed, pushing at his chest.

"I'm back. And Kryvo says I'm a goddess now."

"Almi!"

I turned at Persephone's voice. One by one, the other Olympians were disappearing in flashes of light, but my attention went to where my friend was kneeling on the ground. Next to Lily.

I moved quickly, Poseidon still clutching my hand. Persephone beamed up at me as I reached them. "Almi, look."

I followed her pointing hand to my sister. A tiny spinning whirlwind flecked with drops of water sank into the shell tattoo on her chest.

And then her ribs moved.

I dropped to my knees, putting my hand to her cheek. She was warm. Her skin was the right color.

Excitement thrilled through me, disbelief hot on its heels.

"Almi?" Lily's eyes opened slowly as she said my name.

"I'm here, Lily. I'm here." Tears of joy spilled down my cheeks, as I looked into her bright blue eyes. "We're all here."

I was scared that I was actually dead, and this was all some weird afterlife dream or something.

My sister was alive. And awake. Staring up at me, a weak smile on her lips.

"You asked the font to save the last of the Nereids. It has brought them both back," Persephone breathed through her smile, her healing vines wrapping around Lily's wrists. "She needs water."

Water flowed from Poseidon's glowing hand, precise and gentle as it reached Lily's lips. His power felt different now, and I remembered what he'd said about me being a beacon to him. I felt drawn to it, like it had its own life and sound, and it was calling to me.

As if hearing my thoughts, a stream of water broke away, making its way to me instead. I held my hand out, and a trickle of air flowed from me. When the two met, silver light glowed, and the stream of water and air intertwined with each other, dancing before us.

A sense of utter rightness settled over me. This was happening. This was real.

*"I love you."*

The words were in my head, in Poseidon's deep, beautiful voice. I turned my face from Lily, who was still drinking, to look at him.

"I love you," I whispered. "This is real, right?"

Kryvo squeaked from where I'd hurriedly pressed him to my collar. "One hundred percent real. Look, it's Blue and Chrysos."

I snapped my head left to see the two pegasi galloping into the clearing. Blue didn't stop until he reached me, and I stroked his nose, peppering his long snout with kisses.

"Boy, am I glad you're safe," I told him. Tears were burning at the backs of my eyes, but this time through sheer joy.

"I know this is an emotional time for you all," Athena's voice rang out through the clearing. "But there is the matter of the Poseidon Trials to settle."

Poseidon stiffened beside me, and I focused on the goddess. Ceto was next to her, tentacles squelching on the ground. An uneasy feeling washed over me.

We may have been saved, but Poseidon might have lost his realm.

"Ceto won the most shells. As per the rules of the

Trials, she is entitled to reign over Aquarius." Athena's voice was tight and reluctant. Ceto's gaze fell on Poseidon.

"I am willing to make a deal, sea king."

He bowed to her, still not releasing my hand. "I am grateful. And I have a worthy offer."

She inclined her head at him. "You owe me, Poseidon. I will only consider a grand offer."

"How would you like to rule Atlantis?"

I looked at him in surprise, then back at Ceto. She blinked slowly. "You offer me a city in ruins?" Her words were unimpressed, but her tone belied an undercurrent of what I was sure was excitement.

"Yes. I would like to offer the inhabitants citizenship in Aquarius, should they wish to take it-" he started, but I gripped his arm, cutting him off.

"The inhabitants?"

He beamed down at me, and my knees felt weak. "Yes. They are all alive. I can feel them."

Joy rushed me, and I bounced on my feet involuntarily. "And the victims in Aquarius?"

"We are too far from them for me to tell, but if the ancient people here have been cured, then I think it is, for once, safe to get our hopes up." His face was alive with emotion.

"You offer me a city in ruins, with no population?" Ceto called, drawing both of our attentions back to her.

"Indeed. A city with power. A city with one of the most ancient and powerful artifacts of Olympus in it."

"Poseidon," Athena said, worry in her voice. "The Font of Zoi must be protected. It must never be abused."

ELIZA RAINE & ROSE WILSON

Poseidon kept his eyes locked on Ceto. "This goddess is trustworthy. I will vouch for her. She has been a part of the creation of many creatures of the sea, and she cares for them as her own. She deals in respect. There would be no better guardian for the font's power."

"Very well," Athena said. "You are responsible for this decision, Poseidon."

"Will you take Atlantis, in return for me keeping Aquarius?" Poseidon said to Ceto.

She was silent a long moment. "Can you return the city to the bottom of the ocean?"

"Yes."

"Then yes. I accept your offer." Ceto's voice rang in my mind, straight after her spoken words. *The debt is clear, sea King, Queen.*

With a flash, she vanished. Athena gave Poseidon a piercing look, then she vanished too.

Polybotes stamped up to take her place. He was completely free of stone, and must have stayed out of the fighting once he had been brought back. Given that he had no magic, I couldn't blame him. He fixed his huge eyes on me. "You have saved my life twice. You have my allegiance." He looked at Poseidon. "You are an asshole, and I will only abandon my revenge because your wife is better than you." With a nod, he stamped away, disappearing into the maze. I looked up at Poseidon, eyebrows raised and a grin on my lips.

"You're going to have to tell me the story with you two." He started to answer, but Lily's voice reached me.

"Almi." I dropped to my knees. Persephone's vines

were still around her, and I glanced at my friend. "Is she okay?"

"I'm fine," Lily answered for herself. Persephone nodded at me, beaming.

"Lily." I leaned forward, wrapping my arms tightly around her, pulling her into a sitting position. She returned my hug fiercely.

"I told you so." Her lips were cracked, and her voice was scratchy, but she was grinning at me as I moved back to look at her.

"You told me what?"

"All of it! That you would get your power and be stronger than me. That you would save the world. That the god of the sea was in love with you." She cast a playful glance up at Poseidon.

"It really was you talking to me all that time." Happy tears crept down my cheeks.

"Of course it was. I never left you."

"I love you, Lily."

"I know. I love you too."

# ALMI

"Do I have to do this?" The little nymph straightened the hem of my dress as my sister laughed.

"Yes. You do."

"In front of all those people?"

"That's kind of the point. Turn around so I can see you."

I shuffled around on the little podium I was standing on so that Lily could see me. Her eyes lit up, and she moved so that I could see the full-length mirror behind her.

My reflection stared back, and I never would have believed I could look like I did. The vividly bright shell tattoo, the shining, mother-of-pearl skin tone and the bright blue and silver-streaked hair were one thing. But the wedding dress?

Never in a million years did I expect that.

. . .

It was the palest of greens, with silver and blue—to match my hair—shimmering in the fabric. The top was a stiff corset with completely sheer sleeves that draped low down my arms like liquid. The skirt flowed over my hips, glittering with the hint of bright rolling clouds and cresting waves when I moved.

It was a stunning dress. I looked at Lilly, who had tears in her eyes.

"What's wrong?"

"You look amazing. And I never thought I would see you again, let alone be here with you when you marry the man you love."

"Oh, Lily. I'm so glad you're here too." The nymph moved back, allowing me to step down from the pedestal and gather Lily into a hug.

It had only been two nights since the showdown in Atlantis, and Lily and I had been inseparable since.

Poseidon had been completely occupied in handing Atlantis over to Ceto, moving the citizens into his own realm, and then sinking it back to the bottom of the ocean. Along with Persephone, Lily and I had been helping all the people who had been afflicted by the stone blight, and it turned out that my new magic made me the perfect person for the job. Or perfect *goddess* for the job. I glanced at the little jewel-encrusted starfish sitting on a cushion on the dresser.

Kryvo was the Heart of the Ocean, and his power was mine. And it seemed he wasn't just immortal. He had telepathic powers. Which meant, so did I. With a little guidance from Persephone, I was able to help adjust the memories of those families who had lost loved ones to the stone, so that they never knew anything so serious had ever occurred.

It was satisfying work, and it made me truly happy to help put all the broken families back together again, my own sister and friend alongside me.

But it had only taken hours of being back in Aquarius for me to start missing the sea king. Within a day of not seeing him, I started to feel... wrong. Twitchy and uncharacteristically melancholy.

The lack of his presence made me unable to think straight, or even eat properly. All I could think about, all I wanted, was him.

Then a note had appeared under my door.

Not a note, an invitation. To my own wedding.

POSEIDON, KING OF THE OCEAN, INVITES YOU TO WITNESS HIS FORMAL BONDING TO ALMI, NEREID AND QUEEN OF AQUARIUS. THE EVENT WILL ALSO SERVE AS HER OFFICIAL CORONATION. REGARDS.

There was a scrawled signature at the bottom that was totally illegible.

I had stared at the piece of paper, confusion and a touch of anger welling up inside me, until Lily had taken it from me, and after reading it, turned it over.

There was a sketch on the back, of my shell. It was beautifully done, and it made my breath catch. And in handwritten script beneath was a single sentence. A question.

*Will you become my Queen, before my realm?*

Galatea had arrived the next morning to say the ceremony would take place immediately and that Roz and Mav would be waiting in the dressing room with my dress.

"You'll need a garter," said Lily, putting her hand on her chin and looking me up and down.

I was about to protest that that was old-fashioned and a human thing, but then a thought struck me. "The blindfold."

"What?"

"The piece of his toga he cut for me, to blindfold my eyes."

"Great idea. I'll go get it."

Lily scurried off to find it, and I took a deep breath as I looked at my reflection again. My longing for Poseidon had become as physical as it had emotional. I was connected to him as deeply as if we shared a beating heart.

I understood the need for the ceremony. Both Lily and Galatea had made the point that if I was now a goddess and recognized as Poseidon's wife, then it needed to be made official to the people of his realm, as well as to the other gods.

But I didn't need all this over-the-top nonsense. I just needed him.

I would sacrifice anything I owned to see that smile on

his face. To feel his warm skin against mine, free of cold hard granite. To feel his powerful aura washing over me, to hear his whoop of joy as we soared through the air and the ocean together.

A small noise escaped my lips as I screwed my face up with impatience.

I wanted him here, beside me, now.

The one good thing about having a formal wedding, I thought as I stared at my skirt in the mirror, was that weddings were followed by *wedding nights*.

My dreams had become more intense, and I knew that I was far, far more excited — and nervous — about the evening than the wedding vows or wearing a crown.

I would finally feel the way Poseidon's desire-filled eyes, husky voice and tense body had promised I would. He would be able to do anything he liked to me. I would let him. Anticipation sent thrills across my skin.

"Aquarius will be lucky to have such a beautiful Queen." I saw Galatea standing behind me in the mirror, and I forced the filthy thoughts from my mind. I smiled as I turned to her.

"Thank you. I'm glad you think so."

"I do. Are you ready?"

Lily burst back into the room, holding the strip of fabric triumphantly.

I took a deep breath. "I am now."

The ceremony was held in the throne room, and Persephone was waiting for me outside the door when we ascended the stairs.

"Wow. You look… like a goddess."

"I feel like one," I grinned.

"Hey, Kryvo, way to go saving the day," she said to the starfish, who was adorning my wrist like a big sparkly corsage.

He heated on my skin. "Thanks," he squeaked happily.

"Who would have guessed he would be the Heart of the Ocean?"

"I certainly didn't," I said. "I didn't even know I'd brought him to life. I thought he was part of the palace's magic."

"I didn't know either," the starfish said. "I didn't become what I was meant to be until you embraced your power," he said.

"Fascinating," said Persephone, eyes gleaming with interested excitement. She was wearing a stunning yellow and green dress, covered in black lace made up of roses. Her white hair was braided, and she wore a golden tiara shaped from thorns. "You know, I'd love to study him, see if I can work out how you brought him to life," she said to me.

"I, erm, won't be needing his company tonight," I said awkwardly, feeling my face heat. "Kryvo, do you want to stay with Persephone this evening?"

"I would rather be anywhere than with you and Poseidon tonight," he said.

Persephone laughed. "That settles it then." She looked at Lily standing next to me, wearing a stunning flowing gown of rich sparkling teal, that complimented her hair perfectly. "How are you feeling?"

My sister and my new friend had gotten along great the last few days, and it made my heart sing to be with them both.

"Excited to see my little sister get married. Properly this time," grinned Lily.

"That makes one of us," I mumbled.

Persephone raised her eyebrows. "You don't want to marry him?" She looked at the huge, gilded doors behind her. "It's a bit late to back out now. They're all waiting for you in there."

I shook my head. "No, it's just, I don't usually deal with all this…" I swept my arm out. "Formality. And drama."

"You just participated in the Poseidon Trials, which were shown to the whole of Olympus. I think you're fairly embedded in the drama."

"Hmm."

"You need to give your adoring audience their happy ending," smiled Lily. "And anyway, you love him. Go and enjoy telling the world that."

As she said the words, I realized that that was exactly where my hang-up was.

I had to tell him I loved him and was choosing to be his wife, in front of the whole world. But I hadn't even told *him* that.

Well, I had told him I loved him. Me dropping dead was all the evidence he had needed that the love was real and mutual. But, other than in the chaos that was the last trial, we hadn't had a single moment to actually say the words or work out what they meant to us.

Declaring this newfound love in front of a load of strangers was bound to feel a little uncomfortable.

I nodded at my sister. "Okay. Let's do this."

The gilded doors eased open, and I linked my arm in Lily's and followed Persephone into the throne room.

# ALMI

*W*aiting for Almi to enter the room, waiting to lay eyes on her beautiful face, was going to kill me. Immortal or not, it might actually kill me.

I had refrained from even speaking with her as I cleared up the mess Atlas had left behind, because I knew that I would not be able to maintain my control if given even the slightest temptation. And just her voice, her words, her wit... Speaking with her would have been enough for me to abandon all of my duties, whisk her away to my ship, and spend as much time as I needed to wipe away a decade of resentment and pain.

So instead, I had focused everything I had on doing what needed to be done, and subsequently, the last two days had felt as long as the last eight years. Because now, I knew she loved me back. I could feel it, an invisible cord between us, thrumming with life and hope and love.

She gave me an energy that was boundless, her presence cajoling and freeing, a feisty mass of all the things I had missed so sorely from my long, serious life.

Fuck, I had missed her. I wanted her, *needed* her by my side. After the cursed formality of the vows and coronation were out of the way, the world would not see us for far more than two days, I would make sure of that.

The throne from my throne room was gone, an altar and priestess of Hera replacing it. A large, peacock headdress denoted the slight woman as such, and I noticed she was smiling at the back of the room. Gods and goddesses lined the walls of the room, including my brother, but none caught my attention as I turned.

The doors were open. Persephone glided into the room, beaming. She swept to one side, to stand in place next to Hades, and there, arm in arm with her sister, was Almi.

I had thought that when I saw her, the tension that had plagued my body would lessen. But the opposite was true.

She looked beyond beautiful. Radiant. The Goddess, and Queen, that she always should have been.

My whole body stiffened, and warmth flooded me. When her gaze met mine, I saw my own smile reflected back at me, sincere joy on her face. And desire in her eyes.

Her sister kissed her cheek when she reached me, then moved to stand with Persephone. Almi looked up at me, her expression almost shy. I took her hand, then nodded at the priest to start the ceremony.

*You look stunning.*

Her mouth twitched as the priestess spoke about eternal bonds and lifelong commitments. *You don't look too bad yourself. Now shh, I'm listening.*

*We've heard them once before.*

She narrowed her eyes at me. *I wasn't really listening then, either.*

Regretting bringing up the past, I tried to focus on the priestess. But all I could pay attention to was her. The silver streaks shone in her hair, and her skin glowed. She smelled like the breeze on the ocean.

*I missed you.*

Her voice sounded in my mind, and happiness coursed through my veins.

*I missed you too. More every minute.*

*Why didn't you talk to me then? Or come and see me?*

*Because I do not have the self-control required not to have abandoned my duties and taken you far away from all this. Somewhere we can enjoy each other at our long leisure.*

Her cheeks pinked, and I could see the need in her, as strong and fierce as my own.

*How long is this thing?*

I grinned at her, just as the priestess said, "With this crown…" Galatea stepped toward us. She was holding a cushion, and on it was a crown I'd never believed would adorn any head.

It was dainty, made from seashells and coral, with tiny gemstones set throughout that made it sparkle. I had found time before the ceremony to alter it a little, carving tiny whirlwinds into the three larger shells. Almi reached for it, eyes wide with wonder. She brushed a finger over one of the carvings.

"You carved this?" It was a question, but she already knew the answer.

I nodded. "Yes. You are not of the ocean. But you belong with it. That should be celebrated."

She beamed at me, and I took the crown from her, placing it gently on her head. The crowd clapped and roared, her friend from the bakery louder than all of the others.

The priestess spoke again. "And now, before Olympus, you must affirm your love for one another. Almi, do you assent to the bonding of your soul to Poseidon?"

She looked at me, those bright, determined eyes full of certainty. And joy. "I do."

"And Poseidon, do you assent to the bonding of your soul to Almi?"

"I do." With the words came a release of guilt I hadn't realized had been weighing so hard on me. A sense of freedom washed over me, raising the hairs on my arms and sending tingling sensations across my body. I knew Almi felt it too, because she gave a tiny gasp and gripped my hands.

"By the magic of Hera, you are wed and bound," said the priestess.

I lifted Almi's hand as I turned to the assembled room. "Aquarius, I present to you your Queen."

# ALMI

*an we leave yet?* I sent the telepathic thought to Poseidon as yet another person I didn't recognize bowed before us, extending their heartfelt congratulations on our wedding.

*Soon, my love.*

I gave a sigh, covering it quickly with a cough as our admirer bade his farewells. Poseidon gave me a sideways smile, loaded with promise.

*You've waited a long time. A few hours won't make any difference.*

"Hours!" I exclaimed aloud. His smile widened.

My body had come alive the second I'd seen him at the altar, all my annoyance and reticence vanishing in a flash. There was nothing in Olympus I wanted more than to show him how much he meant to me. And to feel the same from him.

He was right, I had waited a long time. My whole damn adult life, I'd been waiting to find out what a man would feel like inside me. And it turned out I'd waited for exactly the right reason.

Him.

I was ready, and I was done waiting.

If I was a Queen now, I was damn well going to act like one.

I glared at him, my mental words brooking no argument. Husband, take me to bed. Now.

His eyelids dipped, bright blue eyes darkening. How can I refuse a command from her majesty? he said, and the world flashed.

When I blinked, we were in the bedroom on his ship. The huge, shell-shaped bed, covered in black silk stood beckoning us.

Before I could say a word, he pulled me tight against him, both his hands on my face. He drew his thumbs down my cheeks as he stared into my eyes.

"Alone, at last," he breathed.

Heat swept my body, pooling between my legs.

This was happening.

"You are so very, very beautiful."

I wetted my lips, drawing in a breath. "As are you, my king." He flashed me a devastating grin, and I bit my lip. "That smile makes me weak. I can't believe you hid it for so long."

"I can't believe I haven't been able to do this for so long," he replied, before dipping his head and pressing his lips to mine.

It started as a gentle kiss, fitting of two people in love. But as his tongue parted my lips, and the taste of him flooded my senses, it turned into an entirely different kind of kiss. A kiss that showed me how much he wanted me.

A kiss that touched every part of me.

A kiss that made my knees buckle.

He scooped me up, holding me close as he moved us to the bed. All I could do was hold onto him. My mind reeled with the sensation of his body pressed against mine. The heat of his mouth, the smoothness of his skin, the hardness of his body.

He lowered me to the bed, his lips never leaving mine the whole time. When my back came into contact with the sheets, he pulled away, only to rain kisses down my neck. He bit down gently, teeth grazing my skin and making me tingle everywhere.

"You are so soft," he murmured. "I want to hear you scream."

I took a shaky breath, letting the need that his words had created spread through me, willing myself to relax. He moved back, and when he looked down into my eyes, I could see the impatience and desire warring on his face. I reached up and cupped his cheek.

Feeling bold, I moved to my knees slowly, gripping his shoulders. "Help me with my corset?"

Before he could answer, I turned my back to him. I felt his fingers on the laced-up back of my dress, firm but gentle as he untied and loosened the ribbon.

When I felt the heavy fabric was loose enough, I took a deep breath and lifted my arms straight above my head. There was a pause, and my dress slid up my body.

He was tall enough that he had no problem removing it, leaving me kneeling in nothing but lace panties and my blindfold garter. Terrified at my nakedness, and desperate to see his nakedness, I turned slowly to face him, dropping my arms back to my sides.

He hissed in a breath, his eyes blazing as they took in my breasts, my belly, my panties.

I dropped my eyes deliberately to his toga-clad waist. In a movement almost too fast to follow, he rid himself of it.

I couldn't help my gasp.

Every inch of him was hard, sculpted muscle.

Every inch.

He was magnificent. Solid muscles covered his chest, with just a dusting of hair leading down south to the soft-looking skin I'd stroked before. My eyes dropped lower, and I moaned. He was already hard, his cock bobbing before me, long and thick and perfect.

I couldn't help reaching out. He twitched, and I thought he was going to stop me, but then he stilled. I wrapped my fingers around his shaft and looked up at him.

He gave a growl that was pure satisfaction as his gaze bored into mine. I turned my face and licked the tip of his cock.

He growled again, his body tensing. I licked the tip again, and then swirled my tongue around it. He tasted salty and warm, and I liked it. I took him deep in my mouth, sucking softly. His hands gripped my hair, and he spoke breathlessly. "My queen." His cock swelled even bigger against my tongue and his hands tightened in my hair. I grasped his cock firmly and sucked, working my tongue and mouth on him. I felt him shudder, then heard him groan and felt him shudder again. "Stop."

He pulled away, and I gasped, licking my lips and staring up at him as he took a ragged breath.

"I've waited so long for you," he growled.

"And I you," I breathed, my voice hitched. Desire was pulsing through me, so intense it was almost unbearable. "Touch me," I whispered.

"Take off your panties," he commanded.

I felt a fresh rush of heat at his command, and I obeyed, pulling down my white lace panties.

The instant I was uncovered, he was on me.

He picked me up, my legs wrapping around his waist as he pressed me against the sheets. My back sank into the black silk, his weight crushing me into the covers. My nipples brushed against the hard wall of his chest, and I arched into him.

The feel of his skin against mine was electric. His hand moved between us, stroking down my belly as he took my mouth in a fierce kiss. His finger found my wetness and I moaned into his lips.

"You are ready for me." It was a question and a statement together, and he sounded as close to edge as I felt.

"So ready. I love you."

He stilled his stroking, lifting his head from mine to stare at me. "I love you."

He shifted as he said the words, and I felt his cock against my entrance. I bit my lip. "You are mine, now and forever. And I yours."

"Forever."

Gently, so gently, he pressed into me, dropping his lips to mine again.

I sucked in a gasp at the feeling, and he moved, kissing my jaw and my neck. He stretched me, a slight discomfort taking me as he moved deeper. But the pain vanished quickly, and he withdrew a little.

"Okay?" He asked against my skin.

"Yes."

"More?"

"More."

He pressed even deeper into me, and I cried out. He held himself there, even as he covered my jaw in more kisses. "Good?"

"Good," I panted.

"More?"

"There's more?" He nipped at my neck and pressed even further into me. I let out a long moan, and he wound an arm under me, pulling me tight against him. I arched into it, letting the feeling of fullness take me.

He began to move. My gasps turned into moans as he withdrew before slowly pressing back in. Again and again, he moved, taking me slowly, and my arms wound around his shoulders. My eyes closed in pleasure, and I lost myself in the feeling of him buried deep inside me. I felt him shudder against me, his body tensing.

I lifted my head and kissed him hard on the mouth. He groaned, and I felt him shudder again. He moved faster, and I wrapped my legs tighter around him, my arms pulling him closer. He kissed me, deeply, fiercely, his tongue possessing mine.

I was close. I felt it building, the tingling starting in my belly as he moved inside me. My body felt like it was on fire, and I was starting to feel lightheaded, but each thrust of his body filling me was pure pleasure. I moaned into his mouth.

"Come for me," he breathed.

I shook, my body quaking as my orgasm exploded through me, pleasure bursting through me in waves. Lights flashed behind my closed eyelids, and I was only vaguely aware of the cry I had made. Poseidon growled as I clenched around him, and he moved faster. My body burned with the intensity of my climax, and I was still clinging to the edge when he groaned and pushed deep into me, shuddering as he came.

His cock twitched, and again, and again, filling me with warmth. He collapsed on top of me, and I welcomed the feeling of his weight on me.

He kissed me, sweet, gentle kisses as he held me against him.

"Mine," he murmured, his voice deep and satisfied.

"Always."

We lay like that for a long time, my face against his chest, my arms around his shoulders, him still buried deep inside me.

"I believe I said I wanted you to scream," he said eventually.

He lifted himself up on his elbows, and I looked up at him. He kissed me softly.

"Did I not scream?"

"You definitely made some noise," he said, eyes burning. "But nothing I would qualify as a scream." He moved inside me, slowly but solidly.

"I don't know," I said breathlessly. "I'm pretty sure I screamed when I came."

He shook his head. "No, my love. What you call a scream, I call a moan."

He brought his face down to mine and kissed me, his hips stilling. I whimpered at the loss of him, and he said against my lips, "Ah, you see? There it is."

He moved again, his cock sliding in and out of me slowly, steadily. I shivered at the sensation still sparking within me, and I looked up at him, biting my lip. "I want to come again."

He grinned at me. I squeaked as he scooped an arm underneath me and rolled. When we came to a stop, he was on his back, and I was on top.

Gently, he put a hand flat on my middle and pushed me back so that I was straddling him. His eyes devoured my breasts hungrily.

Pushing up onto his elbows, he moved his lips to my hard nipple. I closed my eyes, letting the sensation wash over me, the intensity of the pleasure of his tongue with the un-ignorable feeling of his cock still filling me. I ground my hips, pressing myself onto him hard. He growled against my skin, before moving to my other nipple.

I ground harder, the feeling delicious.

He lay back, staring up at me. His look took my breath away. For the first time, I felt like a really could be a goddess and a queen.

Then his thumb found my clit, and all thoughts abandoned me. He lifted his hips, bouncing me on his hardness, whilst his soft, clever hands worked some sort of magic. The dual sensations were too much, especially off the back of such an intense orgasm.

I cried out, and he froze.

My eyelids flew open.

He smiled at me, then gripped my ass with his other hand. Pulling me forward, then pushing me back, he made me ride his length, stroking me at the same time.

I felt myself tighten around him, pressure building inside me, dizzying and uncontainable.

"Let go. And remember to scream."

I did.

I screamed his name as my orgasm ripped through me, my body shaking. His hand dug into my ass, pulling me down onto him hard, then he thrust into me, hard and fast, his hands pulling my hips down onto him.

He gasped, then growled as he came, pumping his hot, thick release into me.

Him filling me pushed me even higher, and I let out a long whimper, my entire body alive with sensation.

I fell forward, collapsing onto his solid chest, and his hands played up and down my bare back as he breathed heavily.

"That was definitely a scream," he said, his voice thick with satisfaction.

I smiled at him, then let my head fall back to his chest. My eyes closed as exquisite contentment took me.

Everything was right. For the first time in my life, everything was right.

. . .

I started to drift off, and I snuggled into him. His arms wrapped tightly around me, and he kissed me gently on the forehead.

"This is where you belong, Queen Almi. With me. Always."

"And where you belong is in the skies and the ocean, not in a stuffy throne room," I murmured against his chest. "You and I are going to have some fun, Mr. King."

He chuckled, and the sound made me beam. "If you're by my side, I'll do whatever I'm bid. I love you."

"I love you, too. Always."

THE END

# THANKS FOR READING!

Thank you so much for reading The Poseidon Trials! If you enjoyed Almi and Poseidon's story, I would be so grateful for a review.

If you've read my previous series (Olympus Academy particularly) you may have noticed that I have a small obsession with the ocean. I am a scuba diver and have been lucky enough to experience some incredible encounters with marine life around the world (along with my fiercely adventurous mother) and the raw power and insanely massive wealth of life in the sea makes me feel a kind of way nothing else does. So, needless to say, I've wanted to write Poseidon's story for a really long time :)

I hope I did it justice! I enjoyed writing this series so much. A lot of my favorite parts of the story came to me as I wrote them (I'm looking at you, Kryvo), which is always so exciting as the author, because you kind of get to experience it as the reader might.

I also found myself calling my husband crying whilst writing this last book, which is a first. It turns out I'm really bad at killing my characters!!

I want to extend a heartfelt thank you to you, for reading my books. I'm writing every day now, and that's because amazing people like you are supporting your favorite authors by buying their books.

YOU ARE AMAZING.

## WHAT'S NEXT...

I will be making a short departure from Olympus for my next series, but there will still be plenty of mythology, magic and, of course, romance, involved. Along with some seriously manly viking heroes...

You can get exclusive access to cut scenes and first looks at artwork and story ideas, plus free short stories and audiobooks if you sign up to my newsletter at elizaraine.com and you can hang out with me and get teasers, giveaways and release updates (and pictures of my pets) by joining my Facebook reader group, just search for Eliza Raine Author!

# ACKNOWLEDGMENTS

Thank you so much to my editor Dayna, who has been amazing at dealing with my complete inability to work with deadlines and always makes my stories stronger.

Thank you so much to my author friends, Simone especially, for constantly motivating me and helping me talk out all those parts that don't make sense. You've made writing this series so freaking enjoyable.

And thank you to my husband and mum, for dealing with my perpetual nonsense!!! I love you xxx

Made in the USA
Monee, IL
26 March 2024